A SILENT WIND

EUGENE DESANTIS

◆ FriesenPress

One Printers Way
Altona, MB, R0G 0B0
Canada

www.friesenpress.com

ISBN
978-1-5255-7423-8 (Hardcover)
978-1-5255-7424-5 (Paperback)
978-1-5255-7425-2 (eBook)

1. Fiction, Thrillers, Political

Distributed to the trade by The Ingram Book Company

To my wife:

"There is no me

without you."

PROLOGUE

PORT-AU-PRINCE, HAÏTI. 1956

Monique Abelard's mother took the French sailors last name when she had his baby. Tall, thin, and light-skinned with hazel eyes, she had brown hair with reddish highlights laying damp against a high-cheeked face. She walked across the littered street. Should she tell the man waiting for her that today was her birthday? She had only her mother's word for her age. No birth certificate existed: no pictures of her father, no marriage certificate. Everything they possessed was lost in a fire that no one remembered. She walked with measured steps toward the gangplank of the freighter. The workers crouched along a guardrail separating the dock from the murky water polluted by oil slick debris and human waste.

Workmen rested on the rotting planks of the dock swatting away the constant attack of flies drawn by their sweat, dried human excrement, and meager food. The workers' faces were weathered by the incessant sun, their clothing barely more than rags. They paused and gazed as Monique approached the dock. The older men turned away. The young men, jealous of the handsome white man waiting for her on the ship, glared as she walked by.

Monique slipped the lunch pail between her long, slender legs and lowered the sleeves of her print dress just enough so that her cleavage was exposed.

"That should make them even more angry." A slight smile crossed her thin lips. She had two children at home to feed and the white man in the ship's hold paid very well: not in Haitian gourde, but in American dollars. It dressed her children in modest but clean clothes and allowed her to feed them nourishing meals.

"Half white whore," a voice growled from the base of the gangplank.

"Say what you like. My children live well and go to a Catholic school. My children are white as well as Haitian. They will never work like you. If that makes me a whore, so be it. I have no regrets."

At the open doorway, she pulled her sleeves even lower. "Arnold likes this look." Monique walked along the acrid-smelling corridor, pausing at the entrance to the hold.

"You prepared lunch, Monique?"

"I prepare something for you each day, do I not Arnold? I always bring your favorite beer."

Arnold eased back on the bed of immense sacks of rice covered with a clean white sheet he'd brought. He folded his muscular arms behind his head.

A small droplet of sweat slid down the center of her back. "Put the fan on, Arnold. It is very warm in this metal box," she said, slipping out of her dress.

"I am sorry, my dear," he answered. "Can you forgive a foolish man for asking a foolish question?"

"I forgive you, Arnold." For a man who could be almost boyish at times, she also saw cold and calculating eyes shaded under his thick brows. His eyes held no emotion, even when they made love. Like two crystals hanging from a rich man's chandelier, they were always the same.

His body was still muscular, his chest hairless and sloping into a perfect V. His face was different, but not his mannerisms. Perhaps he was hiding in Port-au-Prince. A criminal? She slipped out of her underclothes and placed them on the corner of the makeshift bed.

Two hours later, she was back on the street. The very large roll of bills tied with a long piece of string and tucked into her panty seemed heavier. Was he leaving again? How will I know if he will return? He said nothing after lunch and lovemaking.

"Perhaps he is being generous?" she told herself, ignoring the taunts from the dock workers.

The driver swerved to miss the tall, thin woman and pulled to the curb, which was little more than broken stones, litter, and sand. His passenger started to get out, carefully sidestepping the hole in the floor of the car.

The driver smiled, wishing he'd seen the pothole filled with water before he'd stopped. When the older man coughed, the discomfort on his passenger's face made the driver's grin larger, exposing four blackened teeth.

"Fifty gourdes, sir. Fifty gourdes, plus the tip."

"Twenty-five and not a penny more." The passenger pressed the money into the driver's hand and got out, tucking the worn leather briefcase under his arm.

"Schmutyzie niger," the tall man with pale skin and eyes blue like Arnold but darker, growled with a thick German accent. He noticed the woman that the driver almost hit. She was laughing. "Schmutyzie hure niger."

He turned away, covering his bald pate with a tattered straw hat. The cloth trim of his hat was stained black by years of perspiration. His wrinkled tropical suit too big for his shrinking frame. Even with the heat and humidity, he wore a tie knotted at his throat. At the base of the gangplank, he removed his hat long enough to swipe the sweat bubbling on his forehead. He snorted, turning away from the workers standing against the guardrail staring at him. Two others urinated between the metal strips into the seawater below.

"Schmutyzie."

Monique Abelard saw Arnold step through the open hatchway onto the gangplank and wave to the tall man. Arnold was leaving her and her children. This time he would not return with his changed face. She fingered the roll of bills. When this is gone, I will go out again and find another man with money. I must, for the children's sake.

She wanted to shout across the street: "I have a son by you, born while you were away in Holland." She couldn't. Let it be, she scolded herself.

The tall man in the tropical suit returned Arnold's wave. "Hallo, Groben. Lister Es ist gut, si Kamerad zu sehen." The middle aged Captain of the guard at Sobibor death camp shouted.

At the bottom of the stairs Arnold spoke. "English. Speak only English, Lang. I go by the name Arnold, you know that." Lister frowned"

"My apologies. I am glad to see you looking well. I bring news . . . Arnold."

"Walk with me Ernst Lang. The view of the ocean from the beach is good and the smells are far more pleasant."

Lister's eyes softened and he relaxed. "Take off your jacket and your shirt relax and enjoy the sun. Your skin is as white as a flower." He smiled, exposing even white teeth. "Tell me, Lang, what is this news you bring? Am I finally being moved from this hellhole of an island?" Lister reached into his shirt pocket and produced a camel cigarette. He lit it with a wooden match.

"You are being relocated. The orders came two weeks ago from Odessa . . . Doctor Mengele himself signed off on the move." Lang opened his briefcase and pulled out a thick manila folder. "I am sorry my friend, but . . ."

"I am not going to South America?"

"No . . . Let us get off this beach. We can walk to the hotel."

The overhead fan, missing a light and one of its blades, did very little to reduce the stifling heat in the hotel hidden from the tourist hotels. Lang sat next to the window, fanning his sallow face with the straw hat while he tried without success to quench his thirst with a glass of iced tea.

Lister sat hunched over the small dinette table reading the pages neatly stapled inside the folder.

"New York," he grumbled, "This is insane." He looked up with sweat bubbling on his forehead and glared at Lang whose impassive face made Lister even more angry. "Du sitzt eine verdammte. Schaufensterpuppe, Lang. Wahren meine welt . . ."

"Stop Heir Lister . . . enough of your antics. Lower your tone. I told you it would not matter as far as recognition. Hide in plain sight, the move is a stroke of genius. I must applaud Doctor Mengele for his intuition. Our South American friends are becoming nervous about migration into their little countries, but they take our money and live well while their people starve. If it works as we planned, more will join you. We cannot resist orders . . . So many Jews in New York. It is the perfect hiding place. Who would think?"

"My things from the apartment, I . . . "

"They will be sent, except, of course, anything we feel might cause problems later." Lang continued to fan himself. "I must confess, I am sorry for the accommodation."

"Tell me about this woman I am to live with in New York. What role does she play in this opera you have created?"

"Greta Steiner. Her husband was a major in the Waffen SS: a tank commander. He was killed on Christmas Day a short distance from Bastogne in Belgium. We were hoping she would be a good companion, possibly even a wife if you both agree. She will give you good cover and I understand she is a very good cook."

"Allow me to explain the obvious . . . Arnold? You speak English. You had your facial surgeries in Holland. You know the country. On that premise, the doctor thought it appropriate. The committee agreed. You will see your new clothes fit your passport. Now if there are no more questions, I will meet you in the departure center at the Holland line dock two hours before the ship sails. Read and learn. There must be no mistakes going through customs in Holland or America." Lang drank the last of the tea. "You want to see this woman before you leave . . . The tall one I saw today?"

"Yes. I have a phone number to call some sort of exchange. I leave a message She contacts me."

"What will you tell her?"

"I must return to Holland because my brother is very sick." Lister put his hands flat against his face and waited. "Please. She takes the darkness from my thoughts, Lang, you can understand that can't you? I am taking a chance, certainly you could do this for me?"

"She has seen you as you were before the surgery?"

"Yes of course . . . Why?"

"No. She can see old pictures and identify you?"

"What are the chances of her leaving this island, Lang?"

"In two days, you leave . . . be prepared."

Lister walked over to the window and watched as Lang got into a cab and left in a grey cloud of dried mud. He went to the phone and called her exchange.

"This is Arnold. I am leaving the country very soon. Do not try to answer this call. Do not return to the ship under any circumstance. You are in grave danger. Tomorrow afternoon I will go to the post office. I am leaving an envelope for you . . . It will settle financial needs. Go to school. Learn a trade. Spend it wisely . . . I will miss our lunches . . . Goodbye."

Rolf Lister, now Christian Lucas, faced his new home on Eighty-First Street between First and Second Avenue. He put the suitcase down close to his leg. The gate was rusting and out of alignment. The walkway leading up to the entrance had chipped cobble stones. He looked at the windows: grimy with soot and many were cracked or missing panes.

He sighed. Would the inside look as bad or worse? He was not disappointed.

The lobby was worse than he imagined. He thought of Monique and wondered if she found the large stash of American money. Did she use it wisely? Had one of the few good things he'd done in his life brought happiness to a human being? He brushed the thought aside. The door to apartment one opened. A voice inside called out to him.

"Christian, you must be exhausted and hungry from your long trip . . . come in . . . I have made a pot of potato soup."

"Christian," he said under his breath, "how ironic."

PORT CITY OF HAIFA, ISRAEL. 1964

Tulia Davidoff stood behind her daughter. Below the child's bedroom in the spacious apartment, men with their wives gathered for the child's special day.

"Where is this young woman who only last year celebrated her Bat Mitzvah? Bring her down here immediately."

Laughter.

"Present yourself," Uncle Yitzhak repeated. The music blared through the apartment; the men's arms locked together as they danced.

"That could only be uncle Yitzhak, his voice carries like thunder," Reba giggled.

"Yes. That would be Yitzhak . . . You like your dress?"

"Yes, Mama. Is everyone here yet? Is Benjamin coming?"

"He has duties inside his army group, but he sent a gift."

Tulia Davidoff brushed the loose curls of Reba's raven hair. She pulled the girl's hair back, tying it with a strip of cloth from her dress.

"Perfect," she announced, and laid her hands on the young girl's shoulders. "You will be a beautiful young woman. I see it already in your face and in your eyes . . . They are a soft brown. You have your grand—" Tulia stopped herself, her hands tightening gently on Reba's shoulders.

"What is it, Mama?"

"Not today, my daughter." Tulia rubbed her face with the back of her hand. "You are growing up so fast and I worry. I worry that these troubles with the Arabs, the Palestinians seem like they will never end. I want a safe world for you and for our people. I think four thousand years is enough time to wait."

"Daddy and his friends will keep us safe, Mama." She raised her hand and touched the tattoo on her mother's forearm. Six numbers. "The teachers have explained the Holocaust to us." Reba rested her cheek on her mother's arm and her lips brushed the tattoo. "I know the reason we have no family."

"Be patient. Do not rush away from your youth, Reba. Will you sing for your father tonight? You have such a beautiful voice. When you sing, I think of my mother."

"Mama, I . . ."

Tulia Davidoff interrupted with gentle firmness, "Not now, Reba. Today . . . sing and be happy. Let's go; your guests are waiting, young lady. You have plenty of time to be a woman, Reba."

"yom halide" Glasses of wine were lifted, in a toast, to the young girl.

"The men and women sang out in chorus while the men, arms locked together, continued the dance.

"Thank you," Reba said, bowing to her guests from the bottom step of the staircase. It was her first time in heels. Her father brought her a glass of grape juice. She drank, lifted her glass, and said, "Ad mean v'ersim . . . Dance and be happy this day."

She drained the rest of the glass and moved quickly into the group, swaying gently in her new high-heeled shoes, kissing and hugging the ladies and shaking hands with the men.

"There is plenty of food and wine." Abel Davidoff raised his glass, "Reba, the most beautiful of daughters . . . Yom halide."

Moments away, an explosion was heard. A ship docked in the harbor went up in flames. Her father and her uncles raced to the scene of the debris and fallen ashes. Within minutes of their departure, Abel Davidoff would be dead. Her mother's worst fears were realized on the day of her daughter's birthday. Reba Davidoff's life would also change... Forever.

Abel Davidoff was buried in Haifa Cemetery. Reba sat at the graveside holding the framed picture of her father. Her mother, completing her Chabad, sat next to her daughter on one of the two wooden chairs provided for them. Tulia, her arms folded across her chest, wept silently. Reba did not cry, nor did she hear the rabbi speaking from the opposite side of the freshly dug grave. Her face showed no sign of emotion. There were questions to be asked and answered. Her father was murdered by a Palestinian terrorist. Someone must pay. She would speak to Uncle Ariel after the service; he knew her father best. Both of them had survived the same camp.

"The Daughter of Abel Davidoff will sing."

Reba rose, holding the picture close. "I will sing to my father. I have chosen a century-old classic Russian song called "Someone." It was one of my father's favorites."

Reba began to sing. Her voice was as soft and warm as a spring rain drifting across the cemetery. People stopped to listen; a few moved closer. Their eyes watering and fixed on the young girl.

The service ended. Benjamin brought Tulia and Reba to the grave for a final prayer and a last goodbye. The others began to move toward Jaffa Road, heads bowed with tears welling in the eyes of the women. The expressions of the dry-eyed men were etched in stone.

"Uncle Ariel is taking us home, Benjamin. Aunt Sofia is waiting for us; she will stay with Mama for some time." Dry eyed, her voice drained of emotion, she added, "Uncle Ariel and I will talk."

"He told me . . . Reba, you should be with your mother during Shiva."

"I will be. I will talk to Uncle Ariel. Then, I will tend to my mother."

"You are your father's daughter. This thing we do is not your life . . . "

"You utter the same words my mother used just yesterday," she interrupted. "I am proud to be his daughter, Uncle Benjamin. One day, I hope to be able to walk in his shoes."

"Our plan is to make sure you will not have to."

"It is too late, Uncle. The man who killed my father is my enemy."

"The terrorist is already dead, Reba . . .. I beg you not to let this act ruin your life. Your father would never allow it."

"My youth was buried today, Uncle."

"Ariel will tell you the same thing, Reba."

"I will not be swayed, Uncle." She dropped her hand from his coat and took his arm. "Aunt Sofia has prepared bread, lentils and eggs for the meal of condolence."

"Let me be a friend, Reba. Trust my words!"

"You are my friend after my father. My mother is waiting."

The meal finished, dishes and glasses were cleaned and stored away. The friends of Tulia Davidoff departed. Left behind were Uncle Ariel and his wife, Sofia. While his wife led Tulia up to her bedroom, Ariel remained at the table, his head bowed in the sadness he felt was evident on his furrowed brow.

Across from him, Reba waited tight-lipped with her eyes fixed on him and the dark patches around his brow. He had not slept well if at all. "Uncle Ariel . . ."

"Wait . . . Wait until your mother sleeps, Reba." He opened his eyes.

"I want to know. I must know. My father is dead; my mother mourns. I want you to tell me everything. My mother will never learn of this conversation unless you allow me to tell her." Reba sat straight back, her eyes riveted on Ariel. "Benjamin talked with me at my father's grave. I will repeat what I told him. You cannot dissuade me from my revenge. I want to be like my father."

"You are angry and hurt. It will pass Reba, or it will destroy you."

"Tell me about my parents, Uncle Ariel."

"Reba Davidoff, my dear girl, you must learn to be patient. Patience and forgiveness are gifts from God. Reba, you must learn to accept. We will talk when your mother sleeps and not before."

"She is asleep now." Sofia said from the foot of the stairs. "When she awakens, I will make a pot of tea. I think she will enjoy a cup."

"Uncle Ariel and I are going out for a little while. We will not be long."

"Take a shawl, Reba." Sofia looked across the table. "Is this necessary, Husband?"

"I am afraid so."

The driver pulled the sedan off the roadway and parked near a cluster of wild cypress trees. A second Mercury pulled up behind it and stopped. Two armed men surfaced from the car, their taut eyes moving quickly from the road to the tree line.

In the distance, the caves of Rosh Hanikra stood silent against a landscape of green brush. The afternoon sun cast shadows across the tunnel entrances. The air smelled of parched earth. A soldier passed them, taking position near the left front fender where he had a clear view of the road.

"Do not speak and ask no questions until I am finished; do you understand, Reba?"

"Yes, Uncle Ariel." Reba removed her shawl. She folded the shawl, placing it on her lap.

"Before you begin, I want to walk a bit, Uncle Ariel . . . Can I?"

"If you wish." He opened his door and signaled the guard, "She would like to walk." He sat back, closing the door. She is her father's daughter. A woman in child's clothing, he thought. "Do not go too far, I have much to tell you."

"I promise, Uncle Ariel. I will stay where you can see me."

I want to smell the ocean air; will that be alright?" she asked the guard as she approached. "My name is Reba what is yours? If you are to protect me, at least you should call me by my first name."

"That would be inappropriate considering the arrangement. My name is Daniel . . . Daniel Klein. I am sorry for your loss; your father was a great man."

"Thank you, Daniel Klein, for saying that . . . Tell me, Daniel Klein, how long have you been in the army?"

"Miss Davidoff, you are getting close to the road."

"Are you ordering me to go back, Daniel Klein?" She breathed deeply, taking in the cool scent of the waterway, turned on her heel and faced the young soldier. "How old are you, Daniel? I am thirteen and anxious to serve in the army when I am old enough."

"I will be nineteen in two months."

"Not much difference in age wouldn't you say, Daniel Klein." She noticed immediately the thin shaft of embarrassment creeping up his neck. Reba smiled. She liked what she saw. He was tall and muscular, but not too much. She especially liked the deep brown eyes under thick black brows and waves in his carefully trimmed hair. The young man reminded her of Benjamin. "You are right; I am too close to the road."

Uncle Ariel watched as she returned to the car. He saw her mother in her eyes and it brought back the memory of when he first saw Tulia stepping off the freedom ship in the harbor. Reba had that same look now. "Are you ready to hear about the ordeal your parents faced?"

"Yes, Uncle Ariel, tell me everything." She looked through the windshield at the young man standing by the front fender "Daniel Kline is very nice-looking, Uncle Ariel."

"And you are very young. Reba Davidoff."

Sofia added two level teaspoons of sugar to her tea and brought two cups to the table. "Your mother is awake. I will be in the living room with Uncle Ariel."

"I will be fine, thank you Aunt Sofia." Reba heard her mother on the stairs. Outside the window, the long hot day was turning to dusk. Soon it would cool the air and shade the house in darkness. "In the kitchen, Mama; Aunt Sofia has made tea." Reba listened to her mother's slippers scrapping the wood floor. "I know about the officer, Mama. The terrible one."

"The inmates called him, 'Blue Eyes' . . . ." Her mother stopped herself and put her head down, laying her cheek on the soft cloth of her robe. "We never wanted you to know these things."

"Drink, Mama."

"Thank you, Reba. I will let it sit and cool."

"I know that my father was an agent of Mossad and he was on the team that caught Eichmann. One day I will be an agent. I will carry on his legacy. Mama, do not be angry with Uncle Ariel."

"Shall I one day mourn you, Reba?" She wiped her face with the edge of the table linen. "Shall I pray over your coffin as well, daughter?"

Reba sat back in her chair. "Did they catch this man they called Blue Eyes?"

"No, but he is probably dead. The Russians were killing all the camp guards when they discovered what they were doing."

"I met a young soldier today. He is nineteen."

"You are thirteen my dear."

PORT OF RAYONG - BANGKOK, THAILAND. 1968

A black Mercedes sedan rolled to a stop bordering a cluster of white cheese wood trees. A heavily armed soldier slid out of the front passenger seat. He gave a cursory look to a young couple walking toward the pier a hundred yards from the car.

Four floors up, a heavy drape moved ever so slightly. The muzzle of a suppressed M-14 rifle slipped two inches beyond the drape, invisible to the soldiers and one civilianbelow in the street.

"I have six targets," a voice inside the darkened space stated flatly. A slight adjustment to the scope. "I have a clear image. I have six targets."

"The tall one is the main target. Take the officer out first," the man holding the binoculars said. "The guards will move to cover him. You have a clear field of fire. No foot traffic and no cars. The window is open; head shots on both. You have the count four, three, two, one . . . blow that flip up."

The shooter looked at the woman sprawled on the worn carpet, her hands tied and her face covered with a cloth hood.

"I'm sorry . . . I'm sorry," he said in Kra Dai repeating the words in Siamese to ensure she understood. "Do not mourn the dead across the street they were your enemy as well as mine. I am going to remove the rope binding your hands and the bag over your head. You must not look at me, scream, or try to move. Do you understand?"

She nodded.

"We mean you no harm, but if you make trouble, I will have to silence you, do you understand Mama-san?"

She nodded.

He removed the cloth bag and cut the ties. He rubbed her hands and kissed her forehead.

"Be well, old one."

Standing at the railing of the Russian freighter with Liberian markings, a KGB officer heard clearly the rapid fire from a single weapon. Six shots followed by a pause then another shot. There was no return fire.

"They're dead." His fists tightened on the railing. How did they know? "Сукин сын," he muttered, repeating in English, "Son of a bitch." He took the steel steps two at a time, sprinted down a narrow corridor, and opened the door to the radio room. "I need to get a message to Moscow."

"Of course, Comrade . . . One moment. I must power up."

CHAPTER ONE

Reba crossed the concourse of El Prat Airport clutching her shoulder bag which contained two simple print dresses, a blouse, and one pair of slacks on hangers hooked to the strap of the bag. Admiring eyes followed. Her mother's vision of her young daughter was realized.

Memories began to fill her thoughts. Now is not the time, she told herself. The line moved forward. The tall man in front of her, busily reading a newspaper, remained in place.

"I'm sorry, I wasn't paying attention." He stepped back, still looking at her, his eyes dancing from her face to her breasts.

"You do not need to apologize, sir." She didn't mind men looking her over, just so they didn't push it. He seemed nice though. Handsome, well dressed, with a thick tuft of light brown hair, deep blue eyes and a boyish smile that seemed to engulf his face. She smiled politely, hoping he would turn around.

"Here on business or pleasure?"

"Meeting my husband. I think you are next . . . "

"James Preston. I didn't mean anything by it, please forgive me."

"Reba Klein."

"I am ready for the next person in line, please step forward," the woman at the desk interrupted, for which Reba was grateful.

"That's me. I hope you enjoy your stay."

"C'mon will yah. Take it outside, yeah."

Preston's blue eyes hooded. His entire face changed; the muscles tightened in his neck, straining against the collar of his Paisley shirt. He had the look of a predator. Preston relaxed and his boyish smile blossomed on his face.

He looked at the security officer. "People like that bother me, I'm sorry." He looked at Reba. "I am sorry."

"Let's just leave it at that, shall we?" She said flatly. She wanted him away. He made her feel uncomfortable.

"Enjoy your stay," he said, picking up his suitcase.

"Are you all right, ma'am?" The security officer asked.

"Yes, thank you, officer."

"I hope this will not spoil your visit; Barcelona is a beautiful city."

"Who is next in line? Please step forward."

"That would be me." In the corner of her eye, she spied Preston. A tall blonde woman greeted him. They kissed and quickly left.

Thirty minutes later, Reba was on roadway C-31. The Mercedes was new, and the leather seats had the clean smell of a new car. Reba's heart was beating faster. Tears slipped from her eyes and splashed down her cheeks. When one would slip near her mouth, she ran her tongue over it. The salt tasted bitter. The memory of the loss was growing stronger. She turned onto road B-20. "We are almost there, Daniel." A memory flashed, dampening her eyes.

She walked into the large dance hall, now a member of the IDF. As soon as she signed the register she looked up and saw him. He was even more handsome than she remembered with that shock of black hair cut close to his scalp, a chiseled face, and large brown eyes so deep you could see your reflection in them. Her young heart jumped as he approached in his crisp dress uniform.

"Reba Davidoff, may I have the honor of the first dance?"

"You remember me?"

"Even as a young woman, you would be impossible to forget." He held out his hand. "Dance with me, Reba Davidoff." It wasn't a question.

She paused at a rest stop three miles from the hotel, removed the band holding her hair in place and let it fall across her shoulders. She studied herself in the mirror. "Almost forgot," she whispered, and quickly unbuttoned the top buttons on her silk blouse. Remember this blouse? She walked out into the high sun. You couldn't wait to remove it.

Reba Klein checked in. The middle-aged woman at the counter was courteous and pleasant. Papers in order, she gave Reba her suite key.

"I would like to exchange currency, please."

"Of course, directly across the lobby; you can't miss it."

The suite was exactly how she remembered it. The wicker chairs were covered with thick flowery cushions. The table with inlaid marble. A fully stocked bar and refrigerator. The slider was open to a spacious balcony with the afternoon shore breeze rustling the sheer curtains. She could see Daniel in her mind's eye, feel his presence . . . a knock on the door.

"Bellman, madam."

"Coming."

"I have a shoulder bag and three garments on hangers."

"That's correct. Please put the bags on the bed; I'll hang the garments."

"The lady at the front desk sent up a bottle of Merlot, a very good year. Would you like me to fill the ice bucket for you?"

"Yes, please, that would be nice." She called the front desk. "Thank you for the wine but . . ."

"I thought this might help."

"Believe it or not, my husband and I shared a Merlot on the first night we were here that was . . ."

"Get drunk, my dear. I did, the night I lost my husband to a car accident." I am very sorry for your loss madam . . ."

"Tell me, did the wine help?"

"No, but I did get a good night's sleep."

Just then, the bellman returned.

"Take this and thank you." Reba pressed the folded bills, adding up to forty francs, into the man's hand.

"Madam, this is too much; I can't."

"You can accept it and you will. Good evening, Jordan."

Reba padded to the doorway of the bedroom. She saw Daniel, his eyes moving over her naked body. The memory of that first night rushed up, consuming her. She lay on the bed, the sheets cool against her back, her legs wrapped tightly around his buttocks. His thrusts sent a pulsating excitement through her very being until at last they climaxed. She shuddered, pushing the memory back into the abyss.

The parking lot facing the beach was deserted. She welcomed the solitude, a time to reminisce and cry without arousing attention. The sand felt cool under her feet. The sun disappearing to the west cast orange shadows over the beach and the offshoot of rocks to her right. The rocks with the waves splashing over them and spraying the sand brought memories. The beach, the wet sand scratching her back, her back protected by the single towel they brought from the hotel. The feel of him inside of her. She cried out to him. The memory dissipated like the spray from the ocean. She opened the shoulder bag, took out a tissue, and wiped her face. She removed the shovel and the metal box, dropped to her knees, and began to dig. The wet sand kept the form of the hole.

"Daniel, all that is me and all that we were together is in this box. Hold on to it until we are together again." She shoveled the sand into the hole, stood up, and climbed to the top of the rocks. The spray from the waves pricked her skin. She closed her eyes and threw the shovel into the sea.

Back in the suite, a soft breeze cooling her naked body, she piled the outfits she brought back from the beach and carried them into the bathroom, dropping them into the hamper. She no longer wanted them. She turned the faucet for the shower and stepped into the tub. Finished, she toweled herself off, slipped on the hotel robe, walked out into the bedroom, and dialed the hotel operator.

"Good evening. How may I direct your call?"

"I would like to make an international station call." Reba gave the operator the number and hung up. She rested back on the silk sheets and called out to Daniel. He did not respond. I want to feel you beside me once more. No reply. She squeezed her eyes shut and begged; still no response. The phone rang and she jumped. "Yes?"

"I have your party on the line, madam."

"Thank you, operator . . . Uncle Ariel?"

"Reba, where are you? We've all been worried."

"I'm fine, Uncle Ariel. I am leaving Barcelona the day after tomorrow. It would have been our anniversary. I knew my mother would try to talk me out of returning here, so I told no one. I have a direct flight . . . Tell my mother I will visit her very soon . . . Uncle Ariel, I am ready to do whatever is asked of me."

"Reba, listen to me . . ."

She hung up without allowing him to respond. She padded into the outer suite. The bottle of Merlot stood in the center of melted ice, inviting her to open it.

The next morning, she awoke with no memory of how she got into bed. The empty bottle rested on the nightstand with a stemmed glass next to it containing the residue of wine. Reba smiled through the fog. "You were right," she said out loud, "It did not help, but I did sleep."

NEW YORK CITY

The doors leading out to the lobby slid closed. She had aged well. Her hair was cut short and combed straight back. It was her. She was still as beautiful as he remembered her. The man in the maintenance shirt and slacks watched her from behind a pillar.

The Lincoln Mark 3 stretch limo sat at the curb; her driver waited with the suicide door opened. She climbed in. He closed the door with a distinct click and slid into the driver's seat.

Over his shoulder he said, "Shall I take you home, Mrs. Pratt?"

"Yes please, Michael; I want to be there when the children come home."

He had aged well. His hairline receded. He wore it longer, curling over the collar of his green work shirt. A patch on the right pocket read in block letters "Maintenance Supervisor." He wisely removed the name badge he wore in case she saw him. He walked out of the lobby just as the car pulled out into traffic and hailed a cab. To any passerby he was just another middle-aged working man, a strong man, broad shouldered, with a trim waist; but the eyes were a bit unsettling, a crystal blue, almost transparent.

PRAGUE, CZECHOSLOVAKIA. JULY 23, 1976

A tall man, six feet, thin but solidly built, moved quietly down the steps into the cellar of the Bohemia apartment building at 13 Stare Mesto Street. He wore a long grey coat buttoned up to his neck, a black wide-brimmed fedora pulled down near his eyes, and black slacks. In his right hand was a 9 mm pistol. The thick rubber-soled shoes made no sound on the concrete floor.

The cellar had a lingering scent of cat urine. He waited a moment, allowing his eyes to adjust to the darkness. To his left, high on the damp wall, was a grime-covered window. He stepped forward. He knew the cellar even though he had never been in it. He had studied it from a drawing supplied by a courier. A picture of the layout of the apartment flashed across his mind as he made his way to the stairwell seldom used by the residents. He stopped and listened. He heard only the faint sound of music from an opera: Mozart. Suddenly, the door swung open.

A young man in jeans, sneakers, and a flannel shirt entered the cellar, his chest heaving.

"Peter Shevchenko is gone. He was picked up. You have to leave now."

"Bring the car. I am going to the apartment. Wait outside."

She was blond, young, and naked, lying on the bed smoking a cigarette. He put his finger to his lips and whispered, "Do not make a sound. Where is the man who was just here?"

"Someone came to the door," her voice cracked; hot ash fell on her chest. She ignored the sting. She was focused on the barrel of the gun pointed at her face. "He said something I could not understand; I think it was Russian. The man told me his name was Peter. He left immediately, dressing as he ran out the door . . . I don't want to die." She pulled the sheet up to her throat. "That is all I know, I swear. I will do whatever you want . . ."

"What is your name? Do not lie."

"Francine."

Once outside, he raced down the alley. The Skoda sedan and his driver idled at the curb. A quick check of the street and he dashed to the car, climbing in and flattening himself on the floor behind the driver.

"I just missed him by minutes; did you see anyone?"

"Only a man running. One more thing," the driver said, pulling away from the curb. "The D.O.D. left a message at the embassy for you. I was to tell you to call Langley as soon as the mission is completed."

"I got it."

"That bag on the seat has your papers and travel cash. The key is for a clothes locker at the airport."

"No idea what the message was about?"

"I know only what I am told, number four."

BEN GURION AIRPORT-TEL AVIV, ISRAEL

Reba spied the young man wearing a black suit with a loosely fitting jacket. He was watching her and the crowd with equal intensity. She passed through the security checkpoint. As soon as she cleared the area, he walked briskly toward her.

"I am Simon Peres, Mrs. Klein. The general is waiting." He took her travel bag, slinging it over his shoulder.

"Thank you, Simon; my uncle made a wise choice." *He is right-handed. Walk on his left side.* "It is good to be home."

"There is his car." He pointed to the black Lincoln sedan with the side and rear windows tinted. Simon opened the door politely.

"Thank you, Simon . . . General," she said, collapsing into the seat next to Ariel. She waited for Simon to close the door before kissing him on the cheek, "I am tired, Uncle Ariel. It was hard for me to go there; all the memories came back. I am glad I went...I am ready now."

"Are you sure, Reba? You have to convince everyone that you are ready to move forward. I do not want this for you. No family, no friends, no husband and children. I beg you in your father's name to change this course."

"I seek no husband and no children. Daniel was my life, Uncle. Israel is my life now . . . Tell me, what is next for me?"

"The prime minister is planning a party on the first of August. You have been invited as my guest. Wear your dress uniform. They may want to talk to you or they may not. I have no information beyond that. You will drive me."

"What about Simon?"

"He understands such things . . . believe me Reba."

"Yes, General." Reba leaned back closing her eyes. "How is my mother?"

"How can I put into words what your mother is feeling?"

NEW YORK CITY: JULY 24

The German rocked slowly in the chair Greta Steiner used all the years they shared. The small table next to it still held the butts of many cigarettes. The smoking wasted her life. He thought of Monique. How, after all these years, could this have happened? Ernst Lang was correct; he should have listened. What if she had recognized him in the lobby of the hospital? All this time the isolation was all for nothing.

He picked up the glass of Schnapps and drank it down in a gulp. He knew where she lived; he had followed her and waited for her to enter the apartment building. The doorman supplied her name. He apologized, feigning a mistake. Back at the hospital, he spied the directory on the first floor. She was married to an important doctor. She has come a long way from the young woman who serviced him on that dank ship.

Perhaps the doctor is not privy to her past, but what if he is? I must do something. My existence depends on it. If he could find her by luck in this city of so many, who by luck might see him and remember? A muffled scream escaped his cupped hand.

TEL AVIV: AUGUST 1

Reba maneuvered the car through the center of the city. It was good to see the city alive, the tourists venturing out as the sun set, promising a cool night. The street cafés were bustling, the restaurants already enjoying a constant flow of tourists and locals. The IDF actively patrolled, looking for something or someone out of place or out of character. Once out of the city, the uneasiness settled in. She spent a good part of the day preparing for this evening, long minutes in front of her full-length mirror asking and answering her own questions, looking at facial expressions. Too late now, she told herself, turning into the long, curved driveway.

"Are you all right, Reba?"

"Yes, Uncle—" she caught herself. "General, sir."

"Take deep breaths; relax."

"The guard is coming." She stopped and cut off the engine. A light shone brilliantly from a stanchion near the entrance, flooding the car and its occupants. The guard reached the car and opened the door for the general.

"She is my driver. Her name is Corporal Reba Klein. Reba, show the guard your military ID."

"Yes, sir." She held it up to eye level with her right hand, the holstered weapon visible on her right hip.

"You are expected, General; welcome."

"Come around the car and let me see how you look." She walked to the rear of the car and stood at attention. "Good, you wear the uniform well."

"I pressed it three times. I remembered what you said: no wrinkles and don't sweat. It is like telling a woman not to wear anything above the waist when meeting her boyfriend's parents for the first time."

"You will do just fine. Don't eat . . . Drink water only, understand? And one more thing, do not get comfortable with anyone. Mingle. Stay clear of controversy."

CHAPTER TWO

CIA HEADQUARTERS-LANGLEY, THE UNITED STATES

Seven hours earlier, a private phone in the DOD. office rang.

"This is Cahill."

"It's Ethan, sir."

"Ethan, I am so sorry for the loss of your child. I tried to reach you. Is there anything I can do?"

"Joanne lost the baby and I wasn't there for her. She is moving to be near her folks in Fort Lauderdale. She is packing as we speak. She won't speak to me. I told her I was quitting the agency, she won't listen . . . I'm done. I can't change what's happened."

"Let's meet for supper. I know you like that Redskins quarterback's new restaurant. Maybe I can straighten things out with you and Joanne."

"You're not listening."

"Take a moment to collect your thoughts, Ethan. I can reassign you. Give you a permanent position and stability. Do you think if you move to Florida, it will change things?"

"No. Not this time, Mister Cahill."

"Take a few days, Ethan think this . . ."

"Get me out, Mister Cahill."

"All right, Ethan. There will be things I need to process, papers etc. You understand how this all works. There will be no turning back. I can't recreate you . . . I can . . ."

"Get it done," Ethan interrupted.

"Call me, let's see . . . today is Tuesday. Call me next Tuesday." The phone went dead without a goodbye. Cahill listened to the dial tone for a few seconds and hung up. "Beatrice, we have a problem."

Beatrice Noonan a fixture at Langley. She knew all the secrets, including the names of the seven special operators.

"Yes Adam," she said, stepping into his office.

Something was wrong. She could see it in his eyes and in the way he folded his arms across his chest. More than twenty years working just outside his door taught her to be wary of his every gesture, every smile or frown. She loved this man. She imagined loving him from the first day they met. There were days when she hoped he would need her for more than operational assistance. Those days passed like the passing of the seasons. For now, just being here being needed was all she expected. "What is it, Adam?"

"Ethan Edwards needs to leave. He's finished. I believe him, Beatrice. I couldn't even get him out to supper. We need to remove all remnants of his existence. I don't think it will involve the records section at Fort Myers. His military records include the false General Discharge Honorable Conditions, before Vietnam. We must ensure that any hint of his activities never surface."

"It won't be a problem. Remember, Adam, who we work for."

"Would you like a cup of coffee?"

"Number four has been with us since 1965, if you do not count his sixteen months in Vietnam, by the way."

9 SMOLENSKIN STREET -

Reba refrained from making political statements. She discussed her parachute training when asked, admired the clothing choices of female guests, smiled dutifully, and laughed at minor jokes she didn't think the least bit funny. She wisely excused herself when the conversation turned to the problems with their neighbors.

She refilled her glass with cool water, wondering if she looked as bloated as she felt. No matter. I've waited two long hours. They would have called me if they were interested. Where is Ariel; I want to go home. She spied him crossing the floor toward her, shaking hands and speaking briefly to some guests while ignoring others.

"Is it time to go, General?" she asked, feeling her hopes dashed like a bug crushed under an indifferent shoe.

"They want to see you, Reba. Pull yourself together. Take a deep breath, put your drink down and walk with me. Shoulders back."

"I am nervous, General. I did not think I would be."

"You should be. It is only natural, but do not show it and do not sweat. They will take it as a sign of weakness. If you must go to the bathroom, go now. "

"You are not helping."

"I know my brave little sparrow . . . I know. Benjamin sends his best wishes. Are you ready?"

"Yes, Uncle."

Ariel held the heavy oak door for her. He entered, closing the door behind him. The men stood when she entered. As a child, she knew them as simply Uncle this or that and now they ruled her country on one level or another. She was careful to show no change in her expression or demeanor.

Yitzhak Hof the head of the Mossad, was first to greet her. Yaakov Kahn of Shin Bet followed. Amos Ben-Gil, hero of the 1973 war, was next. The line formed the powerful first. Benjamin was missing. He declined to take part, honoring her mother's wish. Reba understood his dilemma.

They offered her a chair, but she declined it. She wanted to stand, her hands clasped behind the small of her back. She smelled the light scent of a woman's soap and perfume. She recognized the perfume: Chanel. Behind the men, in the center of the cedar-paneled room, a door stood slightly ajar. Perhaps it was the wife of one of these gentlemen. Finally the prime minister, stepped forward to greet her.

"Your father would have come to stand proudly by your side this night. I miss him as I am sure you do."

"Thank you. He is always in my thoughts."

"And your husband of course, a great loss."

"Daniel is always with me, sir."

"Remember me to your mother, Reba."

"I will, sir."

"Good." He turned to the other gentlemen in the room, those that did not approach her: subordinates and advisors, no doubt.

"Shall we begin, gentlemen?"

"Would you like a cognac, madam, and you, Yaakov?" Kahn asked, already knowing the answer.

"I believe I would," Rach Goldman answered. "Two fingers with a slice of lemon."

"What is your impression of the young lady?" Kahn asked, handing her the drink.

"She certainly has a grasp of the situation we face each day. I imagine the General helped, but not enough to overshadow her. I applaud him for that. I read the dossier. Her military and scholastic achievements are excellent. I thought her answers were direct." Rachel sipped her drink.

"But still you hesitate, madam?"

"I am just a simple girl from Brooklyn, my dear Yitzhak. She has seen death, she has suffered heartache, but she has never felt death by her own hand."

"Are you suggesting a test of her skills, madam?"

"I would never suggest such a thing, Yaakov. Decisions of such importance I leave to brave men . . . Like yourself." She swallowed the rest of the cognac. "I would suggest that we might want to look at more women who may be capable of serving our secret agencies' needs in ways that men cannot."

"Just a simple girl from Brooklyn, are we?" Yaakov answered, smiling broadly. "Another cognac, madam?"

"I think one is enough. I'll say goodnight to you Yaakov. Yitzhak, would you give me a moment please." It was not a question.

"Of course, madam."

When the two were alone, she asked, "Tell me honestly, Yitzhak, what did you think of the young lady?"

"I would be much more interested in what you thought, madam."

"Always the same; never divulge your feelings. Wait for others to commit first. Weigh the options and then speak your mind, my old friend?"

"You know me. Tell me, madam. What is the silver-haired one conjuring up in her head?"

"It is no longer silver. I am afraid it is tired and gray like the woman who combs it in the mirror each morning. I remember a young girl new to my country running to the sea to swim after a long day. Now I walk slowly to my bed and collapse.

"One day you will be prime minister. I will wish for you ad me'ah v'esrim, madam."

"One hundred and twenty years. Well, now, enough talk about my health and lost glamour." She patted Yitzhak on the shoulder. "Let us talk of this young woman."

PARIS, FRANCE. DECEMBER 6, 1976

The white van pulled close to the curb, stopping six feet behind a Saab four door sedan. The driver shut off the engine, released the safety on the AK-47 and said, "She is late."

The passenger scrutinized the foot traffic. It was difficult to tell with the temperature dropping to thirty Celsius if they had anything under their bulky coats. The café Au Petit Sud Ouest was quiet. The woman he was to meet chose well. Only two older gentlemen, both engrossed in their newspapers, were seated at the sidewalk tables with small heaters by their feet. He checked his watch: 10:15 am Paris time Thick clouds holding the promise of snow shielded the city, making it look more like dusk then morning.

"Maybe we should go, Abadi?"

"Five more minutes. Tell me her name again?"

"Alia Al Baghdadi. Using the cover of a reporter for one of Assad's newspapers."

"Is she beautiful?"

"Abu Abadi, my friend, we are here so she can interview you and pass messages from our friends in Syria. Do not allow your libido to interfere. Remember: Allah is watching."

"That must be her. Look how she is dressed."

"She is a Syrian woman; how do you expect her to dress?"

The woman approached the café, apparently unaware she was being watched. She wore a scarf covering her hair and most of her face. She wore no makeup, and dark metal-framed sunglasses hid her eyes. Her dress and coat were black, the coat buttoned to her collar, and she wore flat, black shoes with soft heels. She carried a small brown briefcase in her gloved hand. She walked to a table between the two older men and sat down with her back to the boulevard. She lit the small heater under the table.

"She is smart. She sits with her back to the street knowing I would prefer it."

"She was probably warned to do so. Go Abu. You need to get off the street; it is not safe. The Mossad hunters still have not forgotten Munich."

The driver scanned the traffic moving toward and around the Eiffel Tower only a short distance from the café. He studied the Saab in front of the van; the windows were thinly coated with frost.

"Go now Abadi."

"You are Al Baghdadi from the north of Syria?" He asked standing behind her, his eyes moving from one customer to the next. He stepped around the table and sat down.

"I am her and I am from the western region of Syria. I speak three languages, including Farsi, if you are more comfortable with it, Abu Abadi." She picked up the briefcase and placed it on the table, interlocking her fingers on top of the case. "It is very cold here. May I have a coffee?"

"Of course." Abadi raised his hand. The waiter appeared. "Two black coffees and perhaps a pastry, Alia?" His dark eyes under thick brows narrowed as he moved his right hand slowly under the table.

"Pastry is bad for the teeth… I am a married woman, Abadi."

"My apologies to your husband, Alia Al Baghdadi," he said, moving the hidden hand from under the table.

"If you are finished testing me, shall we go on with our interview? I have notes for you in my briefcase."

"Yes."

The driver noticed the two cyclists as they turned onto the boulevard. They wore tight fitting riding shirt pants, boots and small helmets only partially covering their heads.

They moved at a good clip staying close to the parked vehicles to avoid the traffic. "These Europeans are insane riding bikes in this cold," he muttered and relaxed his grip on the automatic weapon.

He looked toward the café just as the two cyclists came alongside the van, pulled out small caliber weapons, and fired six shots through the open window. By the time Abu Abadi realized what had happened, the woman had opened the briefcase, slid out the Walther PPK, and shot him first in the chest and then put two bullets in quick succession into his brain.

"I am the wrath of God.," She calmly put the weapon into the case, stood up, and walked slowly to the Saab. The driver sat up behind the wheel and in seconds the car circled the tower and disappeared into traffic. Reba Klein experienced death by her own hand.

CHAPTER THREE

Two men in khaki shirts and shorts, wide-brimmed safari hats and desert style lace-up boots entered the bar near the Gala Square bridge. The taller one of the two noticed the woman near the end of the bar. She smiled. He smiled back. The bartender approached, his manner and expression cautious.

"Club soda. I am Muslim. My friend here will have a cognac. Will you accept Lebanese pounds?"

"Of course. You are here from Lebanon, teachers perhaps? The way you gentlemen are dressed, you . . ."

"Yes, we just arrived this morning. We thought it best to look like tourists. Would you ask the lady what she would like to drink?"

"She is a woman who lives just beyond the bridge. She caters to men like yourselves." The bartender covered his mouth, "One of the better ones; she keeps clean and is free of disease."

"You know this how?"

"I have never had a customer come back and complain. Is that not enough to satisfy you?"

"Parlez-vous français?" The tall one asked, smiling at the woman.

"Oui, like you I speak French as well." She answered.

"Will you join us for a drink?"

"I do not drink alcohol, but I will be happy to join you." The young woman walked slowly toward them giving them the chance to look at her. She smelled of lilacs and her hair smelled of shampoo. "You both are Lebanese. I like Lebanese men; they know how to treat a woman who treats them well."

She sat on the stool turned just enough to allow the two strangers a glimpse of her legs. "Do my legs please you?"

"Very pleasing."

"Tell me, are you here to work at the university?"

"Yes, we are. My friend is a teacher of chemistry and I teach Persian history." The tall one placed two bills on the bar for the drinks and added a large tip.

"My name is Leila Azad; and your names?"

"I am Moss and my friend is Adi.

"Very good gentlemen."

The apartment was small with furnishings in bright colors. Murals depicting the monuments of past civilizations hung on the walls. It had small bedrooms, one on each side of a dimly lit hallway. A kitchen and a small living area faced the front door.

"Lock the door and close the drapes." She led the tall one down the hall carrying a portable radio turned to a popular music station. The tall man removed his shirt and boots. She entered the first bedroom, stepped around the bed, and pulled the drapes closed. The room smelled of jasmine. The sheets on the bed looked clean and freshly ironed. "Where is Arafat?" he asked, putting his boots on the carpet. He folded his shirt and laid it on the bed.

"You have missed him. I have it from a good source that Moses was warned. He left early this morning." She put a finger to her lips. She took out a Beta max cartridge, slipped it into the recorder and turned on the television. The image that appeared was a pornographic scene with two men and a woman. She turned up the sound just enough to squelch their voices. "I am sure of my source."

"How was Moses informed? Do you know?"

"A man working in the Foreign Service office in Cairo. His name is Haram Amari. My source told me an Englishman is responsible for Arafat being warned, but she couldn't find out his name. I will make coffee. You will stay here for a little while. If you leave too soon a neighbor may get suspicious and alert the guards."

"Where can we find this man . . . Amari?"

"I know he is traveling to Cairo on the railroad sometime today, but I do not know his schedule." The woman on the television began to cry out with feigned enjoyment. "That is all I know. Wait, my source told me he likes to wear seersucker suits . . . I think light blue with bow ties. He is short, shorter than me, dark-skinned."

"Is your source in danger?"

"No, she is too smart. The men she caters to are well placed. They pay handsomely for her services."

The tall man stepped into the hall and in a low voice said, "Moesha, come in here. Arafat is gone. He was warned." Abraham frowned. "We have to catch a man whose name is Haran Amari and get the name of an Englishman. If he is so well placed, my guess is MI-6, but that is for the English to figure out."

"What about me? I was promised by your Mossad courier to be free. She convinced me that I would be able to escape."

"You shall be free, Leila Azad; no one is blaming you. Make the coffee. A plan for your escape has been prepared. I will explain over coffee."

RAMSES RAIL STATION – CAIRO, EGYPT

"Paging Special Envoy Haran Amari to the white phone. Haran Amari to the white phone."

Amari spied a phone and walked over to it. He lifted the receiver. It was dead, not even a dial tone. The wire underneath had been cut. He hung up and stepped back with the look of fear in his dark eyes.

"You are Haran Amari?"

"Who are you?" Fear, stronger now, raised the hairs on the back of his neck and buckled his knees at the sight of the two men, one tall one short. "What do you want with me?" He felt faint.

"Do not be afraid. We are here to warn and protect you and take you to safety. It is the wish of Moses."

"Warn me about what?" He tried to sound authoritative. "Prove to me you are who you say you are, or I will create a scene and bring the police."

"The Englishman is not your friend; he wants you dead," the shorter man answered. "You need more proof?"

"Come with us. I will rent a room nearby where we can wait for our friends."

"Moses sent you?"

"Yes Amari. You must be very clever. I could learn from you. I must know how you were able to convince this Englishman to work with you. Go now. Get off this platform. You are safe with us."

BRITISH EMBASSADOR RESIDENCE - CAIRO: DECEMBER 11

A car rolled to a stop in front of the gate the next morning. A tall man in rumpled khaki shorts, shirt, and lace-up boots got out and started toward the SAS guard standing at the gate. He held his arms slightly out from his side, his palms facing the guard, fingers spread wide. "I am Israeli. I have a message in my upper left shirt pocket. May I retrieve it?"

"Go ahead, but be informed that a weapon is pointed at you."

"I assume that; I am right-handed." The tall man retrieved the neatly folded note stamped with the heading Ramses Hilton embossed on it and held it out for the guard. I have a plane to catch . . . Shalom, my friend."

10 DOWNING STREET - LONDON, ENGLAND. DECEMBER 13

"My dear Francis Murdock, what on earth brings you to my office at eight this evening?" Margaret Thatcher chided the head of MI-6. "Tell me, are we at war, sir?"

"No, madam." Murdock opened his briefcase and pulled out a copy of the note left at the Ambassador's residence in Cairo.

"Francis, we are alone and I did not bring my glasses. Please read it to me."

"As you wish, madam. It says:

"Arafat was warned of a plot and was able to escape.

The man who warned him is one Haran Amari.. He is dead.

Someone in your foreign service may be a double agent.

We were not able to acquire his name."

"It was signed: Shalom."

"Did we verify the note, Francis?"

"A man named Amari was found mutilated and murdered in the Ramses Hilton hotel this very morning. Egypt time, Margaret. Shall I send a note to the Israeli chief of the foreign intelligence?"

"Not at the moment. They will know how grateful we are. You might want to invite their envoy to dinner perhaps. Have you informed the people at the foreign office, Francis?"

"Not as yet, I came to you first."

"Give me time to digest this bit of news."

"I'll say good night, then."

"You have some digging to do, Francis? Let's keep this in house, shall we?"

JOE THEISMAN'S RESTAURANT, ALEXANDRIA, VIRGINIA: DECEMBER 15

"I'm glad we could get together for lunch, Ethan. I apologize for the delay, but you know Beatrice; she has to double and triple check everything. She sends her fondest regards. Of course, we both hope the result is satisfactory."

Cahill tapped the vanilla envelope sitting on the corner of the linen-draped table. "There never was anything to connect you to the agency except as a subcontractor. I filled the payout as monies owed for back V.A. reimbursements. You can thank Beatrice for that bit of work. It is a tidy sum and should tide you over until you find what you want to do next. We have also made arrangements for Joanne to receive a tidy sum."

"I appreciate all you and Beatrice have done for me. Don't blame yourself for what happened. I made the choices."

"We will both have linguini with mussels, medium sauce, and a bottle of your best Merlot, '67," Cahill informed the waiter.

"When did you start liking mussels, Mr. Cahill?"

"Today. Tell me, what are your plans for the future?"

"I have been developing a cartoon character, a conservative type. A bird watcher of all things. I have drawings and written material already submitted. I found an agent who likes my idea. I think I can make a go of it. I've been working on it for the past year."

"Does this character have a name, Ethan?"

"You will love this, Argyle Socks. The idea came to me on the flight after Prague. I finally got around to working it into a strip."

"You used me . . . The socks I wear as your character?" Cahill broke into a long crowd-attracting laugh. "You can't be serious? What if some reporter puts the two together? How will you explain how we know each other that well?"

"We don't. I read it in a column in Newsweek. To be honest, the real story is Beatrice came up with the character's name."

"Beatrice knew about this?" The wine steward popped the cork on the merlot, pouring just the right amount into Cahill's glass.

"Perfect," Cahill said. The wine steward poured three fingers into each glass and sat the bottle down just as the waiter arrived with their food. "Beatrice knew about this and didn't tell me."

"Put some grated cheese on the linguini. As for Beatrice, I swore her to secrecy, but I must say we did have a good laugh over it."

"A toast then to the future. England may very well have a new prime minister soon, a woman . . . We have a newly elected president. We can record whatever we want because of these VCR contraptions. The war, thank God, is over. Gerald Ford saved New York from itself. A big shark is eating people off the coast of Cape Cod… Hand me the grated cheese."

PORT OF HAIFA: DECEMBER 16

The Manta Ray restaurant overlooks the port, serving rich and exotic recipes enjoyed by locals, as well as tourists, year-round. The open balcony is my favorite. It is surrounded by cypress trees and offers a famous breakfast sandwich consisting of eggplant, cottage cheese, ham—for the secular visitor—and olive oil on toasted French bread.

The last thing one would guess seeing her in a long white linen dress two inches below her knee cinched tightly at her thin waist by a matching belt three-inch matching heels, a wide brimmed soft hat shading her eyes and matching small leather purse tucked under her left arm. She looked more like a beautiful Israeli woman than a Mossad intelligence officer about to have breakfast with the grey-haired older gentleman in a dark blue pinstripe suit.

"Reba my dear." He stood, wiping his hands with a linen napkin, and pulled out her chair.

"Yitzhak Kahn, I would have guessed you would be having one of those sandwiches. You should be careful what you eat." She sat down, crossing her legs, and placed the purse on the table.

"I took the liberty of ordering a plate of assorted local cheese and a cava fruit cocktail for you," he said, ignoring her taunt. He wiped a piece of cheese from his chin and leaned forward. "You did very well in Paris. Yaakov was very impressed, as well as was the future prime minister." He sat back, opening his jacket. "How do you feel? Be honest with me, Reba."

"My team was very good with me. It gave me the confidence I needed." Reba picked up her cocktail, stirring it slowly. "I thought it was all about revenge, killing Abadi. I was wrong. Even though I hated that man, I felt uneasy. I still do, Uncle Yitzhak."

"I am glad you feel this way. It is never good to feel joy in taking a life no matter whose life . . . Tell me, Reba, how are your language instructions coming along?" He took another bite of his sandwich.

"I know French. The most trying is the Quranic Arabic, but I am learning. The others, Persian and Western Syria, were easier." Reba took a longer swallow of her drink. "Do I really need to learn Quranic Arabic?"

"Probably not, but one never knows . . . Soon you will begin the final phase of your training, Reba. When you have completed it, you will have a new sponsor. Your mother is well? Have you spoken to her?"

"I am going home after we finish to spend a few days with her. I miss her."

BERLIN, GERMANY. DECEMBER 17

Anna Schmidt gripped the headboard. His hands pressing her buttocks with each thrust. He raised his head, licking her nipples, and increased the pressure of his thrusts until they both climaxed and collapsed on top of him.

"James," she bellowed, short of breath "I do not want to leave but I must. I have a husband to go home to."

"Too bad." Her skin was damp. Her hair was clinging to her face. "You had better shower and get home."

"When will I see you again?"

"I'll arrange my schedule so I can come back soon. Would you like that?"

"Yes." She kissed him lightly, slid off him, and stood up. "Do you still use the same towel when I leave?"

"Of course, I do," he lied.

She padded toward the door looking over her shoulder to see if he was watching her. She liked it when he watched her with that glint in his eyes. He made her feel like a young girl again and not a woman close to sixty.

She padded down the short hall and was about to open the bathroom door when she spied the black overcoat draped over the sofa in the living room. Then she noticed the man sitting there reading a magazine. She froze.

"I am sorry if I frightened you," the square-faced man in the gray sweater said, turning his head and looking at her his brown eyes, admiring her. "I am here to see James; I must say his taste, as always, is impeccable." He smiled a big, toothy joyless smile. "Is James available or should I return later?"

She darted into the bathroom locking the door behind her turned on the shower and jumped under the spray.

"Come out here, my friend, we need to talk." He knew she couldn't hear him. The noise of the old pipes pushing water drowned out any attempt at overhearing conversations. "Are you using your alias? I wouldn't want to spoil the fun."

"Yes I am. She thinks I am a computer salesman. The apartment is small, but it's nice. Thank you for letting me use it. You want a beer?"

"I think they call a woman who looks like that well preserved . . . I will have a beer." He waited while Palmer picked out two bottles from the refrigerator, popped the caps and came back, taking a seat across from him. "Is this something serious between you and this woman?" He took a swallow of beer.

"It is all sex and nothing more, nothing less, Frank."

"Could she become a problem?"

"Nothing I can't handle. She is married to a rich Kraut who has very bad friends. I don't think she will make a fuss. She thinks I travel quite a bit. When I tire of her, I will simply not return. She thinks I live in a hotel. I get calls through the exchange center."

"You shouldn't be here now. I've warned you about leaving Bryansk and traveling outside the border . . ."

"James," Anna Schmidt called from the slight opening in the bedroom door. She had finished her shower, gone back to the bedroom unnoticed, and was fully dressed, already wearing her coat.

"Come out, Anna, and meet my friend. This is Frank, he works for the same company as I do. As a matter of fact, this is his apartment. When I told him I needed privacy for a special occasion, he lent me his place. Hotels can be traps . . . too public . . . Please understand."

"My deepest apologies, Frau Schmidt, I should have called before I dropped in."

"I must be going." Her face flushed.

"I'll walk you out."

"No, stay with your friend, James. I will be fine . . . Will I see you soon?"

"Very soon." They kissed and she went out without looking back.

"So, what's happened Frank?"

"You were seen at the train station in Krakow, Palmer. An American on vacation visiting the death camps with his father who liberated it recognized you. He was the radio operator in your company. I can't believe you were able to cross the border into Germany without being arrested."

"You forget who is in charge in East Germany."

"You weren't seen in East Germany, Palmer. You were seen in Poland."

"Relax, drink your beer. I'm dead, remember? I'm buried in Arlington. Nobody cares."

"I'm here Palmer. Somebody gives a shit."

NEW YORK: DECEMBER 30

Adina Polansky looked out the living room window of the small but comfortable apartment she and her husband have shared since they migrated to New York from Poland after the war. The morning sun did little to warm her thin, almost transparent, face. Her hair is a dull gray and tied in a bun at the nape of her neck; her brown eyes are watery and heavily ringed by long years and terrible memories.

"It is going to be a lovely day. Cold but sunny. I think I will take a walk to the bakery. Would you like apple strudel, my dear?"

She turned from the window; he was smiling and nodding as best he could. Frederick suffered a stroke two years before, this past November. It affected his speech and the right side of his body. His hands trembled and he needed to be fed when the trembling became too much for him to hold a spoon. He could still walk slowly with the help of a walker. He could still manage his bathroom needs. He suffered from dementia.

"I won't be gone very long, but the fresh air will do me good. I will hurry. I will only go to the bakery." She kissed his bearded cheek, patted his shoulder, and left the apartment telling her friend and neighbor Estelle she would be back shortly.

Two blocks from her apartment on Eighty-Fourth Street, she crossed to the opposite side of the street, stopping periodically to rub her knee. The limp was the result of a severe beating by a German officer.

She reached First Avenue. Once across the street, she took a moment to lean on a lamp post and rest her leg. Not much further. Frederick so loved his apple strudel and she so loved her husband she would bear any pain to see a smile on his face.

She stepped behind two ladies and a young man collecting his change and leaving. The door opened behind her. A rush of morning air sent a shiver up her spine, but it was nothing like the shiver of horror that engulfed her when the man stepped around her to get a better look at the doughnuts in the case.

She froze, put her head down, and scratched her nose, partially hiding her face. He turned without even a glance at her and took his place in line. It is him . . . How could it be? He's changed, but his eyes . . . those damned blue eyes. She stepped forward, took a deep breath to steady her voice, ordered two apple strudels a container of coffee black, and sidestepped the man behind her, hoping he would not notice the limp.

Outside the shop she stopped and
looked in both directions, wondering which direction she should choose. It must be left. If he lived on or near her block, she would have noticed him sooner. He was dressed like a maintenance man. He must work or live nearby. Her knee on fire, she made her way toward Eighty-First Street and the bus stopped fifty feet from the corner. She would wait, drink her coffee, and hope to see him.

She dropped onto the bench, her knee aching so badly she wanted to scream. She was now five blocks from her apartment. She sipped her coffee. He was walking toward her, passing her, and walking briskly down the block carrying a box of a dozen doughnuts. She remembered the swagger and those crystal blue eyes. She watched and waited. At the corner of Eighty-First Street, he turned west, crossing First Avenue and disappearing behind the façade of an apartment building. Adina leaned forward, dropping the cup of coffee into the gutter, and fainted.

She awakened in the emergency room of Mount Sinai Hospital. Her thin, small frame on the gurney was covered with a thin blanket. A nurse smiled down at her. Behind the nurse a doctor wrote something on paper attached to a metal board.

"Welcome back, Mrs. Polansky. Are you feeling better?"

"Where am I? I must get home. My husband had a stroke and suffers from dementia. He is not well and he will be worried if I do not get home. I bought strudel for him. He will become afraid if I am not home soon. He may already be . . ."

"We have your address on Eighty-Fourth Street; is it correct, Mrs. Polansky?" The nurse showed her the address she kept in her purse.

"Yes, he is waiting for his strudel."

"We have the strudel in a refrigerator. This is Doctor Pratt. He will be taking care of you. He is a very fine doctor. You fainted on the street and a cab driver brought you here. We are giving you fluids so please do not move too much. Our ambulance is on its way to bring your husband here. We spoke to your neighbor Estelle; she is waiting. We will bring your husband to you, dear lady."

"My husband is house bound." Tears spilled down her face. "I have to go to him."

"We are bringing him here by ambulance. He is on his way," Pratt repeated in a gentle voice, "but you cannot leave until I am finished with my examination." Pratt took her fragile hand in his. "Would that be all right, Adina?"

"Be gentle with him; he is all I have."

"You have no other family, Adina?"

"Yes, we have a daughter, but she lives in Washington. The capital. My son-in-law is a doctor at the army hospital. Walter . . . Walter . . . something."

"Walter Reed. What is his name, Adina?"

"Silver. My daughter is Esther."

We will be as gentle as lambs, I promise." Doctor Pratt pulled the nurse aside. "She has little money and no insurance; this one is on us. I'll be right back. I am going to call Walter Reed hospital and find her son-in-law . . . Put her in a suite so her husband can stay with her. I do not think she should go home today."

"Nurse . . . could I have a rabbi visit me? It is very important?"

"Of course. I will have him paged right away."

"The doctor seems very nice."

"He is the chief of cardiology. He is the best. He lost his wife, so he knows how you feel. I will be right back. I am going to call Rabbi Lieberman. It might be a few minutes; he is probably on his rounds."

JANUARY 3, 1977

A young man with a boombox on his shoulder turned the corner of Eighty-First Street, his shoulders and hips keeping time with the loud music erupting from the radio resting on his shoulder. He wore a wool cap covering his hair, a turtleneck sweater, jeans and a pea coat. He reached the second apartment building with the painted semigloss black iron gate and stopped.

He spied a man on his knees digging small holes in the soft dirt. He put a small bulb in each hole, a portion of fertilizer, and a dab of water before covering the hole with his gloved hand.

He looked up when he heard the music and saw the young man watching him.

"We have no vacancies. Move along," the old man said, taking a few steps toward the gate. He had a knife in his pocket and knew how to use it.

"Just digging the music, old man, and watching you do your thing," His feet, hips and shoulders moved, following the cadence of the song, the fingers of his right hand tapping the side of the box. "You do nice work old man. Got to move along."

"Useless scheibe eines affen," the old man growled under his breath. "Go away you are disturbing the residents."

The young man strolled off. Once he was out of sight of the old man, he quickened his pace. The faded lime green four door Ford Galaxy sat at the curb. He shut off the radio, walked quickly to the passenger side, reached in the open window, and placed the radio on the front seat.

"Rabbi Lieberman, can you drop me at the 2.0 precinct. I got a class before my shift."

TEL AVIV: JANUARY 10

A photography shop, photo studio and portrait gallery stood in the center of Gabriel street. The second floor above the shop a spacious three-bedroom apartment used by the shop owner and his family.

The basement was the key to the structure, shared by Shin Bet and Mossad eighteen feet below street level with connecting tunnels leading from the apartment building across the alley to a private stairwell which led to the cellar.

Inside the space were dark rooms for processing film and snapshots. Rows of file cabinets were filled with files on ex-Nazis, terrorists from all over the Middle East, and also American dissidents. The space held a large, closed room with single beds, bathrooms, and a kitchen. Televisions monitored activities along the street. Work desks and long tables filled most of the remaining space.

The package containing the boom box arrived seven days after it was turned over to Rabbi Lieberman in New York. The crate was placed on a long steel table and opened. Satisfied the radio was not damaged, the photo specialist carried it into Dark Room 3. Slowly, with the use of a small Phillips screwdriver and a pair of tweezers, he removed the camera from the radio.

Just short of two hours later, the photo specialist, sweating profusely, emerged from the darkroom. "Gentlemen," he said triumphantly, "It is him: Rolf Lister. He has had surgery, but not enough to fool an old woman with a long memory."

That evening, the phone rang at the home of Tulia Davidoff in Haifa.

"Tulia it is Ariel. I hope you are enjoying your visit with Reba. I need to speak to her."

"Of course. How is your lovely wife Sofia?"

"She gives me no rest, that woman."

"And you love every moment; I'll get Reba."

"Hello, Uncle."

"Reba, we have something for you to take care of. You remember General Golan?"

"Yes, Uncle. I remember him . . . Do you need me to come now?"

"Enjoy your visit, rest. We will meet for breakfast Wednesday with the general and I will explain."

WATERGATE APARTMENT COMPLEX - WASHINGTON, D.C. JANUARY 10

Adam Cahill padded down the hall to the kitchen feeling refreshed after his shower. He prepared a pot of coffee with distilled water. Just as he lit the gas under the pot the phone rang.

"Calling me at six thirty in the morning . . ." he said out loud and padded over to the wall phone, his slippers flapping on the tile floor. "Hello."

"Mr. Cahill, I just got in from Germany. If the retired soldier saw Palmer, he isn't here now. I don't think he ever was in Krakow either. I've checked every hotel and public housing location. I have shown his picture in every café, restaurant and bar, in an eight-block square of the bus station here and in the town of Krakow. Personally, sir, I think it was a false lead."

"You agree the remains of the burnt body resting in Arlington National Cemetery was Palmer."

"He's dead and buried or someone would have seen him in Russia. The Russians would love to show an American traitor to the world."

"Do you think this marine is lying about what he saw?"

"I think it was a case of mistaken identity, Mr. Cahill, and nothing more."

"All right then, keep in touch." Cahill carried two cups of coffee back to the bedroom.

Beatrice turned over to face him. "He brings me coffee, it smells wonderful, and what a lovely surprise after a lovely night. Who was on the phone, Adam?"

"Number One called, Beatrice."

BRYANSK OBLASTY, UKRAINE: JANUARY 12

Palmer sat on his porch sipping a glass of tea laced with vodka. To his left, the forest. To his right, the city. The day was cold, but not as cold as recent winters. He was used to it and the vodka helped. He started to get up to refill his glass when he spied the black Volga V-12 sedan as it came out of the forest on the only road. He frowned.

He went inside and came out a moment later with two glasses, one full. Under his arm, the bottle of vodka. He set them on the small table just as the car pulled into the gravel driveway. He was surprised to see the driver. "Peter Shevchenko, what brings you to my humble home? Would you like a drink, Comrade Colonel?" He looked the same, except his black hair looked thinner with a sprinkle of gray at the temples. The square face and the eyes, blue like the eyes of a wolf assessing everything in his view . . . A hunter.

"Why are you here?" he asked, pouring vodka into a glass.

"I've come to see you, of course, Palmer." Shevchenko unbuttoned his gray coat and sat on the bench next to the window. "Are we alone?"

"Come inside and see for yourself."

"That will not be necessary. Why wouldn't I trust you?" An obvious slight to the man he detested for selling out his friends for a brick house and an ample supply of liquor and women. "You have been traveling, I understand." He felt the cold wind from the forest. "This married woman, Anna Schmidt, was she worth the risk, Palmer? What if you were caught by the husband? Certainly, you can see our dilemma."

"Are you people following me? Is this the work of the GRU?" The first taste of anger spilled out of his mouth along with droplets of spit. "I will go where I want. I am very careful."

"Of course you are, that is why I am here. You are so careful. You took a terrible risk. Our friends in the GDR wanted to catch you. In fact, they were waiting for you to cross the border. We were able to convince them to allow you to leave. The name of the apartment renter was also most interesting."

"I will go where I want."

"I am afraid not. We have an investment in you. We want to protect that investment. You will travel inside the USSR and only under strict supervision. You will use your false name when travel is granted. Other than that, you will remain here and from what I understand there is plenty of entertainment to fill your needs."

"I don't think you are being fair, Shevchenko."

"Life is not fair, Palmer. I know this from experience. My father died fighting the Germans; my mother died in a cellar in Leningrad. You will do as you are told. Now that we have that out of the way . . . I have a question or two about the new president of the United States: this Carter fellow. You are paid well for your information. If you think differently, you will find yourself handcuffed to a street lamp in London." Shevchenko stood up, swallowed the last of his vodka, and padded to the steps leaving his coat unbuttoned so he could access his weapon if Palmer decided to attempt something.

"I understand an assassin almost ended your career in Prague a couple years back? Maybe you need to stay closer to home as well, Comrade."

"You are expected to watch the television and pass along your thoughts . . . See to it, Palmer."

NEW YORK: JANUARY 14

Lister completed his morning rounds. The day was sunny and cold, the air clean. Lister checked the garden looking for signs of mold then went back inside. He went to the third floor to inspect apartment 3B. He took a quick look to make sure the painting was completed. All the fixtures worked properly. Satisfied, he left the apartment taking the stairs down to the lobby. The last thing he did was initial the printed form with the date the elevator was checked. He made a note to call the elevator company and have the cables inspected.

Back in his apartment, he poured Schnapps into his favorite glass. He peeled off his shirt, washed up in the kitchen sink, slipped on a clean flannel shirt, and padded over to his little rocker to await the new tenant.

At 9:57 a.m., a blonde woman with thick glasses and little makeup, except for a rather ugly pink lipstick, appeared. She wore a white silk blouse, unbuttoned, to expose ample cleavage under a leather coat and black bell bottom slacks.

Lister swallowed the last of his drink, rinsing his glass in the sink just as the doorbell chimed. He checked his watch. Right on time, he told himself, happy to show the apartment. He could process the paperwork and still have the afternoon to do as he pleased.

"I'm coming," he shouted, a bit annoyed by the second chime. He opened the door, his eyes immediately falling on her open blouse.

"Christian, I am Lena Davis. I'm here to see the apartment." She guessed correctly. His eyes moved over her breasts, paying little attention to her face. "I hope you were expecting me. My friend at work assured me you would be available?"

"Yes, of course, Miss Davis. I was called two weeks ago. You were lucky to find an apartment so soon. We had to rush to prepare it for you. I hope you like it." He closed the door behind him. "You know the owner Mister. Dukakis?"

"He is an old family friend of my parents. I never met him. I am sure I will like it. You have a bit of an accent. Are you Dutch, by any chance?"

"Yes I am. You study accents?"

"I have a job at the UN, I have to know how to interpret speech. If I intruded on your privacy, I am sorry."

"No, please do not apologize. Here we are . . . You also have an accent . . . Arabic?"

"Lebanese."

He stepped off the elevator ahead of her and crossed the hall to 3B, unlocked the door, and stepped aside to allow her to enter.

"I like the hardwood flooring. I am not a carpet person. I like the smell of fresh paint."

"You have two bedrooms and two bathrooms; one is for guests. The second is in the master bedroom. All the vacant apartments were upgraded. You will like the storage space. The kitchen is small but adequate, the neighbors are quiet and keep to themselves, mostly older couples. Mister. Dukakis did not mention if there was a Mister. Davis?"

"I am single, my work leaves little time for involvements, I'm afraid. Are you married, Christian?"

"My wife is dead . . . Cancer. Take your time. I will wait in the hall in case you have any questions."

"I like it very much," she said, joining him in the hall. "I am sure I will be very comfortable here. Mister Dukakis told my parents the rent is $185.00 a month under rent control."

"Mister. Dukakis sets the monthly payment. He did tell your parents there is a deposit for one month's rent."

"Yes, of course. I will take it. Are there papers to be filled out?"

"I have all the forms downstairs." He locked the door and together they stepped across the hall to the elevator. "I have two keys for the lock. They have been changed so you needn't worry about that. Do you enjoy your work at the UN?"

"Very much. The hours are long, but the work is quite satisfying."

"Would you like a coffee or tea while I put the papers together, Miss Davis?" His eyes glanced at her cleavage; she did not seem to notice.

"I am afraid I am in a bit of a hurry. I must get back. Mondays are horrific, but I appreciate the offer and I might take you up on it when I move in." She answered with a hint of flirtation in her voice. "I will need phone service and electricity turned on."

"Not to worry, Miss Davis. I will see to it. If you would please tell Mister Dukakis you are satisfied with the work. I would appreciate it."

"I will see that my parents talk to him."

Adina rinsed off the breakfast dishes—placing them neatly in the drip tray—poured water into a glass, and brought her husband his medication. He took his pills with his right hand, which only weeks before would shake, forcing her to put the pills in his mouth. He smiled without drooling or spilling it on his shirt, and thanked her with only a slight slur of the words. His eyes were clear the help of the medication prescribed by that wonderful doctor and the nurse who came three days a week helped improve the short life he still had. Adina blessed them both in her prayers each night.

"We have company coming today, my dear: a young lady. She comes all the way from Israel to visit." She patted her husband's shoulder "Our daughter called. She is coming for a visit and bringing our grandchildren." She kissed him on the lips. "It will be nice to have them here.

"Yes Adina . . . nice to have them here."

"Our guest will be here soon . . . I'll comb your hair."

"I can do it."

The young woman stood in the center of the living room. She removed a pair of gloves from her coat pocket, slipped them on, and reached behind her back slowly. In the small of her back, she felt the handle of the V-42 dagger used by the British SAS and American Special Forces. She slowly took it from the cloth sheath and placed it on her hip. He was turning from the file cabinet just as she slid her other hand into the pocket of her coat.

"Here are the papers to be signed. Come sit down at the table."

"I remember the agreement, you told me upstairs. Will you accept a check?"

"Yes, of course. Please have a seat by the desk."

"I would rather stand, if you do not mind, Mister. Lucas. I think better on my feet." She noticed immediately the look of mistrust in his eyes, probably an instinct all criminals have.

"Forgive me," the pleasant smile never left her face. "It is the work. I sit twelve hours a day, that is all. I seem to manage my thoughts better. I know it is silly, but if I may . . ."

"No need to be sorry; I understand. I once had a job where I was always on my feet, and as the manager here, I am often up and around most of the day, so I understand completely."

"I bet you do, you miserable bastard." She plunged the dagger into his midsection. "You murdered my family, my grandparents, aunts, uncles, and cousins you filthy shit taken from your mother's ass." She pulled the blade of the dagger upward cutting into his intestines, slicing his stomach. "Did you think we would forget Rolf Lister . . . Blue Eyes."

When she pulled it out, he slid to the floor cradling the intestine trying to escape the jagged gaping hole.

Lister began to crawl toward his chair, slipping in his own blood.

"Judah," he cried out. He made it to the chair. He reached down and snatched the throw rug away from the compartment in the floor, his intestine sliding out between the buttons of his shirt. "Judah," he growled, blood running out of him, stealing the last vestiges of his strength.

She was on him before he could raise the section of floor. She held the dagger in both hands high above him and plunged it into his brain.

"Shalom Aleichem. I am a greeter to those who visit."

Shalom." The woman answered. "I am Uma Merkel."

"Aleichem Shalom, I come in peace. My name is Reba Davidoff-Klein. I will be here only a short time, then I must visit Adina Polansky and her husband before I return to Israel. But, first, I want to pray. Please show me the way to the prayer room."

"I know the woman you seek and why you are here. We were told to expect you. Follow me."

"Thank you," Reba answered. "I have clothing in my bag that needs to be discarded."

"I know the Rabbi would want to see and bless you, Reba. Give me the discarded clothes; I will see to them."

Adina puffed up the cushions on the couch and straightened the pillows. Hearing the hiss of the teapot, she started toward the kitchen when the doorbell chimed.

"That must be our guest." She rushed into the kitchen—turning off the burner—adjusted her apron, and went to the door.

"Shalom Aleichem; I am Reba."

"Aleichem Shalom. You are welcome in our home. Let me take your coat. I have made tea." She turned toward her husband sitting by the window. "Frederick, our guest is here."

"Shalom Aleichem." He smiled broadly. It had been a long time since he could say those words without slurring them.

"Forgive me, but I cannot stay. I must get to the airport."

"You are here about that awful man?"

"Yes."

"Was it him?"

"Yes it was, Adina. He will never trouble your dreams again."

"Bless you, child of Israel." Adina, tears streaming down her face, took Reba's hands in hers and kissed them.

"I must leave. I have brought a gift for you both." Reba reached into her coat pocket and brought out a thick manila envelope. "Come home, Adina and Frederick Polansky." She kissed the old woman on both cheeks. "I must go."

She opened the door and went out, closing it behind her.

CHAPTER FOUR

MINSK.

"Boris Molotov. It is good to see you. How are your wife and children?"

"Very good, Peter. You have a nice view of the square from your room, and I have chilled a bottle of Quora for you.

"You always treat me well, Comrade."

"Let me take your bag, dear friend."

"You have done enough. I just want to get to my room, shower, and rest. I have to make a call or two first."

"I took the liberty of putting fruit and candies for you, and Olga has prepared pastries."

"Please thank Olga for the pastries and my apology. Give her a kiss for me."

Shevchenko sat on the edge of his bed and dialed. "Is Anna Lebedev there, please? Tell her it is Peter Shevchenko . . . I will wait. Thank you for your assistance, Comrade."

"Peter, tell me you are in Minsk?"

"I just got in my room. I know it is short notice, Anna, it could not be helped. Are you free tonight?"

"I had plans, but I will break them. Where are you? When did you arrive?"

"The Renaissance Minsk on the square. I just arrived."

"I should have known. How is your friend, Comrade Molotov?"

"He is well; let's meet for supper at the Grand Café."

"I get off at seven. How long will you be in Minsk?"

"I am afraid I must leave in the morning."

"Always on the run. I will be there at six."

He hung up and dialed the operator. "I need to make a call to the office of the directorate in Moscow. Please ring me when you have the line open." He hung up and prepared to take a shower. The phone rang.

"Your line is open, Comrade. I am not getting a dial tone. Shall I try once more?"

"Thank you. It sometimes takes more time for the ring, especially between here and Moscow. I will hold." When the operator hung up, he quickly dialed a second four-digit number.

"Kasparov here. Where are you, Peter?"

"Minsk. I will be back in Moscow tomorrow: Aeroflot 61 at noon. The American is a problem. Contact Mikhail. I want to address this issue with you both."

"Aeroflot 61 from Minsk noon tomorrow. I will see you then."

They enjoyed the appetizer, a Russian crepe, lamb dumplings, and wild mushrooms. He allowed the waiter to choose the white wine. They ate, drank, and talked like a married couple explaining away the events of the day.

They walked through the lobby of the hotel, arm in arm, and kissed on the elevator. He opened the door to his room. "A drink? Boris chilled a bottle of Quora."

"I love Quora vodka." She began to undress while he opened the bottle, poured the clear liquid for both, and sat on the edge of the bed.

She padded naked over to him, sliding onto him, her knees pressed against his thighs. She kissed him hard on the mouth while gently rotating her hips against him. He handed her the vodka. She swallowed it and tossed the empty glass over her shoulder as she began unbuttoning his shirt. "Kiss me, Peter. Kiss every inch of me."

Clouds outside the bathroom window. Fresh snow on the sill. Anna dried herself, brushed out her blond hair—leaving it to dry naturally—and slipped into the bath robe, tying it loosely around her waist.

"I ordered oatmeal topped with an egg, toast lightly buttered the way you like it, and a pot of tea."

"It is wonderful and smells even better . . ." She padded over to the bed, pulled the small table closer, and sat next to him. She fingered her ring finger. "Must you leave this morning? Why not catch a later flight this evening, perhaps?"

"I have urgent business in Moscow; Eat your breakfast before it gets cold."

"This is how it will be with us, won't it, Peter Shevchenko. You have invited me to Moscow only once in the three years I've known you. You place me in a luxurious hotel. I don't even know where you live. You visit me here with no notice, only a phone call?"

"You know the work I do, Anna Lebedev. I cannot promise more; it would not be fair to ask you to wait."

"One of my coworkers has asked me to marry him. He is a good man and will be a good provider. He is a party man and is planning a run for office next year. He has connections with the army and the politburo. If this is our goodbye, make love to me," she whispered, sliding the garment off her shoulders.

Standing in line, he waited for his call to the flight registration desk, seeing the couples with young children. Older couples held their valises and travel papers. Peter Shevchenko sighed., seeing the smiling faces, the children clinging to their parents, reminded him just how empty his life truly was.

"Comrade Shevchenko, are there any special requests you require?"

"I have a request for an aisle bulkhead seat or the aisle seat, third row."

"I have one of those." The clerk gave him the card with Aisle Seat, Number Three.

"You may board when you are ready, Comrade Shevchenko."

"Thank you." He waited until the plane leveled off before closing his eyes.

LENINGRAD: DECEMBER ,1941

Refugees slogged along in the snow, carrying what they could on their backs or pulling two-wheel carts. The caravan stretched over a mile. On the side of the road, in ditches, lay those who could go no further.

The young Shevchenko's mother carried a large cloth she hid potatoes onions, carrots, and almonds amid the women's clothes, the weight of the sack bending her almost in half. She refused help for fear someone might find the food. Peter carried the last six potatoes sewn into the lining of his father's coat, along with pieces of dried fruit and a little meat. Food was worth a treasure in gold.

Hungry and thirsty but afraid to eat, Peter picked up some snow, rolled it into a loose ball, and gave it to his mother.

"Lick it and eat it, mother." He formed another ball of snow and ate the flakes. "Put your hands on my shoulders; it will help rest your back."

He was tall for his age and already muscular from the long hours working on the farm with his father, Alexi Shevchenko. How much further would they have to walk? No one could be certain. They did know they were one day closer to Leningrad.

They reached a crossroad and the line stopped. Peter and his mother were close to the front of the caravan and he could see it was a checkpoint.

"They look to be checking papers, maybe looking for spies."

"I have our papers in order, my son," she answered. "Be careful when you open the bag."

"I know what to do mother. One of them is coming down our side of the line:." The soldier approached. He looked to be sixteen, maybe seventeen. He wasn't tall; he had a square face, reddened by the cold. His eyes were brown and his thin nose ran, the mucus freezing on his chin. His hair was hidden under a cap with fur lining and wing flaps. He carried a long rifle with a bolt action.

"What is your name and age?"

"Peter Shevchenko, Comrade. I am thirteen. This is my mother, Elisa Shevchenko." He put the two bags he was carryin down near his worn boots. "We have been on the road of life a very long time, hoping to reach Leningrad."

"Where is your father, Shevchenko?"

"He was killed fighting the Germans in the forest of Bryansk Oblast."

"I lost my father as well in those forests. You are tall for your age, Peter Shevchenko. Can you prove you are thirteen?"

"I have the proper paperwork, including his birth certificate. I insisted on it when he was born, sir. I will show you," Elisa answered.

"Come with me to the checkpoint. You are close to the city, a little over five kilometers. Let me help you with your bags, Elisa Shevchenko."

"What will happen to the young men being pulled from the line?"

"They will go against the German horde and will probably be killed, Peter Shevchenko."

"What about us?" A voice called out from a few feet away.

"We will get to you soon." He shouldered his rifle, picked up her bag, and said, "Follow me to the checkpoint. If you are being truthful about your age, you will pass through. I will give you an address."

"My mother was born here, and she knows the city."

"Good then you will find it without trouble . . . follow me."

"I can't thank you enough," Peter whispered and kissed the young soldier. "I will never forget this kindness."

"If you survive and if I survive, Peter Shevchenko of Bryansk Oblast, remember this: food is short and the people have become like wild dogs. They steal from each other; they no longer recover those who died in the street; the snow is their grave. Take close care of your mother."

"What is your surname?"

"Molotov . . . Boris of Leningrad . . . Now."

"The flight attendant put her hand on his shoulder. "Comrade Shevchenko, wake up."

"I am awake." The dream receded and he was back in the present. "I am awake." He sat straight up in his seat. !941 and the war pushed back into the recess of his mind

"We will be landing in about forty minutes. Would you like a glass of tea?"

"Yes, I think I would. I hope I didn't cause any trouble."

"You were fine, a little restless but quiet. I will get your tea."

"Is it overcast in Moscow?"

"Light snow only, but very cold."

"Thank you, Comrade." Very cold, he thought . . . Not like Leningrad.

MOSCOW: JANUARY 15

Shevchenko entered his apartment just north of Red Square. It was situated just one hundred yards from the Lubyanka building where his office on the fourth floor overlooked the square. The apartment was spacious, nearly 2,500 square feet and rent free. His furnishings were gifts from members of the politburo, men who owed favors. Men with secrets he kept to himself.

Shevchenko put his valise down on the thick brown carpet and took off his coat. He padded to the kitchen, poured vodka into a juice glass, and padded back into the living room, taking off his jacket and tie and dropping them on his sofa. He picked up the phone and called his office.

"Welcome home. How was your trip?"

"Not as successful as I had hoped, Comrade. Kasparov brought me home."

"I am sorry." She did not ask why. Marina Ivanov knew he would tell her in his own time.

"I will shower and dress. I should be in my office by seven. You should go home. I will see you in the morning."

"I will wait; you may need me afterwards. Shall I prepare a pot of tea it is beginning to snow again?"

"That would be good."

His secretary was waiting at the door to Shevchenko's office, a glass of hot steaming tea in her hand. Marina Ivanov was not tall.. Maria Ivanov wore her blonde hair in a tight bun at the knap of her neck. Light blue eyes, a scar she hid behind the thick rim of her glasses was given to her by a drunken young Russian soldier simply because she was a Jewish woman in Stalin's Russia. "One level teaspoon of sugar, unstirred, as you like it, sir."

She greeted him with a soft North Carolina twang in her voice, one of the American accents she could speak as if she had lived there all her life. She taught him the Carolina accent at the school of languages for students of the KGB from 1953 to 1955. She thought the accent best suited the young student.

"How kind of you, ma'am," he answered, mimicking her accent. It was a small intimate conversation between two people who've been together a long time, even though they were never intimate beyond these simple exchanges.

"You have mail and two invitations: one to a concert Andropov is hosting for the party leaders and another from the general staff. You have been invited to General Pavlov's sixtieth birthday party where a special announcement is to be made. Perhaps he is stepping down, Peter."

"Not him. Pavlov will never step down as long as he can lead an army against the Europeans, whom he hates . . . The American is becoming a problem. He travels. He is no longer interested in sharing his views on American political matters, which was the reason for him being allowed to live in Russia." He took a long swallow of tea. "We have time. Join me in a glass of tea. I brought you something from our friends at the consulate." He produced a carton of Lucky Strike cigarettes.

"Thank you, Peter Shevchenko. Have one with me while we enjoy our tea."

"Have you ever wanted to visit the United States? You could live in so many cities. Your accents and diction are perfect for . . ."

"I am Jewish. Even without Stalin, I am not to be trusted outside the Kremlin. I will not be one of Kasparov's tulips, and who would want me as I am, old wrinkled and scarred like an alley cat? I do love the cigarettes though."

"I am sorry. I was only . . ."

"You are a dear friend. I appreciate the compliment you give me, but here serving you is where I want to be. You saved me. Making me your secretary was a gift from God. If it were not for you, I would never have come this far." Marina dragged deeply on her cigarette "You were my best student . . . did I ever tell you that?"

"Many times, Marina Ivanov, many times. How long has it been?"

"We have known each other since 1953. I have been your secretary since 1970. I was afraid when they sent you to America, I would not see you again."

"I told you I would return. How is this man Uri Chernoff? Does he treat you with respect? Does he know you smoke American cigarettes?"

"You needn't worry. I will tell him tonight. It is seven forty. Time for you to go. I will tell him I bought them on the black market."

"A part truth, I suppose . . . Take the vodka home."

"A partial truth is not a lie, Shevchenko."

Shevchenko entered Cell 15A: Beria's room. The drain was in a depression near the rear of the soundproof room. There were chipped plaster indentations in the wall above the drain. The drain swallowed the blood; the chips in the plaster marked the spots where bullets passed through the victim's head, leaving splashes of blood and bits of brain matter. Two feet from the wall a chair the base cemented into the concrete floor. Prisoners were forced to sit on the metal tube when being, what Beria liked to call, interviewed. A long wooden table, three chairs and a bench were the only furnishings. Above the table was a fan. The fan rotated slowly barely moving the stale air. Wall lights lit the room.

"Good evening, gentlemen," Shevchenko said, closing the heavy steel door behind him. He was reminded of Beria's words to Stalin, "Give me a name and I will find the crime." He pushed the thought aside. "Thank you for giving up your evening, but I thought it most important."

"I have been holding my glass for twenty minutes, and still, it is dry."

"My apologies for the oversight, Comrade Kasparov. I left the bottle in my office." A partial truth is better than a lie. "The American does not seem to fathom his position here, or care. He left the country. He went to Berlin to be with a woman. The wife of a German industrialist . . . It isn't the first time. A mole in the security office told me of the situation. He has also stopped viewing American news programs. He says he isn't at all interested in them. I think he should be turned over to the American authorities. What do you think, Comrade Balandin ?"

"Uri Fedorov will never punish him, I am afraid . . . is cunning, but not wise enough to see the facts as they are. He only thinks in terms of what is good for him and the network of turned Americans and their allies. He also must answer to the Central Committee. For now. If we eliminate the American and the word passes beyond our borders, he will be held responsible. He wants to be head of state. Never forget that. We can no longer keep strides with the Americans without bankrupting our system." Balandin invited his friend Kozlov to the meeting; Shevchenko now understood why.

"Do not let the smile on my face fool you, Comrade Kozlov," Shevchenko answered. He did not know Kozlov well, but a friend of Balandin's is a man to be trusted and respected, or Mikhail would not allow him to sit in on this meeting. "Please go on with your assessment."

"I would estimate no more than fifteen years, Comrade, unless a leader comes to power, who can relate to a political world that is changing."

"What about this Carter fellow in America?"

"It is hard to say. He is an enigma; he is like a brilliant child balancing on the edge of a deep crevice. We cannot be certain if he will fall, at least for now, Comrade Balandin."

"You should have remembered the vodka, Peter," Balandin said with a sigh.

"How was your trip to Minsk, Peter?"

"Not what I expected, Mikhail."

"I am sorry to hear that. Not surprised, but sorry."

LENINGRAD: FEBRUARY 1942

Back in his apartment Shevchenko fell into a deep but uneasy sleep. The dark days in Stalingrad came back just as they had on the plane.

The first strips of sunlight began to filter through the small windows into the basement. The light diminished by the heavy snowfall during the night. Even a shower of snow today would completely block any light from entering the cellar. Bodies began to rustle under worn blankets and threadbare coats. The bombers would come with the first sun of winter, picking their targets. Today the death toll would be much higher.

Peter Shevchenko stretched his arms and legs as far as the bodies near him would allow. He pulled his father's coat over his shoulders and stood up, picked up the pot with a smashed lid, leaned forward, and kissed his mother's forehead. She was shivering, her forehead hot. The fever had increased.

"Come with me? the sun has come out who can tell for how long? The fresh air will make you feel better. We will go to the food station together. You need to know how to find it if something should happen to me . . . Come with me, Mama?"

"I don't feel very well at all. You go and be careful." She sneezed and coughed into her coat, wiping the mucous on the inside of the lapel. "The sun will bring more bombers . . ."

"You need food, Mama, and you need to see a doctor."

"The doctors are with the soldiers." She coughed, sneezed, and wiped her face. Go, son. I will climb to the next level and wait for you. Try to find another place for us."

Young Shevchenko at last reached the back of the truck. He held the small pot in his outstretched arms while it was filled. He pulled it down, studying the meager contents: There were three wafer slices of potato, two slices of bread made from sawdust and cow droppings, and a yellow liquid but no meat. He covered the pot and slowly walked away.

He was nearly halfway through the park, the sun shining brightly and warming his face. His feet were wet and cold. Soon they would be numb if he did not find good boots. He spied a man lying across a bench; his boots looked close to his size. The man's face was frozen gray; he was in no need of his boots. He made the sign of the cross, dragged the body off the bench, and pulled the boots off. He sat down and began to remove his boot. Suddenly, off in the distance, he heard the first drone of the German fighters and bombers coming out of the clouds to the west.

Quickly, he put on the new boots. The drone grew louder. He picked up the man and placed him across the seat of the bench. He spied another body not far from the bench. He dragged the woman and laid her face down along the side of the bench and crawled under to wait out the attack. But the planes did not come over the park; they dropped their bombs to the west of the city center.

"Mama," he shouted, "Mama."

It was quiet. No trucks filled with soldiers, no fire apparatus moving toward the western part of the city. He crawled out from under the bench. The boots were bigger than they looked, but they would do until he could find a better fitting pair. He began to walk toward the west, forgetting the pot of soup. Black smoke and flames rose skyward. He could only hope he would find her and be able to bury her. But where could he bury her and where would he find tools to dig? His only real hope was she did not suffer.

Shots fired from inside the wall of smoke and flame; another and another . . . silence. From out of the smoke, a soldier staggered toward the road. He wore a heavy coat, knee high brown boots, and carried a rifle strapped to his shoulder. He came toward the boy. When his strength gave out, he dropped to his knees, clutching a small leather satchel, and cried out to the young boy.

Shevchenko, seeing no one else coming out of the smoke, got up and ran toward the soldier, dropping to his knees by the side of the wounded man.

"The satchel I carry, take it to the Cathedral… Give it to General Zhukov and no one else." The soldier spit blood. "I'm dying, shot by the people of Leningrad because they wanted my horse for food. Be a good comrade. Take the satchel to the General; it is very important to him. Take my wallet and papers so he knows who died for this leather pouch." He coughed again; a large clot of blood spilled onto the snow. "Stay clear of people, for your own sake." He died, still kneeling in the snow, his eyes staring without sight into the face of the young boy.

Shevchenko put his hand over the soldier's eyes and closed them. "I'm sorry, Comrade, but I need your coat, your boots, and your rifle."

He unbuttoned the coat and slipped it off. He laid the soldier face down in the snow, straightening his legs. The young Shevchenko took the cartridge belt with the holstered handgun and buckled it as tight as he could around his waist. He found the wallet and papers and slipped those into the pocket of the coat. He took off his father's coat and covered the soldier with it. Rest in peace, Comrade. Peter began to walk. Soon resolve replaced fear, and survival replaced the thought of dying.

"Walk Shevchenko," he told himself. "Leave your past on this road . . . Survive."

It was dark when he reached the Cathedral. No more tears to shed. What remained was his resolve to do as the dying soldier asked. The streets were deserted except for soldiers on foot or in carriages patrolling the unlit perimeter. In the cellar of the church were the general's headquarters. Shevchenko approached the perimeter gate. A soldier with a submachine gun came out of the shadows and stopped him.

"I am Peter Shevchenko. I have a pouch to give to General Zhukov."

"Shevchenko, I recognize you. I am Molotov . . . Boris Molotov." He lit a match, so the boy could see his face.

"A small world. You say you have a pouch for the general?"

"For his eyes only; a dying soldier gave it to me."

"Did he give you his coat and rifle as well?" Molotov slipped the sub machine gun from his shoulder and pointed it at the young boy.

"The people of Leningrad shot him for his horse. He gave me the pouch and his identification before he died. I took the coat and boots because I was cold and covered him with mine. I took the rifle for protection, Comrade. I must give the pouch to the general; it was his dying wish. I owe him that much."

"Your mother, where is she, Shevchenko?"

"Buried under the rubble of what was our building."

A second soldier appeared out of the shadows. This one was older. "Corporal, what is going on here?"

"I am Peter Shevchenko." The boy repeated the story.

"I am the officer in charge of this area; you will give me the pouch and I will see that General Zhukov gets it."

"I will deliver it as I have explained. It is my duty to my dead comrade."

"You have a duty to only Stalin. How old are you?"

"I will be fourteen in one week."

"I can vouch for him," Molotov said. "I first saw him on the road to the city. He passed through the checkpoint with his mother and he had the proper papers, sir."

"Where are your mother and father now?"

"My father is dead. My mother is under the building that collapsed on her this morning . . . sir."

"Take him to the general; do not be too long." He looked at the young boy with sad eyes. "I am sorry for you."

General Zhukov, a small man with a barrel chest and flat round face, studied the small arrows and pins on the map. "It seems the pins and arrows moved hourly, but only in one direction, Leningrad." He turned toward the man sitting next to his desk, "Well Fyodor Polos, my dear Comrade, what will we do? Should we abandon Leningrad and retreat across the lake, or should we stay and die here? Of course, we both know the answer to that question, do we not, Comrade? It is warm in this cellar and very cold outside as your brother the Lieutenant knows."

A knock on the door interrupted the general., "Yes, what is it?"

"Sir, it is me, corporal of the guard, my general. I have a young man who has come carrying a special pouch for the Comrade General."

"Bring him in, and stand by the outer door, and let no one pass."

"Sir, the commander of the guard has ordered me to return immediately to my post."

"Shall I repeat my order, Corporal?"

"No, Comrade General."

"Has this young boy been searched for weapons?"

"Fyodor here is a NKVD man; he thinks you are a spy. He thinks everyone is a spy. His mother even fears him . . . Are you a spy?" Zhukov smiled, seeing the uneasiness on Polos' face.

"No, Comrade General; I have a pouch given me by a dying soldier in the western part of the city. He was killed by our own people for his horse. He told me to bring it to you and to not leave it with anyone else."

"Give me the pouch."

"I have his papers. He wanted me to give them to you, so you would know who he was." The boy took the wallet, papers, and pouch and handed them to the general.

"What is your name?" Zhukov stepped behind his desk and sat down, untying the coarse string. He slid a few sheets of paper out and placed them face down on his desk while he adjusted the small heater by his boots which gave off just enough heat to warm the roaches and the mice, as he often reminded everyone.

"My name is Peter Shevchenko and I am from Bryansk Oblast. I was born here and my mother was raised here. My father in the Oblast. He inherited a farm when his father died, that is why we moved there."

"Why did you come back? Why didn't you and your father stay to fight the Germans?" Polos asked.

"Ignore him, Peter Shevchenko," Zhukov said.

"My father was a Partisan. He died fighting the Germans. Why do you not fight them instead of sitting here accusing me of cowardice?"

"A good question," Zhukov said, looking sideways at Polos. "Maybe I will ask Stalin to send you to the front, Polos, along with your brother." Zhukov smiled. "I like you, young man. I think you will need the long coat to hide your balls."

"Stalin is my authority. I answer to him," Shevchenko answered, with all the sincerity he could muster.

"Where is your mother?" Zhukov was intrigued. This one is wise beyond his years, even if he does not fully understand it. A young man to be nurtured, perhaps.

"The German bombers came early this morning; she was killed. I walked all day to deliver the pouch and now I do not know what I will do."

"Would you like to stay here? "

"I would be honored, sir. I will serve you well. I will learn as fast as I am taught."

"I believe you Peter Shevchenko . . . Corporal, get in here! Take him to the second basement; introduce him to Dmitry Kasparov. Tell Kasparov to get him fresh clothes. Feed him and bring him back to me. After that you may return to your duties." He scribbled a note and held his hand out to the corporal. "Take this note to Lieutenant Polos."

"Yes, sir."

Boris Molotov led Shevchenko along a dimly lit corridor smelling of mildew, cigarettes, and sweat. At the end of the corridor, a doorway opened into a large room. Men in ragged clothing milled about or sat hunched over metal tables. Three long steam tables with five-gallon cans of a soup simmering sat behind the last row of tables. Next to each can was a ladle.

"Dmitry Kasparov?" Boris shouted over the voices, "Dmitry Kasparov."

A young man in an army uniform two sizes larger looked up from a table. His face was narrow with high cheekbones, deep-set blue eyes, and blondish hair that was long and matted to his scalp. It was easy to see he hadn't bathed in weeks. When he stood up, Shevchenko noticed the gun belt like the one he was wearing. "Corporal, why aren't you on the perimeter?"

"I bring someone for you to take care of. He is to be fed, given a change of clothes, and then brought upstairs to the general. He is to be our new courier, perhaps."

"What happened to the other courier?"

"He is dead," Boris shouted across the room. "Kasparov is the head of the courier corp."

"He looks so young for such an important job," Shevchenko commented as the young man made his way across the room.

"Trust me Shevchenko . . . Boys become men quickly in Leningrad. You will see."

"I am Peter Shevchenko," the youngster stuck out his hand. "I am happy to meet you."

"Have something to eat. Be careful what you take. The food is in short supply. Men will be watching you. Take only one half of a half potion of potato, only a small piece of meat, one slice of bread, and fill your bowl with broth, understood?" Kasparov took his hand and shook it, "How old are you?"

"I will be fourteen in one week."

"Let us hope so."

MOSCOW. JANUARY 18, 1977

Shevchenko awakened in a cold sweat. The clock clicked forward to 5:45 a.m. He wiped his brow with the sleeve of his shirt and lay back down. His pillow felt clammy. He remembered a promise he made to his mother and father. The guilt of not giving them a proper burial in 1941 remained with him every day of his life. The phone rang.

"Hello, who disturbs me at the ungodly hour?"

"It is Kasparov. Mikhail was correct. The American is very close to the man we report to. His assistant, Comrade Anton, called me only moments ago. It seems Fedorov is very upset with us."

"Moments ago, you say? His interference disturbs me and makes me wonder if something else is brewing beneath the service. I will dress and be in my office in two hours."

"This line is secure, Peter. I suggest we meet in Gorky Park, just you and me, while the offices are swept."

"Bring along two of your most trusted ladies."

"I will have them skate on the pond while we talk."

"Good, my friend." Shevchenko padded to the small kitchen, put on a pot of water at low heat, and padded back to the bathroom. He showered, shaved, and dressed.

He looked at his watch. He did not like to be late and frowned upon subordinates who did not feel the same sense of urgency. It was different in America. Students had no sense of urgency unless it involved drugs, antiwar rallies, or sex. He parked the car near the walking path.

The two men shook hands. They watched as the women stepped onto the ice and began to skate. After a moment, and friendly waves of encouragement, they walked off the path to talk in private.

"Was there anything else Victor Anton said besides leaving the American alone? Did he mention travel, for example?"

"No Peter, only that. Fedorov was concerned and he wanted the American left alone."

"Why is he protecting him? Why would he go against the interests of his top intelligence agents for internal security?" Shevchenko paused, rubbing his chin between his thumb and index finger. "There can be only one answer. Comrade Fedorov and his advisors are planning something and he needs the American to help them."

"The president?"

"Yes Dmitry Kasparov. Brezhnev . . . Do you have two tulips unknown to Andropov or his deputy, women you can completely trust?"

"Two are skating before your eyes, my friend. I have another, but she is engaged with an English Diplomat. I have more at your disposal."

"You keep your secrets well. Remember, I am invited to a party for General Pavlov. I want you there. I will see that you are invited. You could bring one of your tulips as a guest. She might find Pavlov an interesting man to know better."

"The redhead . . . her name is Anile Romanoff. I am sure Comrade Anton would like her. The other young lady is Lilia Chekov; she would interest General Pavlov. In that, I am even more secure."

"I suggest they not meet on the same night, coincidence aside, Dmitry Kasparov. From now on please do not give me the names of your tulips."

"As you wish, Comrade. I think Mikhail should know what we are thinking.?"

"Yes, of course."

CHAPTER FIVE

Ethan found Cahill walking along the stretch of tall grass on the bank of the river just as his driver said he would. His shoulders sloped a little bit more than the last time Ethan and he met. His hands were cupped behind his back. His shoes seemed to shuffle along the damp grass.

"Mr. Cahill, why don't we share a bench, sir?"

"Good idea. I've been reading your cartoons with interest. I must say they are just sardonic enough, without being offensive." Cahill reached the bench, sitting down heavily. "I was wrong Ethan. I didn't think it would get off the ground . . . Argyle Socks: I chuckle every time I read it. Do you think you will top that Doonesbury follows?"

"It isn't where I would like it to be, but it is a living and with my savings and retirement bonus, plus stipend, I'm comfortable. It keeps my mind occupied . . . As far as catching Trudeau, it isn't going to happen. I am in the middle of a remodel. That's my story, what about you, sir?"

"Tired. I'm a relic of the Ethan part of the bygone era. People do not care about us anymore. Not even the new president pays much attention. He is brilliant. He lacks the fundamentals for his position. He worries too much. I do not trust his advisors . . . I guess we will have to wait and see. He has only been president two days."

"Why don't you retire? When is enough . . . enough?"

"This is all I know, Ethan, and as long as part of the country needs us . . . well, you know." Cahill turned and stared for a moment at the river slipping by in endless motion. "Have you talked to Joanna?"

"I sent her a Brenda Lee song from 1972: 'You Were Always on My Mind.' She sent it back with a note: 'It's very nice and very thoughtful, but too late.' "

"I'm sorry, Ethan."

"She is happy and in a good place Adam . . . She has met someone, a lawyer. I hope he can give her what I couldn't. How about that breakfast you promised me?"

"Wonderful idea: a nice bowl of oatmeal, orange juice, and a bowl of prunes. Beatrice insists I eat a good breakfast each day; she sends her regards."

"How is Beatrice, Adam?"

"She is fine, Ethan. Just fine."

MOSCOW: JANUARY 22

"You haven't touched your tea. I will make a fresh pot. Your friends will be here soon."

"Don't go to any trouble., Marina."

"It is no trouble. I put a fresh washcloth and soap in the bathroom."

"Thank you, my friend."

"You were tired. Was it Leningrad stealing your sleep last night?"

"Go home, Marina. The meeting may take hours."

"I'll make fresh tea and then I will go."

"What did Comrade Chernoff think of the cigarettes?"

"He is still my boyfriend."

BRYANSK OBLAST

Mail was delivered to Palmer's door as a courtesy. Palmer took the small stack of mail and waved the man off without so much as a thank you. The man's wife waited in the bedroom. For Palmer, it was thanks enough.

He went inside, dropping the mail in a trash receptacle. Except for one letter sent from Germany. The address was crossed out and forwarded to his home He stuffed it into the pocket of his robe and walked to his bedroom. "Get dressed and get out. Make it quick."

"Have I displeased you?"

"Go home to your husband." He poured vodka into a glass. He was getting the feelings again. The women of Bryansk weren't enough. He needed much more. He drained the glass in a swallow. The vodka helped quiet the voices in his head. "Get out."

His eyes narrowed when he read the note. "Anna Schmidt," he growled. "You foolish bitch." His cheeks reddened. "People who are foolish make mistakes." Palmer shredded the letter, tearing it into small bits. She could ruin everything.

He walked toward the bathroom. "Why can't they just screw someone without all the romance that goes with it." Palmer thought flushing the torn bits of paper down the toilet, forgetting for a moment his other more dangerous feelings and padded back to his bedroom.

"Your father and I keep warning you of these involvements, but you don't listen. You keep getting mixed up with women who torment you.".

"Shut up...Shut up, Mother."

THE CHILD IS BORN

Wayne Morrison was tried, convicted, and sentenced to death for the murder of three young women in the late summer of 1942 in Kansas City. He was led out through the rear dock of the courthouse where a Kansas state police car waited. He lived on death row before being hanged at 12:05 a.m. two years to the day he was sentenced.

Miles away at Fairmont Maternity Hospital in Kansas City, Ruth Samson, age nineteen, a prostitute and drug addict, gave birth to a baby boy conceived while Wayne was on death row. A judge allowed a conjugal visit nine months before he was hanged. The judge was later sanctioned and removed from office. Alicia named the baby Wayne after his father.

Three days after she gave birth, in a fit or morbid depression, Samson attempted to kill the baby. She was caught by a nurse in time to save the child's life. The baby was brought to the hospital's adoption center where he was treated for residual drug addiction. Ruth was convicted of the lesser charge of child endangerment and sentenced to three years in the woman's facility. She hanged herself in her cell with a bed sheet. On that same day, Peter Shevchenko lay in a hospital bed in Leningrad. In New York, Paul Edwards entered Roosevelt hospital in New York carrying a dozen roses for his wife and their newborn son. They would name him Ethan.

MOSCOW: JANUARY 30

Palmer stepped off the train at Moscow station wearing laborers clothes. His hair was longer than he usually wore it and dyed a chestnut brown. He grew a beard, keeping it trimmed, and dyed it, adding a hint of gray. He walked with a slight limp to disguise his height. He carried a heavy canvas satchel tied with industrial string over his right shoulder.

He took a cab to the Crown Prince hotel and checked in under the name Phillip Conte. His identity papers were prepared for him by a forger in Paris named Fontaine. He showered and changed into the clothes he had neatly folded into the canvas satchel. He ordered vodka and a sandwich of ham and tomato with green olives and spinach leaves. The phone rang.

"Hello, hold a moment," he pointed to a small table near the patio doors. He gave the steward twenty rubles. "Thank you. I won't need anything else."

"He will be gone all morning and afternoon tomorrow. He just left; I can't wait to . . ."

"Not on the phone. I don't trust privacy in this city."

"Can you come now?"

"Tomorrow. Give me your room number."

"Suite 617 in the north tower."

"Tomorrow then." He hung up, cursed her under his breath, and picked up the phone.

"Desk clerk please."

JANUARY 31

"James," Anna Schmidt gushed, "what did you do to yourself? Never mind that, you can explain later. How do you like the new fur coat my husband bought me for this trip?" She let it slip off her shoulders into a pile on the carpet. Anna jumped into Palmer's arms wrapping her lags tightly behind his buttocks "Get me on the bed," she squealed. "I like the new look. It will be like making love for the first time."

The cold air stung his face. He was completely relaxed now. The tingle in his arms and legs was gone. His mind was free to think of more important things. He should go home to Bryansk, common sense dictated it.

He couldn't. He wanted to see the results of his handy work. He needed to see the turmoil he had created like his real father . . . Morrison. First see the young man waiting for his money. Take care of that situation.

"Return to your hotel room and stay there. Go home to Bryansk tomorrow. Hold on to the memory, put every thought and action into the book," he said out loud.

The murder of the Schmidt woman brought correspondents from as far away as London, and the Washington bureau of NBC news sent correspondent Maxine Fisher-Barnett. Heinrich Schmidt was connected to Washington politics with men who made policy.

Fisher began her career in journalism as a beat reporter for the New York Daily News. Fisher a statuesque, chestnut-haired beauty with doe like green eyes, high cheekbones and full lips moved quickly up the ladder of New York's most watched news gatherers. It was rumored she made progress mostly on her back and secondly because Maxine knew how to keep a tight lip.

Fisher ended her report with, "We will be here through the evening. Right now, I am trying to make my way into the hotel. Maybe I can get an interview. This is, of course, Moscow and not Washington. The only leaks here come from broken water pipes."

Two KGB officials emerged from the lobby. She immediately recognized one of the men: the brooding intensity in his eyes, the same look she remembered from her days at Berkeley. The name escaped her, but she remembered him, the slow talking southern activist who was her first sexual contact. She froze, wanting to approach him, but thought better of it. Instead, she made her way to the NBC van, climbed in, and took a deep breath.

"I was fucking a Communist with a southern accent in college." She blurted out.

"What's that?"

"Nothing, just thinking out loud."

After a long day of waiting for news updates and a chance at an interview, Maxine was left with Anna Schmidt, wife of industrialist Heinrich Schmidt, robbed, raped, and murdered in her suite. The police were actively searching for clues and reviewing camera footage for the possible identification of her murderer. She added the sidebar on the unrelated murder of the young man found in a dumpster in the alley next to the Bolshoi Ballet. She called her husband of eight years—a lawyer in Washington—hung up, and made her way down to the Crown Prince bar for a nightcap. Exhausted, Maxine collapsed onto a bar stool and ordered a triple vodka with a slice of lemon.

"Looks as if you've had a long day."

"I'm happily married; spend your time on a real prospect."

"Maxine, it is you, isn't it?" Palmer recognized her immediately, his curiosity outweighing his ability to stay away. She would not have recognized him with his hair colored and with the dark beard. He decided to leave the hair long, curled over his collar, but rinsed off the hair coloring and shaved off the beard. He felt safe being himself for the trip home.

"James Preston," she said looking up at him, the shock of seeing him registered and her hand shook just enough to spill vodka on the bar. "You bastard."

Shevchenko poured vodka into his glass and drank. "We know he left Bryansk, but did he come to Moscow?"

"We know he was bedding the Schmidt woman . . . He must be in disguise, Comrade, or he would have been seen arriving. We could check the travel logs, but he is too smart to use his name. I want to see how the man carries himself, how he is built. These things cannot be disguised without drawing unwanted attention. Move the tape to the lobby, just before noon. The report refers to Schmidt's testimony that he left at eleven fifteen in the morning. This is verified by members of the conferences he attended in the evening."

"He could have hired an assassin . . . maybe a mistress is part of a plot?"

"The state police have looked into his life and associates. They can be very thorough, Dmitry Kasparov. If they have cleared him, we can as well."

"Let's move on, comrades."

The recorder marked the time: 11:23 a.m. A man wearing a wide-brim hat over dark glasses carried a long, leather coat over his right arm. He walked into the lobby, his head slightly tilted downward and away from the cameras.

"The picture is grainy. Do you think it is him, Peter?"

"The height is about right," Mikhail offered. "His hair is dark. You can see it partially under the hat. He could have dyed it, along with growing the beard."

"He is getting on the elevator without going to the front desk. He pressed six."

"Let's not get excited yet, Mikhail Balandin."

He stepped off the elevator, purposely avoiding the camera. He looked in both directions. Seconds passed; finally he moved along the hall with measured steps and a slight limp in his left leg. He stopped in front of Schmidt's suite. One more look to the left and right and then he removed his sunglasses. He knocked. The door opened.

"It is him. His limp is improvised for the camera's sake . . . It is Palmer's profile. I'm sure of it." Shevchenko picked up a pastry and made quick work of it. "Move the tape forward; I want to see when he left."

"His disguise was good enough to fool the watchful eyes of our people . . . We know what we know. He killed Schmidt's wife and Uri Fedorov knows he did," Kasparov blurted out.

"Are your women ready, Dmitry?"

"The women will be at the gala next Sunday unless they postpone it again, Peter."

"You have raised grave issues, Peter Shevchenko, concerning Fedorov. If you are wrong . . ."

"We must be sure. He did not come to Moscow today. He must have stayed at another hotel. He may still be there. We must get footage from all three upscale hotels in the city without raising certain eyebrows."

"I can see to that," Mikhail said. "Even if we prove it is him, what can we do?"

"A good question. If he is under Fedorov' s protection . . . Nothing.".

FEBRUARY 1

Maxine stepped into the bathroom of her suite. The man she knew as James Preston was in the shower humming a Joplin song she recognized from the three days she spent at Woodstock in 1969. "You could have said good morning."

"Good morning. I didn't want to wake you." He started humming the tune again.

She studied herself in the mirror. Her breasts were bruised and discolored, the tiny bite marks not enough to break the skin. She looked down between her legs: the same marks and bruises. Turning around, her buttocks, too, were bruised, his finger marks clearly visible where he'd forced her to rotate them. She loved it. "Don't use all the hot water, baby."

"Join me."

"No, I want to smell you on me for a while." She padded back to the bedroom. "Breaking News" flashed across the black screen in large white letters. The clock above the television read 10:20 a.m. She needed to call in and was reaching for the phone when the words spilled across the screen. "James, you've got to see this."

"What's going on?" he asked.

"They say they've caught the killer of that Schmidt woman." She clicked off the TV and sat on the edge of the bed. "I need to call the bureau and talk to my editor."

She dialed the hotel operator as he padded over to her, dropping his towel on the carpet. She put her hand out and began to rub his thick member. "Yes operator, I'll wait. I understand the delays."

She pulled him toward her. "Try not to break a tooth, baby."

Kasparov rushed through the door and into Shevchenko's office.

"Have you heard?" he asked, ort of breath. Perspiration bubbled on his forehead.

"I am watching it now; sit down. Marina, my friend might need a glass of tea."

"What do we do now, Peter?"

"Nothing, we do nothing. It seems the case is closed, the killer found." He put a finger to his lips, picked up a pencil, and wrote a quick note showing it to Kasparov. The note asked when the last scan of the offices was.

"Well, that is a relief to start our day, Peter." The scan was completed only that morning.

"We know Palmer killed the woman and also the dead boy in the dumpster," Shevchenko continued. "We know the captured man is too small to be the killer and looks nothing like the young boy who noted the camera pods in the hotel. I am sure they will release his picture very soon . . . This is Uri Fedorov's work my friend . . . But why?"

Marina brought tea for both men and excused herself, closing the door behind her.

"The report mentions jewels, but not missing cash. Palmer must have kept it." Shevchenko rubbed his chin. "The fake killer could have been found with her jewels only one way."

Shevchenko raised his glass and held it outstretched. "To a conspiracy that is much larger than we imagined," he sipped his hot tea. "Can you arrange a chance meeting between your tulip and Fedorov's second-in-command before the party for Pavlov next Sunday?"

Marina buzzed him.

"Difficult on short notice. I thought you wanted to wait?"

"We will leave it as it is, then, until we are sure of a successful meeting.

"Yes, Marina, put him through." Shevchenko motioned for Kasparov to say nothing. "Good morning, Comrade Fedorov." A pause while he listened, "Yes Comrade. It is very good news. We are very pleased as well . . . Yes. I will be at the gala. Yes, Comrade, it should be an interesting event. Goodbye, sir." Shevchenko put the phone down. "He is testing me. He knows I reviewed the tapes. He must have found out from the state police.

"Please give these tapes to Marina and have her return them. Wait." Shevchenko buzzed his secretary. "Marina, a favor," he said, when she stepped into his office. "I want the tapes taken back to the Moscow chief of police, Comrade Gusev. Inform him we could not discern who the killer is from viewing the tapes and are very grateful that he included us. Also, tell him his capture of the killer is a remarkable piece of police work and he should be rewarded by the state."

"Shall I offer to kiss his ass as well, Peter?"

"I imagine the thank you will do, Marina."

Maxine showered.

"I must leave right away. My boss wants me in Berlin to report on the elections and that Kraut's wife . . . Thanks for last night and of course this morning, James. Perhaps we will run into each other again sometime."

She wanted him to think she saw it as a chance meeting, an interesting conversation over drinks, great sex, and nothing more. The next move would be up to him. "Remember Ohio?" she asked?

"I remember Ohio. I'm sure you may never let me forget it. Why does it have to be a chance meeting, Maxine? You will be in Berlin for at least until the elections are resolved; I might be able to join you." He said, avoiding her eyes.

"You are saying that because I'm married?"

"Partially, to be honest. If we could, would you?"

"I don't want more, James. I am perfectly happy to leave the situation as it is . . . By the way, you are still a bastard."

"Maxine you, beautiful piece of ass. Your husband was in the freaking' lobby. I thought it best to stay away after that close encounter."

"Maybe I'll forgive you."

Don't start this again Wayne . . . big mistake. The voice whispered in his ear. She will be trouble. Let her go.

Shut up . . . shut up.

"What did you say, James?"

"I was just thinking out loud, Maxine. I want to see you . . . Just for the fun of it?"

"Nothing more James. No ties. I want depravity. I get normal at home . . . Where are you going from here?"

"Stockholm." He lied.

"How can I reach you?"

"I have a number. I'll write it down."

Palmer relaxed on the train, content with himself for choosing a carriage room. He could be alone with his thoughts. He wanted to be home. Put Schmidt's death in his book. All the details while still fresh in his mind.

"We are approaching Minsk."

"Thank you, Louise." I remember another Louise from Beria, Ohio. She mocked me and even made a poem about me. John Palmer the funny thing. With arms and legs that resemble string.

"It isn't so funny now is it, Louise. No more poems. You were my first. I hope you like your grave. I wonder if they are still looking for you." He caught himself talking out loud. Be careful, he told himself, cupping his hand over his mouth.

CHAPTER SIX

NEW YORK: FEBRUARY 4

Ethan fixed a sandwich of ham, Swiss cheese, a dab of Gulden's spicy mustard, sliced tomato and lettuce on rye bread, popped the top off a bottle of Budweiser, and padded back to his almost completed remodel of the living room. He sat down on his recliner and switched on the television, flipping through the channels until he found PBS. The station had just completed a story about the rise of Adolf Hitler, for maybe the 200th time. He changed channels just as the phone rang.

"Hello," he said wiping his mouth.

"Ethan, it is Beatrice."

"What is it, Beatrice?" He sat bolt upright. She never called and by the sound of her voice, he knew instinctively it wasn't good.

"Adam has had a heart attack; it is serious, Ethan."

"Where are you?"

"Walter Reed, the new intensive care wing. Can you come Ethan? He asked for you."

NHA TRANG, VIETNAM. 1967

"Good morning, Captain," he glanced at her name tag, "Reichert. I hope I have said it correctly. I apologize if I did not."

"You did fine, Major Rowland. We were alerted to your arrival." She turned to the civilian. "You are Mr. Cahill, the station chief in Saigon. Please call me Margaret. Let me get Doctor Harlow. I assume these gentlemen with you are your security team?"

"Yes, Margaret; is there somewhere they can . . .?"

"We have our cafeteria. They can wait there. It is down the corridor to the right, outside the door you both just came through."

"That will be fine."

"I will get Major Harlow. It shouldn't be long." She disappeared behind a swinging door marked Authorized Personnel Only. Above the door, a sign read Patient Quarters. Silence Please.

Major Harlow emerged a few minutes later. He was a short man of medium build and a crop of white hair that nearly matched his lab coat.

"Your sergeant is a sick young man, but he is responding well to treatment and antibiotics. I do not perceive any permanent damage, at least not physically. He was mistreated brutally during his capture." Doctor Harlow cleared his throat. "Frankly, I don't know how he survived, gentlemen."

"Who brought him in?"

"Some marines with 3rd Recon found him. They radioed for assistance. That's what I know, gentlemen."

"Thank you, Doctor . . . Can we see him. We won't overstay."

"You must be a pretty important guy, Sergeant. There are a couple of heavy hitters outside talking with Doctor Harlow. You feel up to it?"

He nodded, patting the nurse's arm with his bandaged hand.

"I have your beret in my locker for safe keeping. Want some water, soldier?"

He nodded, barely moving his lips, and said, "Thank you, Captain."

"There is no rank here. Call me Margaret and I'll call you Ethan." She picked up the glass and carefully placed the straw in his mouth. "It might hurt, but you need the fluids. Your IV fluids and antibiotics can't fix a dry mouth." She saw the pain in his eyes and thought, Why do we do this? Why do so many young men have to suffer? It is all bullshit.

When he finished, she said. "You must have been a heartbreaker in high school." That took the pain out of his eyes and put the smile, though slight, back on his lips.

"Your visitors are here." She patted his shoulder, stood up, winked, and padded off.

The car needed gas. Ethan pulled his Corvette into the service plaza and drove up to the Sunoco gas island. He went inside, paid the cashier, and walked back to the car. The pump clicked off. He had change coming: forty cents. He hung the hose up and got back in the car. Soon he was back on the turnpike. He pushed the Corvette up to sixty, slipped it into fourth gear, and settled in. The engine purring like a well-fed cat. The road signs were clear. SLOW DOWN . . . ICE ON ROADWAY

He put on his Red Sox cap and opened the driver's side window just enough to feel the cold air. After the miserable January snowstorm that crippled the city and the nine straight days of rain at the end of the month, a clear sky and the promise of better weather made New Yorkers feel the winter doldrums were slipping away. A welcome reprieve before the heat and humidity of summer.

He wanted to drive faster, push the old girl out, and feel her power, but he knew it would end badly. State troopers in the tri-state area had more radar than dog crap had flies. They didn't care if you were a wounded veteran or once worked for the CIA or you wrote a political comic strip.

"You know how fast you were going, sir? Didn't you read the warning signs? License, registration and proof of insurance." He held his speed and allowed his thought s to to flow back into his consciousness.

"Doctor says you are responding well. Major Rowland wants to move you back to Long Binh as soon as possible. We do not need to get much detail today; that will be for later.

Ethan nodded and motioned for something to write on.

"Good. Did they find out who you were and your mission?"

He scribbled as best he could a single word . . . Name.

"What about files, maps, and records: Anything about intelligence you might have carried out?"

He scratched a single word . . . Burned.

"We recovered the KIA'S; they are at or on their way home. We picked up the rest of the team. They looked for you."

"That's enough . . . I'm pretty damned glad you're back Sergeant," Major Rowland pushed past Cahill, gently wrapping his hand around the soldier's hand. "You get better, you hear. We'll have a beer or two on me."

Major Rowland turned back to Cahill. "We're going now." It wasn't a question.

"Yes, I guess we are."

"Give me a minute alone, Mr. Cahill."

Margaret Reichert, tending another patient, watched the major bend over her patient and kiss the soldier on his forehead. She couldn't hear what he said. When he stood up, she saw the Purple Heart pinned on his pillow. Both men then walked out of the ward without a word.

The Corvette passed exit seven, rolling steady at sixty miles per hour. The memory faded.

Margaret Reichert-Stanley entered the Special Care Heart Unit, pulling off her coat and laying it across a swivel chair behind the nurse station. "Annie," she exclaimed seeing the nurse exit Room 5, "What are you doing here?"

"I got called in. It is you and me, boss. Luckily, we have only four patients. The new one is in Room 5, some government Mucky Muck. His wife is in there with him."

"Wonderful, I hope it isn't a congressman . . . baby tears, all of them. They stub a toe and want twenty-four-hour care with a doctor in the room to wipe their noses . . . Shit, this place is going to be crawling with suits and lapel pins. Who called in?"

"Janis White, the newbie from critical care. She's okay, a good nurse. I think we can forget the suits. I don't think we will be seeing many of them. His wife made one phone call. It was personal. I don't think she wants anyone to know; look at the chart."

"No visitors except with her permission and no notifications, wow. Who is attending?"

"Doctor Feinstein."

"He must be important if our boy Mark Feinstein is involved. Wait, I know this guy, he's CIA . . . Cahill, yeah. I met him once when I was in the service. You said one call?" Margaret flipped through the pages of diagnostics, drug prescriptions, and doctor's orders. Suddenly, her body stiffened. For a second, she stood motionless, her eyes fixed on the name of the only visitor allowed to see the patient. "Ethan Edwards," she blurted out, "I'll be damned."

"You know him?"

"If it is who I think it is."

"I thought the name sounded familiar."

"The story of how he got his first name is great. A John Wayne western, Annie?"

"That's it. The Searchers. I loved that movie."

Margaret answered the intercom. "Send him in please. Annie, why don't you tell Mister Cahill's wife that Mr. Edwards is here."

It was him, the soldier she cared for before she returned to the world. He hadn't changed much, a little gray on the temples of his dark hair, some small age lines at the corners of his mouth, and crow's feet stabbing out in tiny lines at the edges of his eyes. "Ethan Edwards in the flesh after all these years. Do you remember me?"

"Maggie."

"I said once you were a heartbreaker; you still are. I never got to say goodbye. They moved you out on my day off. I read your political cartoons. I wondered if it was you; my husband loves them."

"It's me, Maggie."

You know you are the only man who has ever called me Maggie. My husband nicknamed me Magpie because I'm always talking on the phone."

"You have kids?"

"I have a husband I would die for and two great boys. One is in his second year of college, and one in his last year of high school. I would love for you to meet them. You know I always thought of you, during those nine weeks you were in my ward, as the nearest thing to a younger brother I ever had. I won't ask how you are connected still to patient Cahill."

"You don't want to know Maggie. Workwise . . . No."

"Ethan?"

"Beatrice," he answered, turning toward the sound of her voice. He started to walk toward her, but his eyes were looking beyond Beatrice Cahill. He thought for a second he would be swallowed by the large, almost hypnotic soft blue eyes and long thick chestnut hair that she brushed away from her face and tied in a bun on top of her head. The attraction was immediate and mutual.

"He is sleeping now. He asked for you. It is serious, Ethan. I can't bear to lose him, not now." Beatrice choked back a sob.

"I know, Beatrice." He put his hands around her shoulders and held her while she sobbed softly against his chest.

"My name is Ethan Edwards," he said to the nurse standing just to her right.

"Anna Lee is my name: Anna Lee Caputo. Margaret tells me you were named for a character in a John Wayne movie." She felt her knees buckle. "I would love to hear how that came about." She finally forced herself to look past him toward the nursing station. Margaret was standing in front of it, her arms folded across her chest smiling at her. "Would you like to go into his room?"

"Is he responding to treatment?"

"I can't answer . . ."

"Go ahead nurse; he is like a son to my husband. He wouldn't mind and I certainly don't."

"As you wish, Mrs. Cahill. Why don't we step inside his room; we can talk there." She turned in the doorway. "Margaret, I won't be long."

"Take care of Mister Cahill, Annie. No rush. I can handle the floor." The smile stayed fixed on her face.

"She told you the story of how I got my first name?"

"Not the whole story, just a hint about its origin."

FEBRUARY 5

Ethan stood up from the high back chair. The sun was a smear of orange on the horizon. He went around to the side of the bed, placing his hand over Adam Cahill's. He felt the tug of a finger against his thumb.

"Thank God," he whispered and looked toward Beatrice. She was asleep in a pair of scrubs on the fold-up bed. He didn't wake her, but left the bedside and walked to the nurse's station.

"He grabbed my finger." Ethan said outloud walking quickly to the Nurse station

" Are you sure it wasn't just a reflex Ethan?"

"I'm sure Maggie."

 I'll go check on him." Anni said ."

"When was the last time you ate, Ethan?"

"It has been a while, Maggie."

"What's the verdict, Annie?" She looked past Ethan. "Good news?"

"He is alert. He took my hand and squeezed it with authority. I woke up Mrs. Cahill."

"Ethan and I are going down to the café. Wake up Doctor Feinstein and let him know Mister Cahill is beginning to respond; will you be okay, Annie?"

"I'm fine, go."

"This is a nice café."

"Recently remodeled. We love it. They cook to order. Try the scrambled eggs with bacon or sausage. Everything is fresh. It's what I'm having."

"You find us a table and I'll order Maggie."

"Whole wheat toast for me please, Ethan."

They ate, he talked, and she listened. He told her about his years with the CIA without going into detail. He told her about the divorce. He blamed himself.

She nodded without comment.

He lived alone, writing his political cartoons and refurbishing a loft on the second floor of what once was a sewing machine factory on the lower Westside. Maggie liked the idea of the large island and the choice of cabinets. He installed the hardwood floors himself and was in the process of adding two more bedrooms—one with a guest bath—a game room, a formal dining room and a large area left over for the living space. In all, it measured 6,000 square feet.

"I'd wait on some of the treatments ideas, Ethan. You might marry again. Women like to make certain choices about furnishings, if you get my drift. Were you planning to stay in town for a few days?" Without waiting for an answer, she left the table and returned with a pot of coffee.

"I brought enough change of clothing for three days." He fell silent while Margaret poured the steaming black liquid into his cup. She sat down, pulling out a cigarette from her scrub jacket and lighting it.

"I never knew you smoked."

"Ever since I was fourteen years old. My husband makes me stand in the driveway when I smoke at home. You know you were the best patient on my ward. You never complained."

"The screaming came later."

"You had the most resolute face. You never cried, you never changed expressions. I remember Barbara telling me when the orderlies brought you into my unit. You refused help until the other soldiers were taken care of."

"I knew I was better off than the others."

"Only by Ethan Edwards. It was touch and go for a while."

"I still hear the yelling, Maggie . . . I remember Barbara. She was so soft spoken and gentle. She gave me the Jesus look, Maggie. I told her not to look at me that way… Did you two keep in touch?"

"She lives in San Diego."

"Married? Kids? How is she?"

"Sort of, she has a girlfriend. They've been together for years." Margaret tamped the cigarette out in the small ashtray.

"Good, I'm happy for her . . . The soldier next to me on my left was in bad shape."

"He was. He told me and Doctor Harlow he didn't want to go home to his mother like he was. It took some time to understand him. Most of it was childlike dribble. A few weeks after you were sent back to Long Bien, Doctor Harlow brought him a large glass of scotch and a small cup of chocolate pudding. He went to sleep and never woke up."

A single tear formed on the corner of her eye and slowly rolled down her cheek. "He wasn't the first, Ethan, and he wasn't the last. I used to rage at God for allowing the war to go on while ruining so many young lives. I remember how you used to sit on the floor next to his bed and . . ."

"Let's talk about something else."

"Yes, let's do that, Ethan." She lit another cigarette. "I think I feel something going on between you and Anna Lee. I know she was impressed. I also know she will be glad to know you are single. You can explain why while you tell her about your name and John Wayne's character in The Searchers. If you are not interested, the conversation ends here."

"I'm interested. I don't know how much she will be when I tell her my life story but, I'm interested."

"She's a big girl. Time to go. Make time to meet my husband and the boys while you are in town. Promise?"

"I promise, Maggie."

"My father was a huge John Wayne fan," Ethan began. "His favorite movies were The Searchers, She Wore a Yellow Ribbon, Red River, and Sands of Iwo Jima. He liked Wayne as Nathan Brittles in She Wore a Yellow Ribbon, but he thought the name wasn't quite right. My father decided right then and there that in Wayne's next western he needed to call himself Ethan Edwards."

"That would be you?"

"That would be me, Anna Lee. He wrote a letter to that effect to John Ford and of course Mister Wayne. As luck would have it, he received one autographed picture and a letter from John Wayne saying he thought so too. The Searcher became Ethan Edwards. I still have the letter. Did you know the movie is based on a true story about a small girl named Parker taken captive by the Camanche?"

"Yes . . . I have a bit of a history. I am related to Stephen Decatur. He defeated the Tripoli Pirates. My father is Italian; my mother is Scots Irish. I'm babbling."

"Would you like to have supper with me tonight?"

"I can't."

"I'm sorry, Anna Lee, I shouldn't have thrown that at you like a 100-mile-an-hour fastball."

"It isn't that. Ethan. I'm very flattered, just taken by surprise. I have a nine-year-old son. His father left us eight years ago. I am divorced. My parents, bless their hearts, have helped me raise him. Tonight, they are going out and it is a little late to try and get a babysitter."

"I'd like to meet him. What's his name?"

"Vincent; he is named after his grandfather."

"Bring him along. We will let him choose his favorite restaurant. It might put him a little more at ease . . . Maybe you as well." He sipped his water. "I'm also divorced. It was my fault. I wasn't there for her when it meant the most. I worked for the CIA. I was on an assignment. She had a premature birth. She lost the baby. The child had a weak heart."

"I am so sorry." She would tell Margaret months later: I fell in love with him that day. "I won't promise, but I will ask Vincent what he thinks. One more thing: Call him Vincent only."

"I promise. I need to get back to New York soon. I hope he says it's okay."

"I'd better go."

Ethan walked Anna Lee to her car. "I hope you two will come, but if it doesn't work out, I'll understand."

He watched as she guided the car down the ramp to the lower floor. I came on too strong, he thought, angry with himself.

BRYANSK OBLAST: FEBRUARY 8

Palmer wore a sweater on his porch, enjoying the break in the weather. His tea was less bitter with a shot of vodka stirred in. He finished writing notes, scolding himself for not finishing those last moments of Schmidt's life sooner. He picked up his cup and padded back into the house, placing the little book under the floorboard. He was about to fix another drink when he spied the black Volga V-12 through his window. He grimaced, thinking he was about to receive another visit from Shevchenko. He retrieved his notes on the new American president and stepped out onto his porch.

The vehicle rolled to a stop. It wasn't Shevchenko who was climbing out of the back seat; it was Fedorov's deputy.

"Good day, Comrade. What brings you here to this lovely city?"

"A glass of tea, perhaps a little vodka."

"What about your driver?"

"He is a Cossack. This weather is like desert heat to him." Anton walked into the house, taking off his coat. "I think talking on a first name basis will do, John Palmer."

"I am your host and you are my guest, Victor Anton."

"While you fix a drink for us," the deputy answered, sliding his large frame into a stuffed chair, "perhaps you can tell me about this Anna Schmidt incident in Moscow?"

"I have a report completed on President Carter's first month. It is on the table next to your chair. Business first, Victor, isn't that what you always say? The woman was a minor problem."

"Not to members of the politburo and more than a few in the Central Committee. I am asking because I must. We have a man in custody. Our story must be both logical and acceptable." His black eyes narrowed. His lips were a thin line beneath his hawklike nose and thick mustache.

"She was good in bed; her husband was not. I thought that was enough. She did not. She was foolish and stupid. She sent me a note asking me to meet her in Moscow. I destroyed the note. It was our only correspondence. I killed her to protect us. I killed her to protect my plan."

"You are certain no correspondence remains linking this woman to you?"

"I think if there were more, her husband would have produced them."

"Fix me that drink you offered while I look over your report on this Carter fellow."

Palmer returned in a few moments with two glasses of hot tea and two glasses of vodka. He placed both drinks on the table next to his visitor. "You won't find many specifics, but I am sure you will agree with my assessment." He sipped his tea and fell silent.

"You think he is weak, this Carter fellow." Victor closed the file, laying it on his lap, and picked up his tea, slowly pouring in a bit of vodka. "What makes you so sure about this man? The Kremlin has been fooled before. I remember a president who we thought was weak. Harry Truman was his name . . . I noticed you spelled your middle name differently . . . Michael?"

"I decided I wanted to use the American spelling now. About your question. Not weak, Comrade. Over his head a bit, perhaps. He is surrounded by men whom I see as weak and indecisive. The American press will be complicit in his failures."

"He did very well in bringing Sadat to agree to meet with the Israelis in his first month in office?"

"Yes, that is true, but now look at his method of dealing with the rest of the Middle East. His presidency is in its infancy and already has problems." Palmer put the glass of tea down and picked up his glass of vodka. "The American press is behind him in this matter, and because of that, the regime will fall. Khomeini will be put in power and certainly bloodshed will follow. For Russia, it is good. Iran was a listening post among other things helpful to America."

"I know you are making a point. I just do not see it, John."

"You will. The pieces are beginning to fall into place nicely. Iran could be the key."

"Tell me about this plan of yours?"

"When the time is right, Comrade."

"Well then, on a more pleasant note, I met a young woman the other day at the airport. She was on her way to Minsk to visit her mother. We enjoyed a cup of tea together."

CHAPTER SEVEN

It turned out to be a pleasant three days. Cahill was doing much better and would be released from the hospital the next day. His future with the agency was no longer in question. His retirement would become effective as soon as the paperwork could be completed. Beatrice had already cleaned out his private files, removed the private phone, recorder, ledgers, private notes, and personal items from his office, storing them away. She appeared at the hospital on Thursday with brochures on travel campers and luxurious motorhomes to everyone's amusement, including Adam.

The short time Ethan spent with Anna Lee and her son Vincent turned out better than expected. The boy was tentative at first. For a boy his age, sharing his mother was not a preference.

Anna Lee was pleased, and by the third day, the boys found baseball was a sport they both enjoyed and could connect over . . . maybe. Vincent seemed to relax a bit, even asking Ethan if he would like to come back, "occasionally." The word carried a lot of meaning in defining parameters. Ethan made a mental note to include the boy in most activities, at least until Vincent felt comfortable enough to give his mother space.

Ethan and Anna Lee had supper with Maggie and her husband on his last night in town.

MOSCOW: FEBRUARY 13

The party for Pavlov arrived at last. Soldiers with dogs crossed the main floor of the Hotel, paying special attention to the dais carefully set back from doorways and windows. A senseless exercise, Shevchenko thought, only to protect Leonid Brezhnev.

To the left of the dais, 15 long tables stretched forty feet. Food, wine, and vodka covered the length of the tables, enough food and drink to feed the people working on the collectives to produce these luxuries. Malnourished men. Men and women with rutted faces burned by the summer sun and frozen by the relentless winters.

Even for the people of Moscow, the sight of so many soldiers and military vehicles guarding the streets signaled a return to the days of Stalin and his massive parades and rally's. The Bolshoi had been shut down for the night; clubs and restaurants for six square blocks around the famous Metropol Hotel were closed. Rumors floated throughout the city citing Chechen terrorists threatening to disrupt the gala. Killers were in the city. Moscow residents were cautioned to stay indoors; Hospitals were put on alert. The army wanted the streets clear, limiting civilian access to the elitist leaders of the country. Checkpoints were easier to man. The last checkpoint was a block from the main entrance to the hotel.

The guests began to arrive at a long tunnel-like canopy that hid them from view. The women wore expensive furs and long evening gowns provided by the imperialist American and French designers. They wore expensive jewels that would make a princess envious. The men whose arms they held were small men, with pouches under designer tuxedos, men who were balding and wrinkled, men who were powerful members of the ruling Troika. These were couples who lived lavishly in spacious dachas outside the walls of the Kremlin and far from the peasant class who supported their lifestyle.

Shevchenko stood grimacing at the hypocrisy of it all. He made his way along the long tables overflowing with trays of lamb, pork, and beef. There were large ice bowls filled with caviar, fresh vegetables both cooked and raw, shellfish chilling on beds of ice, fine wines from Italy and France served in crystal goblets, and bottles of the finest Russian vodka. Other tables featured pastries, tea, and coffee.

Earphones crackled to life. The chairman had arrived. The champagne-filled glasses stood untouched. His arrival stopped conversation throughout the hall. No one dared to be caught not prepared to greet the party chairman.

When he did enter with his wife and bodyguards in tow, the guests stood as one, cheering and clapping their hands. Like Stalin before him, The Soviet leader would allow it to go on until he was bored with it. He took his seat, the only sound the hissing of steam rising from the food tables.

The general entered on cue, followed by his security guards. His wife, four inches taller than the general, walked at his side, her hand resting in the crook of his extended arm. A statuesque high cheek boned woman of forty-eight. What most caught the attention of others were her eyes, deep-set slate under perfectly shaped brows. Full lips to further flatter her face. Her pictures were an injustice.

Shevchenko and Kasparov watched from an ornate column behind the dais. Shevchenko admired her poise and carriage. She seemed to glide along the floor, her legs concealed under her full-length satin gown. "She is beautiful Dmitry Kasparov. Next to him she looks like a Greek goddess."

"Be careful, Peter Shevchenko. A woman who looks like that could bring the strongest man to his knees, or far worse. I believe the Jews have a name for such a temptress in their testaments."

"Delilah."

"I am impressed. I did not know you were versed in Hebrew history, Peter."

"My dear Kasparov, have you forgotten who my secretary is?"

The couple walked to their table. Soviet Leader stood, his glass of champagne raised and pointed toward his honored guest. The rest of the guests also stood raising their glasses, silent as they waited for him to speak.

"You have come to celebrate a birthday. I do, as well. I have another reason to be joyous tonight. Colonel General, would you please stand and face your guests? Tonight, my faithful general is promoted to marshal of the Soviet armies and commander of the western front. Drink and eat my friends, and share my happiness for our guest of honor."

They clapped and shouted.

Shevchenko and Kasparov stood in silence. The orchestra at the far end of the ballroom played the anthem of the Soviet Union. "Whatever the plan, it begins tonight, Dmitry."

"I wonder if we have seen our last spring without war."

"Possibly."

"Do you think the wife has any clue as to what they are planning?"

"We will see." Shevchenko turned to face the crowd as they rushed the tables. "Look at them Dmitry. Our esteemed leaders and their pampered wives like monkeys attacking a row of banana trees."

"You would think they would at least pause and contemplate the meaning of this?" Kasparov said.

"I have read the Persian philosopher, Baha Ullah, who wrote: 'I have made death a messenger of joy to thee. Wherefore dost thou grieve? This celebration is like that, I am afraid," Shevchenko lamented.

"I am afraid as well, my friend. I was trying to remember the Swahili word for danger."

"Hatari, Dmitry Kasparov."

"Ah, yes, of course. I have word from an informed source that the Camp David meeting will begin before the end of the year. I wonder if the Middle East could be the target? Maybe Fedorov will tell you what he knows when you visit him next. You must be prepared to answer, Peter; I am sure he will test your resolve. Personally, I wonder if it would be a diversion to hide another move aimed at Western Europe?"

"Your logic is impeccable as always, Dmitry. That might be where Palmer comes in. That is why Fedorov is protecting him." The conversation ended abruptly when one of Fedorov's assistants approached the two men.

"Comrade Shevchenko, very good party, yes?"

"Very good, Comrade. You have a message for me, I assume?"

"Comrade Fedorov would like you to meet with him at his private residence at eight o'clock in the morning. Will that be satisfactory to you?"

"Of course." When the assistant walked off. Shevchenko turned to Kasparov. "A distraction . . . a test perhaps, Dmitry?"

"My tulip has arrived. I must get to her first and prepare her with the questions we need answered."

"Be careful. Do not approach her. Not yet."

"The general's wife sits alone sipping a martini."

"I think I will speak with her. I will address her with casual talk at first.

There will be time to delve into whatever knowledge she might possess."

"Good luck, Peter."

"Madam Pavlov, may I join you?" Shevchenko asked, using the table to separate them.

"I prefer my maiden name: Sorokin."

"Please accept my apologies, madam. My name is—"

"I know who you are, Peter Shevchenko."

"I am flattered. May I get you another drink or perhaps a plate of food?"

"You should be, Comrade Shevchenko, especially since you interrupted what I was about to say. The answer to both is no. A waiter is bringing me a salad in a few minutes. Now, as I was saying, you are the youngest man ever to receive the honor of Hero of the Soviet Union. You are a Colonel in the KGB-GRU. You speak four languages and you are a spy held in high regard. I understand, also, that you lost both parents to the war. I did as well. My mother and father were killed in Stalingrad. I also hear rumors that you are quite popular with women. Tell me, Colonel Shevchenko, how many of the women here with their fat little husbands have you romanced?"

"I prefer Peter; it is less formal. Since you insist on sarcasm to pass for conversation, I'll say truthfully, you would be the first. If you will excuse me . . .?"

"Sit down, Peter Shevchenko. I believe it is my turn to apologize for my behavior." She smiled: lost was the bored, indifferent look.

"Maybe I will have another martini. Please join me. First you must swear to me that my husband did not assign you the task of keeping me busy? I would be disappointed if you were."

"The answer, madam, is no. If you think the general will not mind, I would be honored to have a drink with you."

"My husband is in a meeting with the party chairman, talking about whatever they feel is important. It is the only secret he manages to keep from me. I expect he will spend some time with the blond he was talking to. I am sure she is here somewhere." Her eyes never left his.

"I am sorry, madam." It was obvious he would learn nothing from this conversation.

"Since you allow me to call you by your first name, you may call me Ladas." She leaned forward and whispered, "The other women are looking at us with jealous eyes. I am sure they are jealous of me sitting with the famous hero Peter Shevchenko."

"Let them look." She laughed a guttural but pleasant laugh. "I'll get our drinks if you will excuse me."

"Don't get up Peter, the waiter will bring them." She turned toward him, crossing her legs. "You were in America once upon a time, I understand?"

"Yes, five years in the 1960s. I was in California, at Berkeley University, and New York, at Columbia University. I was an activist for free speech, at least that is the key phrase we used. Americans can be very gullible." The waiter brought her salad. "Can we have two martinis please? When you have a chance?"

"Of course, sir."

"What was it like being in America?"

"Well, it was different. The students were different, Ladas. The weather was terrific. The professors are almost as socialist as we are. Some even more. They were our best resource to reach the students. The Vietnam War created chaos across the country; it was easy for us. We used the war and the rising drug culture to our advantage."

"What were the women like?"

"Not rigid like here, nor as beautiful. Too free for the way I see a woman. I will tell you about one if I do not offend you."

"A gentleman; I am impressed."

"She was a real radical student. I had an affair with her. It meant nothing to me, only as far as a resource. Today, she is a news correspondent. I know because I saw her in Moscow when that German woman was murdered."

"I read about it . . . a terrible thing. They caught the man who did it."

"Yes, they believe they have. I didn't speak to her and I doubt if she even recognized me." The waiter brought the drinks. "Allow me to make a toast to a wonderful host and a pleasant conversation." They clicked glasses.

"Tell me, Peter Shevchenko, how were you able to talk to her without raising suspicion as to who you were?"

"Why Miss Ladas, how could you ask? I am truly taken back."

Ladas Sorokin laughed. "That is amazing." The smile left Ladas' face. "They must have gorged enough food to satisfy themselves; they are beginning to come toward us."

"Then I will take my leave, Ladas Sorokin. It has been a pleasure speaking with you." Shevchenko stood up. "Perhaps another time we can talk again about America?" He took her hand and shook it.

"Perhaps."

Shevchenko passed through the broad lobby, reaching for his package of unfiltered Camel cigarettes. He was near the entrance when Kasparov appeared.

"She knows nothing. I am sure of it."

"The meeting is over. Pavlov is with my tulip now."

"Good. I am going to leave. It will be an early day tomorrow."

Kasparov followed him with his eyes until he disappeared into the Moscow night. I know that look Shevchenko . . . She got to you, my friend.

FEBRUARY 14

Shevchenko approached the gate of the dacha. The guard, recognizing the driver, pressed a lever inside the tower allowing the gate to swing open. A guard stepped off the portico and walked across the driveway while waving to a young man to come to the car. Shevchenko pulled up next to the guard, shutting off the engine. A precaution.

"Welcome Comrade Shevchenko. The young man will move your car away from the entrance."

The door was opened by another security guard. He stepped inside and was greeted by a woman in a black knee-length dress, white vest, black stockings, and black lace-up shoes. Typical garb for servants in wealthy families except for the shoes. Normally the help wore soft slippers. He was careful not to make eye contact with the woman.

"Comrade Fedorov is on the phone; he will be with you shortly. Would you like a glass of tea?"

"That would be nice, thank you."

Somewhere deep in the house he heard the whir of a sewing machine. It was either the wife or a maid. He sat down on a cushioned chair in the hallway. His glass of tea arrived along with a small plate of cookies. The woman placed a napkin across his legs.

"Thank you." He noticed the blond hair tied in a severe bun at the nape of her neck. Again, he was careful to not make eye contact. This was no maid.

"Good morning, Comrade. Come in, please come in. I am sorry for the delay."

"I certainly understand, Comrade."

"Please, help Comrade Shevchenko with his drink."

Fedorov took his place behind the oversized executive desk, an indication the meeting would be both personal and serious. Ten feet behind his chair, a fire crackled. On each side of the stone orifice thin long gated windows allowed light into the room from the gardens.

"I need your opinion and guidance on a number of issues that have come up Comrade Colonel. How is your tea?"

"I understand. The tea is excellent; the hint of mint is refreshing. I sent a note to commander Gusev of the state police thanking him for his quick action and capture of the murderer of the Schmidt woman. I made it official by adding the content of my letter to the file."

"Very good, Comrade Shevchenko. I have always admired your preciseness in the way you see problems." He leaned forward, placing his hands, palms down, on the finished wood. "I have a dilemma I want to discuss with you and a problem for which I would like your input."

"I am at your service in any way I can help." Shevchenko took a swallow of tea, picked up a small cookie, and ate it slowly while Fedorov lit a Cuban cigar."

"Let us begin with the Palmer situation, shall we Shevchenko? The American has been quite forthcoming since you last visited him and has given us some interesting insight concerning this Carter fellow. He also commented on someone named Reagan. Have you heard of this man?"

"Yes sir. Ronald Reagan was an actor from years ago: and later governor of California. He is an excellent speaker. I believe he was a Democrat at one time. Carter has a good heart and means well, but as a leader? Time will tell."

"Our contacts in America can help us further with that, especially our friend who heads the intelligence and foreign relations committee. We also have information about some accord that Israel and Egypt may be preparing. I am sure you have heard the talk. What do you think of such an accord becoming a reality?

"My thought is any pact with Israel by any government will certainly upset the conditions and protocols in the Middle East. I believe if it happens, Sadat will be assassinated."

"Again, I must agree. Which brings us back to Palmer. He wants to travel to Berlin. He claims to know a woman, a news person from America, one who is quite familiar with the Middle East. He feels he can procure sound information through her about the political climate in America and the Middle East and how it might affect our commitments. What do you think, Shevchenko?"

"I think he wants to have sex and probably already knows this woman and is using this as an excuse to not only realize a chance to travel outside our country, but to satisfy his excessive needs. On the other hand, I also think he might be correct in his assumption about the woman's value for information."

"You do not care much for this man, do you Comrade Shevchenko?"

"My trust in this man lacks confidence. Once a traitor . . ."

"Always the motherland first, Comrade Shevchenko. I admire this quality in you. I think I will allow him to travel. I agree with your assessment of the situation."

"I think you have made a wise choice, sir. You have another dilemma you wish to speak to me about?" Change the subject, move on. His mind was made up about Palmer before this meeting ever began.

"You remember the two French journalists murdered in Paris in 1975? The terrorist Ramirez Sanchez was responsible for their murders. The French want him dead, no trial. They have asked for our assistance. In return, some trade issues could be resolved and we have been assured information on the NATO strategy in case of aggression against it."

There it was: the clue Shevchenko needed to confirm his worst fears. These lunatics were going to make a move against its neighbors and they needed to know in advance how NATO would react . . . madness.

"What must we do for our French friends to ensure these events will take place?" Shevchenko said, keeping his expression as flat as the taste of the cookie.

"They ask that we intervene in his life expectancy. They would do it themselves, but are afraid his informants would find out before they could carry out a plan. He would not expect a situation involving us."

"Knowing the French, I'll assume they are afraid because they are cowards and giving us the assignment gives them deniability."

"You do not trust many do you, Comrade Shevchenko?"

"Not many, sir. Where is Ramirez?"

"He is going to be in Barcelona, Spain, in four days. There he is to meet with an Egyptian terrorist named Mustafa. I want you to take care of this situation for me. I do not want excessive bloodshed. I know that I can count on you to not let that happen.

CHAPTER EIGHT

CAIRO: FEBRUARY 16

Mahmud Mustafa shaved his beard, shortened his hair, and combed it straight back from his long face. He slipped on a pair of black-rimmed glasses, matching the color of his eyes. The look changed his appearance enough to enhance his chances of passing through customs.

"Are you almost finished with your shower? You are steaming up the bathroom. It feels like I am dressing in the rain."

"Almost finished," the woman answered from behind the plastic curtain. "I want to go with you."

"You cannot." Mahmud buttoned the top button of his white silk shirt, finished tying the gold tie she'd given him for his birthday, and sighed.

"You do not have to admonish me, Mahmud. I could help. I could protect you."

"You are correct, even as I think you overstep your place. I am going to Barcelona to meet our Latin friend. I will return in two days. No more discussion, woman."

MOSCOW: FEBRUARY 17

"You have an update for me, Comrade Kasparov?" Fedorov asked

"Our friend is in Barcelona, along with the team. As far as we know it is the Cathedral of the Holy Cross. Ramirez has chosen wisely: a location with many exits along a wide stretch of streets and boulevards. Ramirez is smart, but foolish. He allows himself room to escape, but by doing so he also gives us the same options and easier access to him. I would have chosen differently.

"Good work, Comrade Kasparov. Please keep me abreast of any changes."

"I will. Your faith in us is most appreciated."

THE CATHEDRAL: FEBRUARY 18

Men in long coats entered through the garden doors at the rear of the cathedral. They followed the narrow corridor, checking doors. They passed the sacristy, nestled behind the main altar. Next to it was the room where the priests and servers dressed.

Five of the men moved quietly to the left and made their way to the third closed confessional from the main entrance. The five men entered the pews, forming a half circle. A man appeared in priests' vestments and walked briskly down the row of pews, disappearing into the confessional.

A sixth man standing in the entrance way to the left of the altar turned to the hallway and nodded. A second man appeared, his face dark and brooding. He was not comfortable in these surroundings. He followed the guard to the confessional and slipped inside. The guard moved into the pew to the right, completing the half circle just as Mother Maria Contreras entered with her little band.

"This is as beautiful as the Di Santa Elisabetta near Santa Maria Maggiore," a nun remarked in a whisper. "I would love you to show us the twelve stations. I would like to pray at each if we have time."

"There is always time for prayer, my dear." Mother Maria Contreras failed to notice as she pointed to the altar that her group passed the fountains of holy water without blessing themselves.

"Could we use the main aisle, Mother Contreras? I do not feel comfortable being close to those men by the confessional. The one male in the group asked."

"They are probably ex patriots from the north. They trust no one. I imagine they are here to protect one of their leaders. He is probably confessing his sins. I do not worry about such men, Father, but we will walk up the center aisle if that is what you wish."

The group reached the third Station of the Cross almost directly in front of the confessional box. All eyes were on them until movement near the great marble altar diverted their attention. Three men one carrying an extension ladder, all three wearing painters clothes, and a third brushes and paint cans.

A nun shoved Contreras to the floor. Her hip glanced off the maple wood arm of the pew, sending a shock of pain through her body. By then it was too late for the guards to react. Israeli-made Uzi submachine guns appeared from under coats. The immediate staccato of noise echoed through the grand cathedral, spent shell casings spreading across the marble floors and pinging off the pews as the guards were splashed with bullets.

They were down in seconds, not one of them firing a shot before being killed. The assassin stepped forward and sprayed the enclosure from the lower third of the box upward. A door to the confessional swung open. He fired twenty more rounds, shredding the door and the man inside. In less than fifteen seconds, eight men were dead.

The priest turned toward the three stunned painters. They looked at him, their bodies frozen. The priest, in a raised voice, said, "Say nothing or we will return."

"I am very sorry for you, old one." The female assassin knelt on bended knee next to the nun, pulled off her head cover, and removed a syringe. "This is morphine, dear Sister. It will make your hip feel better." She injected the fluid and said in a soft voice, "Be well, old one. Do not waste your prayers on these dead men, nor us."

BERLIN

Palmer rinsed the excess shaving cream from his face. He was feeling the old urges building up in the pit of his stomach. He needed to kill something; the voices in his head demanded satisfaction. If he did not answer, he might explode in a torrent of violence against Maxine, who was in bed waiting for him to come out of the bathroom. Control, he told himself. Control the emotion until you are out hunting. He dropped the towel from his waist into a pile on the tile floor and opened the door.

Are we going out now? We have to go out, a voice in his head echoed.

Be quiet or I'll change my mind. Be very quiet. He filled his briefcase with essentials to disguise his appearance before leaving the hotel.

"Up early, baby, and showered. Shall I shower or are you feeling dirty this morning? I thought we might—"

"I have to go out for a while. Business must take precedent over pleasure, I'm afraid. Only for a few hours. I told you the trip might include business when I called. Only a few hours and I promise to make up for it."

The ache in his head was getting stronger the little voices excited and restless. He was becoming erect, but not because of anything she was doing. "Hold that thought, Maxine. I will return as soon as possible."

"Is it one of your computer conferences?"

"A sale, I hope." He bent forward and brushed his tongue across her breast.

"We only have today, you know? I leave first thing in the morning."

"I know and don't think it is easy for me, Maxine." A false smile, a look of sadness and she was satisfied. The voices came back, louder and more demanding.

CAIRO

Reba dialed the familiar number. After a series of blips and static rings, a female answered. "I am answering the ad for a telephone operator position at your news bureau. Do I have the right person?"

"The position is still open. Hold on, please, while I switch you over to our interviewer."

"Thank you so much."

"One question: Do you enjoy traveling?"

"Yes, of course."

"Hold on, it might take a moment or two to connect you."

"Reba," General Golan's voice echoed over the phone line.

"Is Mustafa dead?"

"Yes. We have been monitoring their police center. They have identified Mustafa and another man. It wasn't Sanchez. Six bodyguards are also dead. They used Uzi machine pistols. You can guess what that means."

"The French police and news outlets will blame Israel. Do you have any idea who could have planned the attack?"

"Someone very clever planned this attack right down to the use of Uzi machine pistols. I have narrowed it down to two or three possibilities. There are few agencies equipped for this. Rumor has it assassins dressed as nuns and a priest might be involved, but information is sketchy at best. The American CIA is already in contact with Shin Bet."

"The Americans know we do not murder in holy places of worship, unlike our enemies."

"Listen, Reba, you must leave as soon as you can. Do not waste time packing and cleaning . . . get out now. I don't know if he was carrying identification papers linking him to your address. You can't take the chance. The army will be all over that apartment. You cannot leave a thing that can be traced to you behind, understand?"

"I know what to do."

"Catch a flight to Paris and make contact with Mustafa's associates there, but first call me when you have landed so I know you are safe."

CAIRO

Reba stood on the curb, waiting for the taxi driver to put her valises into the trunk of the Mercedes. Faint at first but growing louder, the sirens from approaching police vehicles to her left alerted her of the short time frame she had to be away from the apartment. She stepped off the curb and climbed into the taxi.

The driver came around, got behind the wheel, and merged into traffic. Military vehicles sped past the cab. You are too late, she thought, just as the first explosive device went off in the bathroom of the apartment sending a plume of grey smoke and orange flames into the sky from the collapsed outer wall. A second explosive decimated the small apartment.

BERLIN

Maxine stepped through the door from the bedroom just as Preston entered the suite.

"Hello baby, bad news." She walked across the thick carpet to him, dressed in panties and high heels. "I have to go now, baby."

"What's going on? I bought a very good bottle of champagne."

She moaned like an animal over a fresh kill. "No time, I'm afraid James. You smell like a woman coming into the bedroom. Have you heard the news coming out of Barcelona?"

"No, I've been in meetings. I had to hug the wives of my clients . . . stupid. I'm going to take a shower. You have to leave?"

"Yes baby, I'm sorry. A terrorist named Mahmud Mustafa, an unnamed associate, possibly the number two man to the terrorist Ramirez, and six bodyguards. were gunned down in some cathedral in Barcelona. My bosses want me to fly to Tel Aviv immediately. They are sending a private jet."

"Do they think the Israelis did this? The Jews don't kill people in holy places, but rival factions in the Middle East scratching for power would have no problem. Saudi Arabia immediately comes to mind. The schools turn out terrorists faster than Ford turns out cars. I can't believe it," he said out loud.

"Remember, I was going there anyway. What happened in Barcelona just speeds up the travel plans. I'm sorry, James. I thought we had time, at least until tomorrow." She filled one valise and started on the second one. "Open the champagne while I pack."

"You were going to do an interview, but you never told me with whom, Maxine?" he said from the doorway of the bathroom. "I'll wash up; I'll just be a minute." He popped the cork on the bottle still wrapped in the towel and disappeared into the bathroom, closing the door.

"A man named Abel Golan, a real right winger, a retired general and advisor to the prime minister." She raised her voice so he could hear. "He was one of the freedom fighters in 1948 and a hero in the '73 war. If it were up to him, not only would there be no Palestinian State, there would be no Palestinians." She was bent over the valise when she felt his erection against her buttock.

"We'll be quick; we have time." He slid his tongue across her shoulder, his free hand on her breast. Using his thumb and index finger, he rolled the point of her nipple while making a mental note of the Israeli man's name, sliding it into the set of files he kept tucked away in his head.

"I could go down on you, James."

"What a wonderful thought." He turned Maxine around and kissed her. He felt sure he washed himself well enough in the bathroom. "Allow me to pour the champagne."

MOSCOW

Shevchenko entered the terminal behind a family of four. "Welcome back, Comrade." Kasparov took his hand and shook it. "I have news: some good and some not so good."

"Let's clear customs first. We'll talk when we are alone."

"Everyone was able to make it out of Barcelona safely. By all accounts, the attempt went perfectly." Kasparov guiding the car toward the main exits.

"I assume you have just supplied me with the good news?"

"Yes, I am afraid so."

"We missed Ramirez. Tell me what happened?"

"Six guards and two men were terminated. One was an Egyptian terrorist named Mustafa, the other one was an underling of Ramirez. A nun was slightly injured, Paula Turgenev—"

"No names, Dmitry," Shevchenko interrupted.

"I am sorry, Peter. She was not shot. The old nun fell on her hip. Our agent gave her a shot to ease the pain. Their use of the Uzi machine pistols placed concern in the world press that the culprits might be Mossad."

"Of course, their bigotry toward the Jewish State always blinds them from seeking out alternatives. Killing this Mustafa fellow only adds to the flames." He put his head back against the headrest. "I do not want to talk anymore. Take me home, Comrade. I need to get some sleep for a few hours only; we'll talk more afterwards."

PARIS: FEBRUARY 20

Reba registered at a small hotel along the Sorbonne. She chose it for the seclusion. The street artists, poets and writers who lived in the area knew her as Lena Davis, a writer from the Normandy country of France. Once in the small comfortable room, she showered, slipped on the robe supplied by the hotel—tying it in a double knot around her waist—and padded over to the phone.

"Hello."

"It is me, Alia." She spoke Farsi, remembering the man's voice.

"You have heard what has happened?"

"Yes, I had to leave Cairo that very day. She remembered the man, his voice. It is him, the bomb maker Rami Al Bahia. A woman's voice near the phone his wife. "Your wife is with you?"

"Yes Alia, we are only here for a week or so. We were to meet Al Aziz, but he returned to Beirut. The Latin has escaped to Libya. He and that sand rat are well suited to each other. They both have the screams of a jackal, but the spine of a lamb. Where are you, Alia?"

"I am staying in a hotel called La Flame near the Sorbonne. It is safe here. The locals think I am a writer from the north."

"Have a late supper with us tonight unless you mourn and wish to rest; we will understand."

"No, I want to be with good friends. I do not want to be alone. Where are you staying?"

"The La Place near the Seine, do you know it?"

"Yes, Mahmud and I found a lovely restaurant near there." She gulped air, imitating a sob. "What time shall we meet?"

"We will be in front of the hotel at eight o'clock."

"I will see you then. Forgive my appearance. I left Cairo in a hurry."

"Never mind that. It will give my wife an excuse to shop tomorrow."

She put the phone down and waited a few seconds before calling the operator. "I need to make a long-distance call."

CHAPTER NINE

BRYANSK OBLAST: FEBRUARY 24

Palmer entered the murder of the prostitute in Berlin into his journal, carefully noting every detail of the crime. Name, measurements, clothing and makeup. How the sex made him feel and, finally, the moment of strangulation. He scolded himself for his inability to remove and store his kill. He closed the journal, slipping it under the floor.

Next, he placed the call to the headquarters of Deputy Anton. "This is Palmer. I have a request for the Deputy; may I have a word with him?"

"A moment, please, while I connect you." There would be a few moments of delay while the call was traced to ensure its source.

"Mr. Palmer, I hope your trip to Germany went well."

"Very eventful, I must say. I know the hour is late, but I just arrived home. I have a request for you. I want a dossier on a Israeli retired general: Abel Golan. Have you heard of him?"

"Yes, of course, but why him? Did your lady friend give you his name?"

"Yes, she did. She is in Israel right now interviewing him concerning the Barcelona incident."

"I would be very interested in hearing more."

"You will, Comrade."

"I will see that you are sent the information you require."

"Thank you, and I will have my bi-weekly report to you by Saturday."

MOSCOW: FEBRUARY 25

"Tell me about Berlin, Dmitry."

"The woman he met in Berlin is Maxine Fisher-Barnett; she is married to a lawyer and lives in Washington, DC. She—"

"I know this woman."

"The visit was cut short. I think by the incident in Barcelona." Kasparov continued. "She was in Berlin for the election coverage. She left by private jet for Israel a day early. According to the desk captain, neither of them left the hotel during their stay at least as far he knows."

Palmer left that afternoon. He has returned to his home. He made a call to Anton last night. I would assume to discuss his trip. Our operator picked up the call, but could not listen in."

"Strange."

"Yes, it is. I am investigating. My report indicates the call lasted less than seven minutes. It may have been redirected to someone else . . . Fedorov perhaps?"

"What about your tulip with Anton?"

"He barely talks to her above, 'Pour me a drink. Take your clothes off.' "

"We have to depend on information gleaned from your ladies."

"So far that pond is dry."

"What has Makail learned?"

"Nothing that we do not already know. The general is preparing for a large military maneuver to the west and north toward Latvia. These are normal actions the military takes each year. Next spring, and again in late June, maneuvers will include more mountain training for our ground forces and air command for interdiction purposes, if needed in the future."

"Do you find that odd, Dmitry, that the military is concentrating on mountain training more than land training for a European war?" Shevchenko walked around his desk and began to pace, his hands clasped behind his back. "Unless he intends to invade Switzerland. Where outside our motherland might our Russian military interference become necessary?" He stopped pacing and dropped his arms to his side. "Afghanistan."

NEW YORK: MARCH 2

Ethan awakened to the alarm. He shut it off and lay still for a moment, enjoying the remnants of the dream about the day he hit the home run off the best high school pitcher in New York to win the city league championship. A good dream. No screams with cold sweats.

Baseball season was only weeks away. The Yankees were expected to win again. Vincent was still a bit standoffish, but softening more with each visit. Anna Lee made it clear that she needed time.

He wasn't going to spoil this thing growing between them no matter what direction it took. He had his writing and thankfully it was going well. His readership percentage was growing. As Doris Day said in a song, "What will be, will be."

He swung his legs over the side of the bed. He needed to get ready. They were coming up for the weekend and he'd promised Vincent a tour of Yankee Stadium, sightseeing, and Italian food New York style. Anna Lee and he would not have much time alone, but that was all right.

Expect nothing, hope for the best, and prepare for the worst. Anna Lee needed to know about his past. She deserved to know.

PARIS: MARCH 3

"The loss of Mustafa has impacted me greatly. I cannot imagine your grief, Alia."

"I still feel him next to me in my bed. We accepted the consequences." Reba's voice choked in her throat. "I am sorry your wife is ill, Rami. I was looking forward to enjoying these days with her." They started down the steps leading to the East bank of the Seine, mingling with other tourists.

"You have lost weight, Alia. You need to eat and regain your strength. We have work to do."

"I will be fine, Rami. Revenge will be my strength." The air was cool; the sun warmed her face. "What shall I do now, Rami?"

"Go to Cairo. Do not fear the military or the police. Use the Sunlit Loft. You will be safe there. Take some time to mourn. Someone will contact you."

"I know the area. Have you heard anything out of Barcelona? Was it the

Israelis who killed Mustafa?"

"I do not think so. It matters little. The Israelis will feel the wrath of Allah very soon. Ask me nothing more."

"I want to go to the hotel and see your wife before you leave. Can I? Can we go now?"

"Of course, Alia. While you visit, I will make arrangements for your flight and drive you to the airport tomorrow."

They started back up the stairs, Reba keeping his attention focused on conversation and not on the sedan approaching slowly along the upper roadway. "These steps are dangerous."

"The steps are old and narrow," Rami El Bahia answered. "Roman steps when this land was called Gaul."

They reached street level. Suddenly Reba was grabbed from behind and pulled aside. The car stopped. A man sat straight up in the back seat, pointed a handgun, and fired. The first round hit Rami in the chest; the second shot exploded into his skull, spraying blood and bone onto the wall. The crowd separated; panic filled the walkway.

Reba was half dragged to the car, a Renault sedan, and pushed into the back seat . Two blocks south, the driver turned the car into an alley and stopped. The occupants jumped out. Gasoline was poured on the interior, followed by a lighted match. They ran to a second car and drove off.

"I am Abram. This young man is Daniel Berg."

"I am Eva," the driver said. "Where is the wife?"

"The French call the hotel Le Lieu. Al Bahia said she was sick."

"She is about to feel much worse. Where shall we drop you?"

"My hotel. I am already packed."

"First you must come to the hotel," Daniel interrupted, "You have to be there as a witness."

"I understand. Where is Sanchez?"

"We believe he is hiding in Tripoli."

"I need you to beat me, Abram. I must make them believe I was taken and questioned. You must leave me with a serious injury. "Did you hear me, Abram?"

"Yes Reba, I heard you."

WASHINGTON, DC: MARCH 5

Beatrice Noonan-Cahill buttered two slices of toast while the water came to a boil. She put the knife down and dropped the tea bags into the glass pot carefully so that the strings would not fall in. The phone rang.

"Hello . . . Oh, Mr. Graham, hello . . . Yes, we are both well. I will get him." She stepped into the doorway. "It is Mr. Graham, dear, try not to be too long. I've made toast and your tea is almost ready."

"Hello," he said without enthusiasm.

"Have you been following the story out of Paris, sir?"

"Yes."

"It was the Russians in Barcelona, as a favor to the Frogs. That's what my sources tell me. It was the Mossad in Paris. The Russians missed the main target: Sanchez. The Mossad in Paris found the targets."

"I thought as much," Cahill lied. "Thank you for calling just the same. Mister Graham . . . Anything else going on?"

"Nothing."

Cahill hung up just as Beatrice came over to his recliner with a tray.

"Want to sit on my lap, darling?"

"Drink your tea, old man, and don't ask for trouble."

Cahill took a bite out of his toast. I wonder how Graham could have gotten such information. Maybe Timmons is his source . . . No, Timmons couldn't be. Graham didn't exist. Could he have a link to Russian Intelligence? It is plausible; the French would never attempt an assassination like this.

"You've got that look, Adam. What's on your mind?"

"My memoir."

CAIRO: MARCH 7

Reba walked to the café a block from the loft. It hurt to breathe. She sat down at a small sidewalk table. A young man went into the café without looking at her. He ordered a black coffee and returned. He stopped and looked in both directions, but did not move. "I am Alia. And you are the Syrian, Sala al Ameen, are you not?"

"I am," he answered. "You should wait to be spoken to. Do you not know your place?"

"The Mossad killers took me." She lowered her dark glasses so he could see her swollen and bruised left eye. "They beat me in places you will never see and left me with Rami Al Bahia's dead wife… My love is dead. My friends in Paris are dead and you question when I will speak? Leave me and send someone . . ." She grabbed her side without finishing her thought.

"I apologize, Alia. It is customary according to Allah who gave us the laws."

"Do not preach to me, Sala El Ameen. I want answers. I want revenge." She groaned. "Instead, they send me a messenger. I am going back to the loft."

A man approached the table carrying two cups of fresh coffee.

"Leave us." He sat down. "You must forgive the young man; he was doing his duty. Tell me, Alia, what did your captors want to know?"

"They wanted to know about my relationship with Rami. I lied. I told them he was a friend. I had no idea who he was, only that he was a kind and gentle man. They beat me and beat me. They murdered his wife in front of me . . . I want revenge, Al Aziz."

"I will send a woman to look at the seriousness of your wounds. If you need a doctor, I will get one for you. Wait at the Sunlit location. Can I provide you with help getting back to the loft?"

"No, I can do this. I was wondering when I would find help. You waited long enough."

"The woman I am sending is a nurse; she will assist you." Al Aziz answered, ignoring the insult.

"The pain is greater now. I want to rest. Send your nurse."

MOSCOW: MARCH 8

Shevchenko sat at his desk reading the notes sent by a KGB agent in Paris. He slid the notes back into the file alongside the final report Kasparov had prepared for him. He picked up the picture of the woman taken by the same agent in the passenger waiting area of Charles De Gaulle airport. "The report stated she was injured, but he does not say how."

"We don't know, Peter. By looking at the picture, the swollen face and bruises indicate she was beaten. She was with Al Bahia when he was assassinated. A Turkish man on his honeymoon snapped a picture of her and Al Bahia and gave it to the French police; they passed it along to us," Kasparov answered. Mikhail nodded agreement. "She must have been beaten after the picture was taken."

"She gets on a plane in Paris with a ticket to Cairo and no one notices." He placed the picture on his desk next to the file. "I agree with Dmitry. Without more evidence, we have no way of knowing where she fits into the puzzle. We must attempt to locate her. We need to know where she is and who visits her."

"Egypt, we know that much. The French found that out from a copy of her passport and travel papers."

"I am surprised they were able to find that information, Dmitry."

"They did not; it was Interpol. She may be Mossad; the beating may be to convince others she is a loyal terrorist. I would not put it past the Jews."

"Leave the file with me. I doubt very much if the Israeli government would share such information with the Americans. To many loose lips in Washington, but it is worth a try."

"If I may, Peter, I would not use the American, especially where it concerns Israel," "This senator could ask the Israelis for confirmation. They, of course, would not reply. Questions would be asked. The American could not answer without giving up his relationship with us."

"You make a point Mikhail."

"May I make another comment?"

"Of course, Mikhail, please do," Shevchenko answered a curious look on his face.

"I suggest you tread lightly in these matters. Uri Fedorov is no fool, and like Beria before him, would not waste one second in cleaning out perceived enemies. Meddling in affairs such as these could create health issues for you." Mikhail put a finger to his lips, stood up, walked over to the radio and shut it off. "Why don't we have dinner soon. I miss our little gatherings and so does my wife Raina. Bring your lady friends as well."

"A fine idea; I also have missed our little suppers. Let me check. I am free next Friday. What about you, Dmitry Kasparov?"

"I will gladly attend. I am looking forward to you both meeting my new girlfriend."

"What about you, Peter, who may I ask will you bring?"

"I think I will treat Marina to a night out. She is the best secretarial worker in Moscow and I want to show my appreciation for all she does. She can take notes on how much you both drink and eat."

BRYANSK OBLAST

Palmer called using the Russian Embassy in East Germany as a loop between Moscow and the call's destination. He gave the operator his name. There would be a delay, as expected. She put through the call to the NBC bureau. It would show the Berlin hotel as the origin of the call.

"If you are not able to contact the party you requested, use this number for messages. Give me the name of the party you wish to speak to."

"Maxine Barnett."

"Please wait."

While he waited, he poured vodka into a tumbler and drank it. He poured more vodka into the tumbler and carried it to his bedroom. The young girl was sitting on the bed, naked, her knees pulled up to her chest.

"Drink this and relax. I won't be long. How old are you?"

"Seventeen. I am to be married soon. My mother told me you would show me how to enjoy my body and my husband. She told me if I can take you, I will be ready for any man."

"Well, we'll have to see about that. No talking until I return. Drink." He padded back to the living room and picked up the phone. "Yes, I'm here."

"The woman you wish to talk to is on assignment and will return this evening, Israeli time. Will you be available?"

"Tell them yes. I will wait for the call, even if it is very late." He padded back into the bedroom. "Relax. Would you like another drink?"

It was past midnight when his phone rang.

"I almost gave up on you."

"I couldn't let your call go unanswered. I've had a terribly long day. You are still at the hotel?"

"Where else? And I was lucky enough to get the same room. The memory of you washed over me as soon as I opened the door. I've spent all afternoon in our room wishing you were here."

"Really?"

"Yes, really." He stifled a laugh and said, "Tell me, how has your trip gone so far? Did you get the interview?" He paused for effect. "I'm sorry I've forgotten his name."

"General Abel Golan. Yes, we had a nice long conversation. He admitted off the record, of course. You can't say anything to anyone . . . It was Mossad in Paris, but he denied any involvement in Barcelona. I believe him, James."

"When can I see you again, Maxine? I miss you against me. I'm erect," he whispered into the phone.

"I miss you . . . damn. I've got to go back to Washington tomorrow. I don't know how long I'll be at the bureau. Can't you come back even for a visit?"

"I'm here for at least a year. It is part of my salary package. Monday, I leave for Holland." The lie spilled out so quickly, with just enough melancholy in his voice she had to believe it.

"I'll think of something."

"Use this number to call me; it can be switched to wherever I am. I will give the hotel my itinerary. Can I call you at the bureau in a few days?"

"Yes."

"I'll call you in a few days." He hung up, stifling a laugh, and swallowed the last of the vodka. The phone rang.

"Hello."

"Mr. Palmer, I am Marshal Aleksander Pavlov. Forgive me for the late hour. You know who I am?"

"Yes, of course, and congratulations on your promotion. What is it you want and how can I help?"

"I would like to visit you at your home, say tomorrow morning about ten, depending on travel conditions."

"I'm flattered, sir, and look forward to meeting you."

CHAPTER TEN

CAIRO: MARCH 10

"I am Alisha Ahmed," she announced, when Reba opened the door as far as the chain would allow. "I am a nurse at Saint George hospital, Alia. Al Aziz sent me . . . may I come in?"

"Yes, of course, Alisha Ahmed." She slipped the chain off its hook and opened the door, stepping aside. "Pardon me, but would you close the door and bolt it? I have to sit down. My left side is very painful."

"I need to ask a few questions. It will help make my assessment after which I will make a physical inspection. Sit down if it makes you more comfortable." Ahmed closed and bolted the door.

"I brought the metal kitchen chair into the living room. It is easier on my back and less painful to get up and down. Please use the sofa."

"I can fix tea for you and food if you are hungry, Alia."

BRYANSK OBLAST

"Welcome to my humble home, Marshal Pavlov. May I offer you something to drink?"

"Nothing for me, thank you." The marshal climbed the steps, ignoring Palmer's outstretched hand.

Palmer followed Pavlov, enraged that this man had refused his hand in friendship. He closed the door, locking it. *I could crush your neck like a grape if I wished to.* "Let me take your coat, sir. Please give me a moment;

the water is boiling in my tea pot." He padded into the kitchen. You won't shake my hand, you dwarf, now you can wait for me. He took his time preparing his drink. When he felt Pavlov was properly annoyed, he returned.

"So, Marshal Pavlov, how can I be of service?" He sipped his tea, looking over the edge of the cup at his guest. A good feeling swept over him, noticing Pavlov's posture. He is a man who is not used to being kept waiting. Well, get used to it. Out loud he said, "Excuse the error. Please have a seat on the couch. It is the most comfortable chair in the room."

"Has Comrade Fedorov called you since we spoke?" Pavlov asked, sitting down and crossing his leg out of habit. He adjusted the crease in his slacks.

"No." He did not mention Anton's visit.

"Good, then let's proceed."

"Are you quite sure you wouldn't like a cup of tea, Comrade?"

"I want nothing, thank you . . . only your time."

MOSCOW

"My woman assigned to Pavlov called. He is meeting with the American at his home this morning. After the meeting, they are taking a flight. He instructed her to bring an overnight bag and her passport," Kasparov began as he and Shevchenko strolled in the garden behind Shevchenko's apartment. "He is taking her to the town of Sevastopol for a short stay before returning to Moscow. Next weekend he wants her to join him at a Black Sea resort. He did not say where exactly. She is not pleased with the offer, as you might imagine. She told me he smells like a goat."

"Is that all she knows about this trip?"

"He is not much for conversation. She is afraid to overstep. You can't blame her."

"No, of course not, Dmitry. Why would he need to travel to Bryansk to see Palmer? Why were we not notified? Has your other tulip any information we can use?"

"Not much, I am afraid. Everyone is being very secretive."

"I do not like this and I especially do not like the secrecy surrounding Pavlov's movements." Shevchenko rubbed his chin. "We cannot listen in where he plans to stay on the Black Sea. I am sure his room will be checked for listening devices before he enters. We need your tulip to give us an address and hopefully some sound information."

"Let me address it. Have you given any more time to Afghanistan, Peter?"

"Yes, I have, as a matter of fact, and it makes perfect sense, Dmitry. Our puppet regime in that country is weak. The army is ill trained. The Taliban is growing in strength. They control the poppy fields; they sell the poppy to Assad in Syria. His people break it down and produce crude heroin. It is then sent to France where it is refined. The profits are staggering. One day, the Taliban will take the country over. I think the fall of the present regime is preordained . . . You are smiling, why?"

"I am smiling, my friend, because I think you may have solved the reason for the visit to Palmer."

"Allow me to buy lunch," Shevchenko said happily. "What would I do without you Dmitry Kasparov . . . what indeed?"

"May I make another suggestion, Peter?"

"Of course."

"These things we spoke of today. I suggest you meet with Comrade Fedorov and make him privy to your thoughts on these subjects. Also inform him of the relationship between Palmer and the American woman."

"I do not think it would be wise to tell him how we found out."

"He was not followed. One of my ladies works at the phone exchange here in Moscow; she speaks three languages. Calls are made or received outside our borders, only the receiver of the call does not know the operator is in Moscow. The numbers are pre-set for each area recorded. A call back will pass through her exchange. For instance, when the American woman called Palmer. She believed she was talking to him where they stayed in Berlin. I have a recording of the call. I must say they are devoted deviants."

"Dmitry Kasparov, you never fail to amaze me. Tell me, does Uri Fedorov know how many tulips you have in your barn?"

"He thinks only three: one in America, one in England and one other. I will not mention her for now, simply because she is not one of mine but he thinks she is. In all they number twelve, nine of which are currently active."

"You are truly a man of shadows and distractions."

"I have gained a pound this week. The cough still bothers me, but it no longer sends shock waves through me and my trips to the bathroom are much easier on me."

"The laxative is working. The cracked ribs are healing. I think we can remove the tape binding on your left side. I do not think you will need it, but to be sure we will do some light bending and stretching while I monitor your breathing."

"The water is boiled," Al Aziz called out from the kitchen.

"Give us a few more minutes. I have to remove the bindings, so I can estimate the pace of her recovery."

"I need to speak to Alia . . . he is calling within the hour."

"Who is calling?"

"Al Aziz has not told me. I do not ask, Alia. It must be someone important." Ahmed rubbed alcohol on the tape and slowly peeled the strips away. "Thank Allah your skin is clearing nicely. Take a deep breath for me. Hold it and then release it when I tell you."

"How can I repay your kindness, Alisha?"

"We are ready for tea," she called to Al Aziz. "You owe me nothing, I have prayed to Allah to rid the earth of the devils that did you such harm."

Al Aziz brought two cups of tea. He said nothing to Ahmed, only gave her a dark look over his shoulder. It was enough to let her know to leave and wait in the garden. When the door closed behind the nurse, he took a seat on the metal kitchen chair across from Alia.

"We must talk."

"What do you need to know?"

"One or two questions only. I am glad you are progressing so well. Tell me: Why did Mustafa leave you behind? I would think he would take you along?"

"I begged him to take me. I would be his shadow. He did not trust Ramirez. He was afraid I might be harmed. I even cried; it only angered him." Reba thought of her husband, Daniel, dead on the Golan Heights. She buried her face in her hands and sobbed. Her shoulders shuddered. "I begged him, but he would not listen."

"Cry for Mustafa. I will ask only one more question." The phone rang breaking the mood of the moment. Reba was glad for the pause and pushed the memory of Daniel away before she might slip and call out his name. "I do not want to talk to anyone."

"I will answer; it might be for me." Al Aziz spoke quietly, his back turned. He held the receiver at arm's length and asked, "Do you want to stay here and rest, Alia?"

"I want to stay in Cairo for a few days. I want to walk where we walked and eat in the small restaurant we both enjoyed." When he turned away, she breathed a sigh of relief.

"She has asked for a few days in Cairo. I see no reason to deny her. It will give her some extra time to mourn . . . I will make all arrangements. Yes, hotel as well . . . maybe you could go to her there . . . I understand, I'll ask her." He turned around. "Would you go to Paris? He wants to meet you. He also needs time for something he must take care of."

"Whatever you decide, I can wait here and welcome him or meet him in Paris. Either option will be fine. I have my passport and required travel papers." She dared not ask why the caller needed time.

"She is agreeable . . . Yes, I will make all arrangements for a flight to Paris. Leave everything to me . . ."

"You said two questions?" She took the wet cloth and wiped her face.

"Why do you think they let you live?"

"They wanted a witness to their act. Who is this man who wants to meet me in Paris?"

"His name is Abdul Nir; he is the supreme head of Black September. He is Mustafa's uncle."

NEW YORK

Mr. Coffee was created for single men. You start brewing it the next morning by simply pushing a button or setting it to brew the night before. Edwards still preferred the old fashion method. Fill the pot with cool water and the hopper with fresh smelling Maxwell House blend. Add a touch of salt. Once it began percolating, the room filled with a pleasant aroma. In the corner, hidden under a plastic protector, sat Mr. Coffee. The phone rang just as he was about to make toast.

"Hello?"

"I hope I didn't wake you?"

"I just put on a pot of coffee, Anna Lee. This is a nice surprise. I miss you."

"I miss you, too. I have news that I hope will make your day. Vincent asked if you were coming down next weekend? I told him I would ask you since he thought it would be okay. He wants to watch a spring baseball game between Baltimore and the Red Sox. I just want you to come . . . Can you?"

"Of course, I'll come, wasn't that the plan anyway?"

"This is better. He instigated it."

"I have news for you Anna Lee. The Washington Post and Examiner are going to print my cartoons. I have to submit seven proposed pieces by next Friday."

"That is wonderful; we need to celebrate. I will tell Vincent you are excited about watching a game with him. You can tell him about the strip. I go to work later. Call me tonight, Ethan?"

"I will."

"Thank you for being patient. I really like you, Mister Edwards."

"I really like you, Miss Caputo."

MOSCOW: MARCH 16

Shevchenko bid his secretary a good night after she announced her marriage to her longtime boyfriend would be in September. He was most happy that she had asked him to walk her down the aisle. He was saddened she could not marry as a Jewish woman.

"I will drink a toast to you and Uri Chernoff. You are my friend, Marina."

"Thank you for that, Peter. I can be a Jewish wife in our home, smoke American cigarettes, and pray to my God. That is enough for me." Her eyes welled up. She quickly masked her embarrassment by feigning a sneeze.

"Enough with the tears; you are a strong woman. I admire and trust you too much for such girlish actions. Go home to your boyfriend and make love to him. I think you should do what is best for you. As far as you being foolish, I think it would be foolish to ignore your feelings."

"Maybe you should take your own advice, Peter Shevchenko." She dabbed at her eyes with a tissue and slipped the tissue into her bag. "By the way, thank you again for the lovely dinner on Friday. Raisa was very gracious and Comrade Kozlov and his wife as well, but the other one, Kasparov. brought the Kamenev woman. I am not sure about her . . ."

"Hard around the eyes?" he asked. They both laughed.

"Maybe, just a little hard around the eyes. I thought she was mentally taking notes when you men spoke."

"Tomorrow we will take a walk. I will explain things. We will talk over a hot tea and biscuit."

"I am going home." The phone on his desk sprang to life. She picked it up out of reflex. "This is the office of Comrade Shevchenko . . . yes, he is here . . . May I ask who is calling? Hold on please. Ladas Sorokin for you." She covered the mouth piece with her hand. "That name is familiar to me; should I know her?"

"Do not be coy with me, woman, you know exactly who she is. Goodnight."

"Goodnight, sir." She gave him a look with raised eyebrows and handed him the phone. "Have a nice evening."

"Comrade Sorokin, hello. How may I be of service?"

"I am on my way to Tapas Marbella. I must have a drink before I return home. I was wondering if you would like to join me. You showed me kindness at my husband's celebration. I returned the favor with sarcasm. Please allow me to make it up to you?"

"It is very kind of you but . . ."

"I know you are not afraid of my husband. It must be something else?"

"I was thinking of you."

"Do not concern yourself Peter Shevchenko. Who was that on the phone?"

"My assistant. She was my teacher in school."

"I must remember that. I have a few things still to do. Would seven o'clock be alright?"

"That will be fine."

"Welcome, Comrade Shevchenko. It is so nice to see you again. I was afraid you were not pleased with Tapas Marbella."

"I was here with friends only last week, Rudy, you missed me."

"I was away and no one told me you were here. My apologies, Comrade. Your party is already here. We offered her a refreshment, but she insisted on waiting."

"I am sure you showed her every courtesy." Shevchenko followed Rudy across the dining room. "Comrade Sorokin. It is a pleasure seeing you again." Shevchenko stuck out his hand. She shook it and smiled up at him.

"Thank you for joining me, Comrade Shevchenko. My driver . . ."

"You mean the young man at the bar in the cheap brown suit?"

"You are very observant. Please tell me he is not one of your people?"

"I assure madam he is not one of mine. I would imagine he is a student at the KGB academy or on the staff of one of your husband's senior officers. He regrets the assignment, but he is thinking of his future and that will override any resentment he might feel."

"Analytical as well as observant. I am impressed." A waiter approached. "I would like a martini."

"May I suggest a Quora? Perhaps a Stolichnaya?"

"The latter will be fine. You have taste, Comrade Shevchenko."

"Now and again I come out of the woods like the bear and mingle." Shevchenko paused, and his face reddened. "Once more my foot has found my mouth. I was trying to flatter you. I've failed again."

"Do not apologize. I am guilty as well. Over the years I have picked up some of my husband's poor habits, so I apologize to you. Please order for me as well."

"We would like a martini: a Stolichnaya Elite with three to one mix, three olives, one half cube of ice in each . . . Is that satisfactory, madam?"

She nodded approval. "Please be patient with me, Peter Shevchenko. I am used to people agreeing with my every thought and finding new ways to pamper me because they fear my husband. I am afraid I have forgotten to act like myself. I was rude to you. I thought you were sent to . . . never mind."

"You've cut your hair; it accentuates your face. I must say it is a very nice look. When the waiter brings our drinks, I will order for us. How hungry are you?"

"I am not very hungry. Perhaps an appetizer, but do not let that stop you." The waiter returned with their drinks; she took a sip.

"You were right, Peter Shevchenko. Perhaps you should spend more time away from the woods." She took another sip, bigger than the first, and set the drink on the napkin. He was smiling at her. He had a nice smile, soft eyes. She liked the grey on his temples and speckled through his black hair. "What shall we have? What would you suggest that might go well with our drinks and conversation, Comrade?"

"Do you like cheeses and mushrooms soaked in butter?"

"Yes, to both."

"Good." He ordered both. He liked looking at her. The makeup she wore, soft hues enhancing an already beautiful face. He pulled back. She was the wife of a very powerful man who could have them assassinated on a whim.

When the waiter walked off, she said, "My husband doesn't like you, Peter Shevchenko."

The waiter returned shortly with the food.

"Not many people do. I imagine my work has something to do with it." He took a swallow of his martini. "I am sure he is under a lot of stress these days considering his new position."

"He has moved to a resort on the Black Sea. He thinks he fools me with his lies about maneuvers and inspections of his troops. He is with his whore. I am sorry, Peter. Can I blame the outburst on the drink?"

"Yes, of course."

"I wanted to meet you again and ask your forgiveness for my rudeness and what do I do. I made you listen to my troubles."

"Try the mushrooms while they are still hot."

"You are right of course, Shevchenko." Ladas poked the fork into a mushroom and put a plump morsel in her mouth. One bite and she sighed with pleasure. She picked up a slice of white cheese, rolled it between her fingers and took a bite, mixing the two flavors together in her mouth. She slid her fork into a second mushroom. "You have to try the cheese and mushroom together, it's wonderful. Try this," she said, taking her fork and stabbing a large mushroom. She carefully wrapped a piece of cheese around it. "Put it in your mouth in one gulp so you get the full value of both."

"That is good," he said between chews. The waiter brought water and quickly departed.

"Before you drink any more of your martini, drink a little water. It will nullify the taste of the mushrooms."

"Do I have to?" she asked in a girlish voice.

"No," he answered, still chewing the final bite of mushroom and cheese.

"I am so comfortable and having such a nice time, I forgot why I called you."

"You wanted to apologize. You have, so let's just savor this good food and good talk."

"I must go, I am sorry. Can we meet again?"

"Yes, I would like that. I will walk you outside. Take the rest of the mushrooms."

"We will split them." He called for the waiter.

She kissed him on the cheek and whispered, "The next time I am in town I will call you?"

"Are we becoming friends?"

"I would like that. I am going to tell my husband about tonight before he hears it elsewhere. He will be angry. I hope so."

"I think you've made the right decision, Ladas Sorokin."

He locked the door and stepped through the living room, removing his tie from the jacket pocket laying neatly across the back of the lounge chair. He removed his jacket; the subtle scent of her perfume clung to its fibers. He put the coat down across the arm of the chair, walked into the kitchen, and placed the mushrooms in the refrigerator. He smiled inwardly and stepped across the hall into the bathroom.

In the light over the mirror, he spied the smudge of her lipstick on his cheek. For a long moment he stared at his reflection. What you are thinking is madness, Shevchenko. It could cost you both your lives. He felt her presence, smelled her perfume, and wondered if she was looking into a mirror at this very moment. "Stop this nonsense!" he said out loud. He turned away, switching off the light, and walked to the bedroom. He removed his clothing and collapsed on his bed, the smudge from her kiss remained on his cheek.

JERUSALEM: MARCH 20

Abel Golan ordered his driver to keep a watchful eye and opened the rear door of his car in front of 3 Kaplan Street. He was met by Abram Ben Lieber, known only to a few in Tel Aviv as "the Wrath of God": responsible for killing Asa Shar the teacher, Haran Amari, Rami Al Bahia and his wife in Paris, as well as two other members of the group that attacked or planned the attack against the Israeli Olympic team in Berlin. "They are waiting for us, General," he said, shaking the general's hand. The tall, thin man wore a black suit and for the first time in three years was clean shaven, exposing an angular European face with dark brown eyes.

"How is Reba?" Golan inquired.

"A little sore still. She jokingly chided me for the beating I gave her . . . She wants to come home, General, to see her mother and rest. Neither Paris, Cairo, nor Beirut are her favorite cities."

"Let's get this meeting over with. I will tell the prime minister what she told me about her upcoming meetings in Paris. We will discuss bringing her home after."

They took an elevator down three stories beneath the main floor of the compound and followed a long corridor with lights embedded in the ceiling. Wall vents pushed cool air into the corridor while similar vents in the ceiling pulled air out. A guard with an Uzi submachine gun stood by the steel door. Behind it was the conference room and war center.

"I have been instructed to tell you General Golan." The guard stated when the two men approached. "Your guest is to wait with me until after the first order of business is completed. There are matters to be discussed . . ."

"Do you . . . do they know who this man is?" Golan's face flushed red with anger. "And they refuse him entry?"

"Never mind, General; I will gladly wait in the corridor. There are subjects I am not privy to hear. You go in, General."

The door swung open after thirty minutes. The guard stepped inside, then quickly reappeared. "They are ready for you. I am sorry that you had to wait in the hall."

"You do your duty . . . have no regrets, my friend." Abram shook the guard's hand and entered, the metal door clicking closed behind him. The men in the room applauded; the young stenographer saluted.

The Prime Minister waved him forward, shook his hand, and motioned the others to stop applauding.

"Do not embarrass our guest, gentlemen," he said, standing in front of a wall covered with maps. Arrows and small flags pinned to the heavy canvas showed the territories inside the occupied zones, as well as the strategic locations of the neighbors to the north and east. We want very much to know what our person in Paris has conferred on you."

"Who is this person and how do we know the information is accurate?"

"No names, no titles, and no gender, Nathen Stein. This person lives in a shadow world in deep cover. Only a few know this person's identity. You may start, Abram."

"Thank you, Prime Minister." Abram looked down the length of the table, catching the eye of Golan. "You see, General, we all have secrets, do we not?" It took just under fifteen minutes to explain all he had learned from Reba in Paris. No one raised a question.

"Thank you, young man; you may leave now."

Abram thanked everyone and went to the door, knocking on the frame once. The guard answered and he stepped out into the corridor.

"Now that our guest is gone, I will entertain questions. Yes, Yaakov, you want to begin?"

"Before I ask a question, I would only like to reiterate that this person Abram talked about is a hero of Israel. I am sure Yitzhak will back me up." Yitzhak nodded agreement. "The enemies of peace will never learn. Just a few months ago, our air force struck and wiped out the camps to the south of Beirut and routed the Syrian army."

"What about Egypt?"

"Let me answer the question," Begin cut in. "I believe Sadat will honor any agreement, excluding forming a two state adventure. He will keep a knot on the Muslim Brotherhood and his second in command, Mubarak, is also on board with any agreement and he, like Sadat, despises the Brotherhood. I think they have finally come to terms with this simple fact. It is better to be a friend of Israel than an enemy."

"I have a point to make. You listen to intelligence reports and wait for the next attack against us. Instead of acting, you react. You worry about the UN. You worry about people who do not care if we exist or are driven into the sea. They hate us no less now than they have hated us for four thousand years."

"Make your point, Abel Golan."

"My point is, Mister Prime Minister, we need to be the aggressor. Hezbollah is a front organization for Syria and Lebanon. In due time, Iran will be our biggest problem once the mullahs have their way. The Shah is in trouble. The American president and the American press despise him."

"What are you suggesting? We attack Iran if the Shaw is deposed?"

"I am suggesting we instigate Iraq into attacking Iran soon after the mullahs come into power. The two countries have been at each other's throats for years over the waterways in the south of Iran. Saddam Hussein is a psychopath who murders his own people at will to subjugate them."

"It would be impossible to create such a scenario, General Golan."

"That is what the British thought just prior to Hitler invading Poland. It is what the American people thought just before the military dropped an atomic bomb on Hiroshima, gentlemen."

"I still do not think it possible."

"Then we find another trigger, Yaakov." He cleared his throat and gulped down most of the water in his glass. "The next step would be a two-pronged invasion of both Syria and Lebanon. We could decimate their armies and air forces and be rid of Assad and Hezbollah forever."

"Aren't you forgetting something, Abel?"

"What, Yaakov?"

"I am thinking of the Palestinians, Abel."

"No, I do not forget that rabble. They want a state, give it to them, and the first time one of those bastards attacks a Jew, destroy them and turn the territory into a staging area for our tanks."

"I think we should call it a day and take time to think about the General's formula. We will meet again in one week. Abel, and you Yaakov, would you spare me a few moments in my office?"

"Yes, of course, Prime Minister," both men answered.

Golan followed the other members into the corridor. He spied Abram waiting at the far end of the hall. He walked to him and whispered "Let's bring her home, Abram."

"Moesha Peres is in Paris with Daniel Berg as we speak. I will let Moesha know what you want. Should Moesha help her get out of Paris?"

"She knows when and how to travel. The prime minister has asked for a meeting with me and Yaakov Peri; wait for me in the car."

"What about Moesha and Daniel?"

"Tell them we need them to stay in Paris while we wait for Reba to tell us if she is meeting with the terrorist on the twenty-second. Is Daniel still sleeping with that pro-Palestinian French journalist Monique Chalet?"

"Yes, he is, and getting good information from her about Arafat and—"

"I am sure he is. I hope he is finding enjoyment with his assignment. We must always find satisfaction in one way or another," Golan interrupted. "I must go."

"He says she smells and does not shave her armpits."

Golan turned on his heel. Over his shoulder he said. "Get that message to Moesha. Tell him to pass it to Freidman at the embassy. Tell Daniel her armpits should not be what he is aiming to please."

PARIS: MARCH 22

Reba decided to walk to the café to have coffee and a boiled egg with a plate of assorted cheese and maybe toast. She bought a newspaper, tucked it into her shoulder bag, and hastily crossed the boulevard.

She was happy to see free tables under the canopy. She chose a table close to the street, sat down, and turned on the heater by her foot. Her skirt rose nearly to her thigh. For effect, she placed the paper on the table and slowly stretched her arms high over her head. The silk blouse under her coat accentuating her ample breasts.

The three men at adjoining tables and a passersby took notice. She picked up the copy of Le Parisien, browsed through the front page, and turned to the next page. If she were remembered, it would be her legs and the nipples of her breasts that would be described in detail and not her face. She dropped an envelope on the sidewalk and placed her shoe over it.

Reba began to read a story about a burglary at her hotel when a young man with blond hair and deep dimples in his cheeks reached down to pick up the envelope.

"Excuse me," he began in French, "Did you drop this envelope?" He picked it up and as quick as a pickpocket placed a note inside.

"I must have . . . thank you," she answered. She laid the envelope on the table, covering it with the newspaper. When she looked up, the young man was already moving toward the curb and waving for a cab. The food came just as a second man approached.

"May I join you?" he asked, his dark eyes hidden behind sunglasses.

"I was told you wanted to talk to me. What shall I call you?"

"Abdul is my name. You dress like a woman on the street."

"Your nephew did not seem to mind . . . I do not do well with insults, Abdul. If I offend you, I will get up and leave now."

"I regret the remark; will that satisfy you?"

"Tell me what you want to know." Her dress, sarcasm, and tone of her voice was not lost on Abdul Nir, nor pleasing to his ears. She rested the newspaper across her chest, carefully placing the envelope between the pages. She took a sip of coffee and a bite of toast before she lowered her skirt. The men seated at other tables lost interest.

"Thank you for the gesture."

"You are welcome. Would you like a piece of toast or this egg?"

"I would enjoy the egg. You were with my nephew in Cairo, but not in Spain?"

"I will tell you what I told Al Aziz. We were in Cairo. We were lovers. We discussed issues. We made love every chance we could. He was to meet with the terrorist the Americans call Carlos. I did not feel good about the meeting. I would have gladly died by his side. Now I can only cry for him. I want to face Ramirez. When I do, I will assassinate him."

A cab rolled to the curb not ten feet from Reba and Abdul Nir. A young man got out, the same man who had retrieved the envelope. He stood on the curb and took pictures of the Eiffel Tower that included the couple sitting under the canopy. He jumped back in the cab, the Polaroid camera hanging from a thin strap around his neck.

"How long will you be in Paris, Alia?" He kept his attention on her, looking for signs of falsehood in her eyes or gestures. Her eyes remained trained on his. He felt better.

"I want to leave tomorrow. I need time to myself. I need more time to mourn. I want a few weeks without interruption to regain my strength. You can help me, Abdul?"

"You had time to yourself."

"It was not enough."

"How can I help you?"

"Find out where Ramirez is hiding. I will contact Al Aziz for the answer."

"I will try."

"Good. I hope I helped you with your concerns for your nephew?"

"You have, Alia." He stood up, "Allahu Akbar." On the far side of the wide thoroughfare a young blonde man with a camera hanging from a strap around his neck waited. Abdul Nir had less than two hours to live.

Reba picked up the newspaper, removed the envelope from inside the morning news section, and opened it. The note was brief. COME HOME in large block lettering.

CHAPTER ELEVEN

"Sir, Mister Patterson from the American Embassy is on line three."

"Thank you, Marina; give me a moment." Shevchenko stood up and walked over to the radio. He turned the channel to the patriotic music station and padded back to his desk. "Thank you, Marina. Please put Mister Patterson through . . . Patterson, has your staff stopped passing along messages or is it that; you do not talk to me for some reason I cannot fathom?"

"It's neither; I have been back home. Today is my first day back."

"Tell me, while you were away did you find out if America is going to have a new president, or are we treated to four more years of this Carter fellow?"

"Months into his presidency and you ask me that. Tell me that is not why you called me, Peter?"

"No, Norm, it is not. I called you to invite you to lunch with me." Lunch, a key meaning the need for a private and serious conversation."

"I will take the subway to the monorail station across from the park. We can get take out and eat in the park. I'd like to have lunch there away from the embassy . . . when?"

"Whatever is your pleasure, Norm."

"Today, Peter, say about noon if you can make it."

"Noon it is."

"I never get over the magnificent style of the Moscow metro," Patterson said, taking a pack of unfiltered Camels from his coat pocket. "You invited me, Peter, what would you like to discuss?" A subtle breeze rustled the thin foliage in the trees.

"Let's sit and enjoy our lunch before we talk."

They walked up the pathway, finding a bench with a trash container and a sand-filled urn. They ate in silence. When they finished, the refuse was put away in the trash bin. Shevchenko began.

"My phone is making funny clicking sounds when I dial out or pick up so before I begin tearing my office apart, I was wondering if you or anyone on your staff might be monitoring my conversations."

"Funny you should ask since your boss asked me the same question this morning." Patterson lit a cigarette. "Seems funny, doesn't it?" His deep-set brown eyes watched for any sign of distress in Shevchenko's body language. The answer is no, Peter. I might have a suggestion."

"I didn't believe it was coming from your embassy. I ask because I trust you, Norm. A traitor to your country lives in a western province. I trust you because you have never requested his name. I like you because you keep your word. There is a more important theme for my inviting you to lunch."

"I thought as much when you agreed to meet on short notice."

"The army is planning maneuvers in the mountains above Sochi. Cold winters and in Sochi much snow that never seems to melt. They are also training in small groups for insurgency work in the snows above Sochi."

"That is interesting, to say the least." Patterson lit another cigarette and dragged deeply. "Afghanistan has mountains and the government is having trouble with the Taliban, a militant group growing stronger every day thanks to a money man in Egypt who is at present setting up a camp in Afghanistan. Have I answered your question or confirmed what you thought?"

"I wouldn't know about such things." Shevchenko put his head back and breathed deeply. "I love this time of year; the air is so fresh and clean. One thing, I would take a long hard look at . . . Iran. The mullahs do not like America. For now, they are consolidating their power; many will die, then they will turn their attention to your country and Israel."

"Is that why Israel is taking out terrorists in Barcelona, Cairo, and Paris?"

"They are responsible for Cairo and Paris, not Barcelona."

"Who did Barcelona?"

"I have no knowledge of that. I can only assure you it was not an Israeli attack." Shevchenko took another breath and sighed. "You said something about giving something back?"

"You have enemies in high places, Peter. It seems some in the politburo still remember your contributions in Leningrad and other activities, such as Berkeley and Columbia. Unfortunately, your detractors are outliving your protectors."

"Is Comrade Fedorov one of the . . . detractors?"

"I have no knowledge of that. I do know that an incident in Prague a few years ago made it impossible for you to travel outside Russia. That made you expendable. I believe your future replacement and possible heir is at this moment studying at the Red Banner Institute in Moscow. Do you know a fellow who goes by the name of Vladimir Petrov?"

"No, I am afraid I do not know this man." Shevchenko lied to protect Ladas.

"Maybe you should get to know more about him, Peter."

"Can you tell me . . . is it someone close to me?"

"No, you are safe there. Believe me . . . I wish I had a friend like Dmitry Kasparov and that other fellow from Minsk, Boris Molotov. Your other friend Anna Lebedev; she is married to a local party man with ambition and connections. What your feelings are concerning her is another matter. I am only passing along information I cannot in all honesty prove. If I hear more, I will certainly let you know."

"Thank you for the information. You are just full of good news; bless your heart, Norm Patterson." Shevchenko said in a soft North Carolina accent.

"I agree with you about Afghanistan. I will also pass along your ideas on Iran, Peter." Patterson stamped out his cigarette while trying but failing to hold back a surge of laughter at Shevchenko' grasp of the southern accent. "I will pass it along, but I fear it will land on deaf ears. Be careful, Peter. Now that we have shared no knowledge of current events, I must go."

APRIL 6

The next day a package was delivered to Paterson's office. Inside of the package he found two bottles of Quora. A small handwritten card came with the package. "Friendship and trust are like good vodka." The card was unsigned.

"Forgive me for yesterday; it was something I needed to do, Marina. Please join me for a walk today around the square."

"I will call the exchange. What time frame shall I give them?"

"I would say an hour at the most." Shevchenko put a finger to his lips, scribbled a short note on his notepad, and turned it around for Marina to read it.

"Give me a minute to call the exchange and we can leave. I must say this is a nice surprise. My boss is taking me out for a stroll on a work day. The other ladies will most certainly be jealous of Peter Shevchenko."

"I cannot answer for other departments. I will meet you in the square, Marina." He tore off the three top pages of the pad and slipped them in the pocket of his gray slacks. "You remember a man named Nicholai Porgorny?" Shevchenko asked, as they entered the square.

"Of course I remember him. I believe he was a member of the old troika." They mingled with the tourists, speaking softly like lovers out for a stroll. "Rumor has it he murdered Beria because he believed Beria murdered Stalin."

"I have enemies in high places. They fault me for not being able to travel outside our borders. They fault me for the failure in Barcelona. It is the political gamesmanship, Marina. Part paranoia . . . part envy. They use fraud, deception, and inflated story lines and gossip from nonexistent entities all for no less a reason than maintaining power while surrounding themselves with yes men they think they can trust and manipulate. Someone is monitoring my calls and passing them on."

"Fedorov?"

"Yes. . . maybe it is, maybe not. I do not know yet. Have you ever heard of a young man named Vladimir Petrov? At this moment, he is studying at the Red Banner Institute here in Moscow. He is Ladas Sorokin's driver."

"Would you like me to see if I can put a profile together?"

"Too dangerous, Marina. Anything we need to discuss, we do it in private like today. I must keep many things from you after our little talk. You have seen Beria's guest room."

"I accept your wish. You never told me why you do not travel?"

"There is a man, a very dangerous man who is highly skilled in treachery and deception. He hunts me. I was in Prague a few years ago . . . you remember. This man came within seconds of ending my life. He is like the wind,

Marina, a subtle breeze that lures you into complacency."

"I would guess you also hunted him."

"Yes, and he has eluded me in each instance."

"I am reminded of an old Hebrew proverb I learned as a child, Peter Shevchenko. 'A silent wind can never be caught in a net.' You do not know anything about him, not even if he is still alive. Still, you think of him and fear him?"

"I do not know and may never know Marina. In a way, he has won even though I am still alive. I live here and only here." I have traveled outside the Motherland only once since Prague. Barcelona, I was afraid of being there for many reasons not related to this assassin. Shevchenko stopped and looked up at the spires of Saint Basil's Cathedral. He fell silent, lost in thought. Finally, he asked, "Would you like a tea and perhaps an apple bun?"

"Yes, I would enjoy that. I think there is more you want to tell me, yes?"

"Yes, there is, Marina."

"May I say something, my dear Comrade?"

"Yes, of course."

"When we return to the office, you should call Fedorov and tell him you think someone is listening in on your conversation. Get his reaction. It might tell you what he is thinking Peter."

"You read my mind. How did you know?"

"You writing notes to me is not normal. Your meeting yesterday with Patterson . . . does that have something to do with it?"

"Wait here, I will get our drinks. I want to walk. It is busy in the square today. We will be able to talk."

He walked out of the bakery after some minutes and handed her the bun wrapped in paper, a napkin, and her tea. "The bun is nice and warm. We came just as they were bringing out a fresh tray."

"Tea should never be served out of a cardboard cup," Marina groused to his amusement, "it isn't the Russian way."

"I agree."

"The apple bun is wonderful. Thank you for both."

"You are very welcome."

"Before, when you were circling me, did you see anyone out of place?" Marina took a bite of her apple bun and washed it down with a swallow of tea.

"No . . . You notice everything."

"I have known you for too many years, Peter Shevchenko, not to notice."

"Let's walk; there is more I want to share with you." Shevchenko ate the apple bun, collected Marina's cup and debris, and placed them in a receptacle with the three torn sheets of paper. "I mentioned the training of certain troops to Patterson. He suggested Afghanistan immediately, which only adds conviction to my assumption."

"You need to know what the leadership is thinking?"

"I think Palmer is hatching some sort of plan. He would have to have approval. I do love this weather after one of our winters. I wish it could be like this all year round."

"For that climate you would have to live in America. California or Florida perhaps."

"What a choice: hurricanes or earthquakes."

"You started to mention one other thing—"

"Yes," Shevchenko interrupted, "the other thing."

"We should go back. Almost an hour has passed."

"Yes, we should, Marina."

"My Uri is taking me to supper and the ballet the day after tomorrow. He is picking me up at work. I want you to meet him. Did I tell you he grew up in Ukraine? He was raised in Donetsk, not far from where you lived."

"No, you did not. It will be a pleasure. I want to size up this man who has stolen the heart of my secretary." He smiled. "I am going to Minsk tomorrow morning. I will return the following day. Come to my dacha."

"Are you going to see Anna? You haven't mentioned her in quite a while."

"She married a man from Minsk, a local political man. I am visiting my friend Boris Molotov."

"Something in your tone tells me there is more to this story, Peter Shevchenko."

"We need to get back to the office. I will be staying at the Renaissance. No more questions Marina."

"No more questions."

"One more favor. Please call Boris and tell him I should arrive tomorrow afternoon early. I will give you the information. Please ask him to meet me at the station."

"Be careful, Peter Shevchenko."

"I am going to spend a little time with an old friend, do not worry."

"I will say it again—"

"There is no need," he interrupted. "I know what you mean."

"Would you like me to see to your apartment?"

"If you would. I will be most grateful."

Shevchenko read the return label on the box: East Berlin Postal Exchange. He unlocked the door to his apartment and stepped inside, placing the box on the sofa. He picked up the phone and dialed his office.

"Marina, I have a package here for you from East Berlin. It must be the order of dishes you asked for."

"Wonderful."

MINSK: APRIL 7

Shevchenko stepped off the train and immediately spied his old friend waiting in his car. When it was safe, he crossed the street, walked briskly to the car, put the small valise behind the front seat, and climbed in. "It is good to see you, Boris Molotov."

"It is good to see you, Peter Shevchenko."

"You received my message."

"I am glad I picked you up. It is best that we talk in private. Your secretary would only say it is a personal matter. I am assuming it has something to do with Anna Lebedev." Boris put the car in gear and easily melted into traffic. "What is the situation and what do you require of me, Peter?"

"Drive slowly and I will explain everything." When they arrived at the hotel, Shevchenko reached behind his seat and pulled the small valise onto his lap. "I am going to invite her to supper with me. We will see from my conversation with her if your services are required."

"I will wait. In the meantime, I have informants telling me one thing and friends something quite different. The situation between this couple varies with whomever you talk to. Be careful, Peter Shevchenko. Your room is ready; you need only to pick up the key." Boris reached into his jacket pocket and took out three sheets of typed pages. "This is a dossier on her husband. He is a party man through and through and well established, Peter. He will be the next member of the politburo from Minsk. I am sure of it."

"You put this together while I was on the train?"

"Marina is the one you should thank. I would not want that woman looking into my life. The American Patterson is also concerned. I have spoken with him."

"I understand, my friend. I will call you."

Shevchenko noticed the bottle of vodka with two glasses and an ice bucket on the bar as soon as he entered the suite. Next to the vodka was a pad with a pencil resting across the page. He put the valise down, walked over to the bar, and read the note. It gave her maiden and married name, her work place, and a direct number to her desk. He picked up the phone and dialed. She answered on the second ring.

"It is Peter. Can you talk?"

"Yes, where are you?"

"I am here in Minsk. I came to see you."

"You know I am married, Peter. I cannot meet you. I know how I would react seeing you again."

"Your marriage is why I am here. I am at the Renaissance hotel, Suite 601 H. Meet me for supper."

"I cannot, Peter. My husband expects me home by six."

"Your husband expects too much of you. I have heard things about your marriage, Anna. I am concerned for your safety. Tell your husband a KGB agent is here. Tell him you expect me to ask questions about him concerning future opportunities. Questions I must ask and must be answered truthfully."

"You know about the possible move to Moscow?"

"Anna, why do you question me? Come to the hotel or I will come to you. Call your husband and return my call." He hung up and waited. It rang in less than three minutes.

"I can be there at five o'clock." She hung up.

Shevchenko called down to the restaurant and ordered two suppers to be delivered in two hours. He hung up, put his things in the top drawer of the bureau, padded into the bathroom, and washed up. He shaved and dabbed cologne on his neck. He slipped on a crisp, white shirt and gray slacks. While he waited, he read Marina's report from Patterson. He fixed a drink, folded the report, slipped it between the mattress and box spring, and sat down to wait.

At three minutes past five, there was a knock on the door. Anna put her head to the side and came into his arms, hugging him tightly without speaking.

"Let me look at you." He pulled back releasing the hold she had on him and immediately noticed the swollen cheek, bluish black against her pale skin. Her lip was slightly swollen as well. "Is this his work, Anna?"

"I fell. It was an accident."

"This was no accident. You told me once he was a gentleman and—"

She put a finger to his lips. "Fix me a drink, please. You look wonderful."

"I ordered supper for us," he said, pouring vodka into a glass. "I hope you are hungry. You look thin."

"You have gone from being my lover to my big brother now?" She took a long swallow of vodka, almost finishing it in a single gulp and held out her glass. "I should not have come. If he found out I was with you, he would kill me. He has friends who will protect him here and in Moscow. Another drink, please?" She put her head down.

"Tell me. I want to help if I can."

"He was a gentle man, kind and thoughtful. He treated me with respect. I agreed to marry him. I only saw him drink twice, Peter. The day he proposed and our wedding day. The honeymoon was very nice."

"Where did you go?"

"A Black Sea resort. It is when we came here to Minsk that he changed. He began to drink more heavily and frequently. One night he came home very drunk. I scolded him. He hit me with such force I was thrown back over a chair. He doesn't make love to me. It is like a rape. He cheats on me. I smell perfume on his skin." The tears bubbled up and spilled down her cheeks, smearing her eyeliner.

"He called me a whore and told me he would fill the courtroom with men who would swear I slept with all of them. Two of them would swear I slept with them after we were married. It is all a lie, Peter."

A knock on the door. "I have your supper, sir."

"Just a moment." Peter hustled her into the bathroom and closed the door. "Ah, it smells wonderful," he said, allowing the server to enter.

"Would you set the table while I wash up?" He folded two rand gave them to the server. "Let yourself out."

"Yes, Comrade."

He went into the bathroom, closing the door behind him. "Are you alright?" he whispered. "It will be a minute. The server is setting our table." They waited until they heard the door open and close.

"He is gone. Let's eat our supper and talk."

"Look at me. I am a mess and I have no makeup."

"You look fine."

They ate and drank a pitcher of water with a glass each of vodka. When they finished, he poured tea for them both. "You know, if you had given me any indication there could be a future for us . . ."

"It is the life I chose. I do not apologize for it, Anna. I have regrets. I am human."

"I know that, Peter."

"Let me ask a question and please answer it truthfully. If you could safely leave this marriage, where would you go?"

"It is impossible, Peter."

"Do you remember who I am and who manages this hotel? I asked you a question. Please answer."

"There is a city on the Black Sea near the mountains; Sochi, it is called. Have you heard of it?"

"I have heard it. I hear the snow is very popular in the winter for a lot of skiers. You love to ski?"

"Yes, thank you for remembering."

"I am going to ask my friend Boris to visit your husband tonight and convince him of the importance of allowing you to divorce him . . . without problems. It will benefit both you and him. What time can he be expected home tonight?"

"Your friend Boris was always nice to me and treated me with respect. Did he tell you about my troubles, Peter?"

"No Anna, I heard it from another source. I called Boris and solicited his help. Tell me the time, Anna."

"He was supposed to be home by six, but he changed his plans. He will not be home before ten, and if he is with a woman, not before eleven, possibly after midnight. Either way, he will have been drinking. He can be extremely belligerent when he drinks, Peter."

"Does he carry a weapon?" Suspicion began to bubble inside Shevchenko.

"He has a weapon on his bedside table. It is always loaded. A few times he has pointed it at me. I do not want to go home tonight."

"Do you have an answering machine at home?"

"Yes, we do. Why, Peter?"

"I want you to call home and leave a message." Shevchenko scribbled the long note, read it, made a few changes, and handed it to Anna.

"You might make tearful sounds for effect. Pause for inflection, you will only get one chance to get it right."

"What are you going to do to him?"

"That is completely up to your husband. If you cannot go through with it, I understand."

Anna took a deep breath and dialed. The answering machine barked to life. The message in her husband's husky voice ended with the machine beeped. She took another deep breath and read the note. "I love you, Anton, but I can no longer live like this. Let me be alone tonight? Let me sleep without fear?" She hung up. "What have I done, Peter? He will ruin me."

"You have made the right choice. I am going downstairs to speak to Boris. Try to rest and do not worry."

Boris sat at the end of the long polished oak bar eating assorted cheeses with crackers. He drank only hot tea in situations where his expertise at soliciting outcomes was needed. He spied Shevchenko coming into the bar and ordered his friend vodka with a single cube of ice.

"Sit down, my friend, and drink to old age and pretty, big-breasted women." His voice lowered to almost a whisper, "Is the arrangement made?"

"Yes, you can finish your tea. I have a request. Anna has left a message on their machine at home. You will need to play it for him. Here is the key. He will be home by ten, no later than midnight. He keeps a weapon in the bedside drawer. I also need a room for her tonight. The check-in time must be no later than six fifteen. Use her married name. It will show her to be honest."

"I can assume you believe her to be honest, Peter? But you hesitate. That tells me something else."

"Get him to admit to the cruelty. If he does, you will make every effort to convince him to allow her to leave him without recrimination. He must also admit in public his indiscretion."

"If he is still unrepentant, Peter, what would you have me do?"

"If he is all she says he is . . . there is only one alternative."

Boris finished the last of the cheese and wiped his mouth with a soft cloth. The tea was brought.

"Peter, do you realize what is at stake here? Have you read the papers? You must be certain of her truthfulness." Boris reached into his coat pocket and produced a small vial filled with a yellow liquid. "It is quick, painless, and quite lethal. It will stop the heart in less than ten seconds and if mixed with tea it is odorless and has no aftertaste." Boris slipped the vile into Shevchenko's coat pocket. "Just in case we guessed wrong about this situation."

"Yes, just in case I guessed wrong." Shevchenko finished his drink. "You better get ready. You shouldn't have much trouble. The people of Minsk go to bed early. Before you enter the apartment complex, call me."

"I am expecting a call, Comrade. I will arrange her room reservation and give her number and key to you. Did you read the papers I gave you?"

"Yes, I did. I have two friends Boris: you and Dmitry. I do not need more. If she is truly against me, I . . ."

"Enough said. Do not leave until my call comes. I hope for your sake, Peter, my source is wrong."

Boris went behind the desk, changed the reservation and time of her arrival and picked up the key for Suite 411K. He was about to take it to Shevchenko when his phone rang, stopping him. "Do not leave yet, Peter. We will have another drink and talk . . .".

"Who were you talking to, Comrade? You look worried." Shevchenko asked, when Boris put the phone down.

"The plan is changing. There is danger, my friend. Remember the trench? Your ankle?"

"You saved my life. You carried me from the trench even with the slugs close behind us. You have the same look now."

NEW YORK

Ethan arrived at the loft just after four in the afternoon. He thought about stopping for a meal, but discarded the idea, afraid that if he called too late Anna Lee might be sleeping. He settled on having a drink and a snack. The drink came first: Johnny Walker Black, neat. He let the scotch sit while he dialed her number.

"Hello."

"Hi, it's me. Did I call too early?"

"No, I was hoping you would call. I usually nap from six until nine. Did you have a nice weekend?"

"I'll tell you honestly. I haven't had a weekend as wonderful in a very long time, Anna Lee."

"Neither have I. I am supposed to ask you when will the Yankee's being playing the Red Sox in Boston. That's a big request I know. ?"

"I'll get a schedule and let you know."

"When you told him about the rivalry, he got really interested. I have the eighth to the tenth off. I want to come alone. I told Vincent it was a conference."

"I would love that."

"See if you can get tickets to a Yankee game. I will bet he would love to see Boston . . . so would I, as a matter of fact." She wasn't ready to tell him something else Vincent said.

"Get some rest; you have a shift tonight."

"What will you do?"

"See if I can swing Boston. I'll be up late, pasting completed segments. I want to write, draw the characters and the captions for new material over the next two weeks. Then I will be far enough ahead so I can enjoy you and not have to worry about work. I will miss you above all."

"You promise? God, I feel like a teenager."

"I promise . . . get some rest."

"Goodnight Ethan. Call me tomorrow."

MINSK: APRIL 8

Shevchenko bought a copy of Zvijezda—the Minsk newspaper—tucked it under his arm, and walked out to the platform. He boarded the late morning train for Moscow. He found a window seat in the smoking section, sat down, unfolded the newspaper, and began to read early reports of the incident. Mister Georgi Lebedev strangled his wife in a drunken rage at a local hotel, returned home, and then killed himself with his own pistol. Shevchenko folded the paper, laid it on the empty seat next to him, and closed his eyes.

"Are you by chance finished with the paper, Comrade?"

"Yes, I am." He opened his eyes, took the folded newspaper, and passed it across the aisle to the woman. "You can keep it if you like."

"I wanted to read about that awful murder and suicide. The stand was out of newspapers. I saw them once at a rally. He was running for office. They looked so happy together . . . One never knows, does one?"

"Yes, one never knows," he answered and closed his eyes.

CHAPTER TWELVE

WALTER REED HOSPITAL, ARLINGTON, VIRGINIA: APRIL 9

Anna Lee slipped out of her scrubs and tossed them into the soiled linen hamper. She walked to her locker, opened it, and pulled out a pair of five-inch open-toed spike heels. It had been so long since she wore heels, she wondered if she still could without spraining an ankle.

She was excited at the opportunity to see Hello Dolly live, but had no idea what was acceptable dress. She liked Carol Channing, however, so even if the play disappointed her, she could enjoy Channing's singing.

"You can't sit here all day, girl . . . make a move." She stood up, wobbly at first but determined not to fall. She stepped over to the full-length mirror, pressed her hands on her hips, and slowly turned.

"Not a good look, girl," she exclaimed. "Might be a little puffy." She turned completely around and over her right shoulder and studied the contour of her calves with the heels on. I still have great legs and no veins.

The door opened and Margaret walked in, already pulling off her scrub top. "I swear these days nurses' brains are as thick as . . . " She spied Anna Lee in a bra, panties, and high heels in front of the dressing mirror. "This could only mean one of three things. You are thinking of a career in burlesque? You got laid this weekend and you're checking yourself out? Or you're planning to and soon. Which is it?"

"This weekend . . . Saturday night. Vincent stayed with Mom and Dad."

"Your home?"

"My home, in my bed, and it was wonderful." Anna Lee looked sideways into the mirror. "That man found places to please me I wouldn't have imagined existed."

"That certainly sends a message, Anna Lee, in both directions." Margaret slipped off her scrub pants, stepped to the mirror, and appraised her reflection. "I still got it." She sat down on the bench. "I need a cigarette."

"I know what you are saying about direction and don't think I haven't worried about it. Oh, and it gets worse." Anna Lee placed her hands on her hips. "Be honest with me: Do you think I'm getting a little puffy around the middle? Is my ass sagging.?"

"Anna Lee, my wonderful adorable friend, if I didn't absolutely adore my husband and most men outside of Willy Nelson, I'd be on you like a dog on a steak bone." Margaret looked at her friend, her brows knitting over her eyes. "Tell me the next bomb you are about to drop."

"Vincent asked me if Ethan and I were getting serious. I'm going to tell him Ethan invited me up to New York to see a play the 20th and meet his agent. I told Vincent we were just friends and I had no idea where it would lead."

"What did he think of that?"

"Never so much as blinked an eye, Maggie. If it came to that, he loves New York and wouldn't mind living there."

"Ethan doesn't know yet?"

"No, not yet, Maggie . . . Margaret, I'm sorry."

"Maggie will do. As far as telling Ethan . . . not yet. There is this pressure thing with men. They like to feel they're in charge of such decisions. It's the perfect trap. Not to change the subject, but what's with the heels?"

"We are going to see Hello Dolly on Broadway and he wants to take me to Carbone's, his favorite Italian restaurant in the East Village. I still have no idea what to wear. What do you think Maggie?"

"A simple short black dress three inches above the knee with thin straps. A push up bra wouldn't hurt either. You've got a great rack: Show it," Margaret answered immediately. "It works every time and with those legs, the night is made. How do you think I got my husband to ask me to marry him?"

"You are something else, Maggie. You never fail to have the answer for every occasion."

"Stick with me. I'll have you farting out of silk, Anna Lee. I heard that somewhere, but I'll be damned if I remember where I heard it."

"Not to change the subject, but someday will you tell me about Ethan when you knew him at . . . I never remember."

"Trang . . . NhA Trang. Feel like a cup? I'll tell you what I know. I take it he hasn't talked about it?"

"Not a word about it at all."

"It's hard for a lot of them. C'mon, let's get a cup of coffee before someone finds us and asks us to do a double shift."

"No double shifts today. The only thing I want to do today is practice walking in these shoes and sleep. Let's go."

"You can't repeat what I tell you, Anna Lee."

"Not a word, I promise. All of a sudden, I'm hungry," Anna Lee announced.

"So am I. You game?"

"Why not. Grab a table."

"I didn't see Ethan when they brought him from triage," Maggie began when they were seated. "I first saw him when he was brought to the ambulatory wing that was my unit. He was cleaned up by then. The nurses and his doctor told me they had to cut away his jungle fatigues, which were covered in blood. Not all his. They burned them. He'd been captured. He was living in his own shit and urine for over four days in a cage. He escaped. How, he never said. He was a mess, Anna Lee."

"My God, how awful."

"Why don't we eat before the food gets too cold even for me to enjoy eating? There is more, let's eat first."

"A simple black dress with thin straps and that will do it?"

"Right as rain."

SHEVCHENKO: APRIL 9

Shevchenko was awakened by the rail car shifting on its wheels. The conductor came to his seat, checked his ticket, stamped it, and asked to see his travel card. Shevchenko reached into his coat pocket, the back of his hand brushing against the unused vile of poison. "Here you are."

"I am sorry, Comrade Colonel, for disturbing you. Might I bring you a glass of tea? Perhaps something to eat?"

"I am fine, thank you. Could you tell me if there is a landline phone on board?"

"There is a phone in the restaurant two cars forward, unless you need more privacy."

"You read my mind, Comrade."

"Come with me."

Shevchenko squeezed into the small space. He dialed his apartment, cupping his hand over his nose. Marina answered on the second ring.

"Hello, Marina; did you find the apartment in good order?"

"Yes, the dust has not been disturbed. Nothing has been touched. I called for service this morning. They will have it cleaned by the time you arrive home."

"Can you reach Kasparov safely?"

"Yes. In fact, he is waiting for my call. Oh yes, before I call him, thank you for the package. The next time you see Mister Patterson, thank him as well."

"Good. Please give Kasparov this message: I am on the train. I am two hours out of Minsk. I want him to drive to Vyazma Station and pick me up."

"I will take care of it. Are you all right, Peter Shevchenko?"

"Yes Marina. I am looking forward to you and Uri coming by the apartment this evening. I must go."

WALTER REED HOSPITAL

"Ethan's bunkmate."

"The medic?"

"Yes. let me finish . . . His Rabbi would visit him two or three times a week and read the English version of the Old Testament to him. If I remember, it was the second book of Moses. On the days he couldn't come, Ethan who was getting better by then, asked the rabbi to leave the book and he would read to him. The rabbi gave him a copy and each day Ethan would kneel or sit on the wood plank floor next to that soldier's bunk. He would lean close to his ear and read to him. He'd kneel on those badly scraped up knees, ignoring the discomfort it caused and never once complained."

"My God . . ."

"I will tell you how the young man was shot. Two women came to this base camp seeking help. I think it was in the highlands. I can't remember now: it was ODA 21 or 23. Another woman was having trouble with labor. He went to assist. After he saved both mother and child, they shot him in the head."

The waiter brought a pot of coffee and placed it on the table.

"I made fresh, Sorry for the wait." He poured coffee into their cups then departed.

"Ethan had no clean clothes; all he had was his hospital pajamas, a robe, and those damned slippers. One day, I asked if he could have anything he wanted what would it be? He was fully ambulatory by then, the infection was almost gone, his wounds were nearly healed, and would you believe the damn fool was actually doing pushups next to his bunk?"

"What was his wish?"

"He wanted an ice cream cone."

"Did you bring him one?"

"No. In that heat it would have been a puddle before I got it to him, so I went to the doctors and they came up with some clean underwear, a fatigue shirt, and pants. I put a piece of tape over the pocket, wrote his name on it and off we went. I bought him a ten-cent, double-dip vanilla cone. He was like a little kid, all smiles from ear to ear. When we got back to the hospital, I gave him his beret. Now Anna Lee, you know things about Ethan."

"Thank you. Are you sure about the dress, Maggie?"

"Trust me, Anna Lee. A simple black dress, thin shoulder straps, and those legs . . . he's cooked."

VYAZMA STATION: WEST OF MOSCOW

Kasparov lit a cigarette. Seeing no receptacle for the match, he squeezed the burnt end and stuck it in his jacket pocket. The doors to the train opened and people began pouring out of the cars all along the platform, scurrying away to make other connections.

Kasparov smoked his cigarette. He knew Shevchenko was a man who did not like crowds or cramped spaces back to his youth in Leningrad. He abhorred standing in line, moving a few paces at a time toward exits. Kasparov could feel his anguish. He suffered the same phobias as a youth.

At last, he spied Shevchenko. He padded over to the edge of the platform and squeezed the lit end of the cigarette until it dropped off onto the track. The remaining butt disappeared into the pocket with the match. "I had to park on the next block. The lot was full."

"I do not mind, my friend. I need to stretch my legs."

"Boris called. The police have determined it was a murder-suicide after all. He thought you would want to know."

"Now it's official."

"Boris said something about poison?"

"She betrayed me. I was angry. She wanted me to make love, knowing an assassin was on his way to kill me. I wanted her to suffer. I wanted her to see the hatred in my eyes before she died. I'm not proud of myself, Dmitry."

Shevchenko reached into his shirt pocket and lifted out the vile containing the yellow liquid. "Keep it in a safe place. Do we yet know who is behind the attempt on my life?"

"Pavlov . . . It was him. We will talk while I drive."

The engine growled and spewed blue exhaust smoke in a steady stream behind the aging Volga-12 sedan. Shevchenko sat back and closed his eyes, a frown on his face. He awakened with a start and for a few seconds stared straight ahead.

"I dozed off; I am sorry, Comrade."

"I think you should request a new vehicle. No. I think you should demand one, Peter. A Colonel in the KGB should at least drive a sedan worthy of his rank and service instead of a car that smokes like the chimney of a factory in the Urals," Kasparov said with an indignant smirk.

"I will surely mention it. To Comrade Fedorov the next time we speak. In the meantime, tell me, Comrade, what do you know about Pavlov and Minsk?"

"My tulip informed me about the assassination attempt. I informed Marina who contacted the American Embassy. The rest you know. It seems Pavlov was very drunk and talkative. My associate was also able to get information from him concerning the other matter while they were in bed together. The information is troubling."

"So, we were correct in our assumption?" Shevchenko rubbed his chin. "Why kill me?"

"Pavlov is afraid of you. Palmer hates you. An exchange of gifts . . . It was Patterson who saved your life. That is not all, my friend. My associate," Kasparov paused to light a cigarette, "she was also intimate with Palmer. He told her the Middle East will explode and America will be drawn in. He has a plan, but that is all she could get him to say. She fears Palmer. He hates women; she has the welts, teeth marks, and bruises to prove it." Kasparov rolled down his window to let the smoke escape. "What do we do, Peter?"

"We will conduct our business as if nothing has happened. We find out who the assassin is. We must make a plan to rid ourselves of Pavlov and all others involved. It will take time, Comrade. We can leave no room for error. Your associate will stay with Pavlov?"

"She says she will. She knows the risk and is willing to keep us informed of events."

"If Pavlov realizes he has spoken out of turn in her presence or he finds out she was intimate with Palmer, he will have her killed. She understands the situation?"

"She understands, Peter."

"All right, Dmitry, if you are confident then I am as well."

"Are you hungry? Shall we stop? We will need gas in this disaster of a car."

"Find a stop where we can have a sandwich, something quick. I have invited Marina and Uri Chernoff to the apartment. I do not wish to disappoint her. She has asked me to stand for her, Comrade."

"A great honor. I almost forgot Marina has a file. She thinks you might find it interesting. She will bring it to your apartment this evening."

"I spoke with her earlier and she made no mention of a file."

"She was afraid you would be angry. She did not want to argue with you."

Shevchenko lit a cigarette.

"I already have a suspect in mind, Peter."

"Who is it, Dmitry? Who is this man?"

"He is a man in Pavlov's inner circle. Oleg Smirnov is his name."

"When you are sure, let me know. I leave the solution in your capable hands."

"What about Fedorov? Is he . . .?"

"We will have to see about that situation as well. Obviously he cannot be murdered."

He knew by the scent of cleaning fluids throughout the apartment that Marina had someone clean while he was on his way home.

He began to heat the water. He placed four scoops of leafy tea into a basket and set the basket into the pot. The doorbell rang three times.

"Welcome Marina and Uri Chernoff. Welcome to my home. I have made tea and bought some nice pastries. I hope you like them."

"You are very gracious, sir, to invite me to your home Comrade."

"Marina is a special friend. I trust her with my life. You are the lucky man she has chosen. I need no further introduction. Please call me Peter." He took their coats and carefully hung them in the closet near the door. "Sit down please and make yourself comfortable. I will get the tea and pastries."

"I must have a word with Peter. I will only be a minute." Marina followed Peter into the kitchen. She removed the file from her purse and placed it on the table. "Was Minsk terrible?"

"Yes, it was. I would never have believed she would deceive me." He picked up the bowl of sugar. "Does Uri like sugar in his tea?"

Later the same night, Shevchenko sat upright in his bed, his back propped up against pillows, wearing pale blue pajama bottoms. His Walther PPK lay on the folded sheet by his side. He opened the file Marina brought and read the heading.

SUBJECT VLADIMIR PETROV
BORN LENINGRAD 1953

Shevchenko studied the picture of the young man clipped inside the file. He smiled. The face was, of course, instantly familiar.

He removed the picture, set it aside next to his weapon, and began to read the history of the young man. When he was finished, he slipped the picture back into the folder, closed it, and set it on the small table next to his bed.

"Petrov," he said out loud. "Mother Russia . . . Be careful of this one."

NEW YORK

Anna Lee unpacked, hanging the simple black dress in the closet, still in the store's plastic cover. The five-inch heels remained in the bottom of the suitcase. The rest of her clothing—except for black slacks with a white silk blouse and two-inch patent leather shoes—consisted of jeans, pull over shirts, socks, and sneakers. He had said dress comfortably and she took him at his word. In the master bedroom's bath, she carefully laid out cosmetics as not to intrude on his space. She opened the drawers and put in a few cosmetics. It gave her a chance to look for lipstick, a phony eyelash, or perhaps a pair of earrings absentmindedly or purposely left behind. She found nothing. Carbone's became her favorite restaurant. "It was their restaurant now."

Saturday, he took her to Chinatown. They ate a casual light lunch at Shanghai Asian Manor on Mott Street. After lunch, they walked across the lower Westside toward Battery Park, stopping at the church of Saint Paul the Divine.

"I can tell you love your city. Can we go inside?"

"Sure, people go through it all the time. They have services on Sunday if you would like to come back."

"Do you go to church, Ethan?"

"Not since I came back to the world. Let's go inside."

Margaret was right, the black dress with thin straps combined with the five-inch heels brought her height up to almost eye level. The careful application of makeup was not too much and her hair pulled up into a soft pillow on top of her head struck a chord with not only Ethan, but with other men in the theater. They made love as soon as they returned to the loft, leaving a trail of discarded clothes scattered haphazardly on the floor.

Anna Lee propped herself against the headboard with a quizzical look on her face. He was dressed in a black t-shirt and what appeared to be fatigue pants but, with straps dangling from the bottom. The boots, deeply shined, were noticeable even in the dark, with laces that looked as if they were forming a ladder. "Please tell me you are not a cat thief or one of those second-story guys you read about?"

"I am not a cat. This is the way I trained. Old habits die hard. Go back to sleep." His voice, barely above a whisper, was soft and reassuring as he slipped a wool cap over his head and sat on the edge of the bed.

"A bit warm for that wool cap, Mister Edwards."

"I want to sweat when I run. Go back to sleep."

"What time is it, anyway?"

"Three thirty . . . Thanks for a beautiful weekend. I wish it didn't have to end today."

"Me too, Ethan." It was as close to "I love you" as they came.

"I won't be long. Try to sleep."

"Too late buster. I'll put the coffee on. It will be ready when you get back. Get going and be careful out there." She kissed him hard on the mouth. "If you are a second-story man, I like diamonds."

"I'll try to remember."

"You do that."

Anna Lee got out of bed, padded naked into the kitchen to fix a pot of coffee using the old drip coffee maker already on the stove, and went back to bed.

"Are you leaving without having a cup of coffee with me?" she said, sitting up. "It smells great by the way."

"I'm back."

"That was quick. The coffee is still percolating. How did you do that? You left clomping around and now you're back soundlessly. How did you do that? I didn't even hear the key in the lock. How did you do that?"

"I didn't know you were awake. I smelled the coffee, but I didn't see you, so I stayed quiet."

"That's quite a little gift you have, Ethan Edwards."

"I'm sorry if I scared you. Have a cup of coffee with me."

"I forgot to bring pajamas." Tears welled in her eyes and she began to cry. "I'll clean the bedding."

"Don't do that. I am really sorry I scared you."

"It isn't that at all Ethan, it's me I'm having a woman's day. On top of that, I'm getting my period."

"James, I never thought I would get through to you. The phone connections to your hotel sucks. My husband will be home very soon. I have news; where are you?"

"You caught me just in time, Maxine. I'm leaving Holland for Vienna this evening. I'll be there for ten days or so; what is your news?"

"I convinced my producer and editor that I would go crazy if they didn't put me on assignment. I'll be in Paris on the twenty-ninth. Tell me you can meet me."

"I'll try very hard. Where will you stay?"

"Hotel Eiffel Saint-Charles. I will be covering the street disturbances . . . My husband just walked in." She hung up.

He hung up and waited for the phone to ring. Seconds passed.

"Yes."

"Was the call clear?"

"You had trouble with the connection, I assume?"

"We needed to pass through multiple lines." Ivanna Kamenev answered. "The area you are in has phone problems for any call over three feet. I apologize for the delay, Comrade Palmer."

"No need." He hung up.

The operator hung up, logged the call under Palmer, and put the recorded conversation into Palmer's KGB file for further study. She placed a call to Kasparov and verbally gave him the content of the conversation.

Palmer returned to the restaurant and sat down. A fresh vodka was brought by the waiter. He sipped it in silence, waiting for Pavlov, who seemed in deep thought, his gaze focused on the panoramic view beyond the floor-to-ceiling windows.

"Is everything all right with your call, Palmer? No problems, I hope?"

"I apologize it interrupted our conversation. The call wasn't important." He took another sip of vodka and put the glass down. "Is your lady friend joining us for dinner?"

"She's resting. She has not fully recovered from her fall and the dog bites she received. The bruises are healing well. I thought she would have recovered fully because of her age but alas, I think it may be a simple case of vanity."

"I am sure it is," Palmer said, wondering if she would come to his room after the old bastard fell asleep. "I think we should talk now."

"Yes, of course. I have information which directly involves your actions here to date. Moscow wants our deployment of aircraft and crews settled in Afghanistan by no later than the middle of December. They want our Special Forces trained and ready to deploy at a moment's notice. I have assured Moscow you will complete the training cycle in time for deployment. I do not think we will deploy ground forces until late next year, but they must be ready."

"I will be in Paris for a few days at the end of the month: a personal matter. You can inform Moscow the troops will be prepared and properly trained for any winter action they may run into." The waiter appeared, interrupting the conversation. Palmer ordered the vodka of choice.

"Shall we order dinner, sir?"

"Nothing for me. Please order for yourself, Palmer. I return to Moscow on an early morning flight. This being my second visit here in less than a month, it will be good to be home for a while."

"Leave everything to me. I will not disappoint you. One more thing. Your troops are good, but they enjoy vodka a bit too much."

"I will see to it, Palmer."

Lila Chekov walked into the restaurant and straight to Palmer's table. "I cannot stay. I told him my stomach was upset and I was coming down to find something to relieve the discomfort."

"Can you come to my suite once he is asleep?"

"I will try. If I cannot, he will be gone by five o'clock in the morning. I will call you so you can come up. It will give me great pleasure to have sex with you in his bed."

"I take it the dog bites are healing well?"

"What was I to tell the old bastard? That you chewed on me? I must go."

The phone rang just past five fifteen. Palmer was sitting in an easy chair looking out the window at the mountains in the distance with their thick cap of snow. The plot finalized in his mind, now that it was approved. He got up, only slightly annoyed that the call had interrupted his thoughts.

"Yes?"

"He's gone."

"Comrade Ladas Sorokin is on the phone and would like to speak with you if the colonel is not too busy . . . her words, Peter," Marina said with a raised eyebrow.

"Thank you, Marina. Do we have any more tea?"

"I'll prepare a fresh pot." She pointed an index finger at her temple with her thumb up, picked up his phone, and said, "Please stay on the line, Comrade Sorokin. He will only be a moment." She put the receiver in its cradle.

"Fool with this woman and you will have no defense against her husband." Marina turned on her heel and left Shevchenko to contemplate her words.

"Comrade Sorokin, What a nice surprise."

"I am going to be in Moscow the day after tomorrow. I wanted to visit the State Historical Museum. I thought since it is a short walk from Red Square, you might join me. I had a lovely time when I last visited Moscow. Do you like museums, Comrade Shevchenko?"

"I would be lying if I said I did." He noticed the nervous tick in her voice. "But I would also be lying if I said I wouldn't enjoy seeing you again. What time will you be in Moscow?"

"I thought about eleven. If we have time, we might have lunch?"

"I look forward to it. I must go . . . I am sorry."

"Goodbye, Comrade Shevchenko."

"Goodbye, Comrade Sorokin." Shevchenko put the phone down and leaned back in his chair. His first reaction: Her husband failed in Minsk. Would he attempt the same ploy? Would she be part of it?

Marina brought in a fresh glass of tea and put it on his desk.

"She asked if I would like to meet her at the historical museum." Shevchenko began. She said she enjoyed our last meeting so much she was hoping we could meet again." He began to rub his chin.

How ironic. You know that museum used to be a Jewish prayer temple. That was before Stalin, of course.... You are concerned that she might be part of another plot, aren't you? She wrote on a pad.

Wouldn't you be, Marina? he answered, laying his hands palms down on his desk while showing her his answer.

"You need a break," Marina answered while writing in shorthand, I do not think Ladas is. She seemed nervous on the phone, not because she was hiding something but because she likes you, Peter. You are both playing a dangerous game. Marina pushed the note pad across the desk.

We will see, he wrote in shorthand. Shevchenko picked up his tea, but did not drink. Instead, he continued to write. Out loud he continued to discuss the weather. You had the same impression as I about the nervous tone in her voice.

Then meet with her. She scribbled on the pad. Out loud she said, "Why don't you take a walk around Gorky Park later? A quiet stroll might do you good as well ."

"Shall I go now, or would it be better later?"

"I would go in the early evening, Comrade Shevchenko."

"I might just do that, Marina. Do one more thing for me: Call the American Embassy. I would like a word with Mister Patterson."

Marina picked up the notepad, "I will be out of the office for a few moments. I will call the American Embassy when I return."

"Thank you. A walk in the park might do me good."

Lila Chekov stood in the shower in her tiny apartment looking first at her bruised shoulders. The welts had begun to fade on her buttocks. The phone rang: two rings, a pause of fifteen seconds and two more rings. She hurried out of the bathroom, wrapping a bath towel around her. It rang again a steady ring.

"Lila Chekov, it is Kasparov."

"Did you get the tape and the message?"

"It is the reason for the call. Say nothing, listen carefully. You must leave Moscow today. There is a second tape. It seems the pig Pavlov has an eye for pornographic material. The machine must have been left on somewhere in the room to capture other occupants. You are on a cassette with Palmer. Listen to me and stay calm. I have made arrangements. You are to go to Moscow station when we hang up. A man will meet you there, a blonde man holding a day-old newspaper. He will address you as Olga Olof. He has a package with false documents, birth certificate, etc., and money for resettlement in Prague. You will be met there and given a place to stay."

"What about my family, Comrade. Who will care for them?"

"Pavlov will only care about you. He will have you killed, but first you will be raped by fifty or so of his officers. Hurry Lila. One day you will be able to return, I promise you that."

"What about Palmer? I know he is important to you."

"Believe me, Lila, you are the only one who will suffer."

Vlad Kozlov stood at the edge of the lake feeding pieces of dried fish to the geese. He spied Shevchenko walking to a bench and sitting down. He lit a cigarette and pretended to read a folded newspaper. Kozlov continued to feed the morsels of fish until the small container was empty. "My little friends do enjoy the fish," he said, dropping the empty container into the trash receptacle.

"What do you feed them, if I might ask?"

"Bites of white fish. I am careful to remove the bones of course." Kozlov stepped over to the bench. "Would you have another cigarette? When I left home, I forgot mine."

"You are a thoughtful man. Please join me; I am sure the geese feel the same way." Shevchenko handed Kozlov the package of cigarettes and a book of matches. My name is Peter Shevchenko. It is nice to meet you."

Two soldiers in uniform passed the bench. He waited for Kozlov to light his cigarette and for the two soldiers to pass. "You have a message for me?"

"Mikhail, it is good to see you, my old friend. I am enjoying a nice cup of tea and these wonderful biscuits. Please join me."

"I would like that."

"Please bring us a pot of tea and a tray of biscuits, Sasha. Sit with me. Sasha tells me you sounded concerned when you called, Mikhail?" Fedorov led his friend to a sofa with a print pattern that faced the Cathedral of Saint Basil.

"It is beautiful," Andropov lamented. "I have often taken a moment each day to thank Stalin for not destroying it."

Sasha brought the tea and biscuits and set them on the low glass table. She began to fix the tea, but was waved away by Andropov.

"We do not want to be disturbed: no calls, no visitors. If I need anything more, I will ring you."

Andropov handed a biscuit to his friend on a cloth napkin and began to fix tea, freshening his and pouring a glass for Gorbachev. "If I remember, you like a level teaspoon of sugar."

"Yes, and you are right; these are delicious."

"My chef will be glad to hear that. Now, tell me my old friend, what disturbs you, and how can I help?"

"First, I must tell you what happened in Minsk. Comrade Shevchenko wanted to tell you himself, but I thought it best if I intervened. There was to be an attempt on his life. He was fortunate enough to discover the plot before it could be acted on."

"Is the matter settled, Mikhail?"

"It is a work in progress, Comrade."

"Good, drink your tea and enjoy your biscuit. My wife has asked me to please ask that you and Raina come to our dacha soon for supper. We see too little of you."

"I will certainly tell her."

"Good, my friend. Tell Comrade Shevchenko I am behind him in this matter and whatever he decides will be my decision as well. Wish him luck."

"That leads me to the real reason I am here."

Fedorov's manner reflected no surprise or shock. Mikhail Balandin relayed his conversation with Brezhnev.

"He has asked me to take a position as his territorial commissioner for agriculture. I thought I was slated for—"

"He is most respectful of you, Comrade. These are difficult times, Comrade. Trust the president. Be patient. There are motives for his actions you are not privy to for your own protection. Do you understand, Comrade?"

"Yes, Comrade. Thank you for this conversation."

"Be sure to tell Shevchenko he has my full support."

"I'll say goodnight, Comrade."

"Goodnight, my friend."

Fedorov waited for the buzzer on his phone. He picked it up on the first ring. "You have the conversation recorded?"

"Yes, Comrade General."

CHAPTER THIRTEEN

TEL AVIV

Esther Silver climbed the stairs to the patio of the Manta Ray restaurant. She spied Abel Golan and the woman sitting across from him at a corner table under Kermes Oak. Silver paused on the landing.

"I asked this lady to join us; she wanted to meet you. When she told me who she was, I could not refuse her. You will understand when you meet her." He stood up—wiping his hands with a white linen napkin—shook her hand, and adjusted an empty chair for her.

"May I order you a coffee, perhaps something for breakfast, Mrs. Silver?"

"Nothing, thank you, General Golan. I will not take much of this lady's time."

Reba was pale, her cheeks drawn, the eyes hidden behind large sunglasses, a wide-brimmed black hat masking the color of her hair. "You are Reba? My name is Esther Silver."

"Yes I am. Have we met, Esther?"

"I did not tell Reba why you are here. I wanted you to explain in your own words."

"You are an American; you have the accent of a New Yorker?"

"I was born and raised there, as was my husband, Mathew. We live in Maryland now. I am the director of women's health services. My husband is a cardiologist and we both work at Walter Reed Hospital. My mother spoke of you often. She always referred to you as the angel who silenced her nightmares . . . My maiden name is Polansky."

"I remember." Reba removed her sunglasses and put her hands over Esther's hands. "I never saw your parents again after they moved to Israel. I am rarely home because of my work. I hope they both are well. I know your father suffered from dementia."

"My father died last month; my mother three days ago. They were happy here, Reba. They came home. You made that possible. I wanted to meet you and thank you for the last years of their lives." She lifted Reba's hands and kissed them. "I practiced this saying, I wanted to make sure it came out correctly: Ad me'ah v'esrim, Reba Klein. I will leave you now."

Esther stood up. "Once more, thank you for my parents, Reba Klein."

"Go with God, Esther Silver, and be happy all the days of your life." Reba watched silently until Esther went down the stairs and disappeared. "One hundred and twenty years, she said. If only that were possible." Reba slipped her sunglasses back on and sat back.

"Have you seen your mother?"

"Yes, of course. She attempts to feed me by the hour. I know what she is thinking without being told."

"Ariel would be proud."

"I am not so sure, General." Reba picked up a slice of his toast and ate it. "I am hungry, I think. I would like a sandwich. Esther Silver is a lovely woman with, I am sure, a lovely family . . . I called you to tell you I saw Al Aziz at the airport before I boarded my flight. We spoke briefly.

"Did you plan the meeting?" Golan asked, his brow narrowed.

"No, he showed up unexpectedly. Why did you ask me that?"

"What did he tell you, Reba? Leave nothing out."

Reba sat forward and leaned on her elbows. "They are planning a missile attack from the border of Lebanon. It is intended to cover a suicide attack in Tel Aviv. The attack will be this Sunday, the seventeenth, in the evening when restaurants are full and pedestrian traffic is high." The waiter brought her sandwich.

"Did Al Aziz mention the West Bank as the entry way for the intruders to launch the attack?"

"No, as a matter of fact, he did not. What are you thinking, General?"

"Eat your sandwich before it gets cold. Give me a minute to digest what you have told me."

She sat back, folding her hands on her lap. "Something is troubling you;

what is it?"

"Al Aziz does not trust you. He is laying a trap for you, Reba. Whether he is planning an attack or not, the issue is you. He is watching to see if security is built up; then he will know."

"What makes you believe he is testing me? I have given him no reason to distrust me."

"Look at the facts through his eyes and not your own. "Your associate," Golan was careful not to use the word lover, "leaves Cairo for a meeting in Barcelona. You do not go with him."

"He would not allow me to go. I wanted to."

"Listen, pay attention, do not talk. He is murdered. You are with a known terrorist and his wife in Paris; they, too, are murdered. You are beaten, but left alive. Again, in Paris, you meet with the head of Black September and shortly afterward he is murdered. Now do you understand his motive and why I am mistrusting his words?"

"Yes, I do, but we cannot ignore the threat. We cannot allow the murder of our people in order to keep me alive and safe, General."

"Yes Reba, I understand . . . better than you suppose. I am convinced this plan is a ruse. The attack will not happen; it was never meant to. We have heard nothing to suggest an attack. We will keep our defenses as they are and tell no one. Our forces will not increase our presence in the city and along the border on the West Bank or with the border of Lebanon. Traffic will be allowed to pass as always with the same checks. I will not bring it up at the next security meeting this Friday."

"What if you are wrong, General? How will you live with yourself?"

"In that case, my dear Reba, I will resign immediately. I will take full responsibility for the error in judgment and then, my dear girl, I will end my life. Are you sure you were able to elude him?"

"I was very careful. I know how to dodge watchful eyes. Al Aziz is not as smart as you think, General."

"We shall see, young lady, we shall see."

BEIRUT: APRIL 18

Al Aziz listened to his courier report on the security presence in Tel Aviv. The restaurants shops and tourist attractions were busy, and traffic was normal all along the checkpoints facing the Palestinian sector. Along the border with Lebanon, the presence of helicopter gunships and military movements did not accelerate. Al Aziz was satisfied.

Later that morning, Al Aziz found in his morning mail an envelope that was sent from Tripoli. He read the note.

"I am wanted in Israel as a member of Black September. There is a reward. I am requesting a name change. I have decided to call myself Alisha Abud. Make proper paperwork available, and will return to Beirut very soon." It was unsigned.

Al Aziz folded the single page note into a tight square and put it into his shirt pocket. Alisha Abud. Interesting choice. No matter. The important thing is she is ready to continue her work.

TEL AVIV: APRIL 18

Reba stepped out of the car in front of 9 Smolensk Street. She adjusted her uniform. The weight loss showed on her face.

She entered the residence and was greeted by General Golan, who led her into the library. The dim odor of long dead cigars and cigarettes still permeated the walls and furnishings. Tonight, she needed to convince them she was still a viable operator. Ariel and Benjamin did not attend.

"Thank you for seeing me." She was ushered to a tall back cloth chair. She kept her back straight and her hands firmly resting on her knees.

The Prime Minister entered, followed by General Meir and General Ben-Friel. Reba stood up, straightened her jacket, and crisply saluted the three men. The generals responded with crisp salutes. Rabin waved her back to her seat. There were no shadows hidden in the room beyond the door. It was closed by an aide.

"Welcome," he said. "Well, I see you have been promoted, congratulations. Would you like something to drink?"

"No thank you, sir."

"Shall we begin? You have been in the field working with and reporting on the activities of our enemies. You have endured unpleasant activities, to say the least. I commend you on your ability to adapt and be accepted by these animals. We have been able to liquidate members of their hierarchy because of your efforts and I can see your activities have drained you."

"A little more rest and good food, sir. I will be ready to return to my duties. I have already altered arrangements to that effect, even changing my identity. I have taken the name of a young Arab girl who died years ago, Alisha Abud. I told the criminal Al Aziz I was wanted by the Mossad."

"It sounds as if you have . . ." The Prime Minister paused. "Are you planning to return soon to your work, Reba?"

"Yes, sir. I was hoping to leave as soon as possible. I need to go to Tripoli and fly from there to Beirut."

"Abel, why don't you join the conversation."

"The director of a movie . . ."

"Deer Hunter."

"Thank you, Yitzhak . . . You stayed at his home once before in Malibu. You enjoyed the time with your mother. He is once more away doing whatever with his film. We want you to go there and refresh."

"What about Al Aziz?"

"That matter has been taken care of. Go to Malibu, rest, and regain your strength."

MOSCOW: APRIL 19

Two men met on a bench in Gorky Park, both carrying small cardboard boxes with bits of white fish. They smoked quietly. The geese fed and the cigarettes stamped out, they discarded the cardboard containers.

"It was Oleg Smirnov, Peter," Vlad Kozlov said, holding one last bit of fish in the palm of his hand.

"We have security tapes. We have records of his calls, copies of travel documents." Kozlov continued barely moving his lips: "It was him, Comrade. We know he acted in consort with Pavlov and Victor Anton, the woman in Minsk and her husband. No one in the Central Committee was involved.

Palmer will be on the move. He has been granted travel papers to Paris."

"You mean no one except Victor Anton?"

"Yes Peter Shevchenko. So far; we know only they are involved. It was the General's plan alone.

"And Fedorov?"

"We cannot be certain . . . We have nothing to tie him to the attempt on your life. He has given us permission to take action. We can now proceed. How quickly like chess pieces the powerful fall, Comrade."

"What does Mikhail think?"

"He does not believe Uri Fedorov is innocent in this matter but without proof. He wonders if his last conversation was secretly recorded."

"I am sure of it, Vlad. What about Palmer? You say he is on the move?"

"Andropov has given him permission to meet the reporter in Paris at the end of the month."

"Paris. We must find out if anyone else is involved besides the three plotters. Who does this woman know? What contacts does she have that might interest Palmer? You are not to get involved beyond our little talks, Vlad Kozlov."

"Enjoy the rest of the day. By the way, have you noticed a decline in services around the park? I think they should put on more caretakers to better maintain it." A message sent.

"I do not agree, Comrade. I think the caretakers are doing quite well. As a matter of fact, I talked to one the other day. He enjoys his work and getting outdoors. I like his attitude." His last meeting with Patterson, confirmed.

"That is good news." Kozlov strolled off, a few geese in tow until they were assured he had no more fish. They returned to the pond. glancing at the man remaining on the bench.

"Where are you, Lila?"

"Brno, Comrade Kasparov. I am driving to Vienna on R461. I fear using the air or the train. I am sure it is the first place the killer will look. The operator asked where I was. I would not tell her. I have only told you, Comrade."

"Very wise choice. You know what happened, of course. Do you know who?"

"It was Smirnoff. I have a slight sprain in my ankle. I climbed out the window when I saw him shoot the driver and twisted my ankle. I side stepped along a ledge until I was able to climb around the chimney. I stood there out of sight and waited for the bastard to do his work. I could hear Nina scream.

He murdered her and her husband. They lost their lives to protect mine. I want revenge, Comrade. I want to look into Smirnoff's eyes when I kill him."

"You shall have your wish, I promise you. Peter Shevchenko is with me and nods in agreement. We are formulating a plan to settle scores against certain people. Smirnoff is one of them. But we must be careful; it will take time. When we speak of the plan or of certain individuals, we will use the prefix "'Cras Volka." Do you understand?"

"Yes, I understand. "The day of the wolf . . . Perfect. I will wait."

"Lila, if you have trouble on the border, insist the captain of the guard call me directly. When you reach Vienna and are settled in our embassy, contact me. Do you have something to write with?"

"No."

"Do not use the exchange for any reason." He handed the phone to Shevchenko.

"Lila Chekov, this is Peter Shevchenko. When the time is right you will be there to witness it."

"Thank you, Comrade Colonel."

"Be well and safe." He gave her the number and hung up. "You said earlier we have an informant with knowledge of the escape plan?"

"Yes, it is the only way Smirnoff could have known her travel plans and how to find her. I do not think . . . I hope it did not come from Internal Security."

"This woman in your office . . . what do you know about her?"

"A good woman. She has been in the agency for thirty years."

"A possibility, Comrade."

"Whomever it is, it is someone close to our operations."

"I agree. This person must be found and removed. Find the person Comrade Kasparov, but do nothing until the day we settle scores. Whomever it is must not live one day longer than the others."

MOSCOW: APRIL 30

"Comrade Kasparov you have a call on your private line, a Miss Zora Laski."

"Thank you, Katerina. By the way, I am glad you are feeling better and back to work."

"Was Nadia capable in my absence?"

"Yes, she was, but I am glad you are back." He picked up the phone.

"Comrade Laski, how are you enjoying your first ten days in Vienna?"

"It is the most interesting city. I am enjoying the cooking and the wonderful music at the Wiener Stadthalle concert hall and Endler Hall Symphony Center. Both are wonderful. A nice young man who works at the embassy has been showing me the city."

"It sounds like you like this young man, yes?"

"Nothing of the sort, Comrade. He is doing his duty as one of the embassy guides."

The young man is her bodyguard chosen specially to make her relax. He knows her past, and she likes him romantically. He could sense it in the tone of her voice.

"I am surprised he hasn't tried."

"I am, as well. I think he is either married or he may be a . . . Either way, he is very nice. I miss home, Comrade Kasparov, my family . . ."

"I understand, Zora. Your family is fine. We explained the circumstances. They understand."

"Perhaps I should let this young man know I have an interest in him. What do you think?"

"I would wait, Comrade. Allow the friendship to grow. You might say too much. We are planning a card game. I miss the action. Comrade Shevchenko told you: We will insist you join us for the event."

"Thank you, Comrade. I always enjoy watching you old crows play cards together."

"For now, enjoy Vienna. Goodbye." Kasparov put the phone back on its cradle without waiting for a response. His secretary brought tea and a pastry and placed them on his desk. "Thank you, Katerina. Would you join me?"

"Yes. I will bring a glass. Comrade Laski . . . I do not know her."

"She is new. I will introduce you to her when she comes back to visit her family."

"Very good. I will bring the pot of tea. I have a message from Comrade Shevchenko: an update." She left and soon returned.

"Shall I begin?" she asked, pouring the brown liquid into her glass and stirring it. It is good to be back, Dmitry. I missed it."

"Why don't you put on some music first?"

PARIS: APRIL 30

"Maxine, you are in Paris, I take it? I understand there is a problem with terrorist acts? I hear the Dutch are sending bushels of potatoes to the DRG and—"

"You are getting a bit of a laugh out of this aren't you, General Golan?"

"You must admit it is a bit funny. What will come of the turmoil? Have you decided who might win?"

"That is not why I called, General, but I will answer you. A socialist, of course. Every day they riot in the streets because of the way the government treats them. On election day, they vote the same people into power. As to why I called . . . I have a friend who would like to meet you. He represents a computer software company in America and he hoped to come to Israel to speak to someone about his products."

"You have a friend?"

"Yes, I do, General." She pressed herself against Preston, her robe open.

"I see . . . tell me more about your friend."

"I am doing it as a favor for a fellow American and nothing more. I thought you might help." She groaned with pleasure and pulled away. "I will be stopping in Jerusalem on my return trip to Washington. Perhaps we could have supper. My husband will be joining me."

"I look forward to it, Maxine. I will give some thought to a discussion with your friend and will give you my answer when you arrive."

"I appreciate it, General. I will tell him when he calls." She hung up. "He is undecided. Do you have a conference, James, or can I have you all to myself?"

"No conference. In fact, they think I am in West Germany. Now, where were we?"

WASHINGTON DC: MAY 1

"I'll save you Adam; I will bid fifty."

"You can't save him, Ethan. I bid fifty-three," Beatrice answered with authority.

"I smell a double pinochle, Ethan. If they take the bid, we're cooked. I have to pass."

"I'll bid sixty, Beatrice."

"We're cooked, Adam. Let's fold and have coffee."

While the coffee percolated, Anna Lee cut the fresh bakery cheesecake into manageable slices.

"You look happy and content, Anna Lee, and so does Ethan. I think it is wonderful that you two found each other."

"Ethan always refers to you as Mister and Mrs. Cahill. I know he has the greatest respect for you both."

"They have a long history, Anna Lee. He hasn't told you about it, has he?"

"No. Only that they worked together for years . . . I won't ask."

"Be patient dear heart. The coffee is ready; let's get in there."

"This cheesecake is wonderful. I have only one question, why do I have a smaller piece then everyone else?"

"Because, my dear, I want you around for a while longer."

"I'll second that," Edwards answered.

"Turning on me, Ethan?"

"Only on cake, sir . . . Well, maybe my choice of partners for this game."

"I regret you feel that way, Ethan, especially since you are the weak player . . . I received a call the other day—"

"I wanted to tell the caller he is retired," Beatrice interrupted, patting her husband's hand, "but then how do you tell President Carter to leave my Adam alone?"

"Jimmy Carter?"

"Yes, Anna Lee, that Jimmy Carter."

"He heard some scuttlebutts about the Russians getting their shorts in a bind about Afghanistan and its leader, a man named Taraji. A nationalist and a friend to the US. That isn't for public consumption. I know you understand. He got it from our station chief in Moscow through an unnamed source. He wanted my husband's thoughts on the matter."

"How flattering. What did you tell him?"

"I told him to mind his business, but keep his eye on it. I said, 'Mister President, you have enough to worry about here with interest rates going up, oil issues with the Middle East, and the Camp David accord.' "

"Good for you, Adam."

"Thank you, Ethan . . . Look at this will you? First she beats me at pinochle and then reduces the size of my slice of cheesecake."

"Vincent is sound asleep," Anna Lee announced, sitting next to Ethan. "I really like Adam and Beatrice; they are so suited to each other. I can't imagine in my wildest dreams the two of them so involved in the work they did and having a president calling Adam to ask advice. I thought my jaw was going to break when it hit the hardwood floor."

"He likes you as well, and he trusts you or you would have never heard the conversation. Kiss me, Miss Caputo. I don't want to talk anymore. I just want to finish my drink and stare at you."

"You can get a much better look in there," she said, pointing a finger toward the darkened hallway and the bedrooms beyond.

MOSCOW: MAY 3

The driver pulled up near the metro stop.

"I will walk with you until you meet your friend."

"You will stay with the car. I do not wish to have bodyguards keeping tabs on me and my friends. I do not think anyone is here to harm a general's wife."

"I have my orders, madam."

"Comrade Petrov, you will stay here and wait, or I will tell my husband you made leading remarks to me and tried to kiss me. Do I make myself perfectly clear?"

"Yes, madam . . . perfectly clear."

"Good. I will watch and if I see a cheap brown suit lurking in the bushes, I will make trouble for you. I will also tell my husband to dress you better in the future. I think that is a fair exchange."

"Very fair, madam."

"Good, Comrade, then we have our bargain."

She spied him sitting on a bench under a full-leafed tree. He looked nice in his blue pinstriped suit, open-collar pale blue shirt and cordovan lace-up shoes. KGB, she thought smiling. He looks like a character in a spy movie. They always want to look as if they are oblivious to their surroundings.

She wondered if he ever, like the English actors in old movies played the part of the disinterested stranger while reading a book and smoking a pipe.

"Good morning, may I join you?"

"Of course." He folded the paper and laid it across the seat for her.

"You picked a perfect day to meet." He reached around the side of the bench and produced a small cooler. "I brought water and juice in case you are thirsty."

"How thoughtful. I would like water. I was wondering . . . did I change your mind about museums?"

"No, I am afraid not. You have cut your hair a bit shorter. It is a good look for you. I think I mentioned that before." He unscrewed the cap and handed her the water. "I do not see a brown suit."

"I told him I would accuse him of trying to rape me if he followed me. Why are we here, Peter?"

"I know why I am here, Ladas."

"What is your apartment like?"

"It has three bedrooms, two baths, and a large dining and sitting area. It is just on the outside of the square and very affordable."

"I suppose you have a trophy closet, Peter?"

"Except for my housekeeper and secretary, no woman has entered my apartment. It is my retreat from the world, Ladas. I hope you believe me because I am being truthful." He opened a second bottle and took a long drink.

She put her hand in the crook of his arm. "I also know why I am here, Peter Shevchenko." She pulled her hand back when two soldiers appeared on the path.

"The weather spoils me. I love to come here and just enjoy the park with the children playing." The soldiers passed by the couple admiring stolen looks as they pretended not to notice Ladas. She turned to face Shevchenko, her arm bent on the back of the bench, her loose fist against the knap of his neck.

"I think it is the children you feel sorry for."

"No, Peter, it is never having them that hurts my heart . . . I want to see you again. I want to see your apartment. I want to see how you've furnished it. Where you sleep. I want to know more about your childhood. I want to know about your parents. I want to be able to express myself without having to whisper . . ."

"In that case, I have only one request. You must swear you will not look in my closets."

MOSCOW: MAY 5

Shevchenko carefully read the notes Kasparov made, highlighting points of interest for further talks. He took a moment longer to reread the cryptic notes before speaking.

"No more notes, my friend. From this moment on, we speak of the situation only." Shevchenko tore the three pages of notes into small pieces, slipped them into an envelope, and sealed it. "Shred these things or burn the envelope when you leave, Comrade." While they spoke, music played in the background.

"Understood, Peter. What do you think of the arrangement?"

"Impressive; you and your staff have thought it out carefully. The time frame will work since one of our poker friends can only be available on Friday." Shevchenko opened his desk date book, turning the pages to May.

"Ah, a good month for our game. Friday has five dates . . . Here Comrade, look for yourself. You choose, since you are arranging the game."

"It might take a few days to coordinate. I will finalize the preparations and let you know."

"Sir, you have a call waiting."

"Thank you, Marina. Please tell the caller I will only be a moment."

Kasparov jumped up and padded to the door, slipping the envelope into his coat pocket. "I have an idea who the caller is. If it is whom I imagine it is. You will be careful, Comrade?"

"Thank you, Dmitry Kasparov, I will be careful. Give me the date."

"Comrade Shevchenko is through with his meeting. I will put you through."

"We mustn't let him slip and fall, Marina. Do you agree?"

"I will do what I can, but he is no longer a child protected in his mother's womb. Do you agree, Comrade?"

"Hello. It is good to hear your voice."

"Do you have time to meet me? I am on my way to Red Square. My driver is filling up the car. I told him to find me a cool drink. I hate public phones; they always smell terrible. I am babbling like a schoolgirl, Peter Shevchenko. Tell me to be quiet."

"I thought you did not want to meet in public any longer."

"I want to come to your apartment. I told the driver to take me to Saint Basil's. I told him to wait there. I told him I might want to walk into Red Square to have something to eat or just spend some time alone in Saint Basil's. My husband has returned from Bulgaria."

"I can see Saint Basil's from my office. I will watch for you, and I will watch to see what he does. If he follows you."

"He is wearing a dark blue suit. He will not follow me."

"That seems like a nice change."

"I told my husband to dress him better."

"Just in case he does follow, you have the address. I will reach the street corner near my house and turn away."

"My driver is coming Peter." Ladas hung up without a goodbye.

Be careful what you wish for, Peter Shevchenko. I know, he reminded himself. He padded to the window and waited for her car to come into view.

"Will you be taking lunch today, sir?" Marina asked from the door to his office.

"Yes, but only for an hour, Marina."

"You have a quiet afternoon except for your staff meeting at four, in case you wish for a longer break."

"No, I think an hour will do." He turned back to the window just as Ladas's driver pulled the car to the curb in front of the cathedral. He watched her climb the steps to the entrance wearing a clinging red summer dress. She soon exited through a side door.

"Will there be trouble with neighbors? I am sure someone who lives here knows me or surely my husband. I do not want to create problems for you," she said in a low voice before stepping up on the curb beside him.

"The people who live here, especially the men, have secrets as well. Nothing will be said. I know them. I have done favors for them; I have turned my back in many cases. You do not have to concern yourself."

"I do not want you to be harmed. I know how these people operate."

"Come inside. I will be interested in your view of my home."

Shevchenko stood in the living room, the scent of lemon from the cleaning fluids still fresh. Ladas moved slowly through the room, then into the kitchen and finally down the hall to his bedroom. She hesitated in the door before moving on to the other bedrooms. The last room was used as an office and library.

"Give me your opinion, Ladas Sorokin," he said when she returned to the living room.

"I see a man whose childhood was filled with chaos. I see a home where once there was only rubble, bad dreams, and loss. I see a child made a man long before his years. I see a man's home today, everything in its place, a clean almost sterile home. This home has no memories that creep up in the night. No children to spill juice on the floor. No wife or mother. I see a spacious home too big for the occupant but necessary to take away the memories of bodies crammed into small spaces. I see loneliness in your face, Peter Shevchenko. I do not have to look in your closets to see these things."

"You read this like looking at a scrapbook. How do you know these things?"

"I have read stories about you, Peter Shevchenko. More importantly, I see it in your eyes. I feel it in my heart when I look at you."

Ladas took a step closer. "I should go; you need to go to work." She took another step closer until she was close enough to feel his breath on her face.

CHAPTER FOURTEEN

"General, I must delay my flight to Tel Aviv until the eighth. My boss wants me to stay in Paris another five days. We want to come on the eighth. Will that be a problem for you?"

"I do not think so. If you were coming on a Friday, it would be. I hope it is nothing serious? Is your husband ill?"

"No, in fact he is happy for the delay. He is presenting a brief before the appeals court on the seventh. I'm happy as well. I love the weather in summer."

"The eighth is good. A Wednesday is perfect. How long will you and Carl be in Tel Aviv?"

"Wednesday through Sunday. Carl has to get back to Washington before the thirteenth."

"Tell me . . . what about you, Maxine?"

"Home, I hope. I don't relish staying in Paris. I miss being home with my husband."

"Good for you." Something isn't quite right, a slight hitch in her voice. A small thing, but if someone is accustomed to voice interpretation, they might suspect an alternative. She's lying. "I'm looking forward to your visit. We'll have supper together while you both are here. I know the perfect place."

"That sounds wonderful, General Golan, goodbye." He doesn't suspect a thing; he accepted my plans he never mentioned James . . . I fooled you, General. Maxine took a long swallow of her white wine while studying herself in the full mirror. She needed to purchase a pajama set with long sleeves just to be on the safe side." I fooled you, old man. I fooled you. You're not as clever as you think."

MOSCOW: JUNE 2

Shevchenko entered Gorky Park carrying the small container of white fish. Vlad Kozlov was on the bench. Geese began to gather.

"Good afternoon, Comrade." Shevchenko sat down, opening the small container of fish. "Come here you hungry little beggars."

"You have news, Comrade? It is still early. Even the geese are surprised."

"Yes, I do. The poker game is on for June seventeenth. One more thing." Shevchenko studied the strollers. "Tell Mikhail to tell Comrade Fedorov to make plans with Brezhnev for that evening."

"How can we know if he will not turn the tables on you, Peter?"

"The corruption in the food industry is far greater than most realize. Fedorov turns a blind eye because he is being enriched. I do not think he would risk the party leader's wrath. I have the proof and he is aware I have it."

"You still think he might be innocent concerning Minsk?"

"No, not anymore, Vlad Kozlov. I am convinced something has changed his thinking about Pavlov. I do not doubt an invasion is on the books. I do think Brezhnev want someone else in command."

"I will pass the information as you requested. What about the informer, Vlad?"

"Kasparov know who it is. That matter will be settled as well."

"Here I am out of fish; these scavengers are terrible, Vlad Kozlov. I must go before they eat my fingers."

TEL AVIV: JUNE 8

It was late afternoon in Tel Aviv. He spied Maxine sitting alone on a leather sofa, her legs crossed, showing more thigh than he was comfortable with. The cut of her dress exposing a bit more cleavage did nothing to improve his views on the subject. Maybe she dressed to please her husband. That thought, too, he discarded. In his opinion, modesty, like the religious beliefs of their fathers, has eluded the modern Jew in America. They have become more secular and less driven by scripture.

Another thing about her caught his attention: a bruise almost faded but visible on the inner part of her thigh. One might think she bumped it. Golan believed differently. The bruise was more than likely the remains of a hand print by its shape and dimension.

"Maxine," he said, greeting her with an outstretched hand. "Please do not get up. Ah, I see you read Cosmopolitan, the magazine of the well placed American."

"You have something harsh to say about all things American, General Golan. Sometimes I think deep in your core you hate us."

"Your husband's flight is about to land. I was hoping the three of us could have supper together. I've made reservations. I will cancel them if you two have other plans. I know how separations can interfere with other things."

"You already know we don't."

"I came out to see you and have a chat, but alas I am late and Carl is arriving early . . . I could not help but notice a bruise on your leg and the scrape on your knee, Maxine. Nothing serious, I hope."

Does he know? Is he guessing? Is he trying to trip me up? Out loud she said, "Why, General, I thought men with your beliefs didn't notice such things."

"You do not leave much to the imagination, Maxine. I suppose it is necessary for your line of work. I do not agree, as you know, but I am not one to judge the needs of others. I wanted to have a little time to speak to you about your friend, this Preston fellow. You say he is in software communication of some sort?"

"He sells software, yes. He has a contract for all of Europe."

"Then he lives in Europe. Where?"

"He has a hotel room in three major cities. He hates the fact that he has no roots. He wants to come back to America, but he is committed until next year."

"It must certainly be difficult."

"Does this mean you might want to meet with him?"

"I do not make these decisions." She has ignored the reference to her bruise. "This man . . . you like him, obviously. Do you trust him?"

"Yes. I think he is worth a conversation."

"Before you leave to fly home, do you have a number I can reach him?"

The game continues and I am winning, she assured herself. "Of course, General."

"I believe that your husband's flight number was just announced. Shall we? He took her arm, putting his hand near her elbow and with the slightest motion of his wrist forced the elbow upward. When she arched her back and grimaced, he released her arm.

"I am so sorry, Maxine. Did I hurt you?"

"I fell in the hotel. I hurt my shoulder and my knees and somehow bruised my leg. I'm getting so clumsy lately."

"I insist you see a doctor." At first, she ignored me. Now this lie is thrown in to divert me from what I believe is the truth. She and this man are lovers. If she can be untruthful about this with a straight face, what other lies could she be concealing?

"I did see the hotel doctor. It is only bruised; it is nothing serious." The memory of her falling out of bed hitting her shoulder on the wood surface flashed across her mind. "The doctor gave me pills for pain. Say nothing to my husband; he worries."

"Of course, my dear." He could only imagine the cause of the fall.

Golan poured a measure of cognac into a snifter. He took a sip and sighed with satisfaction. He ran thick fingers through his longish white hair, parted in the center, and sat down. Another long sip of cognac before he reached for his notepad and pen.

"James Preston, the American, a 988 phone code. I have never heard of it. Perhaps the corporation uses it to contact their sales reps?" He scribbled the name and number on his pad. Notes to self. He wrote on the next line and then began to print in block letters questions to be asked. Answers to be scrutinized. Truths to be sought out. When he was through writing, he dropped the pencil in the center of the notepad and sat back, carefully adjusting the black spongelike pad supporting his lower back.

He drank the last of the cognac, rolling it slowly in his mouth before swallowing. What he needed was sleep. The whole affair with Maxine and this Preston fellow made him feel uncomfortable. Something was wrong, out of place, like a picture hanging crookedly on a wall. His instincts told him to be careful; the long years of looking over his shoulder dealing with enemies of Israel told him to trust nothing, even if it appeared on the surface to be nonthreatening. Finally, he stood up. Time goes too fast, he thought, turning out the desk lamp.

His wife, Irma, lay on her side, her breathing low, soft, and even. He slid into bed beside her and slowly ran his fingers through her graying hair. She made a sound like a cat purring but did not move. He patted her shoulder and rolled onto his back.

"Goodnight, my darling. Forgive an old man for not being home this evening.

CAIRO: JUNE 10

Al Aziz, using the alias Salmon Abedi, stepped through the sliding door of the small home. The patio was surrounded by olive trees, shading him from the intense desert heat. He carried two cups of thick, black coffee and a bottle of mint liquor.

"Would you like a taste of Mint in your coffee, Alia?"

"No, thank you. My name is Alisha Abud now. Please remember that. I like your home. You chose well."

"Ahmed moved with me to Cairo. It suits our needs. It is my retreat from our work."

"My nurse angel. I see you together, and it fills my heart, Salman Abedi." She took a sip of the strong brew. "I must ask: Why was the attack on Jerusalem and Tel Aviv called off?"

"Other matters took precedent," he answered. "Now what about you? How are you feeling?"

"I am ready to return. It has been too long since I've helped our cause. Where is Sanchez, that miserable shit of a man?"

"I believe he is still in Sudan, Alisha. I want you to go to a new camp south of Beirut and train a special unit. It is well camouflaged. A tunnel is being constructed and it will be ready sometime in October. We will use it to gain access to the Israeli border."

"I want to go."

"Your revenge will be the knowledge that many Israelis will be killed."

"Not good enough. You must allow me to not only train the insurgents, but lead them."

"Drink your coffee and let me think about it."

MOSCOW: JUNE 13

"Comrade Sorokin is calling."

"Thank you, Marina."

"May I make a suggestion?"

"Can I stop you?"

"No."

"Well, in that case . . . please, by all means."

"Beware of the shade from a tree. It might hide a hornet's nest."

"So it might, Marina, so it might."

"Ladas, is something wrong?

"My husband is returning to his troops. He leaves this evening."

"It is dangerous, this game we play."

"For me it is not a game, Peter Shevchenko. I am sorry . . . I will not bother you again."

"Wait Ladas. Do you remember what you said in my apartment about waiting for me to call? I am happy you did not wait."

"Will you come to the cathedral to meet me?"

"Yes, Ladas, I will. I have decided to give you my home phone number. It might be safer if you call me there."

"One would think it a little late for that now, Peter."

"Do you want to argue, Ladas Sorokin?"

"No."

Her driver stood on the sidewalk next to the car smoking a cigarette, his back turned to the square. A smart man knows who fixes his meals, Shevchenko thought as he climbed the steps to the cathedral entrance. He saw her at once, standing next to the marble statue of Saint Basil, dressed in a black dress, her hair hidden under a veil. He walked up next to her.

"Thank you for meeting me. I thought my remarks about you and your home when I was there angered you, and you decided not to call."

"You are putting yourself in great danger. A plot to kill me has already been thwarted. I would never forgive myself if some harm came to you."

"I would never forgive myself if I let you escape me, Peter Shevchenko. I fear that more than I fear his wrath." She took his hand and squeezed it. "Let me be with you . . . if only once?"

"Can you come to my apartment on Sunday?" he answered without hesitation.

"Yes, I will. It is my driver's day off. I can drive. How early or how late?"

"Come when you can; I will be there. It is not the right time for us, Ladas Sorokin, but the time will come. You leave first. I will wait for you to be on your way."

She squeezed his hand and placed her head on his shoulder briefly, "Until Sunday" she whispered and left, the heels of her shoes clicking on the stone flooring.

TEL AVIV: JUNE 14

Golan reviewed his notes before deciding to call James Preston. Would the delay cause Preston to be frustrated or would the man have taken it in stride, his ego demanding that he not fall prey to it? He dialed the number Maxine gave him and waited. A series of clicks, followed finally by a woman's voice.

"Communication Associates, how may I transfer your call?"

"I am trying to reach James Preston, a sales representative for computer software with your organization."

"Yes, sir. May I ask who is calling?"

"You may ask, operator."

"One moment please." She connected the link to a voice recorder and came back on the line. "I am tracing his travel agenda. He should be in Prague this morning for a conference. Hold on, it may take a moment."

"I will wait." More clicks. Silence for fifteen to twenty seconds before she came back.

"I was correct; he is in Prague. I can connect you now."

"Thank you, operator. You are very efficient. You must be in central Europe . . . the main hub?"

"Berlin to be exact, sir. It is a new center. Your call is ready; have a nice day."

"You do the same." A phone picked up, silence on the line.

"My name is Abel Golan. I suppose I am talking to James Preston in Prague?"

"I am in a sales meeting. I am glad you called."

"Why don't we cut through the shit shall we? You are not in Prague anymore then I am on a beach in Mexico. I am old, but luckily still able to see through a fog. I have investigated certain areas of your business. Oddly enough, no one in the computer business has ever heard of you. So let us start fresh. First, your connection to Maxine Barnett. And move on to your correct name, shall we? I have a suspicion as to where you now reside. I will not dally on that point."

"My connection to Maxine is purely sexual and nothing more. She has no idea why I wanted to contact you. My real name is John Michael Palmer."

"I will contact you again, John Michael Palmer. I may want to meet. I will not discuss whatever you are thinking on the phone. I am sure many ears besides yours are listening."

"I am very careful about my calls."

"I am not impressed by your indignation, nor false bravado, Palmer. Goodbye."

Palmer slammed the phone down. " Jews," he groused, finishing off his drink with a shaking hand.

"I told you she might be trouble."

"Shut up."

They're all the same . . . sluts."

"Shut up."

WASHINGTON DC

"General Golan is on the phone."

"Thank you, dear." Cahill folded the newspaper.

"General Golan what a nice surprise . . . I'm sitting at my desk in my home office reading the paper and enjoying a large orange juice. What else would a retired man be doing on a Monday?"

"I envy you, dear friend, and miss you at the table. How is your health?"

"Very good, thanks to my wife. I'm flattered you called. I sometimes miss the action. I must admit though, less and less each day."

"I will be in America next month the first or second week. We will be at Camp David, to be exact, for the signing of the accords. I would like to see you and Beatrice. My wife will be with me if she feels up to it. We both know how well those two hens get along."

"Yes, indeed. We look forward to it. How are things with Irma?"

"She has her good days and bad. I think a trip will raise her spirits."

"That is good to hear."

"I want to give you a name. Write it down if you must, but keep it to yourself for the time being. His name is John Michael Palmer."

"The name doesn't ring a bell. Should it, Abel?"

"I am not sure as yet. I will call with our travel plans, Adam."

"I look forward to it. Goodbye

"THE DAY OF THE WOLF" JUNE 17

Oleg Smirnoff, dressed in an English-cut dark gray pinstripe suit, walked into Noor bar and restaurant northwest of Moscow. He liked the tasteful décor. The men were mostly government people, the women well-paid models and well-paid ladies who specialized in the erotic fantasies of the patrons.

He took a seat at the bar, ordered a bottle of expensive white wine, and began to look across the dance floor. His brown eyes scanned the crowd for a new face. The only mark on his chiseled face a scar running from his right lower lip to his jaw.

He made a bet with himself for his own amusement. He was looking for a certain type of woman. She must be tall and thin, long-legged with reddish hair and green or blue eyes. She must have a full mouth. She must be intelligent and . . . His eyes fell on a woman at the opposite end of the bar, sitting alone. She, too, was enjoying a white wine while smoking a filtered cigarette. He was sure he'd seen her at Noor before. To satisfy his curiosity, he called the bartender.

"The woman at the end of the bar drinking a glass of wine . . . who is she?

She has been here before. I believe I've seen her."

"Yes. She has become a frequent guest over the last two months. She speaks to no one, as you can see by the empty stools. A few of the gentlemen here believe she has a taste for the vagina."

"She certainly looks very good. Tell me, what is your opinion of her?"

"I serve drinks, Comrade. She enjoys expensive wines. In fact, you both have ordered the same French wine. She minds her business and I mind mine. More than that, I have no opinion . . . not even a name."

"A wise man never invites one's self where he is not welcome bartender." Smirnoff passed some bills across the bar. He picked up his glass, turning to face the dance floor. Smirnoff made no move toward the woman and was careful not to make eye contact. At last bored by the song sung by a French woman lost in love or some such nonsense. He turned noticed her looking at him. He smiled. She smiled.

The young woman left the top two buttons open: a little cleavage for the old man waiting in a business suit. He spent rubles, he tipped the bartender well, and now he wanted to treat her to a late supper at one of Moscow's finest restaurants. If at the end of the evening he wanted sexual favors, she would agree as long as she was careful. The last thing she wanted was to have him die on her, especially since he was a famous and important military man.

She dabbed a bit of lipstick on full lips and ran long fingers through dark brown hair settling it evenly on her shoulders. She removed her stockings and slipped on a pair of black open-heeled shoes. It made her look taller, but not tall enough to be above his stature. She sat down and her skirt rose to just below her thigh.

"Perfect," she announced to the empty salon.

He was sitting at the bar. She ignored him, looking straight ahead. His driver opened the rear door of the Volga sedan and she climbed in. After a few moments, General Pavlov came out and climbed in beside her. Smirnoff noticed as well. Good hunting, Comrade Pavlov. He smiled and returned to his drink content; he would not serve as bodyguard tonight.

The general's driver and valet closed the door, tugging on the handle. Before he climbed behind the wheel, he checked her door as well. He tapped the roof of the car to acknowledge that he secured the vehicle. He climbed in and removed his hat.

EUGENE DE SANTIS

"My reservation is for nine o'clock, Ivan."

"We have time; the traffic is light, sir." The driver started the car and pulled away from the curb. He drove at a moderate speed, knowing that the general suffered from motion sickness. "I noticed Comrade Smirnoff was close by."

"My friend has needs, as we all do. He likes this particular bar, as I do." Pavlov put his hand on her knee. "Suddenly I am finding it most pleasing."

"The traffic is light; shall I stay on the local streets?"

He never heard the answer. The explosion ripped the car to pieces, scattering shards of burning and twisted metal hundreds of feet from the point of detonation. The concussion from the blast shattered windows and blew open locked doors, flipped two cars onto their sides, and knocked pedestrians off their feet.

"Oleg Smirnoff. I have had an enjoyable evening. There are few men who hold my attention, but something about you . . . the way you carry yourself. Your taste in men's wear is impeccable and of course your choice of wines. I think it is time to go."

"Let me buy you a late supper, Malvina Cheb."

"I am flattered, of course. I will be here next Friday. Perhaps you will be here as well."

"Malvina, I happen to know of a wonderful restaurant not far from here. The hotel is very well furnished and the food is Mandarin. A nice change, I think. I have my car with me."

"You are not prepared to take no for an answer."

"I do not want to lose you, not while I have a chance to—"

"Allow me to interrupt you, Oleg Smirnoff. First, I am only mildly hungry. Secondly, I do not go to hotels with men I have known only an hour or so. Tell me, is there a wife at home?"

"No, Malvina. I have no wife at home."

"Do you have food in your home?"

"A plentiful supply, I assure you. I have never brought a woman to my home. It never occurred to me."

"You buy your love. There is no harm in that if it makes you happy. Well, I am not a whore and do not expect to be treated as one. You do not have a wife at home?"

"I have no wife or girlfriend and as to my pleasures, I assure you Malvina, it never entered my mind." He was beside himself. He never felt anxiety before. Her very presence, the scent of her perfume and her strength excited him. He suddenly felt like a boy craving attention.

"I will go home with you, Oleg Smirnoff. You can fix us a small meal. Do you have a nice wine at home?"

"I have only the finest wines, both white and red. The hour is late."

"So it is, Oleg Smirnoff."

"May I smoke in your car?" she said, sliding into the seat beside him. Two police vehicles drove past, sirens on. He ignored them.

"If you wish; open the window part way."

"You are fastidious. I see it in the care you take of your car. I will wait to smoke, but thank you for being considerate. One thing you did not tell me, Oleg, what is it you do?"

"You tell me first Malvina; what is it you do?"

"I am secretary to the produce commissar. It pays well and I am able to buy food at a reduced rate." Malvina turned to look out her side window. "Are we close to your home?"

"Yes, we are. It is the apartment at the corner of the block. If you are concerned about it, I will take you home when you are ready."

"I am not concerned . . . you must tell me what you do to live here and drive a fine automobile."

"I protect important people in government. I am paid very well for the service I provide." Smirnoff turned into the driveway and stopped a few feet from the garage. He flicked off the lights, but made no move to exit the car.

"Is that why you carry a weapon under your tailored suit? I felt it when you brushed against me leaving Noor."

"And yet you came home with me anyway?"

"I wasn't afraid. Are you going to invite me in or shall we just talk out here in your driveway?"

"My apologies. I was just letting my eyes adjust to the darkness." Smirnoff climbed out of the car, his eyes flicking from side to side. The street was quiet, nothing in or around the driveway seemed disturbed. No cars were shrouded in darkness. He opened her door. When she put out an arm for him, Smirnoff put a hand on the door and with his free hand helped lift her out of the car.

"You are pleasant to look at, considerate, and strong. What more could a woman ask of a man? You may kiss me, Oleg Smirnoff. I know you will not disappoint me." She put a hand on his and slid her arm under his left shoulder, pinning the weapon against him. Her tongue found his parted lips.

Caught up in the unexpected moment, Smirnoff did not see the shadow pass in the passenger seat side window and only reacted too late to the syringe plunged into his carotid artery. The narcotic was strong enough to curtail all resistance, but weak enough so that he remained aware. He was half dragged into his apartment and pinned with tape to a straight back chair in the center of the living room, his dress pants and underwear pulled down to his ankles.

Slowly his vision began to clear. He heard voices, but still was unable to understand what was being said. When his vision cleared at last, he looked down at his naked genitals. A dark line, thinly drawn, caught his attention. The line began at his hip and followed the invisible line of his femoral artery, ending abruptly just above his knee. He tried without success to move his arms and legs. They were pinned by the heavy tape. He growled and looked at the woman who called herself Malvina, sitting not six feet away on his leather sofa smoking a cigarette while sipping a glass of wine. He cursed her. A hand came off his shoulder; the slap formed a welt on his cheek.

"You are Smirnoff, the murderer of innocent women. A woman who was kind to me . . . Nina Povich, her husband, and the driver from the embassy. Do you remember, Oleg Smirnoff the killer for a price? Pavlov is dead and now it is your turn to die, you miserable goat of a man."

"Lila Chekhov . . . the whore?"

"You see the line I have drawn on your leg? It runs like a stream carrying your blood to your extremities. I am going to cut into the artery. When I do, you will bleed out, not like Nina with a bullet in her skull. You can slowly watch yourself die."

Lila stepped around the chair, a thin blade knife in her hand. Her eyes flashed anger as she tore a piece of tape from the roll and wrapped it across his chin taping the ends to the back of the straight back chair.

"Who is the other whore on the sofa?"

"My real name is Paula Turgenev."

"She, like me, is an assassin. Paula was one of the women in the cathedral in Barcelona. You may have read about it.

"Do what you came here to do, Lila Chekov," Paula said with a wave of her hand. "But not too quickly. Allow me to enjoy his wine."

Lila slipped on his bathrobe backward, tying it tightly behind her back. She leaned forward, her hand on his shoulder, her feet on top of his shoes, pressing down to minimize his struggle "Goodbye, Oleg Smirnoff. Give my regards to Pavlov."

Anile Romanoff, her full-length fur coat tucked in the crook of her arm and a Walther PPK with silencer hidden beneath the coat, swung the door wide to the outer office of Victor Anton. "Where is he?" she demanded, "He left me standing outside the theater like a common whore. I demand you let me in."

"Give me your name. I will see that he knows you are here."

"He knows who I am. Tell him, soldier. Tell him Anile is beyond anger. Maybe a word to his little shit wife will—"

"Enough foolish talk. It will get you prison time or worse." The soldier turned, raising his hand to knock on the inner door.

Romanoff stepped behind the soldier and fired a single shot into the soldier's brain. She jumped back, fearing the spray of blood and brain matter would settle on her coat. She heard Anton coming, his voice raised in anger for being disturbed. She pointed the weapon toward the sound of his voice. The door opened just as two men, with weapons drawn, entered from the hall.

"What is going . . .?" He froze in midsentence, staring blankly at the crumpled body of the soldier at his feet. He looked up at the woman with a blank expression on his face. "Anile . . . Anile."

"Step back, Comrade, if you want to live," Romanoff answered. She followed him into his ornate office. Without a word, she walked over to the window, opening it. "We have a few questions for you, Comrade. Answer them correctly and these men will not throw you through the window to the courtyard below."

"Who sent you . . .Who are you? What are you?"

"A trivial question, Comrade. You did not ask when you put your fat slovenly body on me. Let me ask you one of more importance. Who else was involved besides yourself, Pavlov, and the killer Smirnoff in the attempt to murder Peter Shevchenko?"

"I have no idea what you are talking about." Perspiration bubbled above his upper lip. "I do not know these things. Whomever said I had knowledge is insane or manufactures a lie for reasons I do not know. I swear I know nothing. I thought we were—"

"The American known as Palmer . . . why is he talking to the Israelis?"

"You ask questions I cannot answer."

"I believe you, Comrade. To prove it, we will leave. I will lay the weapon on the desk to show you we mean no misfortune will come to you."

Anton scooped up the pistol, pointed it at the woman's chest, and pulled the trigger.

"You filthy bitch!" he screamed, pulling the trigger twice more.

"Perhaps it is jammed? Why not take out—"

"I know what to do." It wasn't jammed, and it did not misfire; it was empty. He dropped the weapon on the carpet.

"I told you I trusted you, Comrade. I never indicated to what degree." Romanoff slipped the fur coat over her shoulders, turned, and pointed to the window. "You know what must be done. I must make a call. General Pavlov is dead, along with Smirnoff, his hired killer. You will join them."

Kasparov sat at his desk playing a third round of solitaire, the only light a desk lamp. The call he expected interrupted his play.

"Kasparov here . . . Yes, I did have a nice evening with friends. Tell me, how did you enjoy the ballet this evening? . . . Wonderful news, I'm glad you called . . . Yes, of course, I will be sure to tell the other poker players you called . . . Goodnight." Kasparov gathered up the cards, put them in the box, closed it, and placed it in the center drawer of his desk. He picked up the phone and dialed.

"It is done, Comrade Shevchenko."

"The telephone operator Kamenev at the exchange."

"A terrible accident driving home. She did not survive."

CHAPTER FIFTEEN

Ethan put the finishing touches on the new character for the strip, Nylon Socks, a character right out of 40s and 50s 8 mm porn films. He wore T-shirts which were made famous in movies by Italian actors. He managed to add a pinky ring, a stub of a cigar, and small spots of tomato sauce on the front of his shirt. Satisfied, Ethan began to fill in the prose. Behind him was the soft drone of the air conditioning unit. The phone rang, interrupting his thoughts.

"Hello, if you are selling something, I don't need, hang up now."

"You need a recording machine, Ethan."

"Good morning, Adam. I hate those damn things; most messages are a waste of time. I refuse to sit and listen to them. That said, I'm working on a new character for the strip. I'm calling him Nylon Socks. I'm guessing you aren't calling about my pinochle play."

"No, I'm not, Ethan."

"Is Beatrice home?"

"No, as a matter of fact she is out grocery shopping."

"I thought so. Adam, if this about the Russians probably cleaning house, I haven't given it any thought. Don't give a crap would be a better analogy."

"I would like your opinion anyway, Ethan."

"I suppose I can't stop you unless I hang up, and I wouldn't do that."

"Patterson, our station chief in Moscow, has made a connection with a person of interest and knowledge in government service. They have a sort of code and drop information which might to the casual listener seem unimportant."

"Tell me why I am supposed to care, Adam."

"Patterson is convinced that the Russian army is planning to invade Afghanistan and remove the current government. They fear American material involvement."

"American involvement would be worse than Vietnam, Adam. Those people still inhabit caves. Why should you care?"

"Patterson also believes the Red Army will move on Latvia and Poland if the Poles keep up the rush to free themselves from the Union. It makes sense, when you think of who was murdered less than two weeks ago."

"I have no opinion at all except to say Carter better not listen to the Neo Cons. I'm past that. I'm in a good place."

There was a long pause, with only Adam's breathing on the line.

"Is there more to know, Adam? This call wasn't just about the Russians invading the Neanderthals or the weather getting hotter."

"General Golan, you know who he is, spoke to a man he believes is living somewhere in Russia, a man who calls himself James Preston, but who says his real name is John Michael Palmer." Cahill waited for a response. "You remember Thailand, the docks, and the flip you killed? I never told you but there were two. The second one escaped. We thought it might have been a soldier in Palmer's company. It might very well be Palmer, if Golan is correct . . . I'm sorry."

"I have to go, Adam."

"I understand."

"No, Adam, you really don't."

MOSCOW: JUNE 26

Colonel Gusev, a man of medium build with deep sunken brown eyes masked by bushy brows and a sallow complexion—most likely from heavy smoking—entered the outer office.

"I am Colonel Ronin Gusev," he announced, with a voice as tight and constricted as his jaw.

"Colonel Shevchenko has cancelled two appointments. He hopes it will give you enough time. May I take your briefcase? Can I offer you something to drink?"

"Thank you, no. I will need my briefcase. It has papers I want the colonel to read. The colonel is very lucky to have you as his assistant. You are most gracious, . . .? I apologize for not knowing your name."

"Marina Chernoff, Colonel. I will let Colonel Shevchenko know you are here."

The door opened.

"Colonel, please come in. Thank you, Marina. Hold my calls unless the Americans are at the gates of the city." He took Gusev's hand and shook it. "All these years and we have never met. Please come in."

"We travel different paths."

"I suppose we do." Shevchenko waited for Gusev to sit down and open his briefcase. "Did my secretary offer you something to drink?"

"Yes, she did. I declined." He pulled out a file and placed it on the desk.

"I have a question, Comrade Colonel, before we begin. Is there any more news on General Pavlov's untimely death?"

"Pravda will publish a story tomorrow calling the misfortune a faulty gas tank in the older Volga-12. There will be a call for that particular model car to be removed from service. A committee will be formed. They will conclude that the tanks should be replaced. Money will be appropriated. Rubles will change hands. The public will see its government taking care to see that their safety is more important than costs. You know how these things work, Colonel Shevchenko. The reality . . . We are still investigating the incident. I can say it was no gas leak."

"Forgive my curiosity, Comrade, and yes, I know how the system works. It is refreshing to hear it from another source. Your father would be proud."

"My father has no interest in politics, Comrade."

Your adopted father, Comrade Gusev . . . I meant your birth father. Only three people in Moscow know the truth of your birth. After today, three will be still three."

"I earned my place in my vocation, Comrade Shevchenko."

"You have nothing to fear from me or the KGB, Comrade. I like to visit on a level playing field. You were frank with me; I am returning the favor."

"You are everything I've heard about you, Peter Shevchenko . . . I am here concerning the death of the Schmidt woman."

"Yes, of course. You are talking about the robbery and murder at the Metropol hotel. Comrade fedorov felt the state police were capable of continuing without our interference. Tell me Comrade Gusev has there been a renewed interest?"

Shevchenko kept his expression in check. Surprised concern perhaps, which in most cases would be a natural reaction.

"A man named Paul Dupree works for Interpol. He's an analyst whose job it is to review files of unsolved murders and ascertain if any are connected by physical evidence or method. He has arrived at a theory about the possibility of a serial killer roaming around Europe. The Schmidt woman is on his list. Most recently, an officer's wife near Sochi."

"I thought the killer of Schmidt was caught."

"May I smoke?"

"Yes, of course," Shevchenko reached into the top drawer of his desk, retrieved a crystal ashtray, and passed it across his desk.

"Paul Dupree: What do you know about him?"

"He is considered one of the best analysts at Interpol."

"I see." Shevchenko glanced at the report, but did not read it.

"I came to the same conclusion as the Frenchman. These women were killed in the same fashion. I wouldn't begin to calculate the odds. I have something else. Please look at the first photograph." Gusev slid the picture across the desk.

"I do not recognize this man. You have more?"

"Take a look at these two from surveillance cameras and compare them."

"Where was this one taken?"

"El Prat airport check-in counter. Take notice of the woman at the end of the counter."

"And this one, Colonel, where was it taken?"

"It was taken at the hotel where they stayed. Now put the three together."

"This man hides his face well Comrade Gusev. I can see a resemblance in his clothes and mannerisms." "I see the same woman in both pictures and a third in line with this man." It was the same woman in the Paris airport. A coincidence? Perhaps. Out loud Shevchenko said, "What is the point."

"She was found murdered, washed up on the beach three days after checking into the hotel with this man. The cause of death is the same as the woman in Berlin, as well as others."

"I must assume this man was questioned. Why was he not arrested?"

"He left Barcelona two days before her body was found."

"Forgive me, Colonel. I am confused."

"I should have addressed it," Colonel Gusev interrupted. "Dupree concentrated on the man and cause of death. I investigated and found that she was in the ocean for at least two days before her body washed up on the beach." The colonel let out a sigh of frustration. "Dupree, by appearance and clothing, thinks the man in question is an American and may be living in our country."

"Why would he think such a thing?"

"The man's passport indicates his home is in this country. I know American dissidents and traitors live or have lived in Russia, that is why I came to you, Colonel Shevchenko. I can see by the look on your face he is not familiar to you."

"I am afraid not, Colonel. I wish I could help."

"I much appreciate you taking time with me on this matter."

"You have a large nut to crack, Colonel. I wish I could help."

"Good day, Gusev said stamping the cigarette out."

"Before you leave, would you allow my secretary to make copies of this report? I would like to read it thoroughly to make a file in case this Dupree fellow is really on to something."

"I will, of course . . . Comrade, Shevchenko. I have privacy concerns?"

"You need not worry, Comrade Gusev."

"Thank you for taking time from your schedule. About my comments concerning the Volga automobile . . ."

"I did not hear any comments. If I had, I would take issue with you, Comrade." Shevchenko walked the Colonel to his door and they shook hands. "Let's not be strangers, Comrade," Shevchenko said, opening the door for Gusev.

He padded back to his desk and waited for Gusev to leave before picking up the phone.

"Marina, would you call Comrade Kozlov and change our arrangement? Have him meet me at six o'clock this evening. Please ask Kasparov to come down."

At six o'clock precisely, Shevchenko found Kozlov on the bench. The geese gathered around his feet.

"Ah my friend, I see your little friends have already gathered for their treat."

"They have been waiting for you, Comrade; look at their happy little faces."

"Say nothing. Listen to me. I have an envelope for Mikhail." Shevchenko, sitting next to Kozlov, placed the copy of Pravda he brought with him between the two men and opened the container of white fish. "Come have your treat, my friends."

He repeated the conversation he had with Gusev. "The material is in the agricultural section of the paper." Shevchenko began feeding the fish to the geese.

"My wife is dragging me to Minsk to visit her sister for a few days so make sure you do not disappoint the geese, my friend," Kozlov said loudly. His voice lowered he said, "When you drop the container in the trash, there is a magazine on top of the pile you might find interesting. It is a profile of the Barnett woman."

"I will take care of the geese. Enjoy your trip and we'll meet here in a few days. He shook Kozlov's hand. "Palmer may be a serial killer Comrade Kozlov let Mikhail know."

When Shevchenko reached the square, he opened the magazine and took out the envelope with a name scribbled across its face: Maxine Fisher-Barnett. He slipped the envelope into his coat pocket, discarding the magazine in a trash receptacle. Back in his apartment, Shevchenko read the comprehensive report. She had come a long way from the thin blonde he knew at Berkeley. A long way indeed. He thought of Ladas. Was she thinking of him? Missing him?

CAIRO: JUNE 30

"I have a message for you. I received it this morning while you were asleep. Our friend has agreed you should go. He is satisfied that you are more than capable of completing the mission. I agree with him, of course; you are the perfect choice."

"This mystery man took long enough to decide. You still have your doubts about me, Salmon Abedi? Is that why you do not name him in my presence?"

"Forgive me; it is because of the Mossad and its aggressive attacks on our groups ever since Berlin. It seems no matter where we show our faces, they find us. It is he who will not come forward. If I did not trust you, would I allow you to come and stay with me and my wife?"

He stopped talking when his wife came to the patio carrying a plate of sardines, hard biscuits, tea in porcelain cups, and a small bottle of mint liquor.

"It is a good morning. Summer is here at last," she said, placing the drinks and platter on the table. "Enjoy the food. While I prepare a proper lunch"

"Won't you join us?"

"After you have discussed your business. Alisha Abud."

"Still separating your lives, Aziz?"

"It is better for both of us under present conditions. My wife is not a strong woman." He took his fork from inside the napkin and stabbed a sardine.

"When can you leave?"

"I have to surrender my rooms in Beirut. I should be at Camp 3 next week."

BEIRUT: JULY 2

Brian Suitor, a tall balding man who spoke excellent French Persian entered the Abu Elie bar in Beirut. He liked the atmosphere, and what he liked more was that the bar was far from the fighting and bloodshed in the Christian section of the city, but close enough so that he could overhear the conversations of the soldiers.

"Mister Suitor, a moment," the bartender waved him to a corner of the bar. "Look over my shoulder to the woman at the far corner of the bar in the white revealing dress and dark tan. She is lovely, wouldn't you say?"

"You are correct, she is lovely, but why would you think she might be interested in meeting a rather ugly American like me? Is she a working woman?"

"She doesn't like the men here; she would like to have a drink and good conversation without the demands. I think you two would get along fine. Give it a try. If nothing comes of it, you will have a nice evening and good conversation."

One hour after the encounter in the Abu Elie bar, the woman with the American in tow entered her room at the Radisson Hotel near the coast. He closed the door, locking it, and with his hand still gripping the knob of the door, he said, "Shalom Aleichem, Reba Davidoff-Klein."

"Aleichem Shalom, Rabbi Lieberman. We meet again. It has been a long time since New York. I couldn't believe my eyes when you entered the bar. You have lost weight, and your hair is grey. I have prayed for you. The café in the hotel . . . a worker, one of our own, told me to go to Abu Elie and a friend would meet me there. I had no idea it would be you, Rabbi."

"You brought peace to the Polansky's. They prayed daily for you until they passed."

"I met their daughter."

"I have prayed for you. Uma, you remember her? We married and she waits in Tel Aviv."

"Of course, Uma Merkle."

"I thought: If this young woman is willing to sacrifice so much for Israel, who am I not to do my share? I studied French Persian because they needed information about Lebanon. I became quite fluent. I frequent the bars of Beirut. You can't imagine the news I can pick up about the fighting. I am afraid a beautiful city is going to die and all of Lebanon will follow . . . Enough about me; now what can I do?"

"I am so proud of you, Rabbi." Reba took his hands in hers, bent forward, and kissed them. "Let us continue the conversation in the language of our fathers… Listen carefully."

BRYANSK OBLAST: JULY 3

More than three weeks passed since his phone conversation and still no call. He told himself it was a waste of time. He needed to find another source.

The phone rang, only slightly lifting his spirits. He put his tumbler of vodka down and answered on the third ring. His heart dropped when he realized the call was not from Golan, but Maxine. He paused as seconds passed, deciding whether to answer it.

"Hello, I was just thinking of you."

"I have news, baby. I will be in Italy the middle of next month."

"I also have news."

"First tell me you can come to Italy."

"I miss you, baby, but I can't, not next month." He almost laughed. "I said I have news."

"Tell me why I shouldn't be disappointed?"

"You want to hear it Maxine or you want to pout like a schoolgirl?"

"Will it cheer me up?"

"I may be coming back to the states. I have to go. Feel better now."

"Maybe."

"Don't you know I would love to meet in Italy? I can't, the company . . . I have to go. I will call when I have more news."

"Promise?"

"I promise, Maxine." Palmer hung up.

We warned you.

"Shut up, Mom."

MOSCOW

Kasparov sat on an easy chair and Shevchenko on his sofa. They listened in silence until the last tape was played. "Was she like this with you?"

"The same: very aggressive and passionate. I would say insatiable. She would scratch me when she climaxed and bruise me with her legs. This Frenchman may have stumbled onto something very dangerous and lurid, Dmitry."

"You think she knows what he does?"

"I do not know what to think. You read Dupree's report of the murders with the mention of scratches, bruising, and biting."

"He was in Berlin with her when the prostitute was murdered. We know she was here when Schmidt was murdered?"

"He was in Paris with her, but no mention of murder by the French press or the soldier's wife in Bulgaria."

"What about the Israeli general?"

"There has been no contact for weeks. I must assume the general, if I am judging him correctly, is a very curious and careful man who is probably compiling information on Palmer and then and only then will he make contact, if at all."

"My question is: How did Palmer find Golan?"

"Through Barnett, Peter Shevchenko. It had to be her."

"My private line . . . Freshen your drink, Dmitry. I shouldn't be long."

He picked up the phone. "Hello, could you hold a moment?" he cupped his hand over the mouthpiece.

"I think I will take a walk around the square. A good stretch of the legs will do me good. I might even visit the bakery before I go home."

"Thank you, my friend." He waited until Kasparov closed the door behind him.

"Hello again. I was having a meeting with my associate. I can talk now."

"I miss you, Peter." Without waiting for a reply, she said, "This morning I had a visitor. Yuri Fedorov came to the dacha. He was very gracious in telling me I was no longer in need of security protection. He has removed my driver from my service. I told Petrov to keep the suits. He was very grateful."

"What will you do now, Ladas?"

"He allowed me to keep the car, so I now have the freedom to go wherever I please without a driver. I can stay in the dacha for up to one year. He is such a kind man; I wanted to hug him."

"They may have recording devices in your home, Ladas. Be careful you do not offend—"

"Not to worry, Peter. They were here yesterday removing phones and all sorts of equipment, cutting wire cables. Very professional. A party man was here to ensure everything was removed. He had a clipboard with check marks. I have a question for you, Peter."

"I thought you would."

"My husband, his whore, and driver are dead. I think I have maintained the required time of mourning for a wife whose husband was a terrible man. When do you think it will be appropriate to visit?"

"I am finished with my meeting, Ladas Sorokin. Does that fit into your schedule?"

"I am on my way, unless Andropov's people need to strip the house of the wall panels."

"I think the panels are safe, Ladas Sorokin."

"Except me…No interruptions today Peter"

NEW YORK

Ethan sat motionless. The characters of Nylon Socks and Argyle Socks stared back, smiling, waiting in silence for the bubbles to be put into place alongside their faces. He thought about the drunk in Battery Park. His reaction to the man shoving Vincent to the ground, cursing the boy for wearing a red Sox cap. His first thought was protection. The sudden swift punch to the man's chest. The man on the ground holding his chest, gasping for air. The police arrived. Witnesses to the drunk pushing the boy to the ground answered questions. He was sure it created fear in Anna Lee's mind, not of him but what he was capable of. Then there was Vincent and his reaction.

"Will you teach me that move, Ethan?"

"Maybe I will someday, Vincent, but not today." He saw the relief on Anna Lee's face. He also saw concern. He thought of Captain Brent Lovett, dead, cradled in his arms . . . Palmer did that. Palmer, the traitor, out there somewhere . . . if he was indeed alive.

He wiped away tears. All he craved was a small piece of earth, a space where he could live in peace. A place where the dreams did not disturb his peace. A place where he could awaken every morning, feel the air on his face, smell the flowers (as they always say) next to a warm, loving body he hoped would be Anna Lee Caputo.

The phone rang.

"I miss you, Ethan. Margaret is covering for me. We have all three days together."

"I'm finishing up now. I should be off by noon." She is happy. She sounds all right with me. "Sooner, if I can. How is Vincent?"

"Anxious to see you. Tomorrow he stays with my parents."

"It sounds absolutely wonderful, baby."

"Hurry but be careful, Ethan."

A little piece of earth, quiet days, and restful nights next to a warm, loving woman named Anna Lee Caputo-Edwards. Just a little slice of earth and peace. He imagined veterans everywhere having the same thoughts.

CHAPTER SIXTEEN

"You choose your restaurants with care, General Golan."

"I love Adelina: the fresh fish and the view of the Mediterranean . . . another favorite is Machneyuda. Octopus fried and then baked in garlic oil and red wine."

"What type of fish do you favor? Never mind. You order for both of us. I must insist that you order a red wine, doctor's orders. You may begin."

"I am grateful you accepted my invitation to meet. I must admit I had given up on you, General."

"A foolish man rushes into danger. Tell me, what is Maxine's role in this. Do not lie."

"We do not discuss politics." The waiter brought the wine, poured a small portion into the general's glass, and waited.

"She brought you to me?... You may fill our glasses," he said to the waiter.

How long will the meal take to prepare? We may be here for quite some time. I will see that you are well rewarded for any loss of revenue."

"That is the most considerate, General Golan. I will ask the chef."

"She mentioned your name after the incident in Paris. It was my idea to contact you to sell computers. That is the extent of her involvement."

"We have the privacy of a booth and time to talk . . . so talk. Tell me what it is you actually do for the Russians, and afterwards convince me I am not wasting my time."

"I thought our meeting would—"

"First things first, Palmer. Let's just call it, as the Americans enjoy saying at baseball games . . . the pitcher is warming up?"

Palmer sipped his wine and began. He described his thoughts on Russian activity in detail. When finished, he said, "This wine is very good, General. I am sure the meal will be as good."

"Tell me, Palmer, what would you calculate in all this diatribe you presented as accurate information?"

"Ninety percent based on the facts."

"Ninety percent? Einstein was correct ninety five percent of the time."

"Hitler was right one hundred percent of the time before 1943-44."

"So, you are saying he was right on the Jewish question?"

"I did not say that, General. Hitler was correct in thinking the Europeans and the Americans would do nothing to protect the Jews. I am afraid he was correct. I believe the waiter is bringing more wine, General."

"I didn't order more wine."

"I was asked to bring the wine compliments of the gentleman waiting with his wife at the far end of the bar, General."

Golan looked over his shoulder and raised his glass, mouthing a greeting and thank you in Yiddish.

"Your supper will take forty minutes to prepare. Will that be all right?"

"Yes, start preparing the meal in fifteen minutes, thank you."

"Who is that?"

"An old friend. He served under my command in the 1973 war. Shall we continue?"

"Are you now ready to hear the plan I have been working on?"

"We can pour when we are ready," Golan said, dismissing the waiter. Begin. Tell me this grand plan of yours, Palmer."

MOSCOW: JULY 8

"Now that you have heard the tapes, Comrade, what do you think.?"

"I find it disturbing, Shevchenko."

"I thought you would, sir."

"For now, let us look into other matters, Shevchenko."

"As you wish."

"Fedorov lit the cigar and continued. "The Pavlov Plan to move against the Polish state in order to put an end to this foolish demand for independence has been suspended indefinitely. The Russian army will not move against Latvia."

"I can relate the news to my staff. Russian tanks will not be sent down Jerusalem Street in Warsaw?"

"Yes, you can Shevchenko. With Marshall Pavlov dead and his top aide guilty of his assassination, the military and members of the Central Committee are suddenly silent on the question of Poland. It also gives the president breathing room to focus on other matters such as Afghanistan."

"We will be fighting an unseen army of people no better than the ape ancestors who spawned them. I fear we will find ourselves mired in turmoil as the American army found itself in Vietnam."

"You should have more faith in our military capabilities, Peter Shevchenko."

"I do not question our military, Comrade. I question the country's leader: Mohammed Khan. He does not look to us for support, but to America. That is what upsets me."

"Why don't we take a walk in the garden. I want to discuss The Day of the Wolf without worry of someone listening to me."

"I would have thought you were above all that nonsense, Comrade Fedorov?"

"Trotsky felt as you do. He and other members of Stalin's inner circle paid dearly for such beliefs . . . I also want your thoughts on Palmer. I have information from Gusev on some investigation of murders by a fellow in France named Dupree. Have you heard of this?"

"No, Comrade."

TEL AVIV: JULY 8

Satisfied she was in no distress after listening to her breathing, Golan silently closed the bedroom door and padded down to his study for a night cap and a call. The international operator placed the call, apologizing for the delay in connections. He put the phone on its cradle and waited. He sipped his cognac, wishing he could have a cigar. The phone rang and he picked it up immediately.

"I have your party, sir."

"Thank you, operator. Adam, my friend, I was enjoying a cognac and thinking what a wonderful time we had with you and Beatrice. I wanted to call and say thank you again and invite you to come stay with us. We have plenty of room and the weather is wonderful."

"We may just do that. I'll ask Beatrice. She will probably start packing before I finish the sentence. That woman loves to go places. I think she just wants me out of Washington. So, my friend, now that we have the invitation out of the way, why did you call me at one in the morning, your time?"

"John Michael Palmer: You will never guess why he contacted me. We met this evening, as a matter of fact, Adam."

"I really do not care, but tell me anyway."

"His birth mother was a Jewish girl, a prostitute in Kansas. She's dead . . . killed herself. Because of this link to Israel, he had the nerve to ask me if he could live here as a Jew."

"He came to Israel to talk to you about this?"

"I turned him down. I called him a traitor to his country. He walked out on me."

"If I know you, you are calling me after he fled the country."

"Not until tomorrow, Adam."

"I'm sure you are correct, General. Live like a Jew in Israel? Disgusting bastard. Thank you for calling, my old friend. I know someone here who will welcome your response and it gives us a lead to follow. Do you think he will try to contact you again?"

"I sincerely doubt it, Adam. I'll say goodnight."

"Goodnight, General Golan." Cahill hung up, put his head back, and sighed.

"Who was on the phone, dear heart?"

"General Golan. He wants us to visit Israel as his guest."

"How wonderful, Adam. He called to invite us to Israel. What else did he call about?"

"He had a story to tell me. He lied to me Beatrice . . . He lied to me."

Palmer entered his room, ordered room service, and stripped off his clothes. When his tea and pastry arrived, he called the operator.

"I would like to place a call to Hoboken, New Jersey, operator. The name of the person I am calling is Frank Graham. I have an international AT&T credit card I would like to use. My name is James Preston."

"Thank you, Mister Preston. I will ring you back as soon as I acquire the person you are calling. Give me your card number."

He hung up, poured a shot of vodka into his tea, and sat on the edge of the bed sipping his tea while he ate a slice of yellow cake with a thick coat of surgery white icing. The phone rang.

"Yes."

"Your call is ready, sir."

"Thank you. Hello, Graham."

"This must be important. A call on an unsecured line isn't like you."

"I've made contact in Tel Aviv. I want you to contact Dukakis. I will need two apartments after the first of the year. They must be large enough to accommodate maybe five or six others. No excuses Graham, make that clear to him."

"Does the Barnett woman know you are returning to the states?"

"I hinted at it, but said nothing is approved by my company. Why do you ask?"

"How are you going to handle her, John?"

"I told you. We like rough sex. There is nothing else."

"You said the same thing about the Schmidt woman."

"I will handle Maxine. You take care of Dukakis."

"Enough said. Anything else you need?"

"Yes, one more thing. Keep in touch with Cahill."

"He is retired and not well."

"No one ever retires from the CIA completely, Graham."

The Israeli operator disconnected the transatlantic line and at the same time shut off the recorder, unplugging it from the phone in Room 1232. She then followed up with a check of the tracer to ensure it was working correctly.

She made a call. When a man whose voice she recognized immediately answered she said, "He called a fellow named Graham in Hoboken, New Jersey, from his room. He used a false ID number. The man it belonged to died twelve years ago. I have traced the call, General. The number and city are correct. I have a clear copy of the taped conversation."

"I must say he didn't waste time, did he? Very good, Sophia Moskowitz. I will expect the recording first thing in the morning."

WASHINGTON: JULY 9

"Supper should be ready soon, Adam. Would you like a glass of wine while you wait?"

"Thank you, Bea."

"Will you tell me what is bothering you? I've been at your side for too many years, Adam Cahill, not to see the distress on your face."

"Bring the bottle back with you, dear." He poured each a half snifter of wine. She sat down next to him. "How many presidents have we served, Bea?"

"Seven presidents. Drink your wine and tell me what's wrong."

"A man, we determined, was killed in a firefight in Vietnam. Golan told me this man approached him. He said Palmer wanted to live the rest of his life as a Jew in Israel . . . A lie. Palmer told him he lives in a hotel in Berlin . . . another lie. He and this man spent the evening together in Tel Aviv last night dining together at a fine restaurant. He was seen by a young man we both met at a dinner for Begin in 1974. You were impressed by him . . . we both were."

"I remember him because he was the general's bodyguard. I believe he served in the Israeli Special Forces. I remember he was a very serious young man and was decorated for bravery in the 1973 war. Funny, I do not remember his name."

"Bernard Aarons. You said he would be a force to deal with in the future."

"What are you going to do, Adam?"

"I am going to finish my wine and enjoy the supper that smells so good. Tomorrow, I am going to call Langley and tell them what I've been informed of. After that, it becomes their problem . . . I'm retired."

"That's my boy… I wouldn't tell Ethan about this."

CAMP 3, SOUTH OF BEIRUT: JULY 10

"Where is Alisha Abud now?"

"Showering and preparing for lunch. She is a strong task master. This morning's training was hard, even for me. Some of the others do not like taking orders from a woman; they find it degrading. Not me or the special team. They have accepted her fully."

"That is good to hear Mahmoud. Your wait will be longer, I am afraid. Bring her here to me. I need to talk with her."

"I would not disturb her when she is bathing Al Aziz . . . A thousand pardons . . . Salmon Abedi. She caught one of the men watching her a few days after she came to the camp. It took three of us to pull her off him. I believe he would be dead today had we not intervened. She fights like a man and is as deadly as the scorpion. I will send one of the women to let her know you are here. I will make coffee for us for three if the woman wishes to join us."

"Do you fear this woman, Mahmoud?"

"I fear only Allah's wrath if we fail."

Abedi fixed a fresh cup for Mahmoud just as she entered the tent, her hair wrapped in a towel and her long black dress hanging shapeless on her thin frame. She wore no footwear, even though the sand baked her soles. She offered no apology for keeping Abedi waiting.

"I have not eaten, I am hungry. Can we have something while we talk?" she announced, sitting on a wicker chair. The seat was covered with a small flat pillow.

"I would appreciate it, my brother, if you would have the women bring us something to eat and a cold drink. You must be hungry as well, Salmon Abedi?"

She fell silent until Mahmoud left the tent. "I was not sure if he was included in our conversation. Does he know your real name?"

"Yes, he knows who I am. I do not see why he would be excluded. There is no more coffee. I can have more brewed."

"Possibly later, after we eat," she answered.

"Tell me . . . how the training is coming along?"

"They are ready when we have the order and they are willing to die, if it comes to that. As I am." Mahmoud returned, pulling the flap open. "Bring the food, woman."

"You have lost weight again. I am sure it is the regiment of training, but you look well. Let us enjoy the food and then we can talk without interruption."

"I need to hear only one thing. Is the attack on schedule?"

"Not quite."

The lunch finished along with talk of little importance. The three gathered close together at the far end of the tent, each with a cold glass of iced tea. The tent with its thick canvas walls shielded them against the desert heat. The only relief was that the nights were mercifully cool.

"Well, Salmon Abedi, it is time you tell us what news you bring."

"The work on the tunnel has been halted due to a collapse. The soil was too soft. We have begun a new tunnel, deeper than the first."

"How long must we wait, Abedi?"

"Perhaps November. The diggers are happy and feel safe. The soil in the new tunnel is much harder. The walls have been insulated with wood and concrete. Seven days before the attack, you will leave this camp. You both will make your way through Jordan into the Palestinian side. The other six will come through Egypt and Syria." Al Aziz-Abedi removed a crumpled sheet of paper from inside his tunic.

"This is the address where you will all meet. From the cellar of this building, you will follow a sewer line linking up to the tunnel entrance on the Palestinian side. The tunnel will have the explosives and weapons you will use in the attack. Look on the back; those are your targets. A courier will come to the camp and he will give you all the travel papers you will be required to carry and money. Is there a question?

"I am satisfied. Sister, and you?" She shrugged, but said nothing.

"I must tell you: This could mean death to you all. Your only escape will be through the tunnel once you have completed the attacks. The Israeli army will waste no time closing the entrances to the West Bank. There is a good chance the tunnel might be discovered. You cannot allow them to capture you. You understand?"

"I said it before and I will repeat it again. If death is our reward, then let it be. Allah will provide."

"There are no virgins in heaven for you, sister."

"No, Mahmoud, but there is a man waiting for me . . . a man who knows me. No matter what I do, this man waits for me. He does not need virgins. If we are through, I want to walk alone in the desert. The hour is late. I want to be alone to pray."

"If that is your wish, sister, do what you must do," Al Aziz answered, with a wave of his hand.

"Who is this man, Salmon?" Mahmoud asked when the two men were alone.

"Mahmud Mustafa. He was assassinated in Barcelona. She still mourns him. That aside, I have an order for you, my friend. If things do not go well, I want you to make sure she is not captured by the Israeli army. Understood?"

"I understand, Salmon Abedi. I will not allow her capture."

The desert air cooled her face. She plunged her hands into the pockets of her dress, scolding herself for not wearing a jacket. She passed the last tent, ignoring the watchful eye of the sentry.

She marveled at the construction of the camp: the tents' low profile lined up against the shifting sand, the roofs painted to match the roll of the dunes.

She took the compass from her shirt pocket, studied the needle pointing three degrees past due east, and continued to walk in a straight line, making note of longitude and latitude. She shivered. Sand from the floor of the desert spurted up in a gust, stinging her face.

She spied him standing twenty feet ahead of her. He was smiling.

"I am sorry for the things I've done for my father, you, and Israel . . . do not be angry or disappointed." He was as handsome as he was alive. "Do you still love me?"

His smile broadened. He nodded.

"I love you, my husband, with all my heart, and I wait for Yahweh to call me home to you." A swirl of sand pricked her face. She closed her eyes. When the sand settled, she opened them. He was gone.

Reba returned to the camp, nodded to the sentry and went to her tent to put the compass under her pillow. She left the tent. Al Aziz and Mahmoud were sharing tea laced with mint liquor.

"May I join you?" she asked, sliding the flap covering the entrance to one side.

"Make it quick. The light from the lamps will shine for miles in this desert."

"You worry too much, Abedi."

"I have lived this long because I worry."

Mahmoud turned to her. "Do you not worry, sister?"

"I worry only when I am awake. When I sleep, what does it matter? You lay awake all night and nothing happens to you. If the worst happens, at least you will not hear it." She took a seat on the wicker chair, declining the offer of a drink. "I do have a worry, however, and I think we should give it some thought."

"What is it that worries you?"

"The travel plan worries me. I am wanted in Israel. The government has friendly ties to Jordan. I am sure they have distributed posters of me in Jordan. The Mossad would insist on it. If I am recognized, the Israeli Mossad will flock to Jordan to find me."

"What are you suggesting?" Al Aziz's tone was suspicious. "Do you want to travel alone?"

"I do not need to travel alone, Abedi. Let the others come through Jordan. Mahmoud and I will come through Syria. You do as you wish, but if it does not go well, you can explain it to the committee." She spit the words out like hot oil sizzling in a pan.

"I am going to bed. Goodnight," she said, ignoring Al Aziz. "Get the team up at four, dressed, and ready by 4:15 a.m. Understood?"

"Understood. They will be ready," Mahmoud answered.

"I am going to open the flap. If you are worried about the light crossing the desert, shut off the lamps." Al Aziz will take the bait, she told herself.

"She makes a point," Mahmoud said, pouring the last of the tea into their cups. "Remember, I will be traveling with her. I will know if she is a traitor."

"Very well, my brother. I accept your decision."

CIA-LANGLEY, VIRGINIA: JULY 10

Ronald Timmons's office on the sixth floor commanded a network of agents and analysts making up the heart of the Global Response Center at Langley. He was a man of slight build, with salt and pepper hair worn close-cropped and light brown eyes under thin brows.

Each day, hundreds of ciphers and analytical data crossed his desk. He passed on most of them, concentrating on suspicious items brought to his attention by a black mark on the upper left margin. This morning was no different. He counted sixteen. The rest, he placed on the cabinet behind his desk in a neat pile.

"After reading the transcripts, I have come to a conclusion, but I would ask your opinions before I give mine. Angela, why don't you begin with your assessment of the material I just read."

"I was intrigued by the number of messages concerning a poker game on a specific night. It sounds unimportant." Angela Manning-Han was considered by Timmons as a person whose could look in the abstract and pick and choose specific items others might miss. She was five feet, two inches, ' with a shock of shoulder-length red hair, hazel eyes and an astute mind.

"A general promoted to marshal and put in charge of the armies of the Soviet Union. I might add that his driver, and probably a play thing of the general, were all killed. At first, the car's gas tank is blamed, then shockingly, it is revealed that his primary assassin, a fellow named Smirnoff, and Fedorov's second-in-command all died the same night as the poker game. You see where I am going with this?"

"I agree with Angela." Sidney Drum, tall, lanky with black hair and dark brown eyes was also a Harvard grad. "What set off flares for me was this special force training in the mountains above the Black Sea. Pavlov was directing the training with a civilian we were not able to identify. I believe, and Angela agrees, that the Russian authorities are concerned about Afghanistan and may invade to secure a hold on the country. I also think Pavlov was not up for the job. I could be wrong. It is conjecture on my part."

"Someone high up in government, possibly Brezhnev himself, may have had second thoughts and to preserve the secret did away with the architect of the plan," Angela added.

"I know who the American is," Timmons said, his mouth twisted in a frown. His thin face tightened. "His name is John Michael Palmer, a traitor to his uniform and his country." He paused and swiped a bead of perspiration from above his lip.

"What I am about to tell you stays in this room. It has come to my attention that he is alive and living in Russia."

"How did you get this information, Ronald?"

"That isn't important. I will tell you everything in due time. Let's continue. Angela, I want you to monitor General Golan, his mail, and phone communications when possible. I want to know who visits him and when. Use our people in Tel Aviv. Do not contact Israeli intelligence agencies . . . Not yet. Sidney we want to know if any agency inside MI 5 or 6 has been contacted by an outside source concerning Russia. Do not give specifics. Ask to talk to Sir John Scarlett only. He will understand and will not ask questions."

"Is something big coming, Ronald?" Concern was on both Angela's and Sidney's faces.

"I don't know. I don't even know who the players might be. Get on it and by the way, I totally agree with your assessment of the events the night of the supposed poker game. I also agree with the possible explanation, except for the Brezhnev connection. I think it more likely is Fedotov. Get to work, both of you."

"Right away, boss."

When he was alone, he used his secure line to dial the operator directly.

"Yvonne, I needed to make a call through to Tel Aviv headquarters, Israeli Special Forces base Q near the Golan Heights. Do not concern yourself with the time difference; it will not matter."

"Who am I asking for, sir?"

"Ask for B. Give my name."

"It may take a little time, sir. I will do my best."

"This call is off the books."

"I understand, sir."

WALTER REED HOSPITAL

Anna Lee pushed the door open to the nurse's lounge. Margaret was already inside, her shoes off, legs crossed, leaning back on one of three recliners smoking a cigarette. Anna Lee stretched her arms high over her head and walked over to the service counter. She poured coffee, added just a hint of creamer, and pulled open the lids on the two boxes of donuts. She chose a maple bar.

"Major Lewis is doing poorly. I don't like his chances," Margaret said, talking through a plume of smoke.

"I think they are going to talk to the wife this morning. How are you doing?" Margaret stamped out the butt. "I know that look, Anna Lee. Something isn't quite right in wonderland? When Ethan comes down for the weekend, you glow like a strobe light. When he leaves, you get down in the mouth. This is different. You two having a bad time?"

"He told me, Margaret . . . all of it."

"Serious shit?"

"You were right, Maggie. I almost wish he never told me."

"You better sit down, Anna Lee."

"I'm okay," she said through tears. "He told me about a job. That's what they called it near a dock. I can't even pronounce the name of the port city, Maggie. I won't tell you what he did, but . . . Oh, Maggie. I can't imagine how he has kept his sanity."

"The important question is . . . Can you live with it?"

"He told me he loved me. He wanted me to know everything about him before he said the words. He said he would understand if I felt differently and wouldn't blame me if I sent him back to New York."

"What did you say?"

"I said, 'Let's go to bed; we don't have to make love. I just want to be held.' I told him what he did in the past can't be changed. That was then. This is now."

Anna Lee picked up the maple bar and took a bite. "I told him what Vincent said about moving to New York."

"How did he take that news?"

"He said he felt like the luckiest man in the world and then we went to bed and before you ask, we did some serious holding. This morning, he asked me if I still wanted to marry him. I said yes."

"Good girl. Grab one of those maple bars for me."

THE TUNNEL: NOVEMBER 12

"I am going through, alone, to make sure the tunnel has not been discovered or damaged. I do not intend on losing lives due to faulty construction. Check your time pieces. The time is 8:15. Mark it. It should take me thirty minutes to reach the dig-out point. Move into the tunnel in fifteen minutes. If you do not hear anything out of the ordinary, it means I've arrived without incident and have marked the exit hole. Any questions?"

"Let me go, sister, in case of trouble. You are too important to us."

"You bring the team. I will meet you if the path is clear. The safety of the parcels is what is more important. I will join you thirty feet from my marker. I will dispense the weapons and make a final look through the tunnel to make sure we were not followed. Wait near the entrance for my return. Praise to Allah, he will guide our plan to success."

She pulled the black wool cover over her face. "Remember, wait fifteen minutes." In a few seconds she was out of sight.

Corporal Amos Hebron checked his weapon, equipment, and radio before stepping out of the bunker into the cold moonless night. He slipped on his leather gloves, adjusted the scarf around his neck, and started off toward his post. The sand crunched under his thick-soled paratrooper boots. The stars above blinked at him.

A hundred yards from the bunker, he reached the flat path used to mark the distance to the wall. He started off after exchanging a few words with the guard he was replacing. A hundred yards along the path, Hebron spied a depression in the sand, almost a perfect circle thirty inches in diameter. He froze. The wind was constant, but not enough to create a whirlpool in the sand. He held his weapon up, pointing it toward the depression, tapped the speaker button on his phone, and waited for the operator in the bunker to respond.

"I see an unnatural depression in the sand. It is out of place. Wait . . . wait a second. I see a metal tube penetrating outward and turning slowly clockwise."

"This is General Golan, Corporal. Return to the bunker at once. I repeat, take no action and report back to the bunker on the double." The general turned to the commander of SOP. Is everything in place?"

"Yes, sir."

"Mark the time on your watch. In twenty minutes exactly, blow the entrance to the tunnel, wait five minutes for the debris to settle then go in firing your weapons. Use the flamethrower. There is to be nothing left to identify the bodies. Make absolutely sure nothing is left except bone, understand? A woman is in the tunnel. She is not to be harmed. She is wearing protective gear. Limit your fire to twenty-five meters. Good luck and good hunting."

CAMP 3: NOVEMBER 13

"Have you heard?"

"Only what I can receive on the radio from Tel Aviv. What do you hear, Remi Amok?"

"Our spotters say there was a series of explosions. The Israeli military went into the tunnel and trapped the assassins. We can only assume the vests exploded. If that is the case, it will be impossible to know who died. The Israelis are reporting twelve are dead. Tel Aviv news is saying one of the terrorists was a woman. The news reports say the woman may have been the terrorist Alia Al Baghdadi, but have not confirmed it as the body was so badly burned."

"What else, Remi? Does the Israeli military say how they were able to find the entrance to the tunnel?"

"Only that it was known to them for at least a week before they attacked it. They could be lying to lead us to believe their intelligence is that good." Remi lit a Turkish cigarette. "One thing is sure. Everyone was in the camp; it could not have come from here. There is a mole or a traitor in our group living in the Palestinian Territory, a trusted one. It is the only answer." Remi helped himself to a glass of tea, "Will you be going back to Beirut?"

"Yes, tonight. We must find this mole, Remi. He must be punished along with his family. We must know if it is one who has compromised us more than once."

"Might I make a suggestion for a second alternative?"

"Tell me, what is this second alternative you speak of?"

"We do not change our transmissions or codes; we do not cloak our phone conversations as we should. We may be our own worst enemy, Salmon Abedi."

"I understand what you say, but it is difficult to do what you suggest. So many groups operate independently."

"That is the problem: too many groups with separate agendas. Every time one comes to the front, our enemies know who and where they are."

"So, what is the solution?"

"You said it yourself. The key, then, is independence of each cell. We limit traffic between groups, use more couriers or we will lose the element of surprise before they have had a chance to succeed, my friend. Only a suggestion, Salmon Abedi. It would be a terrible waste of time looking for a mole who may be our own foolishness."

"I might bring it up at my next meeting with the committee. Now, I must pack. After dark I will leave for Beirut."

"I pray Allah will guide your path, Salmon Abedi."

CHAPTER SEVENTEEN

"It is so cold the cars look like ice sculptures. I must rent a second garage for your car Ladas. Pravda says it is colder than the winter of 1941."

"It is warm in your bed. You stand naked looking out the window. My car will be fine. I do not care about the cold. I must say you have a nice bottom: muscular, not too much hair . . . Come back to bed."

Ladas pulled back the covers and propped herself up on one elbow. "Tell me if this view is not better than icicles."

"You like my bottom; how many have you scrutinized, Ladas Sorokin?"

"Four, if that is what is important to you, Shevchenko . . . only four. "When I was fourteen, I already developed full breasts and a woman's body. I was raped by my uncle. When I entered university. I had an affair with a student. He was my first love. He ended it, leaving me for my friend. I met the general . . . I married him. I was a model from a rich military family. It was easy to see he would be important one day and I would have need for nothing. You, Shevchenko, are my fourth."

Ladas lay back on the bed and covered herself. "I adore you. I have never felt so safe in my life. I have never been made love to with more affection or care of my needs before your own. It isn't sex with you. It is too important to me to settle for the simple pleasure of being with someone. You have entered my soul . . ."

"I am very sorry, Ladas Sorokin." He lay down next to her, cradling her in his arms. "Forgive a fool who has never loved before. I am certain I loved you since the moment I saw you at the gala for the—"

"No more talk of the past or ice sculptures."

JANUARY 1, 1978

"Comrade Major Kasparov, I apologize for the late call. I am Max, the tailor from Bryansk. Do you remember me?"

"Yes, of course. What is the trouble that makes you disturb my sleep?" The woman next to Kasparov shifted in her sleep. He rubbed her buttock slowly and gently until he was sure the ringing of the phone had not awakened her.

"The American. Yesterday he refused the cleaning woman entrance to his home."

"I am sorry, Comrade, but I fail to see the significance of his actions."

"Palmer is gone, Comrade Major."

Kasparov's back stiffened. "How do you know this?"

"I watched the house last night until I went to bed. He never turned on the light. No smoke rose from his chimney. This morning, I went to check; the car was gone. He did not answer the door. I tried to look in the windows, but the frost blocked me. When he did not respond, I hit the door very hard and broke the hinges."

"What did you find?"

"He removed all his clothing and personal papers, disconnected the phone, and shut off the electricity. He's gone, Comrade Major."

"Could he have driven to the train station?"

"The last train to Moscow left at 5:30 p.m. I saw him on his porch at seven drinking a glass of tea. I know how to watch, Comrade Major. He couldn't have left before eleven o'clock."

The woman next to him was awake. He put a finger to his lips. "Do one more thing for me, Comrade. Keep everyone away from that house. I will send people down to search it this morning. I will see that they fix the door. Goodbye, Comrade."

He turned to the woman nestled against his back. "You want to come back to work in our little group, Elsa? Well, you may have your chance. I was a fool to let you go the way I did, Elsa. I still loved you."

"Stop talking. I loved you when I was married, Dmitry Kasparov. I love you now. I will put on the tea. I am sure the call was not to wish you a happy New Year."

The lovemaking over, Ladas put her head on the pillow, her hair damp, tiny beads of perspiration forming a moist pool in the small of her back. "I have never felt this way at any time in my life. It took fifty years to be satisfied like this. It was worth the wait, my wonderful man. I would gladly die this day nestled in your arms."

"Please do not die today—" A muffled phone ringing somewhere in the apartment interrupted him. "It is my private phone; it rings twice and pauses and rings again."

"They call you at five in the morning even on New Year's Day?"

"It must be important. You mentioned vodka before?" he gently pulled her to his side. "I won't be long."

"The suggestion of vodka was more than an hour ago, Shevchenko. I will fix tea instead."

"This better be important to call me on this day," he said, putting the phone to his ear.

"Palmer is gone; it is being confirmed. A forensic team is preparing to leave for Bryansk. My agent is a trusted individual; he would not make such a judgment unless he was sure of himself."

"I will be in Lubyanka prison in one hour. I want Marina and Comrade Kozlov to come as well."

"What about Mikhail?"

"No, I do not want him involved. Not yet."

He hung up, slid the phone back into the wall space behind his desk, and slid the picture of Lenin back over the opening.

"Is everything all right?"

"I have to leave for the office. I have a meeting in one hour. I must clean up. I am sorry, Ladas. Wait for me to return. Will you stay?"

"I will stay forever if you want me to, Peter Shevchenko. Shall I cook? We haven't eaten."

"There isn't time. I will call you. I do not know how long this will take."

"Can we talk about it when you return or are we to have secrets between us?"

"I can't say . . . I will call you." He turned away. Secrets . . . Yes, I have secrets, Ladas Sorokin.

Shevchenko, his coat tucked in the crook of his arm, walked down the hall, stopping in front of Cell 15A. He opened the steel door, hung his coat and scarf on a hook next to the door, and stepped inside.

The exhaust fan hummed. The lights blinked above the table. The only change to the cell, thanks to Kasparov, were the sandbags stacked on the far wall. Shevchenko took a seat between Vlad and Marina. Kasparov sat across from them on the bench.

On the table were a pencil, a notepad, four containers of dried white fish, a bowl of peppers with pieces of cut sausage, and another dish of boiled eggs. There were also four glasses and a bottle of vodka and water.

"Where are the geese? Why are they not with us, Comrade Kozlov?"

"I thought it inappropriate, sensing the severity of the situation. When Peter and I meet in the park, we feed the geese. We simply look like friends enjoying a conversation."

"So simple, isn't it?"

"You taught me, Marina. I apologize for taking you away from your husband."

"He understands, Comrade Shevchenko."

"Good. Shall we begin? Marina, no notes. Leave all conversation to memory. Dmitry, where are we in the investigation?"

"The forensic team left Minsk a short time ago, by helicopter. They are under strict orders to cover not only the house, but also the surrounding grounds up to fifty meters. The group knows what to look for Peter. We are checking airports, trains, and buses, including parking areas in and around these points. An alert has been sent out giving the description of the car. Embassies in our sphere of interest have also been alerted or are at present being alerted. A set of photographs were issued to the proper parties." Kasparov reached for a container of white fish and a plastic fork.

"Allow me to pour vodka," Kozlov said, lining up the glasses.

"I would suggest our checkpoints and state police, of course, in case he really is gone. He may just be playing games with us to see how quickly we would respond."

"You make a very good point, Marina. We must give it a thorough discussion while we eat and drink. If he did leave last night, he will be past the checkpoints by now anyway."

"This sausage is very good, Vlad. Where did you get it?"

"Try the fish, Marina."

"Now that our shopping needs are met, shall we finish the business at hand?"

"Dmitry Kasparov, is there somewhere you need to be? Perhaps you might make a small package to take with you?" Marina matched his look of annoyance "My old friend, one must always find a bit of light even in the darkest of tunnels. I meant no disrespect." Marina picked up two cut broccoli spears and a piece of fish with her fork. "Who outside our influence should be notified?"

"England should be on the list. MI-6 would be a good conduit."

"Did the Jewish agents who attempted to kill Arafat ever find out who the informer was?"

"No. We know who it is. My tulip is his mistress and like all fools he tells her things. His name is Sir Reginald Pepper. He is a top tier MI-6 agent and privy to all sorts of secret information."

"Your fingers are much longer than even I imagined, Dmitry Kasparov. Trusting their leadership is like eating broth with a fork."

"Thank you, Comrade Kozlov."

"It might be to our advantage one day, but not today. The Mossad could not find the leak but we did. If we give the information to 10 Downing Street, it could enhance our chances of convincing them we are being forthright." Shevchenko rubbed his chin. "We say nothing to Israeli security. Let us say Golan is helping Palmer in some adventure. Who can tell how far it reaches into the government? Israel, for the time being, needs to be left in the dark."

"What about the American CIA?"

"Let's wait on that issue, as well, at least until we can determine if he is truly on the run and is planning to return to the United States."

"I believe he is preparing to do harm and it will be the United States where the attack will occur. There is a perceived threat with the Middle East, especially with the rise of the mullahs in Iran."

"Iran wouldn't dare go up against the United States," Kozlov said.

"You fool yourself, Comrade Kozlov. The political climate under the present administration in the United States is ripe for a country like Iran to take action," Kasparov answered.

"I will take it a step further, Dmitry Kasparov," Shevchenko said. "The general's death halted for perhaps a year or more the invasion of Afghanistan. It is the beginning of 1978. If the invasion is going to move forward, I would not see it until late next year.

"I understand now why you wanted no notes taken."

"Yes Marina, and that is why no word of this meeting must ever leave this room."

"What of the guard at the main door?"

"I will see to the guard," Kasparov answered.

"We wait, watch, and listen for the reports as they come in. Then we act accordingly. Dmitry, give me a moment, please, before you leave."

"What is it, Peter?" Kasparov checked the door to make sure it was tightly shut. He took a seat next to Shevchenko and poured vodka into each glass.

"If there is a conspiracy involving the Kremlin and Comrade Fedorov, we had better address the situation now. The woman in your home is Elsa?"

"Yes, it is, why?"

"I am glad for you, Dmitry. I was very sad when you left her."

"I was a fool, Peter. I was young and the tree was full of fruit."

"Fruit only lasts through a season. A good woman will last for all seasons, Dmitry Kasparov. If whatever is going to happen does not work out in Russia's favor, someone will have to take the blame. It will not be Fedorov or Brezhnev or the army."

"It will be us."

"I would think so, which means death to those they feel threatened by. A thought becomes a fact. Old friends become enemies. It could be a blood-bath; nothing like Stalin's cleansing, but for those involved it will not matter."

"What if you are right? What then?"

"Elsa wants to come back into the fold, you say. Take her back. I know you want no harm to come to her. The work is dangerous, but if I am correct, she is safer in your care. I believe a number of people will have to leave the country and go into hiding. Where they go to be safe, I do not know. They will need forged papers and enough capital to sustain them."

"Who and how many are we talking about, Peter?"

"Let's not worry about that now; it may never come to pass, but we must be ready."

"Are you going to tell Ladas?"

"Not yet. I will tell Marina tomorrow. She has a right to know in advance. For now, let's wait and see. I will think the worst and make plans accordingly. If I am wrong, we have lost nothing."

Palmer passed through the checkpoint, leaving Russia behind without incident. He continued to drive without sleep. He allowed for ten hours, perhaps more, before being missed, another hour or so for the residents of Bryansk to notify the authorities, and another hour for them to react to the news of his disappearance. Enough time to drive to Prague and then on to Vienna. Prague was the key. He suspected the KGB would expect him to enter East Berlin and from there attempt to cross the border checkpoint or attempt a flight out of the country. They would not think of Vienna until it was too late.

He turned north toward Prague onto highway D1. His plan was to make Brno 200 miles away and rest before driving to Vienna.

He took off the wide brimmed fedora and checked himself in the rearview mirror. His hair was dyed black with streaks of gray. The beard was neatly trimmed to match the hair. The change was enough to get him past the last checkpoint before entering Austria. He allowed for a second day's delay across Eastern Europe for his picture and physical description to reach the embassies. He was counting on Vienna not receiving any notice. If he was correct in his assumptions, his escape and disappearance were guaranteed.

The Volga drove well, though the heater was less efficient. His feet and calves were becoming numb. He massaged them frequently, making a mental note to buy warmer socks and a blanket. It was just past eight o'clock when the Volga entered the town of Brno.

He discarded the idea of renting a car and decided to eat a good meal and gas up the Volga. At the same time, he would make sure the drive belts were in good enough shape to get him across the border. The last thing he needed was a breakdown on East 46i. He went to an army-navy store just as it opened and purchased an old army blanket and thick socks. By nine o'clock, he was checking into a small motel.

"New Year. Revelers. Easy pickings."

"Shut up both of you."

"My meeting is over Ladas. I was thinking of stopping off at the bakery. Is there something in particular you would like?"

"Surprise me. Are you through with your duties? Can we have the rest of the day?"

"I do not think so. I think it is going to turn out to be a long day."

"I found eggs and two lonely potatoes. I thought I would cut the potatoes and fry them both. Would you enjoy that?"

"How long can you stay?"

"I thought we settled that question, Peter Shevchenko."

"I am concerned for your home. The cold weather could damage the pipes."

"The people who came to the dacha were kind enough to leave the automatic heating and cooling systems in place.

"I am on my way to the bakery and will be home soon. I will start your car while you prepare breakfast. It is a very serious matter, Ladas. That is all I am able to tell you right now."

"I can hear it in your voice. I understand. Come home; do not slip on the ice. I want you in one piece."

She hung up, forcing back the urge to cry. "Not now, God," she muttered. "Please, if you are listening to me, do not spoil it for us . . . not now"

PALMER: JANUARY 2

Palmer was awakened just after four o'clock by revelers in the hotel still celebrating the new year. He decided getting more rest would be impossible. He pushed the covers away and immediately felt a cold shaft of air. He got up and padded to the window. Under the window sill, the floor heater waited. He pressed the on switch and quickly felt the first streams of heat.

The room was small and it wouldn't take long to warm it, he told himself, deciding on a shower before he dressed.

After putting the used clothes neatly into his travel bag, he took a moment to double check his travel papers. He put his papers in his coat pocket and walked out.

"Getting an early start, sir? I apologize for the noise. I started the car as you requested and found difficulty with the heater."

"What was wrong with it?"

"Only a loose wire and a clogged vent. It is working fine now. I will get your receipt and keys since you paid in advance. I will have you on your way in a short time."

"Wait," Palmer said, taking a roll of bills from his pants pocket. He counted the bills, adding up to fifty dollars in Russian rubles, and laid the small stack on the counter. "Take this, you have done me a great service."

"I won't be a minute, sir."

We have time, Wayne. There are a lot of drunken women nearby.

"Shut up."

Palmer turned onto East 46i and settled into the driver's seat. The heater was working perfectly. He reasoned that at the next fuel stop he would need to remove the heavy socks. The road was clear. There were only a few spots of ice where the road was not quite level.

"Socialism, the road is never quite level, is it Comrades?" The Walther PPK was a hand reach away. If his life was to end, let it end at the border of Austria. "I'm coming home to America. I have a surprise for you . . . a big surprise. You're not going to like it either."

MOSCOW: JANUARY 3

Shevchenko awakened with a start, realizing he was not in his apartment, but the bedroom of Ladas's dacha. The smell of strong coffee filled the air. He put his head down, resting it on his open hands. I was only going to see that she arrived safely at the dacha and help move her clothes to the apartment. He smiled, his face reddening as he remembered the lovemaking.

"I prepared coffee. I know you like it strong." Ladas floated into the room like a swan floating above a still lake wearing only her sable coat and carrying a silver tray with a service of cups and silverware he couldn't afford if he spent months eating small cans of cat food.

"You look troubled. Is it that you have not heard from your comrades, or are you sorry we did not return home? You wanted to, but I had plans as well."

"Yes, it troubles me. I must say your sleepwear is magnificent." He sat up and kissed her. "The coffee smells wonderful and you smell wonderful."

"I wanted to smell good in case you intended to use me for your own satisfaction. Drink your coffee, Peter Shevchenko, and tell me how beautiful I am in your eyes."

"Is my saying it that important to you, Ladas?"

"Not always. It becomes boring, but in our lovemaking . . ." The phone next to the bed rang: two rings, a pause of ten seconds, and two more. "They know you are here?"

"Only Kasparov, no one else." He picked up the receiver.

"Yes." When Ladas tried to get up, he took her arm and pulled her back onto the bed. "Go on Dmitry, tell me. Do we know where Palmer is?" He listened intently and hung up the phone without saying a word.

"I must leave and go to Moscow to meet with a small committee. The Chairman doesn't know. No one except Kasparov and my secretary knows about us. I will explain everything when I return. Trust me . . . you must trust me. I will help you pack your things in the car."

"Not now, Shevchenko. You cannot squeeze my ass like you are trying to hold onto ice cubes and then tell me you have to leave."

"This beautiful sable coat could get ruined and the coffee will certainly be too cold to drink."

"Ruin it. I have more. I also have plenty of coffee, Peter Shevchenko."

"I must get back to Moscow."

"Be quiet. No more talking."

"Good morning, Marina. It has been a long two days, yes?"

"We must talk—"

"After the meeting we will talk Marina. It may not be necessary with the drastic moves we discussed, but we must be prepared. You, as a Jew, should understand."

"I understand. I just have a difficult time coming to the realization." She took his coat and hat and hung them on the hook outside the cell door. "They are here waiting for you."

"You brought your American cigarettes, I see."

"It is a little late to worry about such things, Peter."

"I brought a bottle of vodka."

"Good then, each one of us has our own reserve." She let out a nervous laugh before she became serious again. "Does Ladas know?"

"Only what she overheard from my conversation with Dmitry this morning. I need to tell her more when I return home after I shower and change my clothes."

"You should think twice before returning to the dacha. Someone might be watching."

"I have already brought her back to the apartment and brought all of her clothing. If I am being watched, I am afraid it is a bit late."

"You trust her, then?"

"Let's go in, Marina. Time is of the essence."

Shevchenko opened his briefcase and brought out the bottle of vodka. Marina put her American cigarettes and a lighter on the table.

"Lucky Strike cigarettes from America . . . someone has access to foreign interests."

"A friend gets them for me, Vlad. If there is a problem, I will gladly put them away."

"On the contrary, my dear Marina. I was going to ask if I could share one."

"You may have the pack, Vlad, if they are not all smoked before we leave." She pushed the cigarettes across the table.

"I would like one," Kasparov said at the same time, taking a pen from his pocket, opening his notebook, and placing the pen on top of the first page. He took a cigarette from the pack and lit it. "Now, we are all conspirators, yes?"

"Before we begin, if Mother Russia is to see a new era in relations with the rest of the world, Gorbachev must remain an outsider.

Everyone nodded in agreement.

"Good," he said, also taking a Lucky Strike from the pack and lighting it before he spoke. "Comrade Kozlov, my friend, we would not hold it against you if you decide to step aside. Your family interests must come first. I see no reason for you to endanger yourself or your family."

"I appreciate not only your concern but your respect for my position. The future of our motherland on the world's stage means more to me than my life or my fortune. It is only my wife and me. Sadly, we have no children."

"I knew I could count on you. Let us begin . . . what do we know for certain, Dmitry?"

"Have you spoken to Comrade Fedorov, Peter?"

"No. he is away with the Chairman and their families in the Crimea; he is expected back tomorrow. His secretary has made an appointment for me on Thursday. Palmer picked the perfect time to leave Russia. Dmitry, bring us up to date on his movements as we know them." Shevchenko stamped the cigarette out.

Kasparov slumped over the text, his arms folded on the edge of the table. "A thorough search of the house and surrounding property proved futile. Nothing, not even a scrap of paper was left behind. His clothing is all gone, along with luggage. The house was cleaned thoroughly, not a fingerprint could be found. What they did find was a small smudge of a black substance under the right faucet handle in the bathroom sink."

"Hair dye, I would bet. Add that to the description we already released to the embassies, Dmitry. Go on."

"Every embassy is watching for him, with higher intensity in East Berlin and Prague. Those would be the fastest routes into Western Europe. He knows this as well as we do and with that assumption, I added Austria to the list and notified Vienna to be especially watchful. I notified Latvia and Finland. I will add the possible attempt at dying his hair when the meeting ends."

"You mentioned Fedorov is in Crimea. Could Palmer possibly go there and leave with one of the ships in port?"

"You think he is helping Palmer, Marina?"

"When you mentioned him, I never considered it as a possibility, but isn't that how Palmer got here in the first place, Dmitry?"

"You are right, Marina. I should have thought of it."

"I think we need a break. There isn't much more we can do here, Dmitry. I think you need to make another call, yes? Tomorrow is Wednesday. We return to our duties as if nothing has happened. Marina, you and I will talk then. Vlad, use an outside source to get the message to Mikhail. I will meet you at the park after my meeting with Comrade Fedorov that would be the fifth, say about noon?"

"I will even bring white fish for both of us."

"You are worried, Peter." It wasn't a question.

"Yes, Marina, I am worried. I believe Palmer is creating a terrible scenario. I am afraid it involves important contacts in Israel. We must convince the western allies of the danger they face."

"If Israel is the culprit, why do we uproot our lives?"

"Palmer hatched his plan here. Comrade Fedorov is well aware of it. He will have no chance of recrimination. Denial would be fruitless, especially if Palmer is captured."

"We are still the scapegoat."

"I am afraid so."

"Do you want me to contact Mister Patterson?"

"Not yet. We will see after I talk to Fedorov." He put his hands on her shoulders. "We will see if we can do what we have to do without affecting our lives. I promise you."

VIENNA: JANUARY 4

Palmer entered the Grand Hotel Wien followed by a hotel greeter. As they passed the grand ballroom of the 140-year-old historic hotel, the greeter pointed out the 1913 painting by Thomas Etthofer in the ornate grand ballroom.

"Beautiful, isn't it?"

"It is beautiful," Palmer remarked with little enthusiasm.

"By request from the gentlemen who registered for you, we can bypass the line waiting to register and go directly to your suite."

"Very good. I am tired from the long drive."

At the same time as Palmer was being brought to his suite, Daniel Berg deplaned and was making his way through customs. The agent inspected his travel papers, asked the routine questions, and directed Berg to the baggage counter.

Once outside, the frigid air struck him, reminding him he was no longer in Tel Aviv. He pulled the collar of the parka close around his neck and greeted his driver.

"I am Daniel Berg."

"Welcome to Vienna, Daniel. I am Donald Feld. Would you like to see the city before we go to the embassy? Palmer is already at the hotel and in his suite."

"Maybe another time. I want to finalize my instructions, see Palmer, and leave on the flight this evening."

"I envy you, Daniel. I have one more year here. I haven't been home in two years."

"It will go quickly, and Vienna is a nice city, is it not?"

"It is not Tel Aviv."

"I will not argue that point, Donald."

Palmer heard the knock on his door. He poured vodka into his glass—leaving it on the bar—and padded over to the door. Looking through the eye glass, he spied the young man: blond hair, blue-eyed, deep dimples. His parka was draped in the crook of his arm. He knocked once more. Parker opened the door just enough, allowing only a partial view of his face.

"I was expecting someone else." His gun felt heavy in his left hand.

"My name is Daniel Berg. If you will not invite me in, I will leave and report to my superiors you were not receptive to me. You can do whatever you choose. I will not come back a second time."

Palmer opened the door, slipping the hand gun into his waistband.

"Come in."

"That wouldn't have helped." Daniel raised the coat, exposing the barrel of the Walther PPK. "Please step aside so that I can see into your room."

"Can't be too careful, can we Daniel?"

"Please walk in front of me. What is beyond that door?"

"The bedroom and bathroom. I was expecting General Golan. They send me you. Why?"

"You think he would chance a meeting with you here? He will see you briefly when you arrive in Tel Aviv. I have your papers and instructions. I will be brief, so listen carefully. I have no intentions of repeating myself."

"I do not think much of your arrogance or your attitude," Palmer said, reaching for the glass of vodka.

"I do not think much of a man who would betray his country, so I guess on that point we are in agreement. Are you ready or shall I go?"

Palmer opened the leather case, removed the ticket and travel papers, scanned each quickly, and put them back. Next, he browsed the informational packet while sipping his vodka.

"It seems to be in order except for one thing. Why do I have to wait until I am contacted to fly out? What am I supposed to do, sit in my room?"

"I did not make the arrangements. If that is all, I will say goodbye."

Palmer waited until the door closed behind his visitor before flinging the glass across the room, smashing it against the counter of the bar. "A prisoner, that's what I am. I can't chance going out."

"You said yourself they wouldn't think you would come here."

"I can't be certain."

"Let's go out; you're really angry. I know how to relieve the tension. So do you."

"Leave me alone, both of you," he growled, staring with hate-filled eyes at his parents standing next to each other on the broken shards of glass. "Why now . . . why after all these years do you show yourself to me?"

"We asked and were given permission. What else do you need to know?"

"Who gave you miserable excuses for life permission? I want you out of my room and my life."

"There are lots of opportunities out there," his father answered, ignoring the question.

"Shut up. Leave me alone; I need to think."

"I'm right, a day and a half in this hotel and you'll go nuts if you don't go out."

"Shut up, damn you . . . shut up."

Palmer went to the liquor bar. They stepped aside for him to pass. He picked up the bottle of vodka and took a long swallow.

"Keep your wits about you; getting drunk isn't going to help. You need to eat a good meal and relax."

"Giving me fatherly advice again?"

"I'm just being honest with you, Wayne. You are one of us."

"I'm not like you at all."

"You are us, Wayne. You are the egg that cracked before you were whole just like us. You need to come to terms with it."

"Your father is right, Wayne."

"Get out . . . get out."

CHAPTER EIGHTEEN

"Do you speak Egyptian Arabic, Al Aziz?" The tall man was thin-faced, with a thick black beard. His eyes, devoid of emotion, were like a still lake. The tall man sat in the center chair between two smaller men, their identities obscured from Al Aziz by the curtain.

"You use a different name Al-Aziz . . . Salmon Abedi. Which should I call you?"

"Either, as you wish. Why can't I see your faces and know your names? Why must I talk to a curtain while I am visible to you?" Al Aziz answered, struggling to control his temper. The tall one . . . the Egyptian. He has the power. The cash. It would not be wise to rankle his feathers.

"I understand your concern, Al Aziz, but you must understand my frustration. I will tell you I come from a wealthy family. I do not want them involved. They must not be outcasts for my beliefs. I am not a warrior, only a voice for Allah and a pocket book for organizations such as yours. I do not show my face. It is dangerous to be in positions of authority in your group. I am young and wish to live a long life. I read the newspapers. Does that satisfy your curiosity, Al Aziz? Or do you prefer Salmon Abedi?"

"Al Aziz is my birth name."

"Good. Let us proceed. I financed the tunnel and the training of the attackers . . . so tell me and my associates, where did the plan fail?"

"They knew. Whether it was a guard seeing them break to the surface or treason, we do not know. Not yet."

"May I suggest an alternative?"

"Of course you may. Any help you might give is the most welcome, tall one."

"How much chatter was passed through the wonderful technology of phones or perhaps coded messages singing on the wires like a well-fed bird?"

"Someone else mentioned that scenario to me."

"Perhaps we should speak to him, Al Aziz. Where is this man and why did you not bring him with you?"

"My associate only days ago spoke of this problem." Al Aziz s' face flushed with anger at the sarcastic tone of the tall one. He maintained his composure, accepting the insult. "The Jews only put names to three of the attackers. The woman who was wanted by the Mossad was a close friend, advisor, and an agent of Allah."

"You sound very sure it was a family. Palestinians, I surmise. You have just helped to strengthen my point, Al Aziz. I believe no Palestinian would do such a thing. The families of the dead are well treated. You do not realize the problem with your answer. You jab at answers, but you have none. Please wait outside. I want to speak to my colleagues."

Al Aziz lit a cigarette. The tall man intimidated him and made him feel awkward, like a child at his first day in a new school. He repeated his own words, "Someone else mentioned it." He could almost see the smile on the tall man's face through the curtain. The door opened. A man dressed in fatigues and holding an AK-47 raised a hand to stop him.

"I was told you may leave. There is no reason for you to return; they are finished with you. The tall one is leaving Egypt today to return to Afghanistan."

GORKY PARK: JANUARY 5

"It is too cold, Peter Shevchenko; even the geese have fled the lake. The young ones skate where the geese swam. We need to find a warmer place to meet. I am afraid my ass is—"

"We may all be seeking a new environment, Vlad Kozlov."

"I take it, then, your meeting with Fedorov did not go well?"

"Why don't we walk, Comrade, while your ass defrosts?"

They began to stroll toward the square, ignoring the sudden gusts of win.

When they had separated themselves from other strollers, Shevchenko spoke.

"I explained the situation to the deputy. He looked at me with the dull eyes of a man not concerned with events. He is worried. His hands were knitted together, each in a fist. He tapped them endlessly against his knees. Something in the plan this Palmer has submitted is upsetting them. They are not so sure of its success, Comrade."

"You know this for certain, Peter?"

"Fedorov told me to spare no expense or manpower. His words: 'Hunt him like a wild animal and destroy him.' "

VIENNA: JANUARY 6

Nadia Volkov slipped her press pass with her picture and name in bold script over the collar of her coat. She left the embassy and arrived in front of the hotel amidst a group of journalists from across Europe and America.

The American, a young man named Harold Foss working for the New York Times, opened her car door and helped her out.

"So, Harold, are you ready for the big news?"

"The news is always the same, Nadia. I'm already bored and they haven't started yet."

"Join me for coffee, Harold. Do we have time?" Having coffee with a male companion would deflect others from noticing her eyes shifting rapidly over the crowd inside and outside the grand ballroom.

"Let's sit under the old painting. We can see when they are about to begin." She found a small table for two; they ordered coffee and a Danish. Foss talked, and she barely listened.

Palmer went outside and stood by the curb. The cold air washed over him. It felt good to be outside, even for a short time. He lit a cigarette and silently counted the hours until he was to fly out of Vienna.

"Look at all these women, Wayne: like ants attacking a bowl of sugar."

"Shut up." He stamped out the cigarette in a sand-filled urn and went back into the hotel. This time when he passed the ballroom, he did not escape the watchful eyes of Nadia Volkov.

The time seemed as if it stopped. The suite felt smaller, the furniture larger, taking up far too much area. He had to get out even, if it meant putting himself at risk. Perhaps a movie, a darkened theater, would be the safest place, but what about his luggage? Pacing and thinking, "Yes," he said out loud and called the bellmen's desk. They would be happy to transport his luggage ahead and sign it in at the proper gate. It was no problem; they only needed his flight information.

He hung up, relieved he had one less thing to frustrate him. He decided to talk to Maxine. He called the front desk, asking the operator for a transatlantic line. He rattled off the phone number and credit card number. This time he used his own out of fear the false card would alert authorities. He hung up and resumed pacing, his hands folded behind his back. He should pack, go to a movie, get out for a while. He started for the bedroom when the phone rang.

"We have your connection, sir," the operator said.

"Thank you." He asked to speak to Maxine Fisher-Barnett.

"Whom may I say is calling?"

"James Preston with the Chicago Sun Times . . . I'm calling from the NATO meeting in Vienna. I have information she might want."

"One moment, please."

"James Preston. I can't talk. I'm in the middle of a conference. I understand you may have a scoop for me from the meetings in Vienna? I wish I could have been there."

"Me too. Is it difficult to talk, baby?"

"At the moment, Mister Preston."

"Mark your calendar. I will be home in a few days barring difficulty with flights" He hung up abruptly without saying goodbye. He packed and called for the bellman. When he came to the door, Palmer gave him a large tip and the information the bellman needed to check the luggage in at the airport. Just to be safe, he told the bellman to alert the baggage handlers to a possible change in his plans. He followed the bellman to the elevator. Palmer went directly to the front desk. He excused himself and asked if the couple next to him were on line.

"Oh no," the man answered, "We're waiting for the NATO conference to begin."

"Reporters?"

"Yes, we're here to cover the conference."

"Mister Preston, was everything satisfactory with your stay?" the deskman asked.

"It couldn't have been better."

"Good. We like to hear good reports. Your luggage is on its way to the airport. Here is your receipt. Let me be sure I have the correct flight number and gate. You are traveling on El Al flight C1066 to Tel Aviv, boarding at 6:05 p.m. Leaving tomorrow evening."

"That is not correct I thought I would spend some time in this lovely city looking for gifts for my wife and children. I wanted to make sure everything was in order." He placed bills on the desk. "I intend to stay at a hotel near the airport in case I can get an earlier flight."

"Well, that is very nice of you, sir." The desk clerk removed the bills quickly from the counter, stashing them away in his coat pocket.

"You earned it."

"May I call you a car?"

"No, that won't be necessary."

"Let me—"

"Don't bother, I know where the garage is."

"The woman at the counter with the other newsman watched Palmer until he disappeared into the stairwell.

"I am sorry, Harold. That Danish seems to have gone straight through me. Find us a seat near the exit. I'll find you."

"Can I get you anything?"

"Nothing will save me now."

"It is our embassy in Vienna. Palmer leaves on the 6:05 flight C1066 direct to Tel Aviv maybe this evening if he can get an earlier flight. A change of plans: He was not scheduled to leave until tomorrow."

"The embassy is sure it is him. Positive Identification by KGB posing as a reporter for Pravda Comrade Kasparov."

"Who is this person? Could this person have made a mistake?"

"No mistake, Comrade. He matches the descriptions we have."

Kasparov thanked the caller and asked him to hold on. His eyes shifted to Shevchenko.

"You were correct, Peter, the smear on the sink handle is hair dye. He has a full beard as well."

"Can we intercept him before he boards the flight?"

"We can't, not from here. We have to depend on our people in Vienna."

"Make sure Lila Chekov is part of whatever plan they use. She knows him. She must not be part of the intervention, only as a spotter. Make them understand this point...Also make sure they have a facial picture of him as he really looks. He could change his appearance."

"I understand, Comrade. The message will be forwarded with the warning attached.."

"Good . . .Very good. It is up to them to find and kill him. He must not leave the airport alive. What time is it?"

"A little past ten our time."

"Six hours. I wish you good luck, Comrade. Palmer is a dangerous man. Be careful." Kasparov hung up the wall phone inside Beria's room and returned to the table. "All we can do now is to be patient and hope our friends contact us with a positive response. In the meantime, we move on to other more important matters that directly involve us. Peter, why don't you start."

"I assume your meeting with Comrade Fedorov was what we all privately suspected?"

"Yes, Marina, our fears have been realized. Fedorov was very precise with his answers. He wants Palmer liquidated on sight. This story is much larger than a hunt for a deranged individual. They fear him . . . they fear Palmer's intentions. They see the disadvantages and must act. We will be the scapegoats if he lives and is captured. Have I relayed the essence of it, Comrade Kozlov?"

"Yes, my friend, except for one point. Even if he dies in Vienna, some of us will be blamed." Kozlov raised his glass and took a small drink of vodka, enough to relieve the dryness in his throat. "It does not end with Fedorov. He is too smart to take this trouble upon his shoulders."

"You mean members of the politburo and the army?"

"Higher up, Comrade Kasparov."

"Peter, may I repeat something we talked about the other day?"

"Please go on, Marina."

"The other day, after the four of us met, Peter and I had a discussion in the hall. I must admit the brief talk frightened me and I thought this cannot be. Peter Shevchenko must be paranoid." A few seconds of nervous laughter around the table. "But now as we talk and I learn more, I have come to the conclusion that we four and our loved ones are in grave danger. I see it as an excuse to rid the ruling class of old enemies. It is Stalin revisited and like Stalin, it is a cleansing of liberal thought."

"My dear Marina, what are you saying?"

"Let her finish, Dmitry." Marina swallowed a good portion of her drink. Like Vlad Kozlov, her throat suddenly felt very dry.

"We all remember the purges. It has been a long time since Stalin's era and why did the purges take place? Because a paranoid little man trusted no one and saw deceit in every face. It is happening again, comrades." Marina raised her glass to Shevchenko and finished her drink. "My throat is suddenly dry," she said and fell silent.

"What now?"

"We wait for Dmitry for the results in Vienna and while we wait, we plan for our future."

"Another purge?"

"Not yet. First Palmer must be liquidated. Then they will come for us."

VIENNA: JANUARY 7

Palmer washed off the black dye in his hair and shaved off the beard before leaving the hotel. He sighed grateful he could not make an earlier connection. He felt refreshed after a good night sleep. He changed clothes, and added a pair of black-rimmed glasses. He slipped on a grey fedora and flattened it so that it produced a more European look. Satisfied, he threw the clothes he wore the day before into the linen bag, picked up his travel bag and left the hotel deciding to walk the two blocks to the airport. He entered the airport, bought a newspaper walked into the lounge, and ordered a Dry Sack neat. Just as he opened the newspaper, he saw the young woman out of the corner of his eye. He watched her pass the lounge. She looked distracted, as if she were waiting for someone and he or she was late, and then she walked beyond his sight. He sat up straight in his chair. The Hotel. She had been in the ballroom having a coffee. When he had checked out, she had been by the counter.

"I'm a very horny and agitated man."

"Shut up, both of you." He drank the last of the liquor, got up—tucking the unread newspaper under his arm—and joined the people in the concourse. He found her at the El Al gate, looking a bit haggard. It was her. He did not panic. Instead, he leaned against a wall, unfolded the paper, and pretended to read. It might be nothing more than coincidence, but he had to be sure. She had a press pass on a string around her neck. Why would a Pravda reporter be here now with the meetings still going on? She could be KGB using press pass as a cover. Did they include Vienna in their search?

A young man carrying two suitcases walked up to the woman. He put the bags down and they embraced. She was whispering something to him. They kissed. It was more than a friendly kiss. They both picked up a suitcase and together walked arm and arm, passing him.

"I'm sorry I'm late. We have time darling, let's have a drink," the young man was saying.

"Why is she still wearing her press pass?" He folded the newspaper.

"I need to see pain and you worry over a young couple. I need action . . .we need action."

"Shut up . . .shut up Mom." Coincidence, he assured himself, but the press pass bothered him.

"You are being paranoid, Wayne. You do foolish things when you are agitated like this. Remember that Schmidt whore. You need to calm down, Wayne. You need to find relief.

"Shut up, mom. Shut up and stop calling me Wayne." He walked to the white phone on the opposite side of the concourse and asked the operator to page John Palmer. He put the phone down, opened the newspaper, and returned to his place on the opposite wall.

"Excuse me, sir," the young man said, "Sorry to bother you but could you tell me where you picked up the newspaper?"

"You can have this one."

"I couldn't. Let me pay you?"

"Take it. Your friend is a reporter for Pravda. I noticed the press pass."

"Yes, she has been covering the meetings at the Grand Wien hotel. Now we are off to Tel Aviv to cover some sort of conference on the Middle East. It never ends. Goodbye."

"Paranoid, that's what you are." He started to walk down the concourse. The young man was at the bar ordering drinks. Palmer's name was announced. Neither the young man or woman flinched. He turned and walked back toward the El Al departure gate. The press pass: He couldn't let it go.

"You were right. It is Palmer. He has shaved his beard, washed the dye out of his hair and changed clothes. He looks like an English gentleman. I must say I like the glasses. I thought it was a nice touch." He set the two steins of beer on the table and sat down. "When can we expect Nicholai of Kiev?"

"He is here; he arrived moments ago. He needed to use the bathroom."

"I hope he hasn't had a case of nerves."

"He needed to take a piss Andre. "Here he comes. Why don't you ask him if he is nervous?"

"Nicholai, sit down. Is that coffee?"

"It is coffee before my work . . . vodka after. Is Chekov here, Nadia?"

"Yes. Chekov is here. Palmer has been to the gate checking the flight time twice already."

"You look exhausted , you should have slept."

"And who would watch for him if he was able to leave last night?"

"Of course you are right, my apologies…What about Chekov. Describe her to me."

"How she looks is not important. She is not to be involved. Have you studied the plan?"

"It is a good plan."

"She is your backup. I understand she is merciless. She will not be with us. She knows Palmer and he knows her."

"How do they know each other?"

"I do not know, Nicholai, and I do not ask," Andre answered.

Nadia checked her watch. "One hour until boarding. Take a walk through the concourse, try to spot him, memorize his face and clothing. He dressed in English clothes. He wears black rimmed glasses under a hat. No beard. If things go wrong, remember: he must not survive even if it means we die with him. Finish your coffee."

"Meet us at the gate in fifty minutes exactly. Set your watch to mine. We will be able to see where he stands on the line of borders." They stacked their hands one upon another. "For Mother Russia."

"For Mother Russia," the two male conspirators answered. "Nadia, you should have removed the press pass," Nicholai said. He stood up and walked out of the lounge.

Nicholai entered the men's room and found an empty stall. He removed his parka. He removed the silencer from the coat pocket, pulled the 9 mm Makarov from the specially designed holster, screwed the silencer into place, and holstered the weapon. He flushed the toilet and put on the coat. Back on the concourse he bought a second coffee and began to stroll the concourse. He passed the El Al gate. The man he was looking for was not there. He moved on, sipping his coffee and admiring the young women without drawing attention to himself.

He stopped at each eatery looking over the menus while glancing inside the restaurant for a sign of his quarry. He read the menu of the last restaurant and began to walk back over the route, just in case Palmer was behind him on the concourse. He checked his watch: thirty minutes to boarding. Where are you?

Nicholai approached the BOAC gate and looked quickly at the destination board blinking: Bern, Switzerland Flight 1108 now boarding. He looked away for a glimpse of the young woman, tall, thin and wearing a floppy hat. Her eyes were masked by oversize sunglasses: a model perhaps. He turned his attention back to the gate, concentrating on the blank faces. Too late to see the tall man in the English cut suit enter the tunnel while Nicholai was giving one more admiring glance toward the young woman. The sway of her hips held his attention a moment too long. He did not know it was Lila Chekov.

MOSCOW

The phone rang in Kasparov's office. The clock on the wall near the window read 6:33. Kasparov pressed the speaker button and took a deep breath, blowing it out in a rush.

"Kasparov here."

"My car broke down. I am at the repair station now. The mechanic tells me it will take time to repair. I missed the mailman, Comrade Kasparov."

Shevchenko grasped Marina's hand and squeezed it tightly. "It has been a long day. We will go to supper now."

"First things first," Shevchenko began. "Marina, tomorrow morning, as soon as you arrive at work, call the American Embassy to make arrangements for lunch with Norm Patterson. Also call Boris. Call him from a phone on the square."

"Yes, sir. Any instructions on where to meet Mister Patterson?"

"Due to the weather conditions, I will meet him in front of his embassy."

"Why are you meeting with the American CIA man?"

"Comrade Kozlov, who best to acquire a large package of travel papers then the American. I cannot very well go to Comrade Fedorov, can I? He thinks he is getting forged travel papers from Fontaine in Paris for four of us. Do we have a count from each of you what relatives are to leave, should it come to that?"

"Yes," each answered.

"Make sure it is correct. We will not be able to change it later."

"Fedorov will cringe if he finds out."

"You are quite right, Dmitry. He must not find out."

"How much will you tell, Patterson?"

"I will tell him enough to convince him of the seriousness of the situation, Comrade Kozlov. I will leave it up to him. I will give him the name of the double agent to convince them our motives are not a ruse. It will be up to them to do as they wish."

"How do we do this without direct help from the Americans, Peter?"

"We cannot, Dmitry."

BERN, SWITZERLAND: JANUARY 10

"What the hell are you doing in Bern, Switzerland?" Frank Graham asked.

"I think I was spotted in Vienna. I can't be sure, so I made other arrangements. Never mind that now. Listen to me. I will be in Tel Aviv tomorrow and New York on the twenty-third if everything goes as planned. I was going stir crazy in that house all these months waiting for Golan. Have you settled things with Dukakis?"

"I can't reach him because he's out of town and off the grid. I know one apartment was vacated two months ago. I don't know if they held it."

"Call that idiot Senator Spencer. Tell him to take care of it for me. If he gives you shit, tell him I will out him and he can spend the rest of his miserable life in federal prison staring at pictures of young girls and jerking off in his cell. Give that pig the message . . . We can't screw it up now, Frank."

"It will get it done, count on it. Anything else I should know?"

"I told Maxine I will be coming to America. No more travel."

"You think that was wise, John?"

"She's a good lay, Frank. I will need the time with her to relax while I wait for Golan's people."

MOSCOW: JANUARY 11

Shevchenko checked the upgraded Volga-12. The new version had a redesigned gas tank. The interior was upgraded, the seats were thicker and formed nicely against the body of the driver, there was more leg room, a better heater and in some models, air conditioners. There were even larger tires for a smoother ride and a suspension system geared to slip resistant brakes.

"Ladas?" he called, closing the apartment door.

"I am here, fixing us a drink. I have the fire going. I didn't cook. I didn't know if you would be hungry, but I can fix something if you like. We have fresh pork chops." Ladas appeared from the kitchen carrying two glasses, each half full of red wine. She was wearing her sable fur and slippers.

She handed him his drink, kissed him, and looked straight into his eyes. "You look worried; your face is sad. Tell me."

"I will." He took a sip of the drink. "I am very concerned. Let's sit down, Ladas. We need to talk."

"Are you leaving me?"

"No, I am not."

"Then it is settled. Nothing is more important, except me putting my things away. I have taken up much of the closet space. I had to move your things to the closet in the third bedroom."

"Sit down and listen."

CHAPTER NINETEEN

Adrian Stonewall Spencer was called Ass, the insult first introduced by his secretary Mavis Powell. Another name she thought appropriate: asparagus, signifying his manhood. Mavis Powell would know. More than a few senators and their aides had fished in her pond.

Spencer stood in front of the liquor cabinet deciding what to have for his first drink of the day. Today was special so the drink should be as well. Today marked his 44th year in the Senate. He had arrived with a net worth of $83,000. His present worth, in dollars and property, was almost $71 million, only $2 million short of his age. Not bad for a backwoods boy with a falsified sheepskin from U. of Virginia that he proudly displayed behind his desk.

He decided on Kentucky Bourbon. He took his first sip, rolled it in his mouth, and swallowed it. His private phone rang. "Mavis, come in here and let me see you." The good 'ol boy twang, though diminished over the years, was his trademark.

"It is a private call on line one, Senator. Some things need to be private."

"Don't we know that, you precious girl. Is it my wife?"

"No, Senator, he is a gentleman caller."

"Do me a thing will you? Call the majority leader and inform him I will vote yes, and when I'm through with this call, come in here and show me what you're wearing."

He pressed the key and said hello.

"Senator, it's Frank Graham. A friend will be coming to New York on the twenty-third of this month. He needs you to ensure two apartments will be available."

"Where is Dukakis?"

"Mister Dukakis seems to be out of touch at present, so I'm calling you. I know we can count on you. Get it done by the end of next week. Our mutual friend must have access."

"I can't promise. I'll try, but you have to…"

"Maybe you didn't hear me, Spencer," Graham interrupted. "You will comply with his needs."

He was about to respond when the line went dead. Mavis Powell swept into the office. She was a beautiful woman of forty in a red dress cut low enough to make the old man smile. She also had the secretarial skills of a mannequin.

"You look like you've seen a ghost, honey."

"Bourbon neat."

MOSCOW: JANUARY 16

"I will have food sent up to the conference room. Sorry about the delay getting back to you. We'll have privacy and we can talk. I might even offer you a vodka, Peter."

"Why not eat in the cafeteria if it's privacy you want."

"We could eat in my office."

"The cafeteria would be the better choice."

"I understand, Peter. Thanks. Shall we go inside?"

"That one is for Minsk, Norm." They shook hands. "I have more to ask of you. We'll talk."

CIA HEADQUARTERS, LANGLEY: JANUARY 16

Ronald Timmons folded his hands on his desk, his expression grim. "Let me begin by saying nothing in this report leaves this office. Am I clear?"

"Clear, sir," Ham and Drum answered together.

"A move on Afghanistan to prop up a failing regime is still on the table for later next year, depending on events that have yet to take place. Now that you both have read it, what do you say?"

"Above all else, he is a Russian and a man who fought for its salvation as a teenager. Whatever else he became, he loves his country." Angela sat forward in her chair, "I think you agree with us . . . am I right, Ronald?"

"We can't verify any of this. Shevchenko is an enemy of the United States. We've tried to kill him."

"Well, Ronald, in that context, aren't we all like him in one way or another?"

"If we act on this information, who do we turn to for assistance without causing a panic? We must verify at least Palmer's existence and his where-abouts. How do we do that without tipping our hand?"

"The information we have so far is he is coming here through Israel. We don't know how high Israeli intelligence or government is involved, but we know we can trust Bernard Aaron. The question is: Can he verify Palmer is really using Israel as a jumping off point, as Shevchenko says? It certainly would move a piece of the puzzle into place."

"It is a very small piece at best... From now on we will just use the letter B; when discussing Bernard.

"Yes, of course. Angela answered. "We should also alert the State Department and of course the White House chief of staff."

"No," Simmons answered in a stern voice. "They are too involved with the Camp David accords. Plus, we would never get a finding from the president, not with what we know."

"Then what do we do . . . sit on our hands?"

"Of course not, Angela. Shevchenko talks about a person of interest in MI-6 who is feeding information to the KGB through a mistress. He claims to know who it is and has given Patterson the name. Why?"

"It may be his ace in the hole or he is playing the card to hopefully secure our help for his friends," Drum added.

"The nerve is bulging on your forehead. I know the look. What are you thinking, Ronald?"

"I'll tell you what I'm thinking, Angela. I suggest Colonel Shevchenko give us more background as a sign of good faith. Something we can hang our hat on. It must be enough to satisfy us that he is being earnest and this is not a sham."

"I still think we should ask B. He would be able to move about without suspicion and find out when and if Palmer arrives in Israel and who he talks to."

"Palmer met once with Abel Golan, Angela."

"My point is made. B must be involved. Send the cipher to Patterson tonight insisting that Colonel Shevchenko do as we ask."

"What if Shevchenko refuses?"

"Then he ties our hands. Send the cipher."

"We'll meet again when he responds. Also, cable Patterson."

"Hello Ronald."

"I know, and I am sorry Beatrice, but he is the only counsel I trust. The president can't pass gas without the New York Times printing it the next day."

"I know you wouldn't call unless it was urgent. Hold a moment. He is working on his manuscript. I will tell him it is you and it is important. By the way, you can say fart, Ronald. I am not a prude."

"Thank you, Beatrice. I will remember that."

MOSCOW

Ladas curled up next to him, folding her legs under her thighs.

"The fire feels wonderful." She sipped her coffee. "It is almost too warm with this robe on; should I take it off?" She hoped he would take the bait.

"First we must finish our conversation. It is too important to put off any longer."

"At least taste the biscuit I made for you."

"Delicious, the butter is in every corner. Where were you able to get grape jelly?"

"Being the widow of a dead general has its . . . how do they say in America?"

"Perks. It certainly has its . . . perks." He picked up a second biscuit and put it whole into his mouth.

"Tell me, Peter, that I will like America."

"You will like it very much."

"You sound like a capitalist, Shevchenko. Be careful."

"You just proved my point."

"I will fix more coffee; do not go away."

"Stay just as you are. I will fix coffee, Ladas, and bring it to you."

"Thank you, Mister Shevchenko."

"While I fix another cup, think of a name you might like: an American sounding name."

"This is really happening, isn't it?"

"I am afraid it is." He disappeared into the kitchen. He returned with two steaming cups of coffee.

"I have thought of a name," she said, taking the cup from him. "Miriam Baker. I love to bake, so I thought it would go well."

"Why did you choose Miriam?"

"My great grandmother was named Miriam. I asked my mother once why no one in the family was named after her. She told me Stalin would not allow Jewish sounding names on birth certificates."

"I suppose Peter Baker sounds American enough. I used the name Peter Grant when I was last there."

"I like Miriam Grant. Baker will be my writer's name. Where will we live?"

"I thought in a state in the northeast. The climate is close to what we are used to and, of course, your love of good fresh fish. I will ask Marina to teach you some dialect from the region enough to fit in."

"I like your accent, Peter."

BERN, SWITZERLAND

"Maxine Fisher-Barnett, how is the news business these days?"

"James Preston. I'm fine, where are you?"

"Bern, Switzerland. On my way to Tel Aviv. On the twenty-third of this month, I will arrive at Kennedy airport at 5:30 p.m. I expect a very warm welcome."

"Expect a warm welcome. Is the move permanent?"

"Yes, starting on the twenty-third, I will be in America the rest of my life."

"My husband will be thrilled; we'll come and pick you up at the airport."

"You can't talk, Maxine?"

"Yes, that's right."

"When can I call you at home?"

"Any time before five our time tomorrow or any day . . . We'll talk then, goodbye."

MOSCOW: JANUARY 17

"I think I would like a pastry from the bakery, Comrade Shevchenko. My sweet tooth is nagging me like an overprotective mother. Can I get you something?"

"You know, Marina, I might just join you. Transfer the calls to our exchange. Let's both get some air."

"It is zero degrees with wind gusts, Comrade Shevchenko. We could go to Saint Basil's?"

"Ah a possible convert to the Christian faith? What people will do for a pastry, Marina."

"I do not think I can close my eyes," Marina whispered when they entered the great Cathedral. "My face feels like I have covered it in a sheet of plaster."

"Drink the coffee. Rub some holy water on your eyes; it will help them and perhaps save your soul, Marina Checkoff."

"Do not mock what you do not believe nor understand, Peter Shevchenko."

"I understand cold, hunger, and loss. Where was this God then . . . Shall we sit?" He led her to a pew. They drank their coffee. "Patterson sent a message. It seems the American CIA needs more background information. I would assume they are not convinced."

"They have to study everything under a microscope."

"I am sure we do not give them much reason to trust us."

"The more they waste time, the more Palmer becomes a danger to them." Shevchenko sighed and finished his coffee in one swallow, "We gave them the English fellow and the Israeli general as proof. What more do they want from us?"

"You are worried?"

"Yes, I am, Marina . . . quite worried."

"I will contact Patterson as soon as we return to the office."

"Pray, Marina . . .pray."

TEL AVIV: JANUARY 21

Palmer entered the terminal in Tel Aviv, following the hall marked with a four-inch-wide green stripe. Security checkpoints and military personnel armed with Uzi machine guns monitored travelers making their way toward customs. Face recognition cameras embedded in the walls studied each visitor such as passengers who avoided eye contact, people who seemed nervous constantly touching their faces. Cameras hidden in lights recorded rustling hair or adjusted clothing that looked to the watchful eye a size too large for their body type.

Palmer, dressed nattily in an English cut sports jacket and dark slacks, carried a single suitcase, his face impassive until he passed a soldier talking heatedly on the phone to a woman he called Bernadette. Palmer shook his head and walked on.

Major Shapiro shifted his position. "Palmer just passed me. You should spot him very soon." He described what Palmer was wearing and hung up.

Palmer walked to the ticket counter to ensure his flight to New York had been properly booked and his papers and passport properly documented. A young woman behind the counter motioned for him to come forward.

"The neck looks right. She has nice tits," the voice, like acid in his skull said. "We have needs, Wayne. You are disappointing us. Your father is getting angry."

"Shut up, both of you."

"Welcome, sir. Are you traveling today?"

"No, I just arrived. I wanted to check my flight plans. My flight isn't for two more days. Here is my passport and ticket."

"May I see another form of identification?"

"Of course." He produced a false ID card, a driver's license, and an American Express card he purchased from the French forger, Fontaine. "It is me," he said, slipping off the horn-rimmed glasses.

"You would be surprised how many people cannot produce a second photo ID . . ." she looked at the cards, "Mister Preston. They waste their time and ours."

"I completely understand."

"Let me check and make sure everything is in order. It will take a few moments our computers need to be upgraded."

"That is why I am here. I sell and service the latest in computer hardware." he glanced at her name tag. "Miriam, a beautiful name. I always liked the name."

"I am most happy. It is as ancient as our people before Moses or Noah. I suspect, before time."

"You look more Egyptian than Jewish, Miriam. I mean no disrespect."

"Americans, you are a funny people. You are in the Middle East, Mister Preston. We have different customs and religious beliefs. We do not dress alike or treat women the same. Strip all that away and we all emerged from the same desert, isn't that so?"

"You are a very wise and lovely young lady . . . Miriam."

"Thank you, Mister Preston. Let me look into this for you so we can get you on your way. Where are you staying?"

"I've booked a reservation at the Royal Beach Hotel."

"Good choice. The restaurants in and around the hotel are excellent. When we are finished here, follow the signs to our taxi station. Leave time for the ride. It is about two hours, maybe three, depending on the traffic. They accept credit cards."

A beep sounded in her ear that only she could hear.

"Excellent conversation. We have learned a lot about Mister Preston. You handled him very well. Now, listen carefully. He is a friend to Israel and poses no threat. I vouch for him," Abel Golan said. A second beep alerted her the connection was clear.

"Here we are at last. Ah, I've found you. Everything is in order. I can assign a seat now, if you like."

"That would be most appreciated, Miriam."

"Do you have a preference?"

"Aisle and bulkhead, if you can manage it."

"You are finished . . . simply report to the boarding area two hours before departure. Maybe you could fix our computers while you are here?"

"I will do my best."

"Have a wonderful stay and thank you for choosing my country."

"You should have invited her to meet you later. She's got great tits."

"Shut up, damn you. If you keep quiet, maybe I'll go out later tonight . . .

no promises. I can't screw up now."

"What about us?"

"Remember the rule? I choose when and where. Now shut up." He was abruptly interrupted by a man's voice behind him as he made his way to the taxi station."

"Be in your room at 9:00 p.m. this evening; you will be visited." The man sidestepped him. "Make sure you are in your room." He picked up his pace mingling with the other tourists.

"I am not a child to be manipulated, general," he muttered and made his way to the cab stand. He had paid in advance for the cab with his untraceable American Express card.

"Royal Beach Hotel."

"You've made an excellent choice. sir."

"So I've been told."

Major Shapiro stood on the curb and adjusted his tie with three pulls. With the thumb and index fingers of both hands he straightened his hair. He scratched his nose using his index finger. Cab 341 was now under the watchful eyes of the Mossad.

"Miss Loeb, I have to make a call. I will only be a minute."

"Do you need to leave the counter?"

"No, Miss Loeb, I can use the phone at your desk."

"Of course, I will cover for you." The woman left her desk and walked over to the counter. "Go ahead, Miriam. May I help the next couple in line?"

Miriam walked around to the opposite side of the desk, dialed the number she had memorized, and waited.

"Hello, it is Miriam," she whispered when a male voice came on the line.

"Hold on, Miriam. He is right here."

"Yes, Miriam, you have word for me?"

"Yes, sir. He left the airport by cab. He is staying at the Royal Beach Hotel. He is being followed, in case he lied to me. One more thing, you were correct about Golan. He called on my earphone and intervened on the man's behalf."

"You have done very well, Miriam . . . many thanks. You may resume your duties," Bernard Aaron said.

"He asked if I was Egyptian."

"What did you tell him?"

"I told him he is in the Middle East. We are different but all came from the same desert."

"A wonderful response, Miriam. I think I will use it if you do not mind me stealing your line."

"I do not mind at all, sir. Shalom Aleichem." She hung up and went back to her station with a blush on her face. Israel had saved her from a wasted life on the street, and in a small way, she could begin to repay the people of Israel.

"I can finish up, Miss Loeb, if you need to return to your duties."

"I will finish. Why not take your break now before the next flight arrives?"

"All right, Miss Loeb. I won't be long."

"Miriam, my friends call me Penny. Before you ask, it is short for Penelope. I was born in Cleveland, Ohio."

She turned to the people at the counter. "Let's see if we have all the correct information so we get you two on your way."

The small café was not full. She could have a quick coffee and maybe a hardboiled egg, enough to satisfy her hunger until she went home to her small apartment.

"May I buy you a coffee, Miriam?"

"Major Shapiro, you startled me."

"I apologize."

"I haven't much time, Major. Miss Loeb is covering for me. Our breaks are short." Miriam felt flattered and frightened all at once. He was indeed handsome. She had an assorted past she was not proud of. Accepting a cup of coffee would be leading him on. "But thank you, Major."

"I Just now spoke to Miss Loeb. She doesn't see a problem with it and if you do not mind, my first name is Jonah. By the way, did you pass the information along?"

"You do not understand. I am not what you might think. I was a bad person . . . now I am a good person, and yes, I called."

"I completely understand, Leila. We all have secrets. I am a divorced man. My army career kept me away too long. I must also warn you, if you agree to have coffee with me, I will ask you to have supper with me soon. Now, may I buy a beautiful woman of Israel a coffee?"

"You may, Major Jonah Shapiro."

"How did it go with Mister Patterson? You seem distracted or worried, which is it, Peter? I am most curious."

"I gave the CIA the information they requested along with the list of names and photos of who will need the proper papers for travel. I can do no more. We will wait now for their response. One way or the other, the Palmer situation needs to be brought to a solution. When we return to the office, Marina, I want you to call Colonel Gusev. We need to stop this Dupree fellow and his investigation."

"Does Ladas understand the situation?"

"She would like you to help her with a special accent."

"Would it be a southern drawl?"

"I need to talk to Gusev."

"Comrade Gusev, thank you for returning my call."

"Your secretary mentioned the Frenchman Dupree; I assume you have found more evidence?"

"Yes, I have, Comrade. We know who this murderer is. His name is John Michael Palmer. I tell you this because I am sure you will not reveal it publicly. I will explain why."

"I would be most interested, Comrade Shevchenko. Please give me a moment."

"Fixing a glass of tea, Gusev?"

"I have turned off my recorder. I am rewinding it, Comrade Shevchenko."

"He is an American traitor living in Bryansk Oblast."

"How did you come to this conclusion and when?"

"I will explain. Tell me, Comrade, have you ever smoked an American cigarette?"

"Yes, I love them. I believe a Camel was on the package."

"Tomorrow, look for a box in your mail."

"A man in your position would not offer . . ."

"I would not think of it. Accept it as a gift from a newfound friend."

"In that case, I would be a fool to refuse, Peter Shevchenko."

"Good, Comrade Gusev. Now listen carefully."

LANGLEY

"It is a lot to swallow. I cannot believe the Iranian regime would think to do such a foolish thing, let alone actually attempt it."

"What do you think, Angela?"

"I don't know what to think."

"What is your best guess, Angela?"

"I say probably a year or less. The American Embassy will be the target."

"What is your estimate, Sidney?"

"The end of the year. I would bet around a holiday here."

"I agree with you both on that point The embassy has a small Marine guard. A mob could over run it within hours. Sidney, we need to inform 10 Downing Street directly," Simmons added. "No one in MI-6 or 5. It may be just Pepper or it may involve others. Remember 1963. Give John Scarlett the name of his mistress."

"What about Afghanistan?"

"Let the Russians have it. They can't win."

"Is the man in Paris our choice for Shevchenko and his people?"

"No Angela, I do not trust that man. I want you to contact Delmer Hauptman, the Dutch printer in Holland. He has done work for me before. He is the Da Vinci of forged documents. I have a few items he did for me when I was active. Call me after you have taken care of the other matters and I will tell you how to get in touch with him."

"You know something about the man in Paris?"

"The Russians use this man. I would bet Palmer used him. Anyway, Hauptman's work is far superior. I'll show you."

TEL AVIV: ROYAL BEACH HOTEL

At precisely 8:00 p.m., there was a knock on the door of Palmer's room. He paused, waiting for a second knock.

"Let Golan wait for me," he whispered. A second knock. Palmer smiled with satisfaction and went to the door. The visitor was not General Golan and not the same man in Vienna.

"Can I come in? You look surprised. Did you really think the general would visit you here if he wouldn't in Vienna?"

Palmer stepped aside to let his visitor pass. He closed the door, almost slamming it. "Which one are you?"

"I am Joseph Horowitz. I am here to inform you of how this activity will be carried out. I believe you and the general have agreed that the materials you requested would be better shipped by a source not connected to the military. However, the general does not feel comfortable with the address you furnished."

"You want a drink, Joseph?"

"No."

"Would it be okay if I have one?"

"Have as many as you like, Palmer, just as long as you remember this conversation."

"You, Jews, really . . ."

"Choose your next words carefully, Palmer. This isn't 1935. You are in our house. Shall I continue?"

"Yes . . . continue." Palmer filled his glass almost to the brim, but did not drink. "What is the alternative the general suggests?"

"I have everything you need to know." Joseph picked the thick envelope from inside his coat pocket and placed it on the seat of a high back chair. "Do you have any questions?"

"The general . . . will I see him before I leave?"

"That is up to the general. I do not know what his thoughts are. He did suggest you stay close to your room."

"Yes, of course, I know."

"An associate of mine is removing tapes from the cameras in the entrance to the hotel, as well as the lobby and this floor. I am sure you understand the need for security?"

"Yes, of course," a deflated Palmer answered.

"Then I will say goodnight, Palmer. Please read the notes in the envelope and memorize the contents. Someone will remove them from your room tomorrow."

"What do I do for food and companionship, if I desire it?"

"Room service, but you knew that. As far as companionship, I think the hotel can manage that as well."

"Goodnight and goodbye. I'm sure we won't meet again." Palmer picked up his glass and drank.

"We will not, unless, of course, I am forced to return." Joseph opened the door, looked right and left down the corridor. The door closed behind him.

Palmer finished the drink, poured a second drink, picked up the envelope, and padded into the bedroom. He showered and shaved, deciding against a meal. He slipped on a robe, picked up the envelope, tore it open, and pulled out the contents. He sat down on the edge of the bed and began to read. He grimaced, emptied the glass of its contents, and laid back on the bedspread. Six hours later, he awakened.

"You need to get up, get dressed, and go out. We need to go out."

"Do you realize where we are, Dad?"

MOSCOW: JANUARY 21

Marina sorted the daily mail. When she finished sorting the stacks in order of priority, she knocked once on his door and entered. "Your mail, Comrade. You have a note from your friend in Minsk and the book you ordered on American presidents has finally come."

"Read what Boris has written, would you, while I look over this book?"

"He will be honored to be by your side when you hunt the wild Boar."

Shevchenko smiled but said nothing as he opened the package. Inside was a book on American presidents and the cipher he had been waiting for.

"Would you like to respond to your friend Boris?"

"Yes, Marina. Please tell him I will be in touch with travel plans in a few days. Tell him the hunting should be good this year."

"Is that the book you wanted?"

"Yes." Shevchenko held up the cipher from Timmons. "You have spoiled me with your idea of a pastry in the morning, Marina. Give me a moment to read the prologue to my new book and we will go out."

"I will send a note to Comrade Molotov. Shall I close the door?"

"That won't be necessary, Marina. I won't be long."

"By the way, I noticed Boris only mentioned himself."

"His wife does not like to hunt."

"Of course."

Forty minutes later, they entered Saint Basil's. Shevchenko carried the coffee containers and pastries in a small box. Marina sat down, rubbing her hands over her face.

"Is America this cold?"

"Nothing on earth is this cold when a winter like this one comes. They say it is the coldest since 1941," Kasparov volunteered.

"Let us drink, eat our pastry, and then we will talk. I will say this, the answer from America is positive."

"If it comes to that, Peter, my husband and I would like to go to Israel to live. If they will even accept us."

"I thought as much, Marina. Drink your coffee and enjoy this wonderful pastry. I think we will use the prison from now on to meet. Even spending time in Cell 15 is better than walking across the square in this weather, comrades, yes?"

"What about Comrade Kozlov?"

"Get a message to him when we return to the office."

LANGLEY: JANUARY 21

"We have word from our friend in Israel and the prime minister in London, boss," Sidney offered, when he and Angela entered Timmons's office.

"Good, but first a little test for you two. Step over to the map table. I have placed six separate forgeries with my real identity, license, credit cards, etc. Angela, you first. Decide on the one you think is a forgery and the one you think is real."

"No tricks, Ronald?"

"No tricks. Five are false; only one set came out of my pocket this very morning. Take your time. No coffee and no bear claws, Sidney?"

"Sorry, boss."

"Never mind. I had Mona set a tray for us. I'll ring her while Angela decides what's real and what is fake."

Timmons picked up the phone. "Mona, you can bring in the treats and put one aside for yourself?"

"I think I have it."

"Very good, Angela, let's have a look." Timmons walked around his desk and stepped over to the map table. "Show me which ones you've picked."

"I see he has you hooked, too, Mrs. Manning-Ham. I hope you have better luck then I did." Mona smiled .

"This one is Hauptman and this one is yours."

"They were both created by Hauptman. Sidney, why don't you try your luck. I will shuffle the two Angela picked back into the pile. Take your time, Sidney."

"I have ten dollars that says Sidney Drum gets it wrong."

"How can you be so sure, Mona?"

"He showed me the real ones, Mrs. Manning-Ham, and told me to turn my back then he mixed them up and I'll be damned if he didn't fool me."

"I've got it, boss."

"Show me, Sidney"

"You are wrong. One is Hauptman and the other the Frog. I told you he is the Da Vinci of forgers. Now to work. Thank you, Mona."

Timmons stepped behind his desk and sat down, "So, where are we?"

"You aren't going to show us the difference?"

"No. Okay, Drum. Talk to me."

"Palmer is staying in the Royal Beach Hotel in Tel Aviv. He has had one visitor: this man. We think he is with Shin Bet. His name is Joseph Horowitz. He could be a contractor."

"Sir John sent a note thanking you for your message. He informed the Prime Minister. She met with the young lady last evening. In two weeks, she would like you to attend a formal dinner for this fellow, Pepper. The purpose of the affair is to celebrate his forty years of service to the crown. He is to be knighted."

"That should be interesting, especially the part about knighthood. That tells me the queen knows nothing about his other activities. It also tells me the prime minister is no one to piss off. It is both very clever and utterly ruthless."

"There is more. She is also inviting Ronald Reagan and his wife, Nancy, to visit."

"Inform the Prime Minister I would be honored to attend the dinner. Also tell her I think a private meeting outside the eyes and ears of the press with Mr. Reagan is a stroke of genius. I will contact Hauptman."

TEL AVIV: JANUARY 22

The young housemaid finished cleaning the bathroom, picked up her supplies and walked into the living space. She spied Palmer on the deck eating his breakfast.

She padded over to the bar and opened the refrigerator, making a mental note to have food service refill the space. She checked the bottles of liquor on the bar, stepped over to the sliding door, and tapped lightly on the glass.

"I am finished, unless there is something else you need?"

He waved her off without looking up from his breakfast. The phone rang, the irritating sound like a chirping crow.

"Hello?" The door to the hall closed. "Well, General, should you be calling me?"

"Sarcasm aside, Palmer, I hope the room is satisfactory."

"It's fine . . . everything is fine." Palmer looked over his shoulder. The sheaths of papers left for him to read and memorize were gone. "I must say your housekeeping staff is excellent and attentive to detail. The room is immaculate. Even the papers you left for me have been removed."

"Did you memorize the content of the papers?"

"It's all in my head. If we are through, I'd like to get back to my breakfast."

"Not quite, Palmer; something has come up. I am afraid a flight tomorrow from Tel Aviv to New York is out of the question."

Is he out of his mind? the voice in his head growled.

"Shut up."

Out loud he said, "I can't stay here. We had an agreement, General. Let me remind you of the five months you forced me to stay in the Oblast while you—"

"We have picked up traffic between the Americans and London." The general did not want to leave a stone behind that might be discovered later, linking him to Palmer.

"What traffic?"

"Well now, Palmer, do you really think I can divulge how we can track a secret communication between friendly nations?"

"I'm sitting in this room alone and now you tell me I can't leave."

"We can provide female company for you, if you wish, since you are so concerned with being alone. Of course, your sexual needs may preclude intimacy."

"What's that supposed to mean, General?"

"I think we both know Palmer. By the way, have you ever heard the name Francois Dupree? He is an analyst with Interpol."

"No, should I?"

"It isn't important for our business relationship."

"I want to stick to the damn plan, General."

"Too dangerous. At noon on the twenty-eighth a car will pick you up. You will be taken to a private airfield. A private jet will carry you to Jordan, from there to Sweden. On February 3, you can go to America."

"You call that a short stay? What if I tell you to go fuck yourself and leave tomorrow anyway?"

"Then, of course, our relationship will end and the man who visited you on your first day in Tel Aviv will have to permanently resolve the issue. I am putting together a team of mercenaries to assist you. It will take a bit of time."

"You are protecting yourself, Golan?"

"Of course I am. Be patient, Palmer."

"How will I know this driver?"

"You have already met her. She cleaned your room."

SOURASKY MEDICAL CENTER
TEL AVIV: JANUARY 24

"Mrs. Stein, good morning. How is our patient today?"

"She is doing quite well, General Golan. I feel secure Sylvia will make a full recovery. Doctor Levinson and Doctor Marks from New York are very pleased. They are convinced the new skin will not be rejected. There is no sign of infection. Our patient is very excited with the results."

"What about her other injuries?"

"Her shoulder is healing. Her left leg had multiple fractures. The good news is our orthopedic surgeons were able to fix things nicely. She will need extensive rehab, as you might imagine."

"When can I visit her?"

"Sylvia's mother has authority over visitations. Her burns are covered with a special damp wrap. A sterile environment is mandatory in cases such as hers. I will address your request with Doctor Spitzer and her mother. He is charged with her health and his word is final. I hope you understand."

"Of course. Please let 'Sylvia' know I called and let her know she is in our prayers."

"I will, General Golan."

"Does Doctor Spitzer have a goal set for her release?"

"The process is going well, as I said before. I wouldn't expect her release until sometime in June, perhaps July. That is only a guess, General. Rehabilitation will depend completely on her."

"Sylvia is like a daughter to me. You can understand my concern."

"I do General."

Palmer stepped out onto the balcony. He admired the view, the lights of the city defiant against the enemies who would seek its destruction. The scent of the eucalyptus in the air drifted up to his deck. It is just past 4:00 p.m. in Washington, I'll give a little more time before I call Maxine. He sat on the lounge chair and sipped his coffee, below him the traffic noises rose against the darkened sky.

"We are going to Sweden: how wonderful.?"

He looked up. Leaning against the railing, the gaunt terrible figures stared back, "Yes we are," he answered. "Let me think. Leave me alone."

"We've never been to Stockholm. Will you go out?"

"I don't know."

"From what we've heard, Wayne, the women are most affable and free of inhibitions."

"Do not push me."

"We've waited patiently, Wayne."

"I said don't push me." Palmer looked at his watch. "I need to make a call."

"Is it that bitch Maxine?"

"Shut up and get out." He dialed Maxine's home phone.

"Hello . . . Yes, operator, I will take the call, thank you."

"These phones are not secure. We have to be careful. I have news there is a delay in my departure. I must go to Stockholm for the company's big sales meeting. I could earn a lot of money if it goes through. I will fly home on February 3. It's important I go. It can't be helped."

"Dammit James, I've made plans for us." Her voice was loud, emotional, almost a screech. "Delay spoils everything."

"Calm down Maxine, it isn't the end of the world. I miss you, baby, but I have to do this. Then we'll be together whenever we can."

"You don't understand, James."

"So, make me understand, Maxine."

"We really haven't discussed our situation once you come home."

"I thought we had a relationship, Maxine, based on our specific needs and desires. Was I wrong?"

"You are not wrong. It is me; I've changed… I told my husband."

He closed his eyes and put his head back against the cushion of the chair. His face froze. A sudden flash of extreme heat rose out of the collar of his shirt. Control yourself; take control of your emotions while you are still on the phone. Take a deep breath and hold it until you are calm enough to continue.

"Are you still there, James?"

"Yes, of course I'm here." A false laugh. "It is just unexpected; you can understand, can't you?" Calming down shows no sign of discontent; the anger you feel is very real. "I'm thrilled. What a wonderful surprise, Maxine."

"You mean it, baby?"

"Of course, I mean it. I have an idea when I arrive in New York. Let's find a hotel in Jersey, close to New York but away from crowds and people who might recognize you. We'll bury ourselves in bed for days. Now, does that sound like I'm upset?"

"I just climaxed."

"Start canvassing. I'll call you from Stockholm in a day or so. Will you do that?"

"Where are you staying in Stockholm?"

"I don't know yet. The company is making the arrangements; I won't know until I land."

"I could take a few days off and fly there, then we could come back together."

"We wouldn't have the time. You take care of the arrangements there and I'll make this trip as quick as possible, then we'll be together until death do us part."

"Hurry baby . . . goodnight."

"Goodnight." He put the phone down carefully on the cradle and closed his eyes. "You had to spoil it!" he shouted, before knocking his coffee off the table, smashing the porcelain cup to bits on the concrete floor of the deck.

"We warned you about her, Wayne."

"Don't say another word, not another word."

NEW YORK: JANUARY 24

Ethan slipped out of bed and padded to the kitchen, prepared the coffee, and put the pot on low heat. He sat down at the table. The coffee began to percolate. Soon the aroma of freshly brewed coffee would fill the loft and she would awaken and scold him for not waking her up sooner.

The engagement ring he bought waited to be slipped on her finger. Today he was going to make it official. She loves you and you love her. Her son loves you and you love him. Her footfalls sounded on the hardwood floor; he stood up to greet her.

"Why didn't you wake me?"

"I made coffee. You were sleeping so soundly I didn't want to. Sit down. Want some breakfast?"

"Just coffee. Walking around in your underwear, Ethan . . . did you pause by the window so the women across the street can get a look?"

"Yeah, I knew you'd know. Can't put nothing over on you, can I?" Ethan fixed two cups of coffee, put a spoonful of sugar in Anna Lee's cup, stirred it, and set it down.

"You seem distracted, honey . . . is something wrong?"

"I've got something on my mind. Drink your coffee; I'll be right back. He returned after removing his shorts and slipping on a pair of pajama bottoms.

"I don't think I will ever get used to the soundless way you move."

"Here, I hope you like it. I hope it . . ." He brought the velvet covered box out from behind his back and opened it.

Her eyes moistened. "Next to you and our son, my beautiful man, it is the most wonderful thing I have ever seen." Her tears splashed on her cheeks as she jumped up and rushed into his arms. "I love you, Ethan, like the sun loves heat."

"I'll take that as a yes?"

"Yes, yes, yes." She kissed him with all the passion she could muster and just as quickly pulled away.

"Put it on my finger?" She started to cry again. "I knew I should have done my nails." Anna Lee took a step back. "I have to call my parents and tell our son, and then I need to call Maggie."

"You want to call right now? "Are you sure he'll be okay with it?"

"Ethan Edwards, I'm a woman and when a woman is experiencing the second happiest day of her life, she makes calls. And as to our son, he'll be thrilled. You know what he said to me? 'You and Ethan should get married so you won't have to sleep in separate bedrooms.' "

Before he could answer, she ran through the loft, her slippers slapping on the wood floor and her robe billowing out behind her.

"I think she's happy," he said out loud. Good thoughts . . . good times . . . making good memories.

PARIS: JANUARY 26

The headline in Le Monde, a daily Paris newspaper, proclaimed the death of Christian Fontaine, the artist, in bold letters. He was found floating in the Seine face down, his body wedged against a bridge support. Police visiting his apartment found personal belongings, a wallet with 200 French francs, his watch, rings, and other jewelry. There was no sign of a struggle and residents in adjoining apartments heard nothing that would arouse suspicion. Though no note was found among his possessions, his death was declared a suicide.

CHAPTER TWENTY

PALMER COMES HOME: FEBRUARY 3, 1978

The passenger in aisle seat 4A of the 747 first class upper deck finished his drink and opened a pouch filled with chocolates and individually packaged fruit slices. He closed his eyes and reclined, popping a chocolate wedge into his mouth. The memory of the previous night crept into his thoughts. He started to become erect.

"That was nice last night. We enjoyed watching you with that young slut. Your father is happy. I'll be quiet now; you have a decision to make when you land."

"Steward, could I have another martini please? no, wait. Make that coffee with a shot of vodka, a blanket, and sleep covers for my eyes. I'm a bit tired." You are right, mother. I need to think. Go away.

"Would you like me to wake you, Mr. Morrison, when we serve our meal?"

"Yes, if it's not too soon. I'd like the salmon."

"Two hours."

"That should do it. Thanks."

Ronald Timmons entered the Old Angler's Inn.

"I'm meeting a friend."

"Yes, Mr. Timmons, your friend is already here. Come this way."

"Well, Ronald, you are looking fit," Cahill said, standing up. They shook hands. "Beatrice must not find out about our little lunch."

"I understand."

"Why are we here? Is it Palmer? Let's order lunch first."

"Yes, Adam." Timmons addressed the waiter hovering over the table. "Just water for me and a dish of baked catfish with green beans. No bread and coffee after we eat. Please bring me the check."

"I'll have the same except for the coffee, waiter." Cahill looked at Timmons. "The shit never goes away. At least the flies take the winter off."

The waiter brought a pitcher of water and filled the glasses.

"I think I would enjoy a small salad," Cahill said. "Oil and vinegar on the side and no onion or crotons." Cahill took a sip of water. "All right, Ronald. I can't wait until we finish eating. Tell me what I do not want to hear."

"I want to be clear, Adam. I came here for advice and nothing more."

"Yes, of course. I believe that is what Gaius Cassius told Julius Caesar."

SAS FLIGHT 162

Palmer looked at his watch then asked, "Are we on schedule?"

"Yes. In fact, ahead of schedule. The weather is clear all the way in."

"It won't be long now, Maxine. My flight is on time. I'm coming home to settle matters."

"Did you say something, sir?"

"No. Just thinking out loud."

"Are we going to rid ourselves of that slut, Wayne?"

"Shut up."

He hadn't realized how hungry he was until the steward brought the food and he began to eat. He wolfed it down, even scraping the plate for the last bit of cheese sauce. He wiped his mouth and popped in two mints, wishing he'd brought a toothbrush and toothpaste on board.

"It looks like you enjoyed the meal." The steward began to remove the dish. "Would you like a drink? I would suggest a cognac?" The steward reached into the inside pocket of his jacket and placed a toothbrush and a small tube of toothpaste on the tray.

"You read my mind," Palmer said, chewing the mints into tiny fragments. "I think I'd like a cognac with a twist of lemon."

"Of course, sir. I'll fix your drink." The steward cut two wedges: one he ran along the edge of the glass, the other wedge he attached to a stirrer and put it in the glass. He began to pour the cognac.

The lead attendant pulled the curtain and entered the kitchen. "I see the gentleman in 4A is awake and by the looks of this dish, hungry."

"Yolanda, have you noticed anything funny about him?" The steward capped the bottle slowly and stirred the lemon and cognac mixture, adding a cube of ice. "Just before I bring him his drink, watch his eyes. I'll hold the curtain open."

"What am I looking for, Gregory?"

"FourA puts his head back. His lids flutter as if he is having a dream, but he is awake and his lower lip moves as if he is conversing with someone."

"I do that all the time, Gregory, especially when I am angry with my boyfriend."

"I don't know; he just gives me the creeps."

"Take this drink to 2A and I'll take 4A."

"Never mind, in six or so hours he'll be gone and never heard from again. We've had much worse."

"Good boy."

OLD ANGLER'S INN

"I hope Shevchenko received his package. You used the Dutch forger Hauptman, a wise decision. I will not advise you on Shevchenko coming to America. That decision rests on your shoulders." Cahill cleared his throat. "This isn't going to be pleasant, you know"

"Yes, I know Adam."

"I am disturbed by General Golan. I told you he lied to me about Palmer meeting him. This tells me he is even more involved than I suspected. The Prime Minister inviting you to be there when they interrogate this Pepper fellow is reassuring and I love her inviting Reagan for a talk. She is one smart lady."

"I'd like you to look at these and see if you recognize the men in the pictures." Timmons handed photographs to Cahill.

"The young one is Joseph; I do not know his last name. He is Mossad, not

Shin Bet as some think. This one is Major Shapiro sitting in the back seat of the car. I must assume Abram is his driver."

"He is. The picture was taken at a private airport outside of Tel Aviv. We were alerted Palmer flew to Stockholm on a private jet. We lost contact there."

"He would have had to refuel somewhere before crossing. He may have switched planes to escape detection."

Timmons picked up the pictures and slipped them back into his coat pocket.

"I have authorized a watch of the international flights arriving from Stockholm. I am assuming he is on his way here, of course. I sent photos, his real birth name and alias to the FBI Office in Manhattan."

"Good thinking, involving the FBI."

"Angela suggested the same option. Dennis is aware of the gravity of the situation. Dennis has handpicked the agents for the assignment. If it comes to that, Palmer will not leave the airport alive."

"Good. Well done. Manning-Ham and Drum are wonderful to work with. You are very lucky to have them."

"I know that, believe me."

"In one way, I was lucky too. I had an excellent staff of analysts and Beatrice, of course. I also had a heart attack that nearly killed me."

"Can I ask one more question, Adam, and then I will let you go home to Beatrice? Do you still keep in contact with the group of seven?"

"Ah . . . I only seek your advice. Right, Gaius Cassius?"

MOSCOW

"You should have told the Americans about the Barnett woman. They could have watched her in case he made contact. The circumstances require it. Hopefully the Americans will capture him."

"But that is precisely the point, Marina. He mustn't be captured. He must be killed to protect Russia first. When it is finished, we disappear to protect ourselves."

"You believe in your heart that the Chairman has marked you?"

"Not only me, Marina."

"I almost forgot: Colonel Gusev called. It seems Dupree sent him a message. The serial killer struck again, this time in Stockholm. Witnesses say she was last seen with an American. Gusev thought you should know."

"Are the witnesses sure he was with an American?"

"They think—"

"Where was Palmer last seen, Marina?"

"Tel Aviv . . . why?"

"The general . . . I would bet he spirited him out, probably on a private jet. He doesn't want him leaving Israel, so he secretly sends him to Stockholm. It gives General Golan plausible deniability and no one would think of Sweden. You are very clever, General . . . very clever indeed."

"You are convinced the serial killer and Palmer are the same man, yes?"

"Yes, Marina, and I am also convinced Palmer is already in America or on his way as we speak."

"You need to hear from Patterson soon. Time is too short to waste on protocols."

"You should be home with your husband. It is almost ten o'clock. Go home. I will be in the office early."

"Put together a short list of books for Ladas. Give her a history of America: the founding fathers, as they are referred to. The laws under their Constitution. She will need these books. She is doing very well with speech patterns. I have a suggestion. Allow Ladas to travel with me to Israel and stay with us until I think she is ready. I think it will be better for both of you, yes?"

"I agree, Marina."

"What if you are not granted your request to go to America?"

"I must go anyway. It may be time to involve Mikhail. He has a contact in America, a man with influence. Mikhail trusts him and considers him to be a friend."

"You have not mentioned this person before. Can you?"

"Go home, Marina."

KENNEDY AIRPORT-LONG ISLAND, N.Y.

At just past midnight, two six-passenger black vans pulled to the curb in front of the departure entrance. Doors swung open and four men and two women in business suits climbed out, each carrying small carry-on luggage. They hurried across the sidewalk and disappeared into the terminal. The twelve FBI agents missed noticing the man at the cab stand in the long black overcoat and gray fedora hat leaning in the passenger window of a yellow cab. The man in the overcoat did not fail to see and recognize them.

"I need to go to New Jersey, the Hilton hotel, on Route 3 in Secaucus. Can you take me? I'll pay a flat fee of two hundred dollars or whatever the meter reads, what do you say?"

"It'll cost you three C-notes to cover my mileage, plus tip. What say you?"

"I'm ready if you are."

"Hop in."

The phone rang in Timmins's office.

"What's the latest Dennis?" he said, picking up the bedroom extension.

"The news isn't good. We missed him, Ron. The flight was early. I am sorry."

"Don't blame yourself, Dennis. I'll keep in touch." He hung up.

"They missed him."

"I'm afraid so, Mona."

"What else is bothering you, Ronald. You aren't yourself."

"My wife is having an affair, Mona. He is an anchor at ABC news. It's serious."

SECAUCUS, NEW JERSEY

Palmer handed the driver three hundred dollars, plus another fifty dollars added to the tip, and slid out of the backseat. "Thanks for the ride . . ."

"Jerome Milk."

"Well thanks for the ride, Jerome Milk. Don't spend it all in one place." He shut the door, turned on his heel and walked up the steps into the hotel, carrying a small suitcase.

"Are you going to do her?"

"Be quiet, both of you. I need to think." He spied the phone in a small alcove and walked to it, keeping his back to the cameras, his face hidden under a wide-brimmed hat.

"Room 737." Two rings and she was on the line. "I'm in the lobby."

"I'm naked; get up here."

"I'm on my way." His eyelids fluttered. He checked his watch. It was 1:55 a.m.

"Wayne, are you going to do her first?"

"Be quiet, both of you." Palmer stepped onto the elevator. I thought you were different Maxine. I thought we had a good thing going. He got off and padded down the hall. The door opened to Room 737. She was naked.

"I guess you missed me. Can I at least wash my face?"

"Wash your face between my legs-- no more hiding for us."

"What did I say? Until death put us apart, right Maxine?"

Palmer paid the cab driver, entered the port authority, and walked quickly to the row of phones on the main concourse. He put in the correct change and dialed the number in Hoboken.

"Frank, I'm in the Port Authority; is the apartment ready?"

"One ready. The Super is a guy named Strong; he's expecting you. The owners wanted at least one rented, seeing as you changed arrival plans. The second apartment became vacant three days ago."

"It's late, I'll go over there first thing in the morning. I'll take a walk, stretch my legs, maybe get something to eat or I'll take in a movie, I don't know. It just feels good to be back: the noise, the activity, I'll see."

"Have you contacted Maxine?"

"I took care of the problem earlier. Before I hang up, I'll need a handgun."

"I have the perfect weapon for you."

"We'll talk soon." He hung up, walked over to the row of lockers, put his suitcase inside, locked it, slipped the key into his coat pocket, and walked out onto Eighth Avenue, mixing with the crowd. The smells, the sounds, the culture and lights of the city came back in a rush.

He sighed, realizing how much he had missed being away. He had work to do, punishments to mete out. He walked up Eighth Avenue to the Stage

Door Deli. He was hungry for Pastrami with melted Swiss cheese, globs of brown mustard, and a pickle on Jewish marble rye.

Back on the street, he made his way to Forty-Second Street, bright with lights, movie theaters, massage parlors, adult bookstores, male hustlers, and prostitutes. The gutters were littered with refuse. The narrow hollows between buildings with junkies. The Great White Way, he thought ruefully. Not anymore. He spied a movie marquee. It might be interesting to see how Donald Sutherland plays the role of the doctor in the remake of, Invasion of The Body Snatchers, but not here, not in these movie houses. He was exhausted. A movie might be good. He might even catch a little sleep and dream about Maxine's last moments on earth. Theaters were dark. He slid in the back seat when the cab pulled to the curb.

"Where to?" the driver asked

"I'd like to see that movie, driver," Palmer answered, pointing up at the marquee. "But not here."

SOURASKY MEDICAL CENTER: MARCH 7

"Sylvia, your thirty minutes is up." The therapist shut off the treadmill and handed her a clean towel. "You've worked hard this morning; how do the grafts feel?"

"Fine, no discomfort when I move at all, Beth."

"Good, your breathing is regular. Are you feeling any pain in your chest?"

"No. The ribs feel good. It's the legs that become weak."

Beth Rubin made a notation on her patient's chart. "I will report to Doctor Samuelson. Doctor Spitzer thinks you are ready for the next step. I think he is correct, with caution of course. I want to look at the grafts; strip for me."

"What are you going to menace me with next?"

"It is all good to a point Sylvia. The hard part starts tomorrow. You have much more work to do. I think you can go home for short visits. That, of course, is up to Doctor Spitzer. I will expect you to return here after short visits until you complete all phases. I will schedule regular appointments, which I expect you to keep; all right, Sylvia?"

"Just try to be rid of me. How long, Beth?"

"That is up to doctor Spitzer. I wouldn't hope for a complete release for a while."

"Okay, Beth."

"You have a visitor, but he can wait. Let's have a look at you."

She removed her sweats. Reba stood naked, her arms to her side, her legs spread, knees bent. Beth pressed areas that had suffered deep bruises and burns.

"Very good; get dressed. The doctors did a wonderful job restoring tissue. Scarring is all but invisible and you have done an excellent job with the workout. You still have a long way to go. Do not rush it."

"I can't thank you enough, Beth, for your help and kindness."

"I take it you do not have a man in your life. Do not be ashamed of your body if you meet someone. If he notices anything and says nothing, he is a good man. Stay with him. Your visitor is an older gentleman with a scar over his left eye."

"That would be General Golan, Beth."

"Are you in the army, Sylvia? I did not see an occupation on your chart."

"Can I tell you a secret that you will promise to keep?"

"You look fit, Reba. The medical center has treated you well." The general was happy with her appearance.

"The doctors you brought from Mount Sinai Hospital in New York were miracle workers."

"It was the least we could do, Reba. You have been crying . . . what is wrong? Tell me."

"My therapist is going to recommend I be released to my home, Abel. Short visits only."

"That is wonderful news. Why does it sadden you, Reba? Listen to me. I may have something for you."

"What is it, uncle? What new terrors have you created in your mind?"

"When you are finally released, we will talk. In the meantime, do as they say when it comes to your health and strength. We have time to discuss your future. It might require travel to America. For now, do as the doctors say and get well."

"You cannot put a vase in front of me without flowers."

"It is not the right time, Reba. It may never be. Hold onto the vase. If it works as I hope it will, I will fill the vase with flowers."

NEW YORK: MARCH 7

Palmer started north from Seventy-Second Street. He'd slept through most of the movie, waking up just as Donald Sutherland revealed himself.

He left the theater hungry and still sleepy. He spent the next hour and a half nursing cups of coffee, a bacon and egg sandwich at Paul's Diner, and reading a day-old New York Times before starting toward the apartment on Eighty-First Street.

The five-story structure looked clean and well maintained: no soot stains on the brick façade, clean windows. The courtyard with the fountain beyond the gate looked like a postcard from some Italian villa. The shrubs were neatly trimmed covered in winter plastic. The dirt in the planters looked almost fresh with deep ruts to contain the rainwater.

He opened the gate, closing it quietly behind him, and walked the length of the courtyard. Lighted rooms with curtains or drapes above him cast oblique shadows on the path and yard. He entered the foyer. It was clean, warm, and quiet, a single lamp on a triangular table by the alley window the only light. The only sound was the low, even hissing of the radiator.

The stairwell's elevator door and railing looked freshly painted. He spied the door to his right, a brass plate with the block lettered 1A at eye level. He rang the bell, put his ear to the door, and listened. He heard footfalls on the wood floor coming toward the door.

"Good morning. My name is Preston and you must be Ken Strong," he said, sticking out his hand while mustering a boyish smile. "I've come to see the apartments. I was hoping both are ready."

"One of them is ready and furnished."

"Palmer rubbed his hands. "Cold out there."

"It's going to get a lot colder; the temperature is supposed to dip into single digits starting on the ninth. Late spring again. I made coffee; you're welcome to a cup. C'mon in."

"That doesn't sound good: the weather, I mean. I might take you up on that coffee while we review the lease."

The super was tall and broad shouldered, with a thin waist. His white hair was closely cropped, his brown eyes held a lot of memories. His yellow pajamas and obvious marine green bathrobe looked form fitted.

"You were a Marine . . . so was I." It was time to set parameters, "First of all, Mr. Strong, my name isn't Bud or Mack or hey you. It's James Preston."

"No problem, Mr. Preston."

"I'd like to see the apartment and I would like to know when the other apartment will be ready. I'm on a schedule. By the way, I'm impressed with the way you maintain the building."

"The man who came before me kept it tip top. I just followed his lead. Give me a minute to get dressed."

"Did he retire or get hired away?"

"He was murdered. I'll only be a minute. How do you take your coffee?"

"Black please. No sugar. Straight like my women and liquor. Did you cross the pond, Mister Strong?"

"Nineteen sixty-eight. Just in time for the Tet Offensive in Nam. How about you?"

"No, I was out by then." He had guessed right about Strong, a lot of memories behind those eyes.

Palmer sat down in the living room, the lease agreement on his lap. Strong fixed coffee.

"Real estate people . . . they're like politicians . . . parasites." He flipped to the last page of the agreement and signed and dated it.

"Here's the coffee, the agreement okay with you, Mister Preston?"

"All lawyer talk, I don't understand a word of it." He took the mug of coffee. "Thanks. The other apartment, will it be ready to furnish next week?"

"I'll see what I can do. If the residents just got out recently . . . It isn't my business, but . . ."

"No problem, I'd be curious if I were you. We are involved in some work for one of the government agencies. I can't say more at this time. What I will need is your cooperation and tight lips."

"I got it, say no more. Does the owner know about this?"

"Yes, as a matter of fact. I need to contact him as soon as possible. It seems he's been out of touch?"

"He's back. He's always running off with his girlfriend or buying her stuff. It's his life and he can afford it, I guess."

"His girlfriend sounds like a hot number."

"Yeah, she is built like a brick shit house and good looking. It's got to be his money. He's not much to look at. Hell, it's none of my business. He pays me well. I live here rent- and utilities-free."

"You say the previous manager was murdered? Was it a domestic thing?"

"No, he was a widower. They found him right where your feet are, Mr. Preston. From what I hear, he was gutted and his head was the home of a knife of some sort. He was a Nazi. A camp guard: that's the rumor, anyway. They never caught whoever did it. Tenants say it was a woman. You want to inspect the apartment now?"

It had been smart to order the furniture in advance. Tomorrow the cable man was coming to activate the TV in the living room and bedroom. The furnishings for the other bedroom and living room would arrive as soon as the second apartment was ready.

He needed a second bedroom in his apartment for one-night stands. A table and chairs for the kitchen, a desk for correspondence, a couch, a recliner, and reading chairs for the living room. Throw rugs. All to be delivered tomorrow. Today he needed to buy towels, sheets, blankets, a comforter, small appliances, a coffee maker, and enough liquor of different blends to suit what mood he was in at the moment. First things first.

Palmer filled the refrigerator and kitchen cabinets with enough food to keep him fed for two weeks without having to leave the apartment. He had enough changes of clothes to last a few days before he went shopping for a more adequate blend of clothing. The domestic needs filled for the time being, he relaxed and fixed a bourbon.

He picked up a pen, making a note to pick up decent glassware. Good bourbon should be enjoyed from a snifter and not from a juice glass. He deliberately looked over the newspaper to see if he missed anything in the column about Maxine's murder. He closed his eyes. He saw her lifeless eyes staring up at him.

"Till death do us part. I am a man of my word."

He padded into his bedroom. He went first to the radiator under the window and gave the handle a half turn. The radiator hissed. He cracked the window, allowing a small portion of winter to enter. He sipped his drink. There was one more thing to do. He went down to the lobby and used the public phone.

"Hello, Frank."

"Palmer has come home?"

"The other apartment isn't ready. It is understandable, considering my delay in coming over. I spoke to Dukakis. I don't trust him, Frank. He's a weasel."

"Don't worry about him. I see you took care of your lady friend?"

"Yes, and you were right. I made the clean break of it. I made a clean break of it. Get it? Clean break?"

"I know. Nice play on words. You need to lay low for a while. Take it easy."

"Have you been in touch with Cahill?"

"No. I don't want to draw attention to myself by asking him questions about things I should have no knowledge of. I'll talk to him when I think it's appropriate. Do you think the Russians know you are here?"

"It really doesn't matter, does it, Frank?"

"I guess not. What could they do if they knew?"

"Nothing. I'm going to get some sleep. I wanted to check in. I'm going to call Golan when I wake up."

"I'm glad you did her, John. Wait, give me your phone number before you hang up."

"No phone until morning. I'll call you after the installer leaves. Goodnight." Palmer hung up and returned to his apartment, finished off the drink and undressed. He slid under the covers, the opening in the window blowing cold air on his face. His first full day in America since 1968. It felt good.

CHAPTER TWENTY-ONE

Palmer sat on his new couch. He had to get out of the apartment. The walls were closing in on him. The air felt stagnant, even with the windows open. "That's it, I have had enough," he declared.

Thirty minutes later, he was on the sidewalk walking toward First Avenue dressed in a pair of Wrangler jeans, thick grey socks and a sweatshirt he had purchased with the Korean War winter parka at the Army-Navy store on Seventy-Sixth Street. Terrain boots, a green and red flannel shirt, and black scarf.

The super told him about the German bakery up the street. He decided to try it after a good stretch of his legs. He needed exercise. He needed to walk to build strength. He decided to buy weights for the apartment and good walking shoes. He also decided to see Invasion of the Body Snatchers. It was early; he would be back at the apartment in time to watch a newscast. First, the walk to the movie house. A good start.

"What about us, Wayne?"

"I think you both have had enough. Shut up." He answered his voice loud enough to be overheard. He scolded himself. "See what you made me do?" he whispered. "Keep quiet."

The remake did not quite generate the kind of enthusiasm when compared with the original. Sutherland was good as the doctor. He enjoyed watching the lead actress walking through the pod nursery, naked. He would have liked it better if her breasts were larger, but all and all she was pleasant to look at. Leonard Nimoy's character puzzled him. Palmer kept waiting for Spock to say "Live long and prosper." You win, Kevin McCarthy.

He noticed the squat man leaning against a yellow cab, his legs crossed at the ankles, his hands at his side. He was wearing a New York Yankees cap. Does he know me? He looks like someone I should know. He's looking right at me and smiling. Palmer crossed Seventy-Ninth Street. As he approached, he realized who it was. Eight million people in this city and this son of a bitch finds me.

"You know me?" he asked, toe to toe with the guy in the Yankees hat.

"Captain Palmer, you marine in my country. I remember you. I heard you dead . . . killed in action and here you are . . . no dead."

"How did you get here? Let's sit in your cab and talk; it's too cold." Palmer climbed into the passenger-side front seat.

"I came as a refugee after war ended. Man falls off ship, so I become him."

"A lucky break, I'm sure. Now you are living the American dream making money with the cab, married, nice apartment, I bet?"

"No marry, wife in Vietnam. Fuck her, let her stay. I work two jobs in the cab in daylight and salad man at Sparks Steak house six-day-a-week nights. Apartments run down a lot of junkies in the neighborhood. I do not have nice things to steal so they leave me alone. Soon I will be able to afford better apartment and next year I buy car . . . a Mercury."

"I see you've picked up the language pretty well and you are working hard. I have to run, but let's have supper soon. We can enjoy good food and talk." His mind was spinning, calculating narratives. A witness. I can't have this slope

head looking over my shoulder.

"You want to be friends, Palmer?"

"Why not? We both have secrets, don't we?"

"Jack Dempsey."

"What about him?"

"Not him. Restaurant. It is big and open like a mess hall, good food, and big crowds. Nobody listens to us. I like food that is not expensive. Sunday next week my day off, okay?"

"We'll meet in front Sunday at 6:00 p.m., okay?"

"I'll take you home."

"I'll walk. I want to stop at that bakery on Eighty-Second."

Palmer got out of the cab. "I'll see you on Sunday; don't be late. I hate waiting in the cold."

TEL AVIV: MARCH 14

Reba finished her run and slowed to a walk, allowing her body to cool. Her legs were not yet as strong as she would like, but enough to satisfy the doctors and her therapist. She swiped perspiration from her face with a clean white towel and made her way toward a grove of trees. She looked around at the couples and other joggers and remembered the first and last time she'd come here. The day she met Daniel Klein. Reba smiled as the memory washed over her. She even remembered what she was wearing. She wiped her face and ran the towel over her bare arms.

"I have come to you, the souls of Babi Yar. If my mind can endure the violence that I do." She placed the folded towel on her shoulder. "I will hear what you have to say. Break your silence, souls of Babi Yar. I beg you." No answer.

The Silver 1963 Lincoln came to a stop twenty feet from the path. The suicide door opened and General Golan climbed out.

"Reba, my dear, we need to talk. You look well rested, and it is easy to see your strength is returning."

"I have your answer, General. Whatever you want. My answer is yes. When?"

"There is time, Reba. First you must complete your therapy."

NEW YORK: MARCH 20

Ethan missed waking up with Anna Lee by his side. He missed the pleasant conversations. The little talks, they liked to call it. They held hands at breakfast and shared an English muffin or a bagel with a thick layer of cream cheese.

He sipped his coffee, popped two Vitamin D pills into his mouth, swallowed them, and flicked on the small TV. He turned to the local news. He finished the last of his cartoon monologues the night before. It was enough work to carry the strip well into November. He was free now to do as he wished. He made a mental note to call his agent and a realtor to see about selling the loft. He was about to pour another cup when a reporter relayed the story of the shooting in front of Jack Dempsey's.

Ethan put the cup on the and counter calmly picked up the phone. He dialed the number splashed on the bottom of the screen. He asked for Detective Polk.

"I won't waste your time, Detective Polk. Tran Luc Loung is not his real name. He is Dinh Ang Nguyen." He spelled it for the detective. "He was a major with the NVA, a murderer of women and children. A man with the soul of a bat."

"Who is this?"

"I didn't waste him. Good hunting, detective. I feel sure you will never find or arrest his killer." Ethan hung up.

MOSCOW: MARCH 26

The supper finished, the women cleared the table and prepared tea. Uri Chernoff poured vodka for Shevchenko and himself and sat down, taking a pack of Lucky Strike cigarettes from his pants pocket.

"I have a request, Peter. Marina tells me you will go after this man Palmer. I want to join you. Will you allow me to help you find and kill this man?"

"Uri Chernoff, you are a good and gentle man, a man of peace." Shevchenko took a drag on his cigarette and casually blew the smoke out. "I was most happy when Marina found you and you both were married. This thing we must do is not only dangerous—"

"I am no stranger to danger, Peter Shevchenko," Uri interrupted, "A Jew in Russia knows better."

"Let me finish. I do not question your manhood, Uri Chernoff. What we must do leaves no time for reflection. The innocent might suffer with him. Do you understand?" Laughter erupted in the kitchen. "I most sincerely admire you for wanting to help, and you will, by taking Marina to Israel to live without looking over your shoulder for the secret police. When the ladies return with the tea and cake Ladas prepared, I have something to show you both." Shevchenko stamped the butt out in the ashtray, reached into his coat pocket and produced a package of Camels. "Try one of mine, Comrade. You can judge which one suits your taste." They smoked in silence; the laughter in the kitchen continued.

"The tea, gentlemen, is ready," Marina announced, leading Ladas into the dining room.

"We will be trying plum cake. It is a recipe by a woman in America. Betty Crocker is her name."

"She has never been to America and already she thinks like a capitalist," Shevchenko said.

"Ladas, show Peter what you learned while we prepared tea."

"Why, sugar, I just know you are going to love this cake." The parody was perfect, the inflection of tone undeniable.

"A woman bred in the south, my word. There is no finer creature on the face of the earth," Shevchenko answered in a drawl matching Ladas.

"Well bless your heart, sir." The dining room filled with laughter.

"We brought something you both need to see. It is the first work from Holland."

"We will have tea and cake before we see what you have brought. Uri, you get our wallets while I pour the tea and Ladas cuts the cake."

"There is a piece missing."

"Of course, there is. Did you think I would bring out the untested cake, Peter Shevchenko?"

The cake was applauded as a work of art, vodka in tumblers was poured, tea cups refilled, cigarettes lit. Minutes passed as Chernoff studied each certificate carefully. At last, he put them down and looked up.

"Well, Comrade, what do you think?"

"Which one of the two is mine? The right or the left?" Chernoff rubbed his eyes, his face a picture of wonderment. "I see it and still cannot believe what I see. The colors, the printing, the feel of the stiff paper, even the signatures . . . who is this artist posing as a simple man?"

"That is not important, Uri. What is important is how they are accepted. I need both of you to use them as your identification. Use stores you do not frequent. Buy railroad tickets, fuel, and groceries. Do not fear being arrested. We have already allowed for that. Marina, look at your papers. See if you can see a difference, the slightest error . . . take your time."

"Have you and Ladas received yours?"

"Yes, we have: three days ago, Marina. We've used them frequently, even purchasing things we did not need like a change of tires on Ladas's car. I would not put you in any situation we had not already faced."

"How many has he completed?"

"Only these four. The rest will be ready as soon as we complete the list of names."

"You still believe Fedorov is no longer a friend?"

"More than ever, Marina. I saw it in his mannerisms and the tone of his voice. I saw it in eyes when we met last. I am to kill Palmer and suffer the same fate. The final acknowledgement came when he agreed with the names on the team and added one more. He told me her name is Lydia Sokolov. She is already in residence in our embassy in New York."

"The final piece to the puzzle. It is as you said, Peter."

NEW YORK: MARCH 26

He rarely left the apartment past eight a.m. To keep busy, he began early in the morning to build more strength in his arms and legs with pushups and sit ups, followed by riding the stationary bike. He hadn't worked with weights yet. Running toward the East River in the cold early morning just before daylight refreshed him, removing the toxic waste in his body caused by eating junk food and drinking sodas. The better he felt, the less he ate fattening foods Helping him maintain a diet of red meat, salmon, chicken proteins, and fresh green salads.

He allowed himself one treat of a slice of chocolate cake on Saturday after his jog, eating a slice with a cup of tea mixed with a shot of vodka. He read to pass the time, presently reading Chesapeake by James Michener. Later, he would unpack his clothes, which finally arrived from Minsk. Another package would be arriving, delivered to an unsuspecting rabbi in Brooklyn. The second apartment was ready and the furniture was in place, but he refused to call Golan.

It was noon when he finished unpacking and storing away his clothing. He made a mental note to purchase more hangers. The next morning, he took the boxes downstairs. Ken Strong was just coming out of his apartment carrying a tool box. "Good morning. It never ends, does it?" he said with a false smile.

"Are you going to take the boxes outside?"

"I was just about to do that, Ken, before I started my workout."

"Thanks for breaking them down. Just leave them by the door. I'll get it later. When are your people coming?"

"The government works slowly when it works. Always on the taxpayer's dime, Ken. I'll catch you later."

Palmer returned from his run, padded across the lobby into the elevator, and pressed the button for the fifth floor. He wanted to see the layout of the roof, find the fire escape to see if it aligned with the one across the alley, and check the distance between this building and the building next door. The fire escape was on the opposite wall leading down to the alley below. That's good, I can make the jump easily.

She was unlocking her door when he reached the landing. She was no spring chicken, but nothing to be ashamed of either. Palmer put women in two categories: sluts and women he turned into sluts.

"Good morning," he said with his boyish smile always reserved for first encounters. When she turned around, her appeal became more relevant.

"Well, hello. You must be our new neighbor. My name is Joan . . . Joan Henry." She stuck out her gloved hand.

"James Preston and yes, I guess I am the new neighbor. It's nice to meet you." He shook her hand. She had a firm grip; he liked that in a woman. Maxine had a firm grip on all things except her emotions.

"It was nice meeting you, Mr. Preston." She turned away, hoping he would invite her for a cup of coffee or a drink. He was very good looking and that boyish smile . . . take it easy girl.

"It was nice meeting you, Joan. May I call you Joan?"

"Yes, of course."

"Very well, and please call me James." He walked to his apartment, unlocked the door, and went inside without looking back at Joan Henry.

"Quite a woman for her age, Wayne. I like a woman who is full figured, and she isn't that bad to look at either."

"Don't even think about it, dad. She's too close. She's an attractive neighbor and no more than that. Go away."

"You can't stay cooped up in this apartment."

"I said be quiet. I have to be careful. No mistakes. It's all about revenge now."

"What about us, Wayne?"

"I had plans for Maxine. I had to change them . . . Change yours."

10 DOWNING STREET: MARCH 31

Reginald Pepper, with his wife dutifully on his arm, entered 10 Downing Street. The occasion and welcome might have engendered most men to feel embarrassed by the show of support. A red face and a bowed head were common in such instances. Not so with Pepper. His ego would not allow a demonstration of humility. The honor of Knighthood was deserved, nothing short of that would be acceptable.

As more than one of the invited guests noted, "He acts like he is a Royal." Shouts of "Here-here and well done" were replaced by handshakes and apologies for the night being moved back a week.

"Well, Pepper, this seems to be your night and you, madam . . . may I say as lovely as always, Mrs. Pepper." Mrs. Pepper was a plump unpleasant woman whose image of herself was as grand as her husband's. Unnoticed was Sir John Scarlett's not taking his hand and shaking it.

"I must say, Sir John, I am most flattered by your attending this function in my honor."

"To be honest, something has come up that will need our immediate attention. Forgive me, Lucille, but I must borrow your husband for a short briefing downstairs."

"A meeting so important you take him away tonight, Sir John?"

"I am afraid so, Lucille; the business of our country never rests."

"Yes, Sir John." Pepper squeezed his wife's hand, "Have a glass of brandy, my dear. I am sure the ladies will surround you until I return."

No one in the conference room once used by Winston Churchill as his bunker and command center stood to greet Pepper. The greetings were muffled and subdued. There were no grand gestures, no applause, no handshakes.

"The prime minister and Richard Castle, known to his associates and other intelligence personnel as "Baron," are in a meeting with a special guest and his wife. They should join us shortly."

"MI-5 and 6, their associates . . . ah, and Timmons of the CIA. Can I know what has happened to draw this esteemed group together?"

"The prime minister was very clear that the meeting would not begin before she could attend. I am sorry, Pepper, but you know as well as we do that when she gives an order . . ."

"I understand, of course." Pepper was becoming concerned. A special meeting including the prime minister and on this night when he should be upstairs enjoying the platitudes and well wishes. The very sound of it sent a shiver up his spine. The voice in his head told him nothing is as it seems. He took his regular seat at the table. The room remained quiet. Discussion stopped. The only sounds were a clearing of a throat or a muffled cough.

The prime minister entered and everyone stood to greet her. Behind her, a man and a woman hidden from sight were being led out through another door. She greeted everyone with a nod, except Pepper. She asked him to remain standing. A security guard held her chair out for her. She thanked him and sat down. Her eyes focused on Pepper.

"I have a question for you Pepper and I would appreciate a straight answer."

"Of course, Madam Prime Minister."

"You have served with the Foreign ministry for over forty years. I am sure we couldn't count the number of people you transacted with, can we now?" The prime minister's voice was emotionless, the cold stare unrelenting.

"To be honest, I couldn't as well."

"Tell me, Pepper. In all your travels, have you ever run across a woman named Zoya Yano in, say, the last three or four years?"

"I am sorry, Madam. I do not recognize the name. Who is she?"

"A Russian spy you have been having an affair with, Pepper. Perhaps you know her as Janet Hobbs?"

The prime minister poured brandy into snifters and passed them to her guests, starting with Timmons. She took her place on a flowered high back chair. "How do you like the brandy, Ronald?"

"It is very mild on the throat, with a hint of apple and blackberry, I think."

"You know your brandy. Tell me, how is Adam Cahill? I understand he had a bit of a rough go?"

"Very well, madam. I will be sure to tell him you asked."

"I will see that you return home with two bottles of this brandy. Please give one to Adam with my best wishes. I'd like to ask a question and I would appreciate your candor, Ronald."

"I will answer as candidly as I can."

"You sound like Sir John Scarlett." She smiled. "No offense, Sir John."

"None taken, madam."

"Tell me who was your source, Ronald, and how dangerous is this situation?"

"I informed you of Pepper's treachery so when we came together to discuss the situation, you would understand the need for privacy for the time being. I know the problem we face is real. What I can say is it involves a very dangerous individual, an American traitor whom we must stop. I wish I could tell you more concerning the sources while we enjoy a friendly drink, but for now you must trust me and Adam."

"But he is retired? You have made that clear."

"I did indeed and he is. I take his advice only, Sir John."

"I think, gentlemen, Mister Timmons is not revealing his source because his source comes from outside his agency and perhaps outside his country, Sir John. Would you say that is a positive evaluation?"

"I would say so, Madam."

"I think we have what we need for now to take care of Pepper, Sir John. Do you have a question for Mister Timmons?"

"I think we have what we need to proceed."

"What say you, Richard?"

"I must agree with Sir John, madam. I think we will have much success working with Mister Timmons, a chip off the old block shall we say."

"Tell me one thing before you go, Ronald. What do you think of this fellow Reagan?"

"In my position, I cannot comment on politics, madam."

"Perhaps I did not put enough brandy in your snifter. I met him and his wife, Nancy. She seems a bit high strung. Very protective of him, but I liked him as a person. Tell me, Ronald, how would you feel, off the record of course, if you weren't in the position you are in?"

"As a private citizen, I guess I would have to say considering the four past presidents including the man in the oval office presently . . . he might be just what the country needs. He could be a father figure telling us all not to worry, it is all going to be alright. America is still the light at the end of the tunnel. He hates communism and has no respect for the current leadership. He doesn't like big government. At least, that is the impression he gives me when he speaks. Now, whether he runs or not, who can say? Whether I vote for him is undetermined at this moment. I wonder if he is like Truman, who decided some years ago he was sorry he created the CIA."

A brief moment of light laughter.

"I must say, I felt the same way about him, thank you. By the way, since you have been most candid with me, let me share a private word with you. One day, I believe he said December of next year, Ronald Reagan is going to announce another run for the presidency. I think he can win this time."

MOSCOW: MARCH 31

"What have you there, Marina?"

"My Bible, Peter Shevchenko. I have marked the passage I want you to read. It is in the second book of Moses. It is a passage from the Prophet Jonah. This passage mentions a person called "Watchman." I think it fits the moment."

"Then I will read it, Marina, for your sake. What other news do you bring?"

"Our embassy in London has sent confirmation of the arrest of Reginald Pepper. They also have arrested our agent, her name is Zoya Yano, and charged her with espionage. She will waste away in prison, I am afraid . . . she is so young."

"They will use her as a bargaining chip. You know the game, Marina."

"She gave up Pepper. Two of our agents were arrested and four sent home. She would be dead before she stepped off the plane if they sent her back, Peter."

"You may be right. Has Norm Patterson responded?"

"Yes, the books you requested will be delivered as planned and on time. Yuri Andropov has asked that you come to his dacha at eight o'clock on Monday morning. I told him you were having a staff meeting; could he change it?"

"I already know the answer, Marina, but thank you for trying. It is better to get it over with and give us the rest of the day."

"You must be very careful Peter Shevchenko. Marina stepped around Shevchenko's desk; On the far wall a concerto played on the phonograph. "Ladas is preparing supper." She whispered. "Help her with her language homework. Speak to her with the drawl and it will help her until she is comfortable. Now go home to her, Peter, it is almost six. Will there be anything else, Comrade?"

"One question: How is the shopping going?"

"Very well. We bought new drapes and Uri needed tires for his tired car."

"Good. I think we've covered the work for the day. Have a nice weekend. Come in a little earlier Monday. I will go straight to my appointment from home. We will have the staff meeting when I return." He wrote a note on his pad. I think Fedorov's hands are tied. He needs me. He will not act against me until Palmer is dead.

"Very good, Comrade. Goodnight." Marina mouthed the words: Be careful, Peter Shevchenko. She picked up the note and walked out.

NEW YORK: APRIL 1

"Well, the man is engaged for almost a month but he doesn't call. I have to hear it through the grapevine like a pigeon hears his mate chirping at him. Anna Lee called Beatrice the same morning?"

"I've been busy. What about you, Adam, what are you doing to keep busy?

"Well, if you must know smartass, I'm writing my memoirs. A publisher has shown interest and I've spoken to an agent. I haven't decided on a title yet."

"Call my agent. I know . . . why don't you call it Argyle Socks, Adam?"

"I'm going to hang up, Ethan. I get enough abuse from Beatrice."

"Don't hang up, Adam, I need to talk."

"I thought as much. What is it?"

"A killing right in front of Jack Dempsey's restaurant, very professional, a single shot at the back of the head, probably small caliber, a twenty-five. The dead man was Ding Ang Nguyen. He led the raid on the base. The one that got good men dead and me lost for four days."

"Somehow, he was able to come over as a refugee, Ethan. A veteran spots him, remembers him, and does him . . . case closed, Ethan. Live your life. Cherish what you have today. Let the past rest. Come see us. We need to celebrate your engagement."

"I'm thinking of selling the loft and moving to Washington."

"Are you mad? You love your home. You love New York. Why in God's name would you want to move to this godforsaken rock pile on the Potomac? The only thing still good about this city is the departure gates at the airport. Have you talked to Anna Lee about this silly idea of yours?" Cahill put his hand over the receiver. When he removed it, Beatrice was on the line.

"I'll tell you a secret. You didn't hear it from me."

"Yes, Beatrice what is it?"

"Anna Lee and her son want to live with you in New York. I'm putting Adam back on. When are you coming down?"

"Next weekend. Anna Lee has four days off."

"Good, you Anna Lee and the boy are coming here. Here is Adam."

"She's tough Adam."

"You were always her favorite, Ethan. We're looking forward to supper with the three of you. I might let you look at my writing."

"Why didn't she say something?"

"She is in love. Need I say more? I believe you gave me advice once about women, Ethan. You should heed it now. Goodbye."

"What's wrong, dear heart? You look troubled."

"He is troubled by the Viet murdered in New York."

"What did you tell him?"

"I told him it probably was a veteran who recognized him and took his revenge. He doesn't need to know anything else."

"Good. I've made a salad for lunch with fresh salmon. Are you ready to eat?"

"Not right now Bea, but I would like a glass of wine."

"There is more to this story, Adam. I know you . . . It's the call from Balandin, isn't it?"

"Yes, it is."

"You can't get involved, Adam. Call Timmons. I'll be right back with two glasses. I think I'll join you." Beatrice disappeared into the kitchen. She put her hands on the counter, bowed her head and whispered. "He's had enough She fixed the drinks and walked to his study, taking a deep breath. "Here we go," she announced.

"If the book is published, Ethan suggested I call it Argyle Socks."

"I think that is an excellent idea."

"I think you're both goofy."

"But you wouldn't trade me for anything?"

"Not anything, my dear."

NEW YORK

"I was just about to call you," he said, thinking, I needed to pace and clear my head first. I needed to feel normal. Adam was right, no sense in getting all worked up about nothing. Ethan let out a long sigh.

"How is your day going?"

"I have a few questions. I miss you. I miss your—"

"I'm going to need a shower if you keep talking like this."

"I miss you like hell too. Business first. Will you wear a wedding ring?"

"Of course. Why would you ask, baby?"

"Some men do not like to wear them. I'm checking off that one. I don't want to have to ask, but I have to . . . church of choice, or do you prefer a secular wedding in front of a judge?"

"What would you want if you were choosing?"

"Well, we are Catholic."

"Call the priest. I would love to marry you in a Catholic church."

"You will have to meet the priest and sit through a volume of questions since you are not Catholic."

"I look forward to it. I think it would be good for me."

"You mean it, my wonderful man?   Now for the big question . . . honeymoon?"

"Let's see, honeymoon . . . hmm."

"I would like to speak to Detective Polk, please."

"He is in interrogation at the moment," the PA answered. "If I could have a number."

"It concerns the shooting on Broadway. I don't have time to wait for a phone call."

"Hold on, sir." The PA pressed the hold button and dialed the viewing room to Interrogation Room 3.

"I have a man on line five who says he has info on the Broadway shooter. I can't get a return number."

"Put him through, Fran. Start a trace and a recording." Polk picked up line five. "This is Detective Polk; who am I talking to?"

"I killed the slope head you people call Tran something or other, Detective Polk. If you check with missing persons, you will find a young woman Toni Lombardo is missing. She's thirty-two, black hair and brown eyes . . .You won't find her, Polk. I've made sure of that. Goodbye."

"Wait, don't hang up . . . shit!" Polk shouted into the dead phone.

Palmer stepped out of the booth and crossed the street to the taxi stand on Thirty-Fourth Street and Broadway. He gave the driver his home address and unbuttoned his coat. He put his head back against the seat. Even before the driver pulled away from the curb, his thoughts turned to the last moments of Toni Lombardo's life.

He let out a low growl like a predator protecting its kill. His lower lip moved; his eyelids fluttered. He saw her face, the choked hysterical look in her eyes as he pressed his big hands around her neck, squeezing the last breaths from her shaking body. A second growl caught the attention of the driver.

"You okay back there, mister?"

"Yeah, I'm okay. I had a flashback about the war. I am sorry if I scared you."

"You okay now?"

"Yeah, I'm fine. I'll just open the window a bit. The air on my face will be good for me."

"You should see someone and talk it out."

MOSCOW: APRIL 17

Shevchenko, showered and dressed, padded into the living room.

"I smell lamb. It smells wonderful." He stepped over to the bar and poured two tumblers of Wild Turkey. "Have a drink with me, sugar. Try this bourbon. You need to get used to American liquor, girl."

Ladas stood in the doorway of the kitchen and looked appraisingly at him, the Bible Marina had given him in her left hand.

"Do I look like an American woodsman?"

"You look like one of those capitalist cowboys I learned about in school. Supper will be ready in half an hour. I mixed broccoli spears, mushrooms, and a sweet potato together," Ladas put her arms around his neck and kissed him, "but you still feel like a communist, darlin'. I will try American liquor. Never offer me beer . . . terrible."

"Well, gee now, you have to know a bottle of beer is sexy in a woman's hand. It tells a man she's no phony. The practice is going well," he said, dropping the drawl. "You will fit in nicely. You are wearing a dress?"

"Tonight, I am a Russian housewife. I will study later and the dress fits my mood. I hope we are past the fur coat or do you still need me that way to be stimulated?"

"I need only to look at you to be stimulated, Ladas Sorokin."

"Good, now give me my drink. I have to get used to the taste, yes? Tell me about this book. Is Shevchenko wanting to become a Jew?"

"If I do, what would you do?"

"I would become a Jew, yes. I am fascinated by it, thanks to Marina . . . drawn to it would be better."

"It is a passage from the prophet Jonah. Marina marked it for me to read."

"I already read it while you showered. I believe the prophet is speaking to you, Peter Shevchenko. I am going to check on my lamb. Read darlin'. Can you tell me what Comrade Fedorov wanted?"

"I will explain everything while we eat." He swallowed the last of his drink and tentatively opened the Bible to the passage Marina marked for him. He read it a second time and a third. When he finished, he closed the Bible and held it against his chest.

"He means you, Shevchenko. You are the watchman Jonah speaks of, aren't you?" She leaned on the doorframe, her arms folded across her chest. "The lamb is ready. I want you to marry me, Peter, before you go to America. Fix me another drink. Tell me what you see in the words and do not eat too much supper. I want you to love me tonight."

"I think you are the most beautiful woman I have ever known," he said, looking at her silhouette framed in the doorway, "and yes, to all three questions, Ladas Sorokin, but only if you take my name."

"Gladly . . . Ladas Shevchenko. I do not wish to use any other name."

"In America you will have to."

"Miriam Baker. I told you I wanted it to honor the woman who could not pass it on in Stalin's Russia and for her husband who taught me to cook. I will hate it. I will hate my country because I will have to hide my identity to protect the man that I love."

"Maybe one day soon that will all change. We can hope."

"You remember my driver Petrov? He is a dangerous man. A man to notice and take precautions against. He is a Stalinist and he has the ear of Brezhnev, and others of the old Troikas. Nothing will change, Peter. I've listened when they talked among themselves in Pavlov's dacha, after they had had too much vodka."

"You know Mikhail Balandin, Ladas?"

"Yes, of course, what is your point?"

"Because of him we can hope."

"That is enough for me, Peter Shevchenko. Now, what do you think of the prophet's words? Am I correct? Does it fit the situation?"

"I want you to hear a song from an Canadian singer whose name is Gordon Lightfoot. I first heard him sing before he was famous. He recorded his first album called Sundown. A friend stationed at the embassy in New York sent it to me because he knew how much I enjoyed the singer. On this album there is a song I want you to hear since we are on the subject of prophecy. It is called "The Watchman's Gone.""

NEW YORK: APRIL 20

Joan Henry unlocked and opened her door just as Palmer reached the landing. "Well, I see someone has been to the bakery and that could only be a German chocolate cake. I recognize the box." She smiled, exposing even white teeth.

She's ripe, Wayne, and well preserved. I'd like a piece of her cake."

"Shut up." Out loud he said, "My downfall. It gives me incentive to exercise. I'd be glad to share a slice if you like?"

"What a nice thought but no, thank you. Some people haven't learned to mind their business." She nodded at the door directly across from hers.

"Please forgive me if I gave you the wrong impression," he interrupted. The disarming smile was etched like stone on his face. "I didn't mean anything more by it."

"I'm sorry, I was being silly and pretentious. Let's start over, shall we? My name is Joan Henry."

"Hello Joan Henry. I'm your new neighbor, James Preston. I live just down the hall." The boyish smile returned. He could see by her expression it had the desired effect. "If you like, I could cut two slices of cake: one for the lucky man in your life and one for you."

"I'm sure he would enjoy that, but he is out of town and won't be back until Sunday evening . . . late."

"In that case, I could cut a piece for you and leave it by your door." The boyish smile never wavered.

"I suppose you could, James."

CHAPTER TWENTY-TWO

General Golan carefully negotiated the steps to the upper deck of the Manta Ray restaurant. He should not have been climbing the steep stairs, but he needed space and privacy. He managed the pain. His doctor insisted on a knee replacement.

"Not today." His standard answer.

He reached the platform of the upper deck, balancing himself by leaning heavily on his cane. He took deep breaths until his breathing normalized enough for him to bear it. One more deep breath and a moment to let the pain subside to a dull ache and he was ready to greet his guest.

He spied Reba sitting under the Kermes Oak, her eyes hidden by dark glasses. Her hair, a shade lighter, was cut short under a wide-brimmed white hat. She wore a simple black and white dress which could not disguise the woman beneath it. He gave a short wave and made his way through the crowded tables.

"I've ordered breakfast, General. Your knee is worse; you need to have the operation."

He put the briefcase down next to his aching leg and propped the cane against it.

"I love this time of year," he said, ignoring her comment. The waiter brought breakfast, refilled Reba's coffee cup, and poured a cup for the general. "How did the meetings go with the young men who will join you in New York?"

"Abram is a strong man. I will depend on Abram to stand up to the

American with me. Daniel is fearless, he will follow Abram. Joseph and Moesha will as well. I do not know about Daniel taking orders from the American. We will have to see. I like the idea of bringing a woman along. I know Eva Cohen . . . good choice. The men like her. She will make a good companion or backup if needed."

"She may not join the team; it hasn't been confirmed as of yet. Did you read the dossier?"

"Yes. Palmer seems a bit unhinged, if I read your thoughts correctly." Reba spread a dab of cream cheese on her bagel and added a thin sliver of smoked fish.

"You will have to watch him carefully. He murdered the Barnett woman." Golan cut a wedge of apple and popped it into his mouth.

"How do you know this?"

"Her husband is a friend. He called to tell me she left him to be with another man. She was murdered the night Palmer arrived in New York. "

"It could be coincidence."

"Palmer admitted to me they were having an affair. She did not know him as well as one might think. My guess is she became too involved and had to be dealt with. Control him with whatever means you need. Monitor him closely. If his actions become erratic and you believe the mission is lost or threatened, you are to kill him and return here with the team . . . understood?"

"Yes, General. I understand completely."

"I spoke to Ariel. He of course does not the details of the plan. He is concerned but understands the situation as I presented it to him. He will not interfere."

"I was hoping he would not be privy to this."

"I had to include him for your mother's sake. If something goes terribly wrong, she—"

"I understand. Let's eat before the food is too cold to enjoy, General."

"What do the doctors say concerning your recovery?"

"I will need a little more time, but they are very optimistic."

The plates removed, a fresh tablecloth was placed on the table with fresh napkins and a small plate of pastries. Coffee cups were refilled. The general placed his briefcase on the table.

"I have your passport, New York driver's license, ID card, and an American

Express card with a high limit a few countries could use. More than you should require. Put it in your purse."

"I assume you have taken care of the others?"

"Of course. The arrival will coincide with yours. Your living arrangements etc. It is all in the envelope."

"You do not show me a picture of Palmer; why, General?" She picked up the manila envelope and put it in her oversized bag. She took out a plain white envelope.

"I want first impressions. Is that envelope for me, Reba?"

"My will and all paperwork showing this Jewish girl as she was. Give it to my mother in case I do not return."

"What is the meaning of this, Reba?"

"If I do not return, the reason is obvious. I will be hated by my own people."

"We can arrange a transformation of your face."

"The network has pictures of me, General. The Americans will have them as well. I cannot return. "

"The doctors who fixed your burns will make a new face more beautiful than this one if that is possible."

"A new face. A stranger in my mother's eyes."

"But not her heart, Reba Klein."

"Be sure my mother gets the envelope."

NEW YORK

"That was some piece of chocolate cake, and that," she pointed to his member, "I haven't had anything that size in my mouth since I ate a hoagie in Philadelphia." Joan Henry propped herself up against the headboard and lit a cigarette. "I have to say in all honesty, you are every girl's dream, Mister Preston, and nightmare all rolled into one."

"I'm glad you enjoyed it as much as I did. I'd better go. When is your boyfriend arriving?"

"His plane doesn't get in until late tonight."

"Maybe I could come by later since he won't be in until late?"

"Not a chance. Once is wonderful, I will not forget it, I'll probably dream about it, but at my age I can't do it. Now if I was twenty-five, I'd be on you like a bear on a spawning salmon. Go away. I need time to recover."

"I think she just saved her own life."

"Keep quiet, Dad." Out loud, he said, "We'll be just neighbors down the hall from each other. I will abide by your decision, Joan."

"Well, don't close the door all the way . . . just in case."

KENNEDY AIRPORT: JUNE 19

The El Al 747 landed at Kennedy airport carrying 404 passengers, one of them a woman traveling alone in first class. She waited while the other passengers scurried to the exit. She checked her papers, making sure her passport travel documents—including a birth certificate and a visa, all forged—were all placed in the same pouch. She slipped on the fur coat, thanked the flight attendants, and deplaned.

Carrying her two small pieces of luggage, she made her way to the customs counter. The area was warm. A mixture of perfumes and lotions invaded her nose. She slipped off the fur draping it over her shoulders. At last, she was waved forward.

"It is a very busy airport," she commented while producing the envelope.

"Reba Davis-Klein?"

"Yes ma'am."

"A little warm for that beautiful coat…What is the purpose of your visit?" The woman closed her eyes and shook her head slowly and said, "We have to ask. I think it is ridiculous. If someone was going to come here to harm us, does the government really think they will tell me?"

"Don't apologize. In my country it is more difficult because of our borders. Frankly, I am glad you asked. I am hoping to live in America for my remaining days, that is why I requested a visa for only one year. It is enough to give me time to adjust and prepare . . . I have cancer." More information than the questioner needed but it worked. The questioner's facial expression changed.

"I am so sorry to hear that, Mrs. Klein. Is your husband traveling with you?"

"My husband died in the 1973 war. I wear his ring so I will never forget."

"One more question and I will let you go. Do you have anything in your bags to claim?"

"No. Only cosmetics and clothing for five days. Most of my things are being shipped and should be arriving very soon."

"Here are your papers. Do you have a good doctor?"

"Yes, he is very good. I have been assured I will not suffer. I forwarded my medical history so it would not get lost."

"Good luck, Mrs. Klein. It is warm outside, but very nice."

In another area of the terminal, an Air France 747 landed. On board were two Egyptian students on sabbatical at Columbia University to study advanced economics. Later in the evening, an SAS flight would arrive from Denmark carrying two other Egyptian graduate students on sabbatical at Columbia University to study implementing modern architecture into old-world neighborhoods.

By 1:00 a.m., all five members of the group were asleep in separate hotels in midtown Manhattan. Palmer was called at seven in the morning to inform him of their arrival. Arrangements were made for him to meet with the leader of the group for supper at 7:00 p.m., on June 22 at Carmine's restaurant on West Forty-Fourth Street.. He was to wait at the bar. He was told to reserve a table. He was not told it would be a woman.

"I was told the leader of the group would come straight here to the apartment."

"The person decided against it. Give me a description of what you plan to wear so the person will recognize you."

"I don't like or appreciate this treatment. I don't like change on a whim, understand?"

"You don't have to like it, Palmer, but you will accept it. Understand?"

Two hours later, Palmer lay in bed. He hadn't slept since the phone call. He was angry and frustrated. The cool air rushing over his face from the small air conditioner in the window did nothing to calm or reassure him.

"What if Golan is planning to eliminate me?" He was talking out loud. "That is easily handled. I could have Frank Graham alert the authorities. The General must know that . . . I'm overreacting. I need to think rationally." He sat up and swung his legs over the side of the bed.

"We need to go out, Wayne, you're all wound up."

"Quiet, I need to think. You two have had your fun. As for my feelings, it's a little late for that now, Mom." He poured vodka into a glass and swallowed half of it before refilling the glass.

He laughed, picked up the bottle and glass, and walked out into the living room. His heart racing, he sat down and slipped on a pair of surgical gloves, set a single sheet of paper on the blotter, and began to write.

"Dear Detective Polk."

WEDNESDAY, JUNE 20

Reba entered the deli at 12:30 p.m. She stepped into line at the counter and waited for the counter man to call her number. She had never eaten a pastrami sandwich, but had heard so much about it she insisted the consulate man pick a deli. She ordered pastrami on marble rye, Swiss cheese slices melted with pickles, brown mustard and a bag of Wise potato chips.

She walked to the table wearing a long leather coat with no makeup, not even lipstick, and a New York Yankee cap pulled tightly over her hair.

"It smells wonderful, but how do you bite into this? It must be six inches tall."

"You don't, unless you are a construction worker. Use the plastic knife and fork to cut it unless you want melted cheese on your cheeks. How is your first day in New York?"

"Good. The hotel is very nice. The city is too crowded. Very loud."

He lowered his voice. "I spoke to Palmer yesterday. He will be wearing a blue shirt with an open collar. A tan jacket, dark brown slacks, and brown loafers. He will be at the bar at seven. I told him to acquire a discreet table so you two can talk. Be mindful of him, Reba, he is not a pleasant man."

"I can be unpleasant as well." Reba took her first bite after cutting a wedge, chewing it, and rolling the flavors in her mouth. "This is truly heaven sent. I shopped this morning. I bought a dress that will attract attention. My luggage has not arrived. I have two trunks."

"Your things will be at the apartment today, but you are not to go there. The general wants Palmer to be surprised."

"The general already made that clear. Is Eve Cohen coming?"

"No, she is not unless it is required. You are to act as if you are meeting your husband for supper. Do not let your guard down, Reba."

"Can I eat my sandwich now, Harold Goldman?"

"Of course, my dear. Enjoy."

Palmer, dressed in a perspiration-stained sweat suit with a wool cap and leather gloves, walked into the Midtown police station. He paused long enough to remove the white envelope from his sock before stepping up to the sergeant's desk.

"I'll be right with you, sir."

Palmer nodded, counted to twenty, and placed the envelope on a stack of papers in front of a female officer who was paying no attention to him.

He stepped back and walked quickly out of the precinct, crossing the street to a waiting yellow cab.

"Take me to the Port Authority, driver," he said, and sat back, glancing at the entrance to the precinct. No one came out to the street and looked about with curiosity for the man in the sweat suit.

Palmer walked directly through the main concourse. He hailed a cab and gave his destination to the driver, a mirthless smile on his face.

"Attention to details . . . Always work on the side of caution on the outside chance you were seen leaving the precinct." His lips were moving as he congratulated himself. He imagined detective Polk reading it.

"I killed the bitch in Secaucus and Lombardo. Now I am planning a bigger kill. My crown jewel. She is famous, statuesque, and loved around the world. She will be my last act, Polk. I am not going to hide her; I am going to show her off to the world. What's left of her."

"Where to, sir?"

"Let me off on Seventh Avenue, driver. It is such a nice morning; I think I'll run across town."

"Whatever you say."

"Tell me," Palmer glanced at the drivers I.D., "have you ever been to the Statue of Liberty?"

"I took my kids over to the island when they were young. She's beautiful."

"Yes, she is, Monty, yes, she is."

Palmer signed for the two trunks and gave twenty dollars to each man, then closed and locked the door behind them. Showered, shaved, and dressed in clean shorts and T-shirt, he fixed a glass of apple juice. He sipped his drink, standing in the doorway of the guest bedroom. The owner of the trunk's name did not appear on the shipping papers or the tags, only his last name appeared and an address. He thought that odd, but what really attracted his attention was the scent on the trunks . . . a woman's scent. Palmer got down on his haunches and sniffed the handles and locks. He detected a very faint scent.

He stood up, retrieving his glass, and took a drink.

"He sent a woman. Why? Is she supposed to sleep with me and keep me in line? Is she Amazon-looking to prove a woman's prowess or simply a monitor to learn the plan and go back? She isn't a monitor for information, not with two trunks of clothing. She's part of it."

He was talking out loud, feeling the frustration turn slowly into anger. He finished the drink.

"Calm down . . . Calm down. Nothing is going to change. Patience . . . Control." He felt better.

CIA HEADQUARTERS - LANGLEY: JUNE 20

Manning-Ham and Drum entered the office. Timmons was sitting back in his chair, his hands folded on his lap. On his desk were three cards in each stack of cards set exactly three inches apart. Sydney Drum closed the door behind him.

"I made notes." He sat up, putting his hands on the desk.

"How did the trip go and when did you get back, boss?"

"I stayed over. It was good to get away from all this. I even went shopping. I bought three English cut suits. I drove out to the country and stayed at a bed and breakfast. I visited Paris. Dirty, I did not like it . . . Let's get on with it. Whatever Palmer is planning, it will happen in New York."

Timmons turned over a card from the first stack and placed it face down directly behind the other cards.

"I want you to monitor all local police traffic in New York City and northern New Jersey, Sydney. I want you to look for missing women cases. If he is a serial killer, he may be still active."

"You agree with Dupree?"

"Yes, I do." He turned a second card over. "I've given Shevchenko permission to come to America. He will come straight here to Langley when he lands. He is making a stop in Israel first. He will not be alone. He is bringing associates. He swears he can prove collusion with Senator Adam Stonewall Spencer of West Virginia."

"I know that fool. His initials couldn't be more perfect. Wasn't he in the Klan at one time?" Manning-ham said, with disdain in her voice.

"He was a Grand Dragon with the KKK, I've heard," Drum added. "Do we have a finding, boss?"

"No, we do not. I never asked." He turned over the last card in the first stack. "This conversation never happened and is not being recorded. I wanted you both to have a window of deniability should the situation with Palmer end badly." Timmons picked up the stack and one by one put them through the shredder next to his desk, "Let's continue. I have another meeting in thirty minutes." Timmons placed the two remaining stacks aside. "I need to speak to Adam. I am sending a driver to pick him up. We will review—"

"Are you all right, Ronald?"

"I'm fine Angela. I appreciate your concern."

"You seem to always catch me as Beatrice is preparing lunch. If you are waiting for an invitation, you, of course, know our door is always open to you."

"It may not be welcome after you hear what I have to say, Adam."

"Is it about Palmer?"

"Yes, it is."

"You know I met with Robert Kennedy when he was attorney general; I always liked this desk, I'm glad you have it."

"Shevchenko is coming over to hunt Palmer—"

"Is this being recorded, Ronald?"

"Absolutely not. My personal machine is off. What I'm about to tell you . . ." Timmons moved the second the stack of cards, centering it on his blotter. "I do not have a finding, Adam. I never asked the president for his okay. It is all on me. I didn't even tell the Prime Minister when I visited. She understands, of course."

"Have you spoken to any of the senators on the intelligence committee?"

"I can't. Shevchenko named the chairman Senator Spencer as a leak. He has been turned for years."

"Do you believe Shevchenko?"

"Dennis Oats is helping me create a model to present to the senator. I trust Oats and he trusts me . . . And yes, I believe Shevchenko."

"So why am I suddenly involved as part of this grand plan? You are not asking for advice, so it must be something else."

"Shevchenko has asked that he be allowed to work with your group. One of them especially."

"Impossible Ronald. He was just down here for the weekend. I can't do it."

"Will you meet with Shevchenko when he arrives?"

"I told Mikhail Balandin I would consider it. Shevchenko's other request is off the table. He needs to understand that."

"We will table the request for the time being and move on."

"We will table the request to: never will I give him up, Ronald. He is out of it. He never existed."

"Tell me, Adam . . . do you still wear argyle socks?"

"Son of a bitch, Timmons."

JUNE 22

Graham took the 14B exit off the New Jersey Turnpike and drove east toward Liberty Park. Palmer looked out the window. He hadn't spoken since they entered the Turnpike.

"We're here," Graham said, guiding the white Dodge van with the Jay and Sons Plumbing logo on the doors three rows from the entrance to the boat dock. "You haven't said anything about the van."

"It will do fine. Let's go and see what we came to see."

Palmer stared at the Statue of Liberty, his mind a jumble of scenarios. In reality, only one fit the outcome.

"When are you planning to do it, John?"

"My first thought was September twenty-ninth. It's Yom Kippur. I thought it would be a lovely gift for our Jewish friends. It was just a thought. I haven't decided. The water will be calmer and warmer. The ride over less jarring, I wouldn't want the explosives to go off before I'm ready. I built a scale model. I know exactly where to set off the device for maximum effect. I'm going to make a big goddamn mess of her, Graham.

"That letter you wrote to that cop . . . Big mistake, Palmer; they're not stupid."

"They'll be looking at Hollywood. I made sure to make it sound like I was going to kill some famous actress. I know what I'm doing. You should watch from here, Frank. Best seat in the house. They'll be picking up body parts and dredging that estuary for years."

"Your plan is missing a part . . . escape?"

"I'm not leaving the island Frank... I have to get back. I'm meeting the leader of the Israeli team for supper this evening."

Palmer entered the building, darted across the foyer, and took the steps two at a time until he reached the landing of the third floor. He paused, catching his breath just as the door to Joan Henry's apartment opened and an older gentleman—balding, with puffy eyes and a noticeable pouch—emerged.

"Good morning," Palmer said with a boyish smile. They shook hands. Palmer ignored Joan Henry. "My name is James; I live down the hall."

"Raymond Craft is my name; nice to meet you."

"Well, have a nice day you two," he said, never giving Joan so much as a sideways glance.

At eight minutes to seven that evening a cab pulled to the curb in front of Carmine's and stopped. Reba paid the fare and climbed out, closing the door. She took off her coat, draped it over her shoulders, ran her fingers through her hair—stringing out the loose curls—and entered Carmine's like a princess entering her private dining room.

Interested eyes were on her as she expected they would be.

"I'm expected," she said at the reservation desk and spied the man at the end of the bar with the tan jacket and brown slacks. "That is him. Darling, you daughter is making me crazy," she exclaimed, putting her arms on his shoulders and kissing him on both cheeks. "You were in the airport in Barcelona?"

"Would you like a drink? Our table should be ready soon." he answered, ignoring her comment.

"A martini, very dry." Reba put her coat across his lap, the bra effectively producing a deep cleavage.

"I've seen larger and better."

"You can't very well tell by looking, Palmer, and since you will never see these outside of a bra, comparison is out of the question. Order my drink, I'm thirsty."

The host approached, stopping a few feet from the couple pretending to study a seating chart. The man was ordering her a drink. Years of working with customers and studying body language told him the façade of happiness did not fit in this instance. When her martini and his vodka arrived, he stepped forward.

"Your table is ready. Please follow me, unless you would like to finish your drinks?"

"No, we are fine, we'll come along now; I'm famished," Reba answered.

He led them through the tables with the finesse of an ice skater managing a difficult turn. Behind him, she quibbled about the daughter he fawns over and his lack of discipline with her. Jewish couples were like Italians, they fought only about two things: their children and money.

"Here is your table. Is it satisfactory? You mentioned privacy, sir? May I take your coat, madam?" He pulled her chair out for her.

"Why thank you, I'd like that." A waiter approached with a water flask and filled their glasses. "What do you suggest we try. . . ," Reba quickly glanced at the hosts name tag. "May I ask your full name?"

"Salvatore Russo, madam."

"I want to compliment you, Salvatore Russo. I wish to write a note of thanks to your employer." The gesture would be remembered.

"Thank you, madam. Paulo, your waiter, will guide you through the menu." He wore no wedding ring. Did the woman? The gentleman shook his hand and thanked him. He felt the folded bill in his palm and quickly slipped it into his pocket. "Thank you, sir."

"This table will do just fine."

"Your menus." The waiter put one in front of the woman. Opening it, he placed a large linen napkin across her knees. "Look through them and take your time. Any questions you have, I will be glad to answer." He left them, tending to his other guests.

"You were supposed to be at the apartment a few days ago."

"I decided to see the city. I was right about Barcelona, wasn't I?" Her voice was barely above a whisper. "You were in the airport. I even remember the name you used . . . Preston, wasn't it? A woman was murdered there, a blonde. She washed up on the beach. She was with you in the airport."

"Yes, it was me in Barcelona. You were revisiting a honeymoon, if I remember. Was that bullshit to tell me to keep my distance?"

"No, it was not. My husband is dead. I am here to do what is necessary to see that my country is safe. The others are here as well. Are you using the name Preston at the apartment? I wouldn't want to call you Palmer by mistake."

"You look comfortable in your surroundings; have you been here before?"

"If you are asking about the city, I've visited New York once before briefly. The reason is none of your business except to say it was personal."

Reba looked down at her menu. "In case you wonder why they sent a woman instead of a man, I am very good at what I do, Palmer, and I have been doing it longer than you know. I'd like to order now."

"I had a suspicion the general sent a woman, you know why?"

"No, I do not."

"I smelled your perfume on the trunks: jasmine, is it not? The same as you are wearing tonight." Palmer signaled for the waiter. He, too, could play the cat and mouse game while letting her know that he was not one to be trifled with.

"It is Chanel, Palmer, not jasmine. Order the veal parmesan for me, and I'd like a nice red wine."

The apartment was painted a sterile light grey with white trim. One picture, a nature scene, an empty farm. Reba expected as much. Palmer never felt close to anyone beyond physical need. She expected to hear a low howling like an animal in distress somewhere on the brick wall outside the living room window.

"Where do I sleep? By the way, I liked the restaurant."

"I'll show you the room." He led her down the hall to the bedroom. He opened the door and stepped aside. "The furniture is new. You will be the first to sleep on the bed."

"I appreciate it. I hate hotels. Who knows what went on in those beds." Reba lifted her dress and began removing her panty hose. His expression never changed. "One pillow is good. I do not intend on sharing my bed."

"I get up early and run to the East River and back." His voice, a mirror like his eyes, was blank.

"I like to run early as well . . . may I join you?"

"If you want; I leave at six."

"I will be ready. Close the door, please. Goodnight. "

"Your bathroom is down the hall to the right; I have my own." He closed the door and crossed the hall. They were leaning against the windowsill, holding hands.

"What do you want?"

"We don't like her, she's not very nice. Great body, nice looking, Wayne. We don't like her. She will try to control you like that, Maxine. While we are on the subject of bodies . . ."

"I told you we can't do that anymore; I thought I made it very clear"

"You know your father Wayne, you've spoiled him."

"Get out. Both of you, I need to get some sleep." He wanted multiple drinks and maybe a visit to Joan Henry down the hall. "I'll chase her balding boyfriend out and do her on the floor, mark her up good." He giggled like a child who had gotten away with something very bad. But deep inside, where reality still lived, he knew both actions would be a mistake. Instead, he called Frank Graham.

"They sent a woman. That bastard Golan is playing games with me."

"What choice do you have, John? I'm not alone. Call me tomorrow afternoon. I'm calling Cahill in the morning."

"Is she hot, Frank?"

"You have no idea, Palmer. Goodbye." Graham rolled over on his back. The young blond man put his head on Graham's chest; his hand moved, palm down, to Graham's member.

"Should I worry about the call?"

"No baby, he's straight . . . and you are my gorgeous secret."

MOSCOW: JUNE 23

"You never told me what Comrade Fedorov talked to you about in this latest meeting, Peter." Marina took old pictures out of frames, placing them neatly in envelopes and marking each one.

"It isn't important, Marina. What is important is that you and your husband have a train to catch this afternoon. It will take you both to the station outside Minsk. You will be in the station only one hour. The train will then take you to Vienna, nonstop. You must be there in the morning or miss the rest of your immediate family. Any deviation could bring the police. Do you understand, Marina?"

"Yes, I understand, Peter."

"They will be waiting for you at the airport. You all should be in Tel Aviv by tomorrow evening. The consulate will have your clothes and trunks and will escort you to your new temporary housing. A major in the Israeli army will take care of all your needs until you are established. His name is Shapiro."

"Our papers in order. When will we meet with Ladas?"

"She is coming here and should be here shortly."

"Does Fedorov know who is leaving and how many?"

"He only knows what he knows. I will stop in Tel Aviv to see her." He held Marina in his arms ignoring the warm tears on her cheek. "Care for her until she comes to America."

"Do not worry about Ladas."

"Thank you, Marina."

NEW YORK: JUNE 23

Palmer set the table and prepared coffee, orange juice, and toast with peanut butter and boysenberry jelly while Reba showered. He had to admit he was impressed with her stamina. She had stayed with him, breathing in through her nose out through her mouth, as she jogged alongside him to the FDR drive and back without a break. She did not seem winded and was even polite and gracious when he introduced her to Joan Henry in the foyer.

"I made toast and coffee."

She stepped into the alcove of the kitchen, rubbing her hair with a thick towel and wearing pajamas under a thick bathrobe. She opened the fridge.

"Well, isn't that nice. No bagels?" She spied the chocolate cake. "Is that how you seduced Joan Henry? All it took was a slice of cake?" Reba wrapped the towel around her head with a satisfied smile. "That won't work with me, you know, but at least you could have plied me with a bagel, cream cheese, and a slice of salted fish."

"No to both questions, Reba. I fix this breakfast for myself. I only made more because you are here." Tit for tat, two can play this game.

"Of course, you did. I saw the look on her face when she saw me, Palmer. You did her. I do not care what you do, just do not try to fool me."

I hate that Reba. She doesn't respect our son.

Your mother doesn't like her and neither do I.

"Be quiet, both of you."

"Did you say something, Palmer?"

"I was just thinking out loud about things."

"When were you planning to show me the target?"

"I thought after we eat and get dressed. " She made him feel uncomfortable, in less control; he did not like the feeling.

Palmer pinned the blueprints on the wall showing the outer buildings, perimeter, and inner structure of the statue and docks. Small yellow pins marked the areas of interest.

"The pins mark placements of the vest explosives for maximum effect. I made a replica of the island to scale." He left her looking over the blueprints. When he returned, he carried a scale model of the island and statue mounted on a plywood platform. "I think it will be easier if you see it, rather than imagine it from blueprints and the Battery Park dock." He was interrupted by the phone. "That might be the call I was waiting for." Palmer walked through the hall to his bedroom, closed the door, and picked up.

"Hello."

"We may have a problem."

"Did you call Cahill?"

"They know you are here."

"That doesn't concern me if they know, Frank. They don't know the plan and they don't know where I am."

"Shevchenko is on his way here with assassins. Cahill asked if I would assist if called upon."

"Assist with what, Frank?"

"He didn't say. If Shevchenko is coming, they must know something. Perhaps they found out where you are staying. I know there is more. Shevchenko wouldn't be coming here blindly. Langley would never allow it."

"The government would never allow it, Frank. This is strictly CIA work. They are going dark on this. Maybe a call to the State Department would disrupt the CIA's intentions. What do you think?"

"What about Russian plants? Women who sleep with and handle people like Dukakis and Spencer. Cahill knows more than he is saying."

"I don't think so, Frank. I don't think he knows himself. That's why he asked you to help if need be. You haven't answered my question."

"It would be a waste of a dime. The State Department is more screwed up than a donkey with two dicks. Dukakis is another issue."

"I will deal with Dukakis. When you know more, get a hold of me. But just to be on the safe side, maybe you should look for another location."

"I'll start looking today. I know a realtor."

"That took some time. Is there a problem?"

"No, just an associate of mine. Guy talk, is all. He has nothing to do with our arrangement. So, what do you think of the blueprint and the scale model?"

"So that was not the call you were expecting, Palmer?"

"It was."

"Do not play games with me, Palmer, or I will pull the team out and you can do what you want."

"Okay, Reba . . . The blueprints, what do you think?"

"I am just starting to review it. What is my role in this? What about my people?"

"You will get me to the island. Your friends will drive onto and blow up a section of the George Washington Bridge. The bridge is our distraction. Police, firemen, and ambulances will converge there. Clear enough?"

"Very clear, Palmer. I would like a piece of the cake."

"Good. I will fix a piece of the cake while you study."

"Could I have juice with it?" Be subtle but firm, He can be managed.

CHAPTER TWENTY-THREE

THE FALL OF GENERAL GOLAN

The Learjet landed on schedule. It rolled off the main runway, turned left, and came to a stop. The engines shut down. No one exited the aircraft and no one approached.

Inside the hangar, General Abel Golan, two suitcases by his side, stood in the middle of a group of six army commandos. Shots in his knee afforded him the luxury of not having to walk with a cane, temporarily. Major Jonah Shapiro was in charge. Perez, Yitzhak Hof Amos Ariel, and Yaakov Peri emerged from an office at the far end of the hangar. Menachem Begin appeared with Golda Meir.

"Has there been a change in orders?"

"A change, yes," Yaakov answered. "The old man will explain."

"Everyone is here. Good . . . We can start. Madam, would you begin?"

"You are not going to Camp David, General Golan. There are no plans for signing in the next few days. Depending on the results of this conversation, you will not be leaving this hangar." Two IDF officers took hold of the general's arms.

"I do not understand."

"My dear General, I think you do. Why don't you look outside? I think you will recognize the Russian exiting the aircraft. You do see him, General?"

"Yes, I see him, madam."

"In that case we shall begin. This group is here for General Golan, to be a jury of a sort. The decision on guilt or innocence will be final and binding. Tell us about John Michael Palmer, the American traitor, and this insane plan you came up with to destroy our enemies with the help of the American military?"

"There is nothing insane about it, Madam," the General answered. "You always want to believe . . . give it a chance. People change, you chant. Six million dead and many more before the Holocaust and still you think it will be better. Do you know what that man on the tarmac represents?"

"Yes, we do, General," Yaakov Kaln an answered. "We know about Afghanistan. We know about the plan. Not all the details, of course, which we hope you will tell us. You want to get us involved, along with the United States, in a great Mideast war. You are like the neocons in America. In your insane vision, we will finally rid our nation of its enemies. At the same time, the Soviets can do whatever they want without interference. Both sides win . . . We know."

"Tell us the target in America so we can stop it."

"You are all mad."

"You are stalling, General. We want to know the plan and who amongst the Mossad is involved with Palmer."

"I can't help you. I do not know the plan and never was I privy to it. I will never give up the agents who worked with me . . . They are the true children of Israel."

"I am afraid you leave us no choice. Major Shapiro, take the general to the office now. Here is a list of questions we need answered. Do what you must."

"Yes madam

"You never listen. You never learn."

Moments later, the echo of Golan's screams shattered the silence. The screams stopped as abruptly as they started within minutes. The only sound comes from the turbo fans as they draw out the fumes of aviation fuel and stale air. The door of the office opened and Major Shapiro stepped out. Behind him, a ribbon of white-gray smoke drifted from the open door carrying with it the odor of burnt flesh.

"Did we learn anything?" he was asked when he joined the group huddled in the hangar.

"I have the names of those who have joined the plot. Five. Four reported to our embassy in New York. We have people in our embassy also complicit in the plot. Here is the list.

"I will see to this," Yitzhak said, holding the list by his side.

"Let me see the list, Yitzhak." Ariel's face turned white when he scanned the list of names. "My God, it is our Reba," Ariel gasped.

"They must not be brought back . . . and certainly there can be no trial." Ariel put his hands on Shapiro's shoulders. There were tears in his eyes. "Our Reba. Benjamin will need to know."

"If they are captured, I want to see the end of them."

"Granted, Major Shapiro."

"Why is Shevchenko here?" Shapiro asked.

"He has asked if he could marry while he is here. Her name is Ladas Sorokin. She was married to General Pavlov before his demise…He is going on to America to hunt and kill Palmer."

NEW YORK: JUNE 24

"It's me, Mrs. Henry, the super."

"One moment please, Mr. Strong. Thank you for coming up," she said in a raspy voice.

"What seems to be the problem?"

"The apartment is fine. I'm concerned with that new tenant and that woman he has living with him. Then there are the four Arabs upstairs. You are smiling as if I'm deranged, Mr. Strong. The other day, I was getting off the elevator and that woman was in the hall smoking. The door to his apartment was open and I saw these blueprints hanging on the wall and a plaster model of Liberty Island on a long table in the living room."

"The woman is a government agent. She works in the office of land management with Preston. They are studying the structure, finding weak points after all these years and coming up with a cost analysis for repairs. Her name is Reba Davis. She is a very nice woman. You might enjoy getting acquainted . . . it's all very legal."

"I'm sorry I bothered you, Mr. Strong."

"You didn't bother me, okay. I'm glad I have tenants who watch out for the place, especially with these bombings by the FALN." Strong waited for Joan to close her door and lock it. He smiled, shook his head and started down the hall toward the elevator. He pressed the button just as the door to apartment

3B opened and the woman stepped out holding a package of cigarettes and a book of matches.

"Good morning, Miss Davis." Even in sweats, she cut quite a figure. "Working out, I see."

"Got to keep in shape; this is a tough town."

"The city just likes to act tough," Strong answered. "By the way, while we are on the subject, you might want to get to know Mrs. Henry. She seems to be a bit itchy about things. I know I shouldn't have said anything about your work. I think if she hears it from you, it might quiet her nerves."

"What seems to be the problem?"

"She saw the Liberty statue and the blueprints. It made her nervous."

"I see. I'll make a point of it. I'll ask her over for coffee. I thought she was on a trip to Japan."

"Thanks, I'm sorry to be a bother. I think they are leaving tonight."

"It's no bother at all Mr. Strong."

TEL AVIV: JUNE 24

A loud knock on the door then four more in rapid succession: a man's voice. "Ladas Sorokin, would you make me break down this door?"

"Who could that be, Ladas?"

"My love," her eyes filled with tears. "Excuse me, Rabbi." She hurried across the room, her shoes clicking on the tile floor. "Peter Shevchenko," she cried out breathlessly, pulling the door open. "My sweetheart . . . my sweet love." She kissed him hard on the mouth and pulled him into the room, shutting the door.

"My Ladas," he said, "I must leave you . . . I've missed you."

"Peter, I want you to meet Rabbi Noah Presser. He has been helping me understand the Hebrew history."

"It is a pleasure to meet you, Peter. I understand you wish to marry? I am overjoyed for you both."

"Time, I'm afraid, is short . . . I am a communist, Rabbi. I have no religious affiliation, not because of being Russian. I lost both my parents in the great war. I have done things I am sure no deity, if one exists, would forgive."

"The subject of God and his testament we will let rest for another time, Peter. You wish to marry this lovely woman, and I wish to help you. Is that fair?"

"It is most fair, Rabbi. If Ladas wishes to continue to learn of your faith, I will not stand in her way. I think it is good for her, if she finds peace in its offering. Who knows, perhaps, as you say, we can discuss God and his bearing on men at a future date." Peter squeezed Ladas's hand. "We have a couple who will stand with us, so what must we do?"

"All you will need to do is arrive at the American Embassy tomorrow morning. The proper paperwork has been filed. You are not citizens of Israel, so no blood test is required. They need only your signature, Peter. An American judge will marry you. Arrangements have been made for a small party of celebration to be held at the embassy, if that is satisfactory. I will leave you both."

"One more thing, if I may. I think I speak for both of us . . . Would your beliefs allow you to marry us, Rabbi?"

"That is an interesting question, Peter. I would think that a marriage between two people is a contract for life and should not be interfered with by religious doctrine. Of course my beliefs, which we call Halachah, will hinder me from certain portions of the ceremony according to Jewish law. Saying that, I would be honored to marry you both. I have a question. Would it be all right with both of you if I said a prayer for you both?"

"Yes, of course . . . Is it alright with you, Peter?" Her face reddened. "I shouldn't speak for both of us; I—"

"You never have to apologize for your feelings, Ladas. Yes, Rabbi, a prayer would be wonderful. Neither of us have family. Only our friends. Her parents were killed in the great war as well. I would ask if you would remember us in your prayers while circumstances force us to be separated from each other."

"I will remember you both in my daily prayers as long as Yahweh keeps me on his earth."

"Can I hug you, Rabbi?"

"There is nothing in our laws against hugging, Ladas."

NEW YORK: JUNE 25

The elevator door opened, and Palmer stepped out. He put his boot on the bottom wheel rung and tipped the dolly back toward him. He pulled it out and started across the foyer toward the entrance just as Ken Strong came through the front door.

"Heading for work, James, at 3:00 a.m.?"

"You look like you've been to a party, Ken."

"A few Nam buddies in town . . . My head hurts."

"Going to work, Ken. The trunk is full of sensitive gear we need for our project. You didn't happen to see a white van out front? I left the other trunk on the sidewalk."

"Shit, I don't know if something white is out there. Shit, I don't know how I got here."

"Let me help you there, Ken." Palmer stood the dolly up, took the keys out of his hand, grabbed Strong's arm, and pulled him toward his apartment.

"I got a secret; you want to know my secret?"

"Sure, Ken," he answered, opening the door. "I'm putting your keys back in your pants pocket, Ken."

"Joan Henry has the . . .," he belched spittle on his shirt, "for you, man."

"Where are we taking the trunks, Palmer?" Daniel Berg asked as Palmer guided the van south on Ninth Avenue toward the turnoff to the Lincoln tunnel.

"Secaucus, there's tall grass in the marsh and soft dirt good for digging. The river is too shallow. Did you bring water?"

"Two gallons of water, a change of clothes for each of us, clean socks and shoes, a package of chocolate chip cookies, four candy bars, two shovels, and a pick in case we hit an obstruction when we dig." Daniel opened the wing window. "I am going to smoke."

TEL AVIV

Rabbi Presser asked Marina to read from the Old Testament, Ruth 1:16-17.

"I know the prayer, Rabbi."

Marina presented the bride to Rabbi Presser, opened her Bible to Ruth: 1:16-17, and read from the scripture.

"Rabbi Presser opened his book. "Before I begin the civil ceremony that will bring this man and woman together as one heart shared by both, I ask God to bless this union." Rabbi Presser smiled, patting each on the head, and began the civil ceremony.

"I will love you; I will protect you, and be faithful to you all the days of my life." Peter slipped the gold band with an opal inset onto her finger. He remembered her telling him opal was her mother's favorite stone. "This is my bond to you."

"Ladas, share your thoughts with Peter."

"I am your wife, your best friend and confidant, and I will always be." She slipped the gold band with an onyx inset onto his finger. They kissed, and Ladas put her lips close to his ear and whispered, "Not too much celebration, Shevchenko. I will be making demands on you until you leave me."

"When do I rest woman?"

"You can sleep on the plane, Peter Shevchenko."

HOBOKEN, NEW JERSEY

"This is a complication you do not need, Palmer. Who is in the van?"

"Daniel Berg. He is one of the Israelis."

I don't care about him; who is in the goddamn van?"

"A man and a woman: couldn't be helped. They were in the way."

"We do not need this shit, Palmer. You have to stay focused."

"I did not want you involved, but we had a problem. Some drunk ran over a pedestrian on the service road in front of the Hilton hotel in Secaucus."

"All right, go. Take whatever personal stuff you have in the van. I'll make sure it is wiped clean. I've found an apartment overlooking the Hudson River in Fort Lee. It's perfect and has easy access to the bridge, turnpike, and Route

4. Now go, Palmer. Get back to New York, stay put, and wait for my call."

"We need Cahill."

"I know we do. Where is the van?"

"Outside."

"Pull it down to the lower-level garages." Graham hung up and cupped his hands behind his head.

"Is there some kind of trouble?"

"Yeah, dammit. I have to go out soon, Christopher."

"Can we talk about it? You want me to come with you?"

"Not this time, baby."

"CIA stuff, huh?"

"Yeah, CIA stuff."

CIA HEADQUARTERS - LANGLEY: JUNE 26

"Mr. Timmons, you have B on your green phone."

"Thank you, Mona." Timmons took the small key from a tin of cough drops and opened the bottom cabinet of his desk. He took out the private phone, centering it on the desk blotter. "I'm ready, Mona, put the call through . . .Benjamin."

"There will be breaking news shortly on the death of General Golan. I am sending pictures of five Israeli agents already in your country. They are working with Palmer. Four are posing as students, the woman as a cancer patient."

"Where are they? Did he tell you?"

"In New York, that is all we know. I do not believe Golan knew. The announcement will be made by the prime minister at nine o'clock your time. As you know, we can be of little help with manpower in your search under the current circumstances. Four of the five had been staying at the embassy, and at present, members of the embassy staff were being shuffled back to Israel for private trials."

"I realize the position you are in, sir. Ask for Bernard Shaw. I think he is already in Tel Aviv. He can be trusted to be honest in his coverage."

He put the phone back in the cabinet and buzzed his secretary.

"Get Manning-Ham and Drum up here, Mona. Hold them in your office until I buzz you. I have to make a call."

"Yes, sir. Will you need refreshments?"

"No. There'll be an announcement of importance at nine or shortly after. We'll watch the Israeli response together." Timmons hung up and dialed.

"Good morning, Beatrice."

"He isn't here, Ronald. He's out for his morning walk; he should be back very soon though."

"Put on CNN at ten minutes to nine, Beatrice." He said goodbye and hung up. He sighed, rubbing his hands together, and leaned back in his chair closing his eyes. There was a slight tremor in his hands. Timmons took two deep breaths. "What would Adam do?" Timmons whispered. Adam isn't here, you are here. You need to pull yourself together. Make decisions rationally, without fear of failure . . . Lead. The country depends on it for their safety. It does not matter what Adam would do in this situation. What matters is what you do, Timmons.

He opened his eyes, sat up straight, straightened his tie, put the pencils and pens in their proper place on the blotter, and buzzed Mona. "Are they here? Good. Have them come in."

"What's up, Ronald?" Manning-Ham asked, leading Drum into the office.

"Put on CNN, and take a seat. I'll explain while we wait for the official story."

"This can't be good," Drum said, taking his seat. "No coffee and now this?"

"After I'm finished, a coffee may not be strong enough, Sidney."

TEL AVIV

"Do you have your papers in order, Peter?" Ladas's eyes welled up. She promised herself she wouldn't cry.

"Yes, in my coat pocket. Please do not cry. I need that radiant smile in my head until we can be together. No more separations after this, I swear it." Shevchenko pulled Ladas into his arms. "I am going to miss the feel of you against me, the scent of your perfume, the smell of your hair . . ." He slid his hands slowly along her sides, resting them on her buttocks. "This wonderful ass."

"I'm fat. I've become a fat Russian wife. I swore I would not cry like a schoolgirl. This is your fault, Peter Shevchenko. You are not supposed to leave your bride." Ladas buried her face in his chest. "I'm getting tears on your jacket."

"Good, it will keep you in my thoughts. Has Timmons arranged housing for you? You haven't said anything about it."

"I am to meet a realtor in this place called Bangor, Maine. Her name is Danielle Putnam. I am to meet her on Saturday. Maybe you will be finished with this Parker by then."

"Maybe, I will. I must go."

"One more minute and don't move your hands."

"I have taken something of yours."

"Have you taken a picture of me to keep close to your heart?"

"That and one other thing. I took a pair of your panties to keep under my pillow when I sleep." She began to laugh. "What is it? I thought you would like my gesture, Ladas?"

"I love your gesture, Shevchenko. I was picturing you wearing them to bed." She pressed herself tightly against him, "You must go. Come back to me safe, Peter Shevchenko."

"I promise I will return. We will live in this place called Bangor, Maine. Mr. and Mrs. Baker. My wife sitting in the enclosed patio, typing out your short stories and me in my pickup driving into Bangor for groceries and gas for the mower," he said in his finest southern accent.

"Why bless your heart, darlin.' "

NEW YORK

"Been on a run?"

"Got to keep in shape, Ken. I think I'll take the stairs." He reached the first-floor landing and stopped. "What do you want, Mom?"

"I came to say goodbye. Your father and I will not be bothering you any longer. It seems your father has a new friend, a man from Oregon, or is it Washington state? I hate it when I don't remember things."

"You mean like feeding your baby?"

"Your father bonded with this young man." She giggled a hideous cackle. "He kills these young women like you, but he goes back after a few days and he screws them and eats bits of them . . . anyway, I wanted to say goodbye."

"Goodbye, Mom." He no more believed her than he believed in the tooth fairy.

"Where were you?" Reba was on the couch in her robe; it was open and loosely tied. Her legs were tucked under her hip, her hair wrapped in a towel. An anchor was getting ready to update the public of an important news story coming out of Tel Aviv. It was easy to see she was indifferent to his presence. "You went jogging without me."

There was a moment he thought seriously of slapping her.

"You were sleeping . . . What's so important?"

"I'm waiting to find out." She reached for a package of Marlboro's.

"I thought I asked you not to smoke in the apartment Reba."

"I didn't want to miss the story. Here, it is coming on in a second." She lit the cigarette. The smoke rose, forming a small cloud over her head "If it bothers you, open a window. But be quiet, I want to hear this. I made coffee, but it's old."

"This is Bernard Shaw reporting from Tel Aviv. We are waiting for the Prime Minister to address the people of Israel on the death of General Abel Golan. The general was a freedom fighter in 1948 and considered . . . Wait, here is the prime minister now."

Reba unfolded her legs and sat up. She tapped out her cigarette, took a fresh one from the pack, and lit it. First there were tears as the prime minister described how the general died. The tears soon melted away to anger as she smoked the cigarette down to an early stub, tamped it out, and sat back. When the prime minister completed his statement and left the podium, she screamed, "This is bullshit . . . nothing but bullshit!"

"Hezbollah has taken credit for the murder. They are cheering in the streets of Beirut," Shaw was saying. "The anger in the Israeli community is palpable. Revenge is the cry from the crowd."

"They know. Somehow they found out."

"They know nothing."

"You are wrong Palmer." She stood up, cinched up her robe—to his dismay—and started to walk to the kitchen, pausing in the doorway: "I need a brandy. They know who and what you are Palmer, and they know we are here."

"Hezbollah has taken credit, end of story."

"Yes, they took credit. They take credit for a lot of things they do not do. You forget I was part of that, Palmer. They have played into the hands of the government. A nice neat package tied in a nice tight bow."

"You are overacting, Reba."

"Am I? What was he doing that put him in such a precarious position? You hear, Palmer, but you do not listen." Reba disappeared into the kitchen.

"His helicopter malfunctioned and crashed."

"Bullshit, Palmer."

Palmer walked over to the window and turned on the fan, moving the dial to exhaust. He coughed as the acrid smoke dried his throat. "This works into our hands. The prime minister said it himself. Hezbollah is the culprit: case closed. The story will be out of the press after today and forgotten."

"Yes, the news will die while Mossad agents search for us here, Palmer. Golan gave us up. I am sure of it."

"I would worry about the Russians sending assassins, but not the Mossad. Your government will not hunt for us. They will never admit one word of this publicly. It would be a disaster for Israel to admit its government was complicit in such an incident."

"You cannot blame a nation for the actions of a few, Palmer."

"Who isn't listening now, Reba? Do you see what has happened in Iran? Stalin had more friends in the State Department, the press, and Hollywood during the forties and fifties than Israel has today. Their hands are tied. Drink your brandy and, please, no more smoking in the apartment."

"I suppose you have a point, Palmer."

"Can't you call me John?"

"I am not sleeping with you. If I call you John it will be then. I am going to get dressed. I want to know about the security on Liberty Island. I want to discuss your plan for the bridge. I want to see the bridge up close. I want a brandy."

"Not you. I will take Joseph and Daniel. Will that be all, your grace?"

"For the time being."

CIA HEADQUARTERS - LANGLEY: JUNE 26

"You have a call coming in on your private line It's B."

"Thank you, Mona, put it through. Hold calls and I want you in here. Hello, my friend. We heard the address." He motioned Mona to a seat across from him. "Before we begin, my assistant, you met her, will be listening in."

"Welcome, Mona."

"Good morning, sir."

"You have listened to the broadcast? Allow me to express my concerns about his death and other matters."

"I think I know where you are going with this, sir. This call is about a mutual enemy: John Michael Palmer."

"Yes, it is."

"I am glad you understand, B. We will take care of Palmer. As far as the agents with him . . ."

"You are not telling me everything, are you, Ronald?"

"I can't. I will need a second set of pictures."

"Your request will arrive tomorrow by courier. Mona, what do you think of all this?"

"I think Mr. Timmons has made the correct decision for all involved, sir. Of course, you will be updated daily on his progress."

"Yes, of course. Cahill had Beatrice and Timmons has you, Mona. Both men have chosen wisely. Please give my regards to Adam and Beatrice."

"I will and thank you for the compliment." She was blushing, her cheeks almost matching her hair. "Shall I call Manning-Ham and Drum, Ronald?" she asked, waiting for Timmons to put the green phone back in the cabinet.

"What would you do, Mona?"

"I would not involve them beyond their regular duties, Ronald. The less people involved in this situation, the better. I certainly would not mention the call you just received from B. It would be like dumping oil into the Potomac."

"Excellent analogy." Timmons leaned across his desk to check his appointment schedule.

"You have an Intel briefing with "POTUS" at eleven. I penciled it in your notebook in case he cancels it again. You should tell him what's going or at least a sketch."

"No, he wouldn't give us a finding anyway and he would blow a gasket if he knew we were bringing in a Russian KGB agent to hunt Palmer. No. He must never know. What else have I to do, besides prepare for Shevchenko?"

"Twelve thirty to one thirty, lunch in the café. You have the weekly department heads conference with the director at three. What does the director know, by the way?"

"He is also out of the loop."

"You are amazing, Mr. Timmons. Everybody is in the clear but you."

He put his head back, closed his eyes, and once more clasped his hands on his lap. "Put Manning-Ham and Drum down for two this afternoon. My wife presented me with divorce papers, Mona. She is moving out to be with her lover."

"How does that make you feel?"

"Free. We do not have to mask our feelings any longer. I don't want to go back and forth. I want our own place. Our own life."

"Be patient. After the divorce is final, she cannot claim she is the injured party."

"She can't. Who would believe her? The evidence is clear."

"For a man as brilliant as you, you are naïve my love."

JUNE 28

Palmer paid the toll and entered the upper level of the George Washington Bridge, slipping easily into traffic.

"You want to come early for a maximum killing field, Joseph. I want you to drive. Abram, when you reach the second weight-bearing girder on the upper structure, set the radio timer, get out, and run forward. Moesha, you will plug the wires into the cylinder on the side of the first drum. Use the ramp to exit. Daniel, you will be waiting on the city side. I'll show you where to wait."

"I have studied the blue prints carefully," Joseph answered, interrupting Palmer. "A van with a large cargo bay and enough explosives driven into the bus terminal would have a higher killing field, if it exploded in the center of the building. A section of the floor would undoubtedly collapse. Vehicles on fire would fall through the floor. The survivors would have no escape routes."

"I agree with Joseph," Daniel added, "the death toll would be higher and the damage greater."

"Well, let's test your theory." Palmer edged the car into the right lane and exited the bridge. He turned right onto 175th Street and pulled into a commuter parking garage. "Let's take a walk," he announced, bouncing out of the car.

"What is that train station?" Daniel asked, pointing to the entrance to the subway.

"New York subway. I believe that is the A. I do not know the routes."

"Wouldn't that be a better way to get away from the area?" Berg asked. "I am thinking the bridge will be shut down. We will not be able to cross in any case."

"You are not allowing for the panic the explosion will cause. You could be trapped in the building."

"I agree with Daniel, I think we should consider every possibility to escape, Palmer."

"Fine." Reluctantly, he accepted the notion of survival. "You must remember gentlemen . . . survival is never an absolute."

CHAPTER TWENTY-FOUR

WATERGATE APARTMENTS: JULY 3

"How is your drink, Ethan?"

"It's wonderful, Adam—a hint of almonds very smooth on the pallet . . . Where did you find this?"

"Timmons brought a gift from the Prime Minister. Timmons was over there for the Pepper affair, nasty business. Have you two set a date?"

"Soon. We want to get Vincent settled in a school close to the loft. We were thinking of La Salle as a matter of fact, my old alma mater. We both gave it a lot of thought. We both agreed to get out of Washington. Vincent is ecstatic, and Anna Lee has already found work at Saint Vincent's hospital. She starts in October. She gave notice at Walter Reed. Maggie, you remember her? She is devastated, but happy for us, and it gives her and her husband an excuse to visit New York."

"I, for one, couldn't be happier, Ethan. Did you happen to read about General Golan? It seems to me it wouldn't be an act Hezbollah would or could accomplish without help."

"Okay, Adam, let's have it. You've been playing Ring Around the Rosie with me for the past hour."

"Now why would you think that, my boy?"

"We've known each other a long time, Adam. Get to the point."

"The Viet who was killed in New York . . . Timmons believes it was this Palmer fellow who killed him. They may have met by chance."

"What has it to do with me?"

"Do you remember a Russian by the name of Dmitry Kasparov?"

"No, should I?"

"ODB 51, he was there. He is in Washington."

"Get to the point, Adam."

"Timmons has learned that Palmer is going to do grave damage unless he is stopped. He is working with a Jewish commando team who are here to assist him and force the story that Arab terrorists committed whatever atrocity he is planning. Timmons has it from two very good sources: the Israeli Government and the KGB."

"Golan is dead because he was part of it, Adam?

"As far as I know."

"Timmons involved you to get to me?"

"That is also correct, Ethan. I told him it was out of the question."

"But you have changed your mind?"

"Yes, Ethan, I have—after I talked to Mikhail Balandin."

"Lunch is ready. Bring your drinks."

"We are coming, my dear; the stew smells wonderful."

"I'm not getting involved."

"Timmons knows who you are."

"This sounds like a script for a Hollywood movie."

"In a way you outed yourself, Ethan."

"How?"

"Argyle Socks."

"Let's go, you two. I have gossip I want to share."

"Domestic, I hope. I really do not care about the lives of the royals or their offspring."

"It's domestic, I swear."

NEW YORK: JULY 5

"I am going to need a cargo van, Frank, now that the other van is no longer available. It will have to be bought from a dealership in Jersey. The bus terminal uptown will be the secondary target. Have you heard or spoken to Cahill?"

"No, I was planning to call him later today, if he doesn't call me."

"I will talk to you soon." Palmer hung up without waiting for a reply and walked out into the living room. "Where is Joseph, Reba?"

"He went to Crown Heights to pick up the shipment."

"I said I wanted to pick it up, Reba. I wanted to check the contents myself."

"We decided he would go instead. A Jew would not garner much attention and the rabbi knows Joseph. They met in Israel last year."

"I do not like change without at least telling me."

"We do not like your private calls." See if he backs down. Take control. "We do not make a fuss over it," Reba retorted. "We assume whomever you talk to is part of this, but not directly involved with the act. So, you see, trust is essential. You understand, don't you, Palmer? Why don't we discuss the plan now. Quibbling doesn't help; do you agree, Palmer?"

"You are right, Reba. Arguing gets us nowhere. The man I called is a good friend. He has connections in the CIA and has been a big help to me. He is our eyes and ears." He felt his power waning, the feeling infuriated him. He needed to go out. He needed a release. No, he told himself, control . . . keep control of your feelings. The Lombardo woman was the last; you promised yourself.

"That wasn't so bad now was it, Palmer? "Moshe added. "We need to eyeball the terminal on foot. The walkthrough was not enough."

"Palmer poured orange juice in a glass and added a soup spoon of vodka. "Where is Abram? He should be part of the conversation."

"He is upstairs completing his prayer." Make him relax. If you could sleep with the likes of Mustafa . . . No, she told herself. Let him learn restraint. One pillow on the bed. He has given in. The pillow was the first step.

"Did you have trouble with the rabbi? Did anyone in the building see you come in with the crates?"

"No to both questions, Reba."

"Good. Moshe, help Daniel put the crates in my bedroom."

"Where is Palmer?"

"He went to the bakery. I want you, Joseph and Daniel, to go to the Uptown bus terminal; use the subway. It will be good to learn more about it. Take Moshe and have him go by bus. Later we can discuss the viability of the subway as an escape vehicle. Daniel will explain the reason for the trip. The crates: Did you check the contents?"

"The count is correct. Why do you stay down here with him, Reba? I do not trust him."

"Neither do I, Joseph, and neither did the general. He is a dangerous and volatile man. I stay here to watch and control him."

"He doesn't like control, unless he is the controller."

"I know that, Joseph, and I know you have questions about the death of the general. Be patient. Concentrate only on the mission. What we do here will help Israel. Now go and do as I ask." Reba poured a glass of brandy, picked up the newspaper, and walked back into her bedroom, closing the door. She took off her slippers and lay on the bed with the newspaper on her lap. She finished the brandy and closed her eyes. In a whisper she began a prayer of sorrows she learned from her mother.

"Are you in there? It's me, Palmer."

"Not now, Palmer."

"It's important, Reba. Did the shipment arrive?"

"Yes. I have them in here."

"I want to see the explosives. May I come in?"

"No, Palmer; I am taking a moment to pray and rest."

"This isn't right, Reba. You can rest when we finish what we started." He should just barge in, but something in the liquid chaos of his brain made him stop. "How long will you be?"

"Not long if you stop talking, Palmer. The others have gone up to the bus station to see what area would be best for maximum effect. They will be gone for a while. Abram has gone upstairs."

"I wanted to go with them."

"You need to fix a drink. They know perfectly well what they are doing, Palmer." Reba listened to his footfalls and then the sharp thud of the shutting of the door. She smiled. "You are learning who is really in charge, Palmer."

Thirty minutes later, Reba went to his door and knocked.

"I am ready now, Palmer, for you to show me what you have." She knocked again when he did not respond. "Can you hear me?"

"I can hear you; maybe I am not quite ready."

"Suit yourself. If you must play your childish game, I'm going to have a brandy and a nice piece of chocolate cake." She walked off into the living room, fixed a glass of brandy, and padded into the kitchen. When she came out, she spied Palmer, sitting on the couch with a glass of vodka in his hand, his robe open.

"I've seen better, Palmer . . . and had better," she said, showing no interest, except for a smirk. "Would you like a piece of cake with your drink?"

"Yes, I would." The boyish smile never left his face, but inside he was seething, fighting his personal demons clamoring for him to lash out at her. At least he did not have to deal with Mom and Dad, he told himself. His robe open, showing not the least bit of respect for her, would have to do.

"Good, I do not like to eat alone." She returned with a large slice of cake for him, noticing with satisfaction that he had tied his robe and crossed his legs at the knee.

She thought to mention her disdain for his actions, but let it go. Mentioning it meant victory for his ego.

Harry Dukakis walked quickly through the lobby. Dukakis is a small man, heavyset, with black-rimmed glasses balanced on bubbling sacks of loose skin under his medium brown eyes. "Well, Ken, good morning. May I come in?"

"Of course, Harry. I didn't know you were back in town. I just made fresh coffee."

"Ah, no coffee. The building grounds and lobby look very nice, Ken; you are doing a fine job. I think you are do a raise, am I right?"

"It's about that time, Harry. You sure you wouldn't like a cup?"

"No, thank you. I'll be in town for ten days. I'll see to that raise while I'm home. The reason I dropped by is to ask how the new tenants are doing."

"Nice people, quiet. They stay pretty much to themselves. They seem happy. Government people. They have been studying the main structure on Liberty Island. They tell me the Feds are looking to restore the old girl. They are making a financial feasibility study of the island. They have blue prints and a model. That isn't for public release, Harry."

"Interesting, Ken." Stunned by what he just heard, Dukakis pulled a small cloth from his jacket pocket, dipped his head, and feigned cleaning his glasses in hopes Ken Strong hadn't noticed the change in his posture. "You know, Ken, on second thought . . . a cup sounds good. May I use your phone?"

"Sure, Harry. If you need privacy, there is one in my bedroom."

"That'll work." Dukakis padded off. "I won't be long." It took a minute before his call went through channels to ensure it wasn't a crank call. "It's me, Senator," Harry Dukakis said in a muffled voice. "Can you talk privately?"

"Give me a moment, Harry." Senator Spencer opened the bottom right drawer to his desk and shut off the recorder. "Alright, Harry, what is it?"

"I'm here at the apartment building on Eighty-First Street."

"Did our guests arrive safely?"

"Yes, they did, but that isn't why I'm calling."

"Is there a problem, Harry?"

"They told the super they were government employees studying the feasibility

along with the cost of repairing the Statue of Liberty. They even have a mock-up model in one of the apartments. Did you know about this, Senator?"

"I know they are here for a special reason. It is not to damage Lady Liberty. We have a family living there. We have around the clock surveillance, trained guards posted on the island along with electronic surveillance covering all the seaward entrances. They couldn't get to the island without being seen and ordered away and if they should attempt to land, they would be killed. My dear Harry . . . Wait. What is it, Mavis?"

"Nothing, I just wanted to see if you needed anything before you left for the weekend."

"You could fix me a drink and then come sit by me. Okay, Harry? Hold on." Mavis handed him his drink while he ran his spindly hand up her dress. "If that's all, Harry, I have things to do."

"Ken Strong is due for his annual raise."

"See to it."

"Thank you, Ken," Dukakis said, returning to the living room.

"You want to meet them, Harry? They should be back by now."

"That won't be necessary. I have it on good authority they are first rate people, Ken. By the way, how is that lovely woman on the third floor . . .Miss Henry. Have you . . .?"

"She's fine; Her and her boyfriend went out of town for a few weeks."

"I'm sorry, Ken. I thought she would be perfect for you."

"It wasn't to be, Harry. I'm happy for her, wherever she is."

"I'd better go. Irma is planning something special for my birthday tomorrow. Expect the raise in a week or so."

"Thank you, Harry, and happy birthday. The mail is here, I'll walk you out in case he has packages for the tenants. I don't like to leave them in the entrance. I can't be everywhere at once."

"Are we having a problem?"

"No, Harry, and I'd rather not invite one."

"I just talked to Cahill. He doesn't need my direct assistance. He has another person in mind, but he still wants to keep in touch. The old man needs an outlet, someone to communicate with."

"It sounds like he is more involved than he lets on."

"He'll talk to me in time, I'm sure of it."

"This isn't a forever situation here, Frank."

"I might have a clue. He mentioned a cartoon in the newspaper. He called it Argyle Socks. He asked if I ever read it. I don't know if it was a slip or just simply a cartoon he likes."

"Okay, so what Frank . . . he likes cartoons?"

"It could be. Cahill always wore Argyle Socks; it was like his thing. I'm wondering if one of the group of seven became a cartoonist. I'm going to follow up."

"That's a waste of time and time is important, Frank."

"Not if it is a certain person whose group number was four. If it is him, Palmer, you don't want him on your ass."

"He's that good, huh?"

"I'll keep in touch, John."

"You don't have a name?"

"None of us did. Cahill was one shrewd customer and still is, Palmer."

"Then how do you figure you can find this guy, Frank?"

"Let me worry about that. Oh, that apartment I told you about . . . it's yours. I talked to the manager; his name is Underwood. Keep it in mind."

"I will. Let me have the address in Fort Lee and Dukakis's address." Palmer wrote down the information, hung up, and walked out into the living room.

"Was that your friend on the phone?"

"Yes, it was."

"You look concerned, Palmer. Tell me why."

"He's a worrier, a real detail guy. He thinks his previous boss has information on the Russians, but he isn't talking about it."

"Don't lie to me."

"I'm not. He has found another apartment for us in Fort Lee, New Jersey, very close to the bridge, just in case."

"You are dodging my question, Palmer."

"He is talking about an operator who almost killed me . . . I was lucky. The reason he came after me isn't important, Reba. Graham says he is like the wind he's that good."

"Joseph is completing the diagram of the terminal by foot measurement; he will be down once he has completed his evaluation. Why don't we take a ride to Fort Lee and see this apartment, as you say, just in case."

"Not today. I want to go over these estimates Joseph is bringing to us."

"Then tomorrow?"

"Tomorrow, yes. I want to see Dukakis also. Now you look worried."

"Curious perhaps, and careful . . .just in case." A knock on the door interrupted them "That will be Joseph now."

Ethan and Anna Lee left Arlington Station and began the trek into the national cemetery.

"You come often, Ethan, to visit the friends you lost. I can understand you being distant. This has to be hard on you. You've been acting differently since we had lunch with the Cahills. Is it something I said or did?" Anna Lee tucked her arm into the crook of Ethan's.

"No, it isn't anything you did. Let's visit the stones. We'll stop for a drink and I'll explain."

"We're okay, right?"

"We're fine. We both like a good martini. How about we stop at the Quarterdeck restaurant?"

"Sounds wonderful . . . I love you, Ethan Edwards."

"I love you, Anna Lee Caputo."

"How much further to the sites? I want to say a prayer for your friends."

"We're almost there. They are grouped together, just twenty feet from the Kennedy memorial."

"So many stones. So many died. I wonder what would have become of them had they lived."

"Sometimes I wonder what would have become of us if Adam had not had his heart attack. Here we are . . . up this path." Ethan stood at attention and saluted each engraved stone. Anna Lee knelt, saying a prayer. They walked away, each with their own thoughts.

The restaurant was as crowded as always. They ordered a second martini. Ethan began to explain his conversation with Cahill.

"Would you like something with your drink?"

"No thank you. I'm fine Ethan."

Anna Lee was about to ask a question when she spied a man getting up from a table on the opposite side of the dining room and starting to walk toward them. "There is an army colonel coming toward us, Ethan, from his dress. I'd say he is a pilot. I think helicopters. He has been looking at you since we sat down. I think he must know you or thinks he does."

The colonel stopped a foot from the table. "My name is Patton, Alfred E. No relation to the general. Forgive me for interrupting you. You are Ethan Edwards." The colonel stuck out his hand.

"Yes, I am." Ethan stood up and shook Patten's hand. "This is Anna Lee Caputo, my fiancée. I am sorry, sir, should I know you?"

"It is an honor to meet you, ma'am, and congratulations to you both. My wife thought I should leave you both alone, but I had to say something. We met years ago on a chopper pad in Vietnam. I was flying you and members of your Special Forces team to Nha Trang for your departure flight back to the world. I was a warrant officer back then."

"After all these years you remembered me?"

"How could I forget you? Do you remember what you gave me that day?"

Ethan paused a moment, thinking back. Suddenly it came to him. "It was a piece of wood from my short timer's stick. My God."

"May I explain?" he asked, seeing the quizzical look on Anna Lee's face.

"Of course, please do Colonel."

"Soldiers . . . not all, but many of them, when they were thirty days from the end of their tour, would make short timer sticks. They were long pieces of wood, cut to thirty inches. Your future husband told me he would cut an inch off at the end of each day. On the day I flew him out, he handed me a one-inch piece of wood and told me, "My name is Ethan Edwards. I'm going out today. Don't fail me now."

"I remember what you said, colonel. I still remember."

"I told you I would keep it as a reminder to me of all the soldiers I was able to bring out of that hellhole." Colonel Patten reached into his pants pocket and produced the one-inch piece of wood, which he'd stained and varnished years before, and held it out in his palm. "I never go out without my little piece of wood." The two men shook hands and then embraced each other while the curious looked on.

Anna Lee wiped a tear away. She would never know or feel the special emotion these men felt. "I would love to meet your wife, Colonel. Would you both have a drink with us at the bar when you've finished your meal? What is your wife's name?"

"Felicia and we would like that very much, ma'am . . . no war stories."

"No war stories, Colonel." Ethan sat down, and Colonel Patton made his way back to his table.

"Ethan, I want you to do what you have to do. Do it for that soldier you read to in the hospital. For the three buried here . . . and that Colonel. Vincent and I will be waiting for you."

FORT LEE - NEW JERSEY: JUNE 6

"This view of the bridge, the boats in the river, and Manhattan is wonderful, Mister Underwood. I can see why the upper floors are more expensive to purchase. What do you think, James?"

"I do like the layout, Reba, it's roomy. The furnishings are very nice and expensive, I'll bet. The lease option and time frame are perfect for our needs. We can take care of the important work we are doing on Liberty Island. Use the river to the island instead of fighting traffic. We can have our equipment left on the boat. We do not have the taxpayers fund our expenses except for the rental costs and meals."

"We have very good security here at night, especially with the owners' boats. You might want to rethink using a private boat. The guards on the island are pretty strict about that."

"That is important to us, Mister Underwood, thanks for the tip. We better alert Washington." The boyish smile hid his interest in how Underwood looked at Reba. How he might be useful. His obvious attraction to Reba as motivation. "I like it very much. Tell me, Mister Underwood, do you live here in case we need assistance?"

"No, Mister Preston. I have my home in Ridgewood." His eyes never turned from Reba by the window. "I am here from seven until five Monday through Friday. My relief person lives here. He can follow up on any requests you have after I leave. On weekends, we have maintenance people and a relief manager."

Palmer had his answer and possibly a secondary place to hide if the opportunity presented itself. "I Like Ridgewood, a nice established community. I'm sure your wife and you must be happy there."

"My wife died six years ago . . . cancer. We never had children. Now I live in this big home with my memories."

"I am so sorry, Mister Underwood," Reba said, turning toward him.

Palmer also expressed his condolences, but what mattered more was the way Underwood continued to look at Reba, never looking past her. What did Lenin say about useful idiots?

"I think you both have made up your minds. You said there were six in your party?"

"Yes, but four will be staying at a hotel nearby. Perhaps you could recommend one?"

"The Double Tree Inn is close by. From what I understand, it is a favorite among some residents who would rather not bring special guests to the complex."

"I guess we all have our little secrets, Mister Underwood." The boyish smile returned. "We will certainly look into it and thanks."

"I like the Marriott Hotel in Teaneck as well. I stayed there two winters ago when we had the big snow. It was so bad they closed Route 4 temporarily. Well, shall we review the terms?"

"Would you mind if we talked alone for a moment before we come down, Mister Underwood? When you work on a government project, you have to account for every penny unless of course you are in the House or Senate, if you get my meaning."

"I understand completely. Did I mention the owner of the apartment is in Europe and has assured the co-op board he will not return unannounced before the six month is up?"

"That is good to know. I think we will pay the rental in advance if we decide to stay here. We will be down shortly," Reba answered, placing her hand gently on his shoulder. His reaction, and the blush on his face, was all she and Palmer needed. "I think you can prepare the proper papers for us to sign." Her voice dropped an octave, as if they were having a private moment. The effect was what she expected. Even Palmer was moved.

"Well, what do you really think, Palmer?" she asked when they were alone.

"It is just what we need. My friend was right; he chose well. The view of the bridge is perfect. We have easy access to major roads. We can rent a boat here . . . maybe the owner of this apartment has one of his own? We can cruise down to Liberty Island. I want to go late one evening to see just how strong the security is. And what is more important . . . you have a puppy to pet, Reba. Use it to your advantage."

"I like the idea of a secondary address. What about the apartment in New York?"

"I've been thinking about that. I am going to see Dukakis after we have finished here. I have his address. In the meantime, you go back to the apartment. I'll come after I meet with Dukakis. He could be a weak link. I want to be sure the Russians have not found him first."

"How could they know about him?"

"Details, Reba; it's always a missed detail that brings problems…Check us in at the Double Tree Inn, I'm going to see Dukakis"

Palmer parked in an open lot a block from the apartment. "How much do we really need Dukakis? Something to think about." He climbed the steps, padded into the lobby, and took the elevator to the fifth floor.

Before knocking, he put his ear against the door and listened; he heard nothing. He knocked and listened: still no sound. He padded down to the next apartment and knocked. A young man holding a baby answered.

"I'm sorry to bother you, but my friend next door invited me to visit. He isn't answering. I wonder if you could call the super and have him come up. I doubt if anything is wrong, but just in case."

"Wait a second, I'll call him." He closed the door. A moment later, still holding the sleeping baby, he came back. "The super says to come down to his apartment; he'll tell you what happened."

"Thank you." Don't panic and don't make it bigger than it might be. He took two deep breaths and walked quickly to the elevator.

"Are you the guy looking for Dukakis?" The super opened the door to his apartment, leaving the chain fixed in place. He smelled of stale smoke. His face was a mass of deep lines with a bubble nose and watery eyes. A picture of a doomed soul. "He isn't here, bud."

"Is he out of town or out for the evening?"

"Who wants to know? You a cop?"

"An old friend. He invited me over and we were supposed to go out to supper and catch up. I'm just curious why he isn't answering his door."

"He got sick. His girlfriend said he fell. He had this gauze patch over his left eye. It was bloody and these other guys were helping her half carry him out. I think she said they were taking him to Saint Luke's trauma center in Harlem."

"Thanks. May I use your phone, please?"

"Forget it, pal."

"Saint Luke's Trauma center, how may I direct your call?"

"Emergency services, please. I'm checking on a patient." He knew the answer. Dukakis was probably already dead. At last, the phone was answered, "I'm trying to find someone. I was told he was brought to your hospital. His name is Harry Dukakis."

"Are you a family member?"

"He's my brother."

"Hold on, sir. Moments later, he got the answer he expected.

He slammed the phone down. "Goddamned Russians. I didn't give them the credit they deserved. The woman was probably KGB using Dukakis for information. I should have guessed. It is all tied to that asshole Spencer." He picked up the phone and dialed the number of the apartment. "Get out of there now, Reba, all of you. Take everything of importance with you. Leave nothing of value they can trace to us. Leave only the furniture. We wouldn't have time to move it anyway. I'm talking hours. Go to the DoubleTree Inn and get rooms. I will meet you there. Hurry, Reba."

"What's happened, Palmer?"

"If I'm right, Dukakis is dead. They must know where we are. I'll explain when I see you. No more questions. Get out now . . . all of you." Palmer slammed the receiver down, stepped into the small living room, and stared at the lifeless body of the manager. "Thanks for letting me use your phone."

He walked to the corner and hailed a cab. Don't take the car. Leave it. They can't know the model, but just to be safe, leave it. Get off the street.

The cab pulled to the curb, Where to buddy?"

"Take me to Seventy-Second Street and First Avenue driver. The movie theater." Hide there for a few hours and then take a cab uptown to the bus terminal. Get out of New York. "Driver, could you tell me what's playing at the movie house on Seventy-Second?"

"I think it's still The Godfather Part 2."

"I've heard a lot about that movie; have you seen it?"

"Yeah, I liked it a lot. Better than the original."

It was dark when Palmer walked out of the theater. The night air felt refreshing after sitting in the smoke-filled auditorium. He gave some thought to walking, but soon discarded the notion. He needed to get over the bridge and out of the city. His enemies could already be at the apartment, perhaps before they were able to get clear. He needed to find a phone. He needed to be sure they were safe.

He stepped back into the theater lobby, found the bank of phones, and dialed the number of the apartment on Eighty-First. No answer. They were dead or gone. He dialed the operator for the Double Tree Inn.

"Hello, my name is Preston. I am inquiring if a friend has checked in. Her name is Reba Davis."

"One moment, please."

He tapped his foot on the carpet; his nerves were beginning to splinter. Hurry will you, c'mon . . . how long does it take to—"

"You are in luck, Mister Preston. She is just checking in now. Would you like to speak to her?"

"Yes, please, if I could." A rustling of papers and clothing and she was on the line. "Did it go well?"

"Very well. The children and I are waiting for you. I put them up at the Marriott in Teaneck with my mother so we could have a night to ourselves. Are you on your way?"

"I'm on my way right now, Reba." Palmer hung up, sighed, walked out of the theater, and hailed a cab.

CIA HEADQUARTERS - LANGLEY

Timmons quietly reviewed the files, matching each one with photographs. On a couch to his right, Manning-Ham and Drum were doing the same thing. Exchanging ideas in muffled tones.

Sitting alone near a window, Constance Bell listened to the banter of Boris Molotov with his interpreter. She looked for signs of distress in Molotov's body language.

Molotov spoke English like his friend Shevchenko without the drawl, but for the sake of conversation spoke only Russian to his aide who, like Bell, monitored the Americans. Both men complimented Timmons on his choice of tea and of being kind enough to serve them in glass.

Timmons closed the files, stacked them neatly in the center of his desk, and placed the pictures side by side in front of the Russian.

"Mister Molotov, do you recognize any of these people?" He waited for the interpreter to ask the question. Timmons followed the dialogue. Being fluent in Russian, he thought it best to not let Molotov know.

"Nye. No."

Timmons' phone buzzed. "Mister Edwards is here, sir."

"Thank you, Mona. Please send him in."

Before Timmons put the phone in its cradle, Molotov was on his feet. There was no denying who this man was.

"I am Boris Molotov and you are the man who put such fear in a Russian's heart?"

Edwards did not respond. When Molotov offered his hand, Edwards kept his hands to his side. "As you wish, Mister Edwards. My friend apologizes for not being here. He had other business to attend to concerning a fellow named Dukakis. He will call."

"I appreciate the candor," Edwards answered. "I am here because a very good man whom I hold in high esteem has asked me to come. I will listen to what you have to say out of respect for him."

"I can ask for no more. I would act the same if our roles were reversed. Let me begin—"

"Let's save time, shall we?" Edwards interrupted. "I'll tell you what I already know. John Michael Palmer, the captain who flipped and gave my team up, was taken to Russia by Kasparov. He screwed up and made things uncomfortable in a way that you and your boss are now in my country looking to kill this piece of shit. I know you speak English, Boris, so let's not waste any more time with interpreters, shall we? Shevchenko wants my help to save your ass. Am I getting warm? You don't have to answer; a nod will do."

"I will be frank, Mister Edwards. A plan was instituted in the highest chambers of our government. Palmer's involvement was to help train special forces in mountain warfare. The purpose of the training was to prepare troops for the invasion of Afghanistan."

"We already know that," Timmons quickly interrupted.

"Do you know . . ." Molotov turned and looked over his shoulder at Ronald Timmons. "Your embassy in Tehran will be attacked?"

"So, it is true . . . Do you have a date?"

"After the issues with Iraq are settled . . . December, around your Christmas holiday." He turned back toward Ethan. "We think we know where Palmer is. First, you must agree to one more meeting."

"Shevchenko wants to meet with me, am I right?"

"He has great respect for you and a fear of you. He needs reassurance you will allow him sanctuary."

"I am no longer active; that is the only assurance I can offer. What happened to General Pavlov and his assassin? I guessed it was manipulated by Shevchenko."

"That is correct, yes."

"The trouble you are up against . . . The reason you are here?"

"That is close. His assassin was killed over another matter. Pavlov engineered the attack, but it came from a higher source we believe but cannot prove at this time. That is the difference."

"Will he tell Mister Timmons where Palmer is?"

"He will tell you and ask for your assistance. He has information. That is the wrong word . . . He has concerns that your movements and the movements of the CIA have been compromised. Now you know what I know. What is your answer?"

Ethan looked past Molotov toward Timmons, who simply nodded, alerting Edwards that the conversation was valid. No one was taking notes except Mona in the outer office. Ethan noticed the beeping light on Timmons's phone. No one else did. "I'd like to finish this."

"We would, as well," Molotov said. "I need only your answer."

"It would certainly move things forward. Time is of the essence, Ethan. We do not know what Palmer will do," Timmons said, cutting into the conversation.

"Set the meeting."

"He's in the bubble waiting for your answer. Mister Cahill is with him."

"How easy you people have made it for me. I'll talk to him. I want only our interpreter and Mister Molotov to come down. Everyone else stays away."

"I need to be there, Ethan."

"You set it up, Ronald, your work is done. What you don't know or hear cannot be used against you. I'm giving you a window. Jump, Timmons. If Adam wishes, he can fill you in on his dime. Shall we go, Boris?"

When they entered the auditorium, Cahill and Shevchenko rose to greet them. The air was thick with anticipation as Edwards led Molotov and the American interpreter down between the rows of cushioned seats to the stage, which was only slightly elevated from the main floor.

The two men faced each other. Cahill stood between them. No words were exchanged.

"I am ready when you are," Constance Bell said.

"This man does not need interpretation," Ethan said, his fists clenched in his jacket pockets. "You can follow the conversation, Miss Bell."

"I will do as you wish, Mister Edwards."

"So now I can put a face to the shadow . . . Mister Cahill has informed me you write a cartoon. A brilliant stroke hiding in the open. A cartoonist . . . who would suspect?"

"I am not an active, Shevchenko. I haven't been since the incident in

Prague. I also know why you are here and all the background music that comes with it."

"I have come here to rid my country of embarrassment. If the world found out about this intrigue, my country, Israel, and America would suffer. China would grow strong. A mistake neither one of our countries can make. Israel has partially taken care of their problem. They have killed the germ that infested their government and now they expect and hope America will kill the infection raised here.

"You are talking about General Golan?"

"Yes. You see, unlike you, Ethan Edwards, I can never return to my country. The CIA has granted me a favor I can never repay. To do that, I ask for your help. If your answer is no, I will understand completely. You have a woman, I am sure. So do I. Before I can offer her a life, I must complete this task. I am recently married."

"Your personal life has no meaning to me."

"I understand."

Edwards turned to face Cahill. The eyes stated what the old man's expression couldn't. Edwards saw the depth of sadness in those eyes, pleading for understanding and one more favor.

"I will do this for you, Adam."

Shevchenko put out his hand. Hesitation by Edwards . . . breathing seemed to stop until he took Shevchenko's hand and shook it. "So, tell us what you know."

"A man named Harry Dukakis. He takes the place for a senator as owner of an apartment building on Eighty-First Street off First Avenue. One of Kasparov's women has, shall we say, made her body available to him. She informed us that Palmer and the Israeli agents are at the apartment. Kasparov and an associate visited Dukakis at his residence. That is how we learned of the arrangement."

"Where is Dukakis now?"

"I am afraid he is unavailable for further comment. It would have been imprudent of us to not take extra steps to ensure Dukakis did not warn Palmer."

"The senator . . . what part does he play?"

"He is a different story, I am afraid. He knows of Palmer, but not specifics. We have a file on Senator Spencer. His likes include young women . . . very young women. Let us concentrate on this matter."

"With all this knowledge, why am I here?"

"Let me speak to this if I may, Ethan?"

"Okay, Adam. Help me understand."

"First of all, Mister Shevchenko and his associates have done nothing without the CIA's prior knowledge. Timmons gave the order on the action taken on Dukakis for obvious reasons. I think it is time to finish this now that the entire affair has been laid at your feet. Shevchenko's people are close by the apartment, waiting. They arrived thirty minutes ago."

"That would be a mistake. We must concern ourselves with the safety of the other tenants. We must be sure our quarry, all of them, are in the building. I suggest we find out who the super is. Do a background check on him, in case he is part of the conspiracy, and then make our move when he can assure us they are all in the building." Ethan looked at Shevchenko, his eyes narrowing. "I understand the motive. This is still America and we don't put innocent people in peril to catch or kill one."

"How long will this take, Ethan Edwards?"

"Not long, we're pretty good at this. We have updated special computers while you have typewriters and Lubyanka prison, Peter Shevchenko." He looked at Cahill, sitting hunched forward in the seat. "Are you alright, Adam?"

"I think I should go home. Beatrice will be worried."

"My thanks, sir," Shevchenko said. "I will get a message to Mikhail through our mutual friend in Moscow when this is finished."

"Just so I can feel comfortable . . . who was the terrorist in Barcelona?"

"Comrade Fedorov gave me the plan at the request of the French government. A special team of Russians carried it out. The original target was not present. In fact, Mister Edwards, at least one of them is here now to assist me."

"The Frog forger in Paris?"

"That would be the Mossad. I engineered the demise of the three Russians. We called the operation The Day of the Wolf. Will there be anything else?"

"No. I will go along, Shevchenko." Edwards pointed a finger at Cahill. "For his sake."

Within thirty minutes, Mona was ready to present a file. A detailed ownership history of the complex and an American citizen. The current super is a retired marine. He is unaware of the mechanisms of ownership. We believe he is as innocent as the tenants he takes care of.

"Shall I read it, Mister Edwards, or would you prefer not to share it with Mister Shevchenko?"

"You go ahead, Mona."

"I am curious; how did you acquire this information so quickly?"

"We all have our little secrets, Shevchenko. Go on, Mona. Stick with present ownership and the manager, Dukakis."

"He owns no part of it. He is what Cosa Nostra calls a front man. The super's name is Kenneth Strong. His apartment is on the first floor facing the courtyard. His responsibilities include upkeep, repairs, and the collection of monthly rents from the residents. He was married. His wife is dead, and he now lives alone. His connection to Dukakis is nothing more than his job requirement. He is a retired decorated marine, Vietnam era. He has no criminal history and no connection to the real estate corporation. I was unable to find any connection to the senator. He's just the super, Mister Edwards."

"Thank you, Mona. Do we have a phone number for Mister Strong?"

"Yes, it's 555-5145; would you like me to try and call him?"

"Please do, Mona." Edwards turned to Timmons. "You might want to go to the bathroom . . . what you don't know."

"I'll take my chances, Ethan."

"I have Mister Strong on line two."

"Okay Ronald, you know what you are doing.," Edwards picked up the phone. "Hello Mister Strong, my name is Ethan Edwards. I am sort of a contractor. I am calling from Washington DC. We are arranging as we speak for a flight to New York this evening. We are very interested in a group of tenants who recently rented at least one apartment in your building."

"Are you with a government agency, Mister Edwards?"

"Sort of, it is very important that we speak to you. Why did you ask if I worked for the government?"

"The people who were here worked with land management and I just assumed you did . . . I might as well tell you they left, moved out."

"When, Mister Strong?"

"About three hours now. The woman turned in the keys, said they were being recalled and a moving company will be here in a few days to pick up their furnishings."

"Describe her." Ethan wrote down the description and handed it to Timmons. "Have you been in their apartment?"

"No, I haven't inspected it, I was—"

"We will be there in a few hours. Wait for us, Mister Strong, I believe you were in the Marine Corps. If any of those people return, you may be in danger. Under no circumstances are you to answer your door. Please do not attempt to go upstairs."

"What the hell is going on here, whatever your name is?"

"Edwards, Ethan Edwards. Be a good marine and don't ask questions, and don't make any calls either."

"I have a call waiting for you, Mister Shevchenko. A fellow named Kasparov."

"Hello Comrade. What news have you?" He listened. "Hold on a moment. Dukakis has been put in the ground. Kasparov wants to know what is to become of our agent?"

"Has she contacted Moscow, Dmitry?"

"No."

"She cannot communicate with Moscow or the embassy here in New York. Have Sergei see to the situation. No harm is to come to her Dmitry Where are you three now?"

"Across the street from the apartment."

"Stay where you are. Make no attempt to enter the residence. We are on our way." Shevchenko hung up.

"Is it her Ronald?" Ethan asked.

"Yes."

"Do you have a picture of the woman with Palmer

"It is her. It is the woman in Paris where Al Bahia and Abadi were killed. She was also in Barcelona in the airport when Palmer arrived. We believe it was a chance meeting. There was no connection then. She is Mossad, gentlemen." Timmons slipped the pictures into his folder

"You are sure it is the same person?"

"It is her," Ronald Timmons answered. "I have pictures of all the players."

"Give them to us." Shevchenko said.

DOUBLE TREE INN - FORT LEE

Reba knelt down beside the foot of the bed, folding her arms on a pillow. She began to pray.

"Yahweh let my husband speak to me in my dream." A sharp knock on the door startled her.

"It's me, open the door, Reba."

"What's happened?" Her makeup, streaked by tears, her hair matted, were ignored by the urgency of his tone. "Tell me what has happened?" He brushed past her, his face red with anger. Reba closed and locked the door. "Have a drink and calm down. The vodka is on the desk. I am going to wash my face and then we'll talk."

"Dukakis is dead," he said, when Reba emerged from the bathroom. "It was the Russians."

"How can you be sure?"

"I'm sure." The vodka, his third glass, helped to quiet him. His hand shook noticeably. He knew what he had to do. One thing that made him feel better. She was out there in a bar alone or with a friend.

"How do you know this?"

"I went to his apartment, remember? The super told me he was taken to the hospital by his girlfriend and two men he'd never seen before. He had a bloody patch over his left eye and was having trouble walking."

"Did you call the hospital?"

"What the hell do you think?"

"Calm down, Palmer. Finish your drink. We will get nowhere arguing. You are sure it was the Russians and not the Americans?"

"Positive. Putting a water-based needle in the eye is one of their favorite tricks. That is why I called you. I imagine they are already at the address of our apartment, or close. Are you sure you removed everything?"

"Would you like me to answer your foolish question the way you answered mine, Palmer?"

"No. I'm sorry, Reba. Where are the explosives?"

"In a safe place, I assure you."

"I need to go out. I need to be by myself and think." He needed to kill to pacify his darkened mind. He needed to do this to make sure his parents were really gone. He needed to do this to be able to concentrate on what he must do without clutter. "I'm going out. I will call my friend to see what he knows, if anything, while I am out."

"Do you want me to come with you?"

"No, Reba, I'll be fine." Palmer finished his drink; his hand no longer shook. He was calm. He had reached a decision and was ready to act on it. "If I am back soon, I'll tell you what my associate knows; if not, I'll see you in the morning. Good night, Reba."

"You are not yourself; you shouldn't go out tonight. Let me fix you another drink. I will have one with you. I see trouble in your eyes. You need a release from the pent-up anger. When a person is so troubled, they lose their sense of direction and act erratically."

"So now you are a mind reader? You think you know me?"

"I am not saying that at all. You can't go out like this."

"I can't just sit, Reba. You have no idea . . ."

"Sit down, relax. Let me fix us both a drink . . .John."

CHAPTER TWENTY-FIVE

EIGHTY-FIRST STREET APARTMENT: JULY 6

Ken Strong stood in his living room, a cup of coffee cooling in his hand, his breathing shallow. For an instant, in the dark, he flashed back to 1971 and the silence before the shooting started. The fear returned.

He sipped the coffee. Suddenly they were at the gate. Strangers. The flashback receded. This was real. Four men in long coats and a woman in a business suit and flat shoes. One stayed at the bottom of the steps just outside the entrance.

"Help me Jesus" was all he could say, his voice as shallow as the clock ticking on the wall. He put his hand in his pocket, fingering a set of keys, when the knock came. He switched on a lamp, padded to the door, and opened it. Two men faced him.

"My name is Edwards; are you alone, Mister Strong?"

"Yes."

"We need to see those apartments, Mister Strong," the man next to Edwards said. Both men produced false FBI identification.

"Yes, I'm alone." He repeated. "I have the keys in my pocket." He pointed to his pants pocket with his index finger. "Can you tell me what is going on. Should I call Mister Dukakis?"

"We will explain once we've looked at the apartments," Shevchenko answered. "I'm afraid Mister Dukakis is not available."

"You are from the south . . . the Carolinas, aren't you? How are you adjusting?"

"It is a challenge, Mister Strong. May we have the keys please, sir? Time is important."

"Would you like me to join you?"

"Give us the keys, please, and the apartment numbers. We will see you before we leave and explain what we can. One more question . . . which apartment was the woman using?"

"She stayed with Preston in 3B."

"Thank you, Mister Strong."

"Did you feel they were intimate?" Shevchenko asked.

"No, I don't. They acted very professional with each other. I could be wrong. I think he may have had a short fling with a neighbor down the hall."

"We may want to speak with her."

"She is out of town with her boyfriend. Now that I think about it, she should have been back yesterday. I guess they decided to extend their trip." He pulled out the keys and handed them to Edwards.

"One more thing, Mister Strong. Do not, under any circumstances, answer your phone until we return."

Strong closed the door, walked into his kitchen, and poured four fingers of whiskey into an glass. "No raise this year Bud" was all he could manage to say.

DOUBLE TREE INN - FORT LEE

Reba rolled onto her side, propping her head on her bent arm, and stared at Palmer, who was still asleep, his face peaceful and his breathing level. A mental health professional would have described him most likely in this way. He was a caricature—a man as empty as a cup without coffee.

He did not make love to her; he used her to fill some unexplained void. He went down on her even when she told him she was nearly at the end of her period. When he was finished with her, he simply rolled away and went to sleep.

Reba slid out of bed, put on her robe, and stepped into the kitchenette. She fixed a pot of coffee, sat down at the small table, and waited for it to brew. She prayed.

"Reba? It's 4:30." Palmer flicked on the bedside light.

"I prepared coffee; would you like a cup? I have nothing to go with it." He looked different. She noticed the change immediately. The phony boyish smile was gone, replaced . . . by what? Was this real or just another character to amuse himself? "Would you like me to find out if we can get something?"

"Just coffee please, Reba. Come sit with me."

She fixed two cups, adding one measure of vanilla creamer.

"Are you sure you do not want pastry at least?" she asked, sitting on the edge of the bed. She took a sip of coffee. "Not bad." She took another sip.

"I'm sorry for last night. I treated you like a whore. It seems the only women in my life are." He stopped and took a long swallow of coffee.

"All women in one way or another are whores. A wife is a whore to her husband or lover. Some women enjoy men for what they are. I was thirteen when I became a woman according to Jewish law. My father was killed by a terrorist that very day. It was that day I chose the life I would lead."

"After the seven days of mourning . . . shiva."

"Yes, how did you know?"

"My mother and stepmother were Jewish."

"We must go down the Hudson to the statue and watch."

"This evening, after dark, Reba."

"Yes. Thank you, John Palmer." You have him in control. Use it wisely. "Why do you think of all women as whores? Don't shut me out."

"My birth mother was a prostitute and a junkie. She tried to kill me when I was three days old. My father was a murderer. He was hung for his crimes. My birth name is Wayne Morrison. She named me after my father . . . nice touch, don't you think? She died in prison . . . hung herself. I was adopted by the Palmers. You now know more about me than any woman I have been with."

"Find a boat so we can see the island at night. See just how well guarded it is. Call your friend and I will move us into the apartment. I will also flirt with the manager. Just in case, as you like to say John."

Across the river, the task of searching the two apartments through the night was nearly completed. Pictures were taken of everything left behind, even the small holes in the walls were photographed. Furniture moved, drawers removed and stacked on the floors, nothing was left to search and nothing of importance was found except a used tampon with small traces of blood.

"Maybe she knew we were coming and left a gift for us," Olivia Sokolov, the woman from the embassy, offered.

"They must have known," Ethan said, sitting on the desk in the living room. "But how?"

"I am afraid you may have a hole in your CIA umbrella. A more plausible explanation would be Palmer went to Dukakis's apartment after he went missing and assumed Dukakis gave him up or was murdered."

"One moment, Edwards. Leona, the men upstairs should be ready to come down. Would you please give us a moment?" Silence until the door closed behind her. "It might be both scenarios."

"I must agree."

"The reason I mention it is I had a confidential talk about you with my secretary, a brilliant woman. Her talents were wasted because she is a Jew. She taught in KGB school when I was a young boy. She taught me language, among other things. Marina is her name. She was like an older sister to me."

"Is there a point here, Shevchenko?"

"She called you a silent wind, Edwards. We killed Dukakis. His mistress was one of our agents. She will never see Moscow. It will save her life. The young woman was put in our embassy by Fedorov. I am sure he wanted her to keep him informed of our movements. He must not have that ear to the ground. That is why I cannot send her back"

"Okay . . . I understand."

"My point is, working with you, searching the apartment, I never heard footsteps. I felt your breath on my neck. I imagined many felt it just before they died. Marina is correct, you are a silent wind . . . a ghost."

"We aren't going to find the culprit sitting here. What shall we tell Mister Strong?"

"He can have the furniture."

"I agree. He needs to know only what he needs to know. This traitor you mentioned is close. He doesn't live here, but he has connections to both Palmer and Spencer. He may have found this apartment for Palmer."

"Through Spencer?" Shevchenko asked.

"I think we should talk to the senator very soon and find out just what part he plays. If I am correct, the traitor is someone Cahill used before and may still be in contact with. I think he has the ear of Cahill without the old man's knowledge."

"I hope you are wrong, but it does make sense, Ethan Edwards."

"Ethan, you sound like you are on a plane."

"I am, Beatrice, we're coming your way. We should be on the ground in a couple of hours. How is Adam?"

"I think he overdid it on his walk yesterday. He came home exhausted. He is better this morning. He is awake. He wants to work on his book . . . You are in it, you know?"

"I needed that news."

"Don't you worry, Ethan," Beatrice laughed, "I am his agent and chief editor. Your identity is safe. I'll tell him you are on the phone."

"Thanks, Bea." A moment passed, waiting for Cahill to come on the line. "Adam, I know it's early, but we need your help."

"What can I do?"

"Call Timmons and tell him to invite Senator Spencer to a quiet supper. Call it a national security issue. He needs the chairman's advice before he presents it to the president."

"What's going on Ethan, why are you shutting me out?"

"For your own good, Adam. Trust me. You do not need to know. We searched the apartments. They were meticulously cleaned, not one scrap of paper, pictures . . . Nothing Adam. We were very thorough. We may very well have a mystery man helping them. We missed them. It was close. Palmer has information he shouldn't have. Someone on the inside, Adam. I'm sure of it. I think Shevchenko fears one of his as well."

"You think it's Spencer?"

"No. Do not come yourself, Adam. Stay out of this. I will keep you updated. Think about what I said. Trust no one. Good bye, sir."

"Wait, Ethan. What if Palmer had the same idea and when he found Dukakis missing . . ."

"We thought of that, Adam. We got a mole. Trust me."

"I want to be at the meeting."

"Bad idea and you know it. If we have a mole in our midst, I do not want to think about what he or she can do to disrupt the operation. If anyone contacts you with information he or she should not have, that's the mole."

OLD ANGLER'S INN: JULY 8

Edwards and Shevchenko entered the Old Angler's Inn . The manager greeted them.

"Mister Timmons is expecting you, something about a surprise for the senator.

"He will be surprised," Shevchenko answered. "I hope you serve Southern Comfort, sir?"

"We do indeed, sir, mixed or straight up."

"Straight, up of course, sir."

"Leona, you see the woman at the bar, the one with less dress than breasts talking to the young man? She is with the senator . . . his secretary. Why don't you take a walk over there? Have a drink."

"If you think it will be helpful, Ethan Edwards."

"I have a good feeling about this, Leona. If I am right and I think I am, the senator is going to be quite angry with her. I'll watch for your signal if the conversation is sexual."

"And what if they should leave?"

"Follow and watch them. If you see something more than conversation, return. Shevchenko will rub his chin. Come to our table gushing and flush with embarrassment to tell us all about it."

"I do not have money for a drink."

"Charge it on Mister Timmons's account: the man in the double-breasted suit directly behind my left shoulder, sitting across from the older man in the blue suit. If the bartender asks, point to the double-breasted suit."

Edwards turned to Shevchenko. "Are we ready to join our friends?"

"Let's do that, by all means, sir."

"You fooled me, Longstreet. I would have sworn you'd be a bourbon man."

"What is that name?"

"Keep walking, Peter Shevchenko. Tonight, your name is Longstreet. Don't worry about the name, he was a famous general in the Confederate army during our civil war."

"They lost the war, did they not?"

"Okay, Shevchenko, how about we call you Grant?"

"That is better. The name on my passport is Peter Grant."

They negotiated the crowded dining room. "Good evening, Mister Timmons, and you are Senator Spencer? My name is Ethan Edwards." Ethan lowered his voice. "My friend here is Peter Grant. What's in a name, right, Senator? The important thing is, we need to talk to you. We can do it here in a friendly and comfortable atmosphere or we can go to less pleasant surroundings."

"What is the meaning of this, Timmons?" Spencer looked past the two men toward the bar. The young man Mavis was talking to was not in sight. "I'm leaving. You have no idea who you are dealing with, Timmons. I wouldn't be comfortable with your present Job " He felt Edwards's shoe pressing against his ankle.

"Don't try to get up, Senator, or I will break your ankle. You might want to excuse yourself, Mister Timmons."

"Not a chance Ethan. I'll just enjoy my super, if you do not mind?"

Mavis walked up to the table carrying a package of cigarettes and her small handbag "I'm going outside for some air and a smoke, Senator. You look like you will be a while." She turned and strolled off, moving slowly enough to hear whispered compliments. The woman at the bar got up unnoticed and followed her out.

"Let's talk, Spencer. You are in a partnership with a corporation that owns apartments. We are interested in one of them . . . the one on Eighty-First Street in Manhattan. The one John Michael Palmer is occupying, or was, until recently."

More pressure was applied this time, sliding along the senator's ankle, tearing the skin. The senator grimaced in pain. "We need to know where he is and if it was you, who secured a new address?"

"Please do not attempt a lie," Peter chimed in, "we have a dossier on you. Your secret real estate holdings, gifts, favors, and your obsession with young girls. Do I make myself clear?"

"What is this Timmons? Are these two your spooks? I'll destroy you, Timmons, you have my word on it." He felt Edwards's foot lift and crash against his ankle, tearing the skin further. A rush of air escaped his mouth.

He wanted to cry out. He felt faint and started to slip away. A hand held his shoulder, keeping him from falling.

"Drink water, Spencer, put your thoughts together."

A waiter appeared. "The senator is fine. He is a little overheated. Would you bring him a brandy and more water? Answer the questions," Timmons said, picking up a forkful of salmon.

Leona stood in the entrance to the dining room. Shevchenko noticed her first. He tapped Edwards's shoulder. He signaled her. When she reached the table, Shevchenko said, "This woman is a friend of ours and I am KGB. She is the agent who compiled our dossier on you from another agent you are most familiar with. So, you see, we must know what else you know... Leona, I assume you have some information you would like to share with the senator?"

"Yes, I do. I followed his secretary into the parking lot. She climbed into a car with the young man she was having a drink with. They are presently fucking each other." The waiter brought brandy in a silver container and water.

"Drink some brandy, Senator. Thank you, Leona." Shevchenko smiled and poured a glass of brandy for Spencer. "It seems you have more trouble. Drink, regain your strength. We will continue our conversation."

Spencer gulped down the brandy. Timmons poured another shot into the glass. Spencer took a sip of water and cleared his throat. "I have no idea where Palmer is. I was called by—What the hell does it matter? A friend of Palmer's. I think he used to be on the farm. I directed Dukakis to make the arrangements. He wasn't available, so I had Mavis do it. I swear that is all I know." Spencer looked past Edwards's shoulder. Mavis had returned to the bar. "Talk to Harry Dukakis. He is the registered owner of the property. He lives—"

"He is a dead, Senator," Edwards answered.

"My God help me . . . What have I done? What have I done?"

"We need a name, Spencer. Who called you? Who made the arrangement through you for the apartment? You can't put this solely on Dukakis. Give us the name or I will break your goddamn ankle."

"Frank Graham."

"Get out of here, Spencer," Timmons scowled. "Tomorrow, you resign from the Senate. I don't give a shit what excuse you use. You will make your announcement no later than ten o'clock in the morning or I will release this information to the Washington Post and Examiner." Timmons poured the last of the brandy into his own glass and drank it. "You can pay the bill, Spencer, on the way out."

Palmer slowed the boat in the choppy water parallel to the island. He turned slowly toward the statue. The small craft was now being buffeted on both sides. He picked up speed, watching the shoreline: fifty yards, then forty yards . . . at thirty yards, lights appeared below the surface of the water. He pulled the throttle back. Lights on the island went on, flooding the small craft and its two passengers with blinding light.

"Come no closer. You are inside the perimeter of Liberty Island. Turn your craft away. Make no attempt to come closer."

"We only wanted to take pictures up close of her lit at night," Palmer shouted, holding his bullhorn close to his mouth in his free hand. He held the camera up for the guards to see.

"You are inside the safety perimeter. Turn back or we will be forced to fire on your craft."

"We'd better turn back, John. We found out what we needed to know."

"We are leaving. We didn't know." Palmer put the bullhorn aside and slowly turned the craft around. At forty yards out, he pushed the throttle forward. "Well now, what do we do Reba? Got any ideas?"

"Let's discuss options when we get back to the apartment. The important thing is we will be together." See the smile on his face. You have him in your grasp. Be together. Good choice of words.

"Yes, Reba, together."

"Have you spoken to your friend?"

"I'll work it out, you'll see."

"I knew you would find a way, John." Manipulate and control. Keep him thinking he is in charge. Flatter, but don't make too much of it.

"You look exhausted, Ethan. Can you talk about it?"

"I am exhausted, Anna Lee, and you can't know, not yet . . . Maybe never. I'm waiting for a call. It will be on a secured line and can't be traced to your number."

"When the next call comes—"

"I'll answer; you mustn't listen." The phone rang—two rings, a pause, and it rang again. "It's my call."

"I'll fix us a drink."

"Thanks, baby . . .Hello, Ronald."

"Mister Cahill confirmed the name Spencer gave us. He is very upset that he was fooled by Graham. He is particularly concerned that he may have given you up and put loved ones in danger as well. He said he mentioned Argyle Socks. He was only making a comment about the strip, but he is afraid Graham may have taken it as a slip up. Mister Cahill is beside himself, Ethan."

"Tell him he need not worry. I'm not angry."

"I have an address in Hoboken, New Jersey, and a photograph of Graham. Who is with you?"

"Everyone. Give me the address."

"Where the hell have you been, Graham? I've been calling the apartment. We're in Fort Lee. They got to Dukakis, Frank . . . he's dead. We had to get out of the city in a hurry."

"Who cares about him as long as you are safe, right? Put on your television, Spencer. He and his secretary are dead, he crashed his car on the beltway. I have other news . . . I've been following up on Argyle Socks. My hunch was right, pal. Number four is Ethan Edwards, the cartoonist. He has a loft in the city. I have the address and I've seen him. He's got a girlfriend in Washington, DC. She's a nurse at Walter Reed hospital and she's got a son. She has a condo; I have the address. I've seen her. I've followed her. I've got her routine down. He's with Shevchenko."

"I don't give a shit about his personal life."

"You should. I'll take care of this problem. You concentrate on yours."

HOBOKEN, NEW JERSEY: JULY 11

The high-rise building was dark except for the lobby.

Two women entered. They walked slowly to the desk. Lila produced a handgun. "Say goodnight and hang up. Do as I say, or I will shoot you."

"I have to go. One of the tenants is having a problem."

"Tell whomever it is you will call back when you are finished."

"I'll call you back." He hung up, his eyes bulged and the front of his tan slacks darkened, the stain widening. "Don't kill me. I got a wife and kids. Please don't kill me."

"I have no issue with you. My friend here is going to take you to the basement. You will be tied up and gagged. Go with her now. Tell her where the door to the basement is. Tell me how to dim these lights."

"They go off automatically at two o'clock."

"Good. You have pissed yourself. You smell, Mister Berry; fear is a very strong feeling. My friend has little patience for stupidity. Do we agree?"

"Yes, ma'am, I won't make any trouble. The maintenance people have lockers and there is a linen room."

Leona walked around the desk and took Berry's arm. Her free hand held a 9 mm Makarov against his lower back. "I will get you cleaned up, What is your first name?"

"Curtis. I swear I won't give you any trouble . . . Don't kill me."

Well Curtis Berry, I will have to tie you up once we've washed you. When we are finished with our business here, I will call the police and tell them where you are. You have my word."

Armed men entered. They walked swiftly across the lobby, Edwards glancing up at the lights.

"The lights turn off automatically at two. They should go out very . . . Ah, there we go," Lila said. "Leona will be up in a few minutes."

"How is the night man?"

"He understands the situation. I have his driver's license. He pissed himself. I do not know why when men have fear, they piss themselves."

"Is there a question here, Lila?"

"It is an observation, Peter Shevchenko." The door to the basement opened. Leona came out and walked quickly over to the elevator. "Fifth floor, Apartment 525."

"Did it go well, Leona?"

"He will tell the police he was overwhelmed by four masked intruders all dressed in black; they wore masks. He can't describe them. I told him to show the police his stained pants as proof."

"Let's go. Sergei go to the roof as a precaution. We will send for you."

The elevator reached the fifth floor, and the women got out. Sergei pressed the button taking the elevator to the twentieth floor. "Five two five is to the left." The men stood by the elevator. Shevchenko raised his hand, signaling them to knock.

"Hello there. We were told you are having a party." Lila pressed her ear to the door. Leona took out her weapon, resting it against her buttock. "Hello?"

"One moment, I was in the shower."

The men came down the hall. The door opened to a young man: tall, blond-haired and very thin, dressed only in a pajama bottom. "We were told there was a party here tonight. This is Mister Graham's apartment, is it not?"

"This is his apartment. I am afraid you've had a joke played on you."

"Step back." Lila brought up her weapon and pressed it against the young man's chest. "Is he here? Where is he?" The two men rushed past him.

"He isn't here. If you are here to rob us, take what you want and leave us alone. We won't call the police." He started to tear up.

"Bring Sergei down."

"He's not here."

"I told you he wasn't. Please . . . just take what you want."

"Who are you and what are you doing here?"

"My name is Christopher. I live here. Frank and I are in a relationship."

"I am going to ask you questions about your lover."

The door opened, Sergei and Leona entered, locking the door behind them.

"Sergei, show Christopher that little trick you do with a piece of garden string." Shevchenko pulled two straight back chairs close to the young man.

"Sit, Christopher." Shevchenko sat down, opened the medical bag, and took out a roll of masking tape. "Why don't you ladies search the apartment for information that might help us while I discuss certain aspects of Christopher's relationship with Graham?" Shevchenko placed a piece of tape on Christopher's chin. He took out lengths of cord. "I'm going to tie you to the chair; do not resist me."

"I won't . . . Tell me, what has Frank done?"

"Your friend is a very bad man, Christopher. This is a friend of mine he is going to tie something of yours."

Sergei knelt next to Shevchenko pulled down Christophers pajama bottom and tied the string to Christopher's penis, double looping it.

"There we are." Shevchenko said in a soft voice. "Now we can talk. Speak only when I ask a question that requires an answer. Otherwise simply nod or shake your head. If I think you are telling me the truth I will smile. If I think you are lying, I will let Sergei tighten the string. Be honest and you will not suffer. Try to protect your lover and Sergei will see to it that you are no good to any man. Do you know where he is?"

"Washington, he rented a car and drove. Please don't hurt me. I swear I only know he is in the CIA and can't talk about what he does for them."

"Does he treat you well?"

"Yes, he is very good to me."

"How long have you and Graham been lovers?"

"Four years."

"Did he say anything about his trip? What was it for?"

"He only said it was CIA stuff. Something to do with a woman and her son. He was going to protect them and would return in a few days. He tells me only what he can."

Shevchenko spied Edwards moving closer, his eyes bulging. He waved him away. "Let me finish, Ethan. Do you love him, Christopher, and does he love you?"

"Yes. He told me this is his last job. He wants to move to Holland."

"Did he mention the woman's name by any chance?" Christopher was becoming more relaxed and less fearful. He might have a friend in this man, someone who understands. Shevchenko sighed and patted Christopher's knee.

"No. I can't be sure, but I think he mentioned she was a nurse."

"Ethan, why don't you call your friend and see if everything is all right." He looked back at Christopher, reached over, and patted his shoulder. "We are almost finished."

"Anna Lee, it's me."

"Well, this is a nice surprise call at the hospital. Are you coming back soon?"

"Where is Vincent? Is he at home?"

"He is with his grandparents; why, Ethan?"

"You may be in danger. Listen to me. Call Cahill. You have their number. He will contact the proper authority at the agency. Arrangements will be made to protect you. Do not leave the hospital. Keep an eye out for strangers around the unit. Call your parents and tell them to expect people coming to their home. I'll give you a code word to tell Cahill his people are to use it when they get to Vincent: 'mailman'; don't forget it."

"Ethan, talk to me."

"There isn't time, Anna Lee. I'm coming straight to you. I am sure Cahill will send people to the hospital and your parent's home. Someone will give you a storyline for your parents: Memorize it. I've got to hang up. Remember the code . . . mailman."

"We have found a few interesting files and papers. I thought there would be more."

"Frank has a safe under the floor in our bedroom. I know the combination."

"Why don't you give it to Lila. Sergei, after Lila opens the safe and removes the contents, we will leave. We will wait for you in the car while you clean up here. I think Christopher has had enough excitement for a lifetime."

"If Frank has done something terrible, I do not want to be here when he returns."

"You won't be seeing or talking to him again. I can promise you that. We are going to move you to the bedroom. Do not make trouble."

"I've called for the plane and it is already checked out and refueled. We need to get out of here. Now."

"A moment, please. We are getting things from Graham's safe that may lead us to him and Palmer, Ethan. We need ten minutes at the outset. Did you reach Anna Lee?"

"Yes, Peter; I told her what to do."

"I have what I found in the safe. Christopher is on the bed. I told him, we were leaving and not to worry."

"Very good, Lila. Leona is getting the elevator-- Sergei?"

"I will be along on the next lift."

"Is this necessary, Shevchenko? That young man is innocent."

"That young man is more woman than man. He has the emotions of a woman. He has been betrayed by a trusted lover."

"The elevator is here."

"Take him with us. He won't be in any trouble; I'll see he is put in Langley. He will not be able to reach Graham. Trust me, Peter."

"Sergei, get Christopher dressed and bring him down-- hurry."

"Thank you."

"We have a strong tailwind; we should be landing at Andrews earlier than expected."

"Good news for us." Shevchenko rubbed his chin.

"I hope so," Ethan answered, closing his eyes. His lips barely moved in silent prayer.

"Mister Edwards, you have a call from a Mister Cahill," the pilot said over the intercom. "Use the ground to air phone behind your seat."

"If Mister Cahill needs assistance, tell him to call Kasparov. Tell him these names: Molotov and Ivanov. They will give their lives to protect your woman. Trust them both, Ethan."

Ethan forwarded the instructions to Cahill.

Anything else Ethan?"

What about the CIA and Christopher?"

"They will pick him up when we land, Ethan, and hold him at Langley."

"You should go to the hospital Ethan when you land. Leona will go to Anna lee's Parents home once we land."

"I like the way you think, Shevchenko"

"Of course you do, because we are the same."

WASHINGTON, DC: JULY 12

Leland Colby entered Mac's Southern Fried at 10:30 a.m. Leland slid his six-foot-three, two-hundred-and-twenty-pound frame into a booth. Food came out almost before he had adjusted the belt on his trousers: a platter of fried chicken, fries, and a pitcher of ice water.

"I'm expecting a friend." The short sentence brought a second glass immediately to the table.

Colby once had a promising career as a boxer. He was twenty-eight, carried a record of thirty-four and zero in the ring. He was ranked number two and slated for a shot at the title when people who decided such things told him to lay down.

Colby poured water into his glass and drank it in two gulps, wiping his chin of grease. He picked up another leg and finished it off, tossing the bone into a separate dish just as his visitor arrived.

"Hey man, have some chicken: the best in Washington. Bring my friend a plate, Mac."

"Nothing for me, thanks. I haven't enough time. That's Mac, the owner?"

"Nah, everybody in this place is called Mac, Mister Graham."

"We are ready, Leland." Graham took a set of keys from his coat pocket a thick brown envelope and placed both on the table. "You drive to the hospital. Park on the first level of the visitor parking garage and wait. Make sure you can see the outdoor parking lot clearly. The men will arrive in a green van. They will park in the fifth row of the visitor lot. When they finish what they came to do, you can leave. You will never speak of this day again, understood?"

"What do I do with the car?"

"The registration and proof of ownership are in the glove compartment. You can sell it or keep it for your own use."

"A bonus. Sounds like a plan, man."

"Bag your meal; drive safely. No screw ups. You must get there without incident. You can finish your meal while you wait in the visitor's garage."

"It'll be cold by then, Mister Graham."

"Put the envelope on top of your food it will warm it."

"I need a bag for the chicken, Mac. I got to go."

CHAPTER TWENTY-SIX

WALTER REED HOSPITAL

"Anna Lee, you have a call."

"Thanks Denise. Hello, this is Caputo."

"It's me, Anna Lee. I'm on my way to you. Have you heard from Timmons?"

"Yes, they are with my parents and Vincent. He explained the cover story to me. Are they really here to harm us?"

"We think the threat is very real. Is anyone with you?"

"Two very large, dangerous-looking men with Russian accents. I'm going to cry, Ethan."

"No, you're not. Under no circumstance do you leave the unit until you are clear of danger. The two men are your best protection; trust them and do as they say. Everything will work out. I promise."

FORT LEE, NEW JERSEY

"Joseph, pick me up at 8:30 at the hotel. We're taking a ride to the Chevrolet dealership."

"What are we looking for?"

"Cargo vans to start with. We're looking for availability. We need at least one for business purposes. You and I just became plumbers." Palmer hung up. "Can you hear me, Reba?"

"Yes."

"Joseph is coming for me at 8:30. We're going to Paramus to look at vans. I want you to go to the apartment. Get our things moved in, but don't unpack just in case. Try to get close to Underwood. Find out where he lives in Ridgewood, size of house, access to frontal roads and privacy."

"You make it sound so easy, John. He already mentioned he is alone and the house is big."

"When you are alone, a house can be bigger than it is. Make up a story he will believe."

"Just in case of what? You didn't tell me Graham's plan."

"I don't have details. He wouldn't tell me."

"You make sure you do not make decisions without consulting me."

He waited before answering, closing his eyes. No voices, no hollow-faced crows. They were gone. At last, he was free of them.

"Come here, John. Give me a reason to miss you."

WALTER REED HOSPITAL

"Mister Cahill is waiting in the administrator's office; he has information you need."

"You are Cahill's driver . . . we met last year at the Old Angler, I believe."

"Taylor Broom. I don't park cars any longer. Please inform Mister Cahill that I will be on the roof, above the cafeteria awaiting instructions."

"Tell me, Broom, what's your weapon of choice?"

"I like the German made PSG-1 with the 6x42 mm scope. It gives me a wide view."

"I have always wondered if arrogance is better or worse in our line of work. It seems to me arrogance can cause one to error. One day we should go to the range together."

"I look forward to it."

"I'm sure you do. I'll give Mister Cahill your message, Broom."

"Ethan, I'm glad you're here. You haven't had any sleep? I am so sorry for making.."

"We haven't much time, Adam."

"Yes, of course. I have pictures and histories of the men who most likely will be involved. I have an updated photo of Graham. I gave a set to the Russians and hospital security. I told the head of security and the administrator that they are not to be involved, above notifying us of a sighting." He handed the file to Ethan.

"I have a copy. Who are these guys, Adam?"

"The black man is a retired boxer named Colby. Graham introduced him to me a few years ago. I suspect he is a driver, possibly a backup shooter. But that's a long shot. The other three are members of a street gang in New York's west side. Graham recruited them for assorted activities. He enjoyed the company of thugs and gangsters."

"He had a boyfriend, Adam. Did you know that?"

"I suppose I suspected it. Is the boyfriend part of the plot?"

"No, Adam, he simply fell in love with the wrong man. Whatever makes a person happy. I don't judge personal lives."

"Where is he now? In custody, I hope, Ethan?"

"He's in custody, Adam. He's volatile and very emotional. They took him to Langley. We planted a story with the Hoboken Police in case Graham calls or shows up."

"It will be light soon Ethan. If Colby is the driver or even a backup, we need someone in the visitor parking garage to eliminate him."

"I took care of that Adam when I arrived. I will radio his description. I sent a woman, less suspicious to look for an older model car. She flew in with us. She is very good. I need a moment to see Anna Lee. Your boy Broom is on the roof of the cafeteria waiting for instructions."

"Of course, you do need to see Anna Lee and she needs to see you. I will alert her guards. Ethan, don't forget Graham knows who you are and what you look like."

"You know me, Adam. I will be as silent as the air he breathes."

"Take my phone, Ethan. Keep me posted."

"How did you get past Beatrice?"

"She understands certain circumstances require certain actions, Ethan."

Molotov standing on the landing alerted Ivanov, who was guarding the stairwell. He put up three fingers, indicating the elevator number. Both drew their pistols in case someone other than Ethan Edwards stepped out. The bell sounded. The doors opened.

"I am Ethan Edwards. Can I come out?"

"Put your arms out to your side and step out slowly ---two steps only." Boris raised his weapon. He relaxed, seeing Edwards, and signaled Ivanov. "You can put your arms down, Ethan Edwards. The woman is in the nursing manager's office, just to your left."

"Thank you, Boris Molotov of Minsk?"

"He is Ivanov of Sebastopol. The woman waits."

"Thank you both." Ethan turned and walked quickly to the office, disappearing inside.

Boris slipped his weapon into the shoulder holster. "You see, Comrade, it is nice to have a good woman to take care of. Who takes care of you?"

"Maybe one day, when I am old like you, Comrade. For now, I prefer my freedom."

"It is better when you are young, I think."

Lila Chekov stepped off the elevator on the ground floor landing, taking a moment to study the row of vehicles. She immediately spied a 1964 Grand Prix sitting in the aisle behind a parked car. The paint, once a dark blue, was faded to the point the primer was exposed on the hood. The driver's side window was open. Smoke drifted out. She noted the tires were new. There was one man in the car, a black man—big shouldered with a shaved head. The description Cahill gave her fit the driver. She took out a parking ticket she had found on the ground and started to walk toward the car, looking from right to left, studying the overhead signs. The rising sun cast long shadows across the enclosure.

She moved to the center of the driveway, walking slowly, continuing to study the signs until she was even with the driver's side door. It was him, Colby. She stopped, cursing under her breath.

"I am lost. I cannot find my car." Lila glanced at her ticket. She looked at Colby. "Can you help me?"

"Do I look like a tour guide?" Colby flicked the butt of the cigarette out onto the concrete floor. "I'm busy."

"I do not understand the signs. Can you please help me? I cannot find my car."

"Like I said, bitch, I'm no parking attendant either."

"I know you from someplace. I know that face." She stepped closer to the car, removing her glasses, her right hand hidden in her coat pocket.

"Yeah, I'm Jimmy Carter." Colby pulled another cigarette out of his shirt pocket and lit it.

"You're the fighter that threw the fight against that other Herp. You are Leland Colby, the phony, 'Smash guy.' " Lila pulled the Makarov 9 mm pistol with the elongated silencer out and aimed it at Colby just as he pulled up the handle of the door.

"What is this? Who you calling a Herp?.. What's a Herp?"

"Lower your voice, Colby. I know why you are here. Other men are coming here...killers. You are here to watch the---Tell me where they are and I will set you free."

"Screw you, bitch. I don't know what you're talking 'bout. What's with the gun? You some kind of assassin? That shit doesn't bother me."

"Colby, is it worth death to not tell me? I will ask once more. Where are they and how many are there?"

"I guess you will just have to shoot me." Colby spit the cigarette out onto the ground.

"It is your wish." Lila fired three rounds into the head of Leland Colby, removed the silencer—tucking it into her coat pocket with the gun—picked up the shell casings, and walked out of the garage into the bright morning sun.

A green Chevrolet van entered the parking lot the driver found a spot in row five and parked. Lila began to pace, sipping her tea while her eyes stayed focused on the van. The passenger door was open. There was a sign on the door: Donahue and Son's Paint.

Shevchenko walked up behind her, brushing against her shoulder. He excused himself.

"I am so sorry young lady," he said, offering to get her a napkin to wipe the spilled tea off her coat. In a low voice he said, "What about the Herp in the visitor's garage?"

"He is dead." The driver's door of the van opened, catching her eye. A young man climbed out and stretched his arms over his head. "The green van five rows to your one o'clock, Peter. I am suspicious of it." A rear door opened. "We were told to watch for three men together in the lot. What time is it?"

"Eleven o'clock."

"It is time for her to leave the hospital, yes?"

"Wait here; I am calling the guards down. We will see about this activity. Ethan Edwards should be in the lobby. Watch the van. Count occupants if you can."

"I have. I counted three."

"Do not let them out of your sight." He found Ethan in the lobby talking on a hand-held phone. "We think we may have a suspicious vehicle, a green van."

"Broom, did you get that?" Edwards said into the phone.

"I'm on them. I see at least three subjects."

"What are they doing?"

"Two are by the rear of the van, another one is moving in your direction. Wait . . . the two climbed back into the front seat of the van."

"Don't let them out of your sight. The one coming toward me--- describe him."

"Five seven, blond wavy hair, a round face, clean-shaven just like the picture Mister Cahill gave me. He is wearing fatigues. No name tag or rank. He's got a 101st airborne patch on the wrong shoulder. He's wearing sneakers. He's also carrying a heavy winter coat draped over his right arm. A little much for this time of year."

"How far out is he Broom?"

"Third row out. He's stopping, looking around. I can't see a weapon. I can take him out, no problem."

"Wait. If he looks up, can he see you?"

"Not in time to save himself."

"Okay, wait for my signal."

"What will that be?"

"We'll be on the two in the van. Shots will be fired; your guy will turn to see what is happening."

"Got it."

The three Russians came up behind him. "One of them is three rows out, center stage, two more inside that green van five rows down at our one o'clock."

"We should come at them from both sides. Lila will get the car. What do you think, Ethan?"

"One of your men should get the car. Lila should be with one of us--- less suspicious." Ethan paused a moment, frowning.

"What is wrong?"

"It's Graham; where the hell is Graham?"

"He is gone. If he were here, he would have recognized you. He would know the black driver is dead and warned the others off. Kasparov is on his way to Dulles in case he dumps the rental and decides to fly out. Kasparov will kill him. These three do not suspect a thing. Boris, you go for the car and wait to pick us up."

"I know the tread on my tires are worn, but—"

"Make your point Boris, my old friend. Time is very short."

"This man Graham--- he is not at the airport. Dmitry will not find him. If I am correct. He is already gone."

"I hear a very wise idea from a very wise man, Comrade," Shevchenko said. "Call Kasparov before you pick up the car."

Edwards's phone crackled to life. "What is it, Broom?"

"Our boy is still on his heels in row three. I think he may be the shooter, the way he carries himself along with the wrong coat."

"We're coming out."

The young man, standing in row 3 ignored the man and woman walking to his left talking and laughing, arm in arm, absorbed in their own lives. Or the two men shaking hands on the patio, exchanging small talk, saying their goodbyes, one of them walking toward the visitor garage the other coming straight toward him holding a parking ticket in his hand. He looked past them, waiting for the woman to come out. He checked his watch. He turned and watched the man holding the ticket as he made his way through the rows. He turned back, facing the patio: still no sign of the woman. He couldn't have missed her.

The man in row three heard the shots fired behind him, turned, but before he could take a step, a bullet fired from above the cafeteria exploded through his head, penetrating the windshield of a car in row four.

"I have to see Anna Lee and tell her it's over. She is okay and so is Vincent."

"Call her when we are clear. I will call Timmons. We have to go, Ethan. Let Cahill handle it. We have to go now."

Frank Graham drove up to an open spot near the door of the snack bar. He thought about topping off the tank, but decided to wait until he was closer to the Pennsylvania turnpike exit. By then, he would not only need gas but something to eat and drink. Now he just wanted to call Christopher to let him know he would be home by early evening. He turned off the car's engine just as the oldies station was breaking for the hourly news updates and a weather report.

Inside the snack bar, he purchased a package of gum and got enough change to call Christopher. He took a napkin with him to the bank of phones, wiped the earpiece and grip, and dialed the operator. After inserting the proper amount of coinage, he dialed the number of his apartment. A voice he didn't recognize answered, startling him. His first reaction was jealousy.

"My name is Graham and you are in my apartment. "Who the hell are you?"

"My name is Dale Muncy. I am a homicide detective with the Hoboken Police department, Mister Graham. Do you know a man named Christopher Hadley?"

"He's a friend, what's happened?"

"He's dead, Mister Graham, someone shot him. Where are you? We need to talk to you."

Graham hung up, walked out to the rental car, and climbed in behind the wheel. He began to rock back and forth. He turned on the engine and radio just as the announcer interrupted the music and began talking about the shooting at Walter Reed hospital.

Graham shut off the radio and engine. Minutes went by as he contemplated his next move. He couldn't go back to the apartment. Cops were there. Christopher was dead . . . murdered? Events were unfolding; plans once thought impenetrable were at risk. Palmer was in danger. He had to be warned. Did the hunters know about the apartment in Fort Lee? Did they know about his rental car, signed for in Hoboken before he left.? Was Palmer already compromised, or worse, already dead? He climbed out of the car, locked it, and went back into the snack bar. He dialed the number of the apartment in Fort Lee. A woman answered.

"Is this Reba?" he asked, trying to calm the shakiness in his voice.

"Yes, and you must be Frank Graham. Is the massacre in Maryland you're doing? Your people are all dead, Graham."

"I have no idea how they knew." A lie to protect Christopher, but he was dead too. The CIA murdered him. "We're all in trouble." He said out loud.

"Nothing has changed; we have a new place to hide. I will know more this evening. Can you come here? Are you being followed?"

"I'm on the turnpike. If they were on to me, the highway would be compromised. The apartment is safe for now, I'm sure of it. I'm on my way. Where is Palmer?"

"He is looking for vans. You see, nothing has changed. Come join us. I think your options are less favorable now, wouldn't you say?" The operator interrupted the call. "Charge the call to this number, operator," Reba said, "we are not finished talking."

"I'm driving a rental I picked up before I left Hoboken. I should drop it off and come in by train. They might be checking rental agencies as we speak."

"That was foolish to put yourself in this position."

He flinched. A ribbon of fear ran through him. The tone of her voice, cold, calculating. It was a veiled threat. He was alone now, on his own. He was no longer of use to Palmer. "I'll figure something out." Palmer killed Christopher not the C.I.A.

"Come to the apartment. Someone will meet you."

"I'm coming. Will you be there?"

"Someone will be here---waiting."

Frank Graham was in a vacuum. Think rationally and don't panic. First things first: Get rid of the car. Find a hotel, give yourself time to think. "I'll call when I reach New Jersey." He hung up without waiting for a reply. "Palmer killed Christopher. He came for me and found Christopher. His revenge for my failure. I'm next." He whispered as he walked swiftly to his car.

PARAMUS, NEW JERSEY

"I don't like buying cars, Joseph. Tell me, Harry, how much longer do we have to wait?"

"I'll tell the manager to verify your application as quickly as we can." The salesman jumped up. "Would you both like a soda or maybe coffee?"

"I want the truck, Harry. We don't need a soda. I'm paying cash. The clock starts now."

"Why are we buying a truck? Tonight, I could easily take it from the back lot."

"You heard the same crap I heard on the radio. Graham's brilliant idea turned to shit. We can't take the chance, the CIA or FBI will monitor local cop advisories. The first thing they'll look for is robberies. Graham lived in Hoboken. They will monitor every cop shop in Bergen County, you understand?"

"I understand . . . better to be careful."

"You like hamburgers, Joseph?"

"I love them."

The sales rep came back and looked in the door of the office. "Your application went right through. You are golden, Mister Preston. You've been out of the country. How did you like living in Europe these past years?"

"My advice Harry? Visit, don't live in Europe---How much longer, Harry?" Palmer looked at his watch. "Tick tock. You have a phone I can use? I want to call my wife."

"Right on the desk: dial nine for a private line."

"Hello."

"Reba, it's me. We're almost done here, buying a cargo van. Have you heard?"

"Yes, it is all over the news. Graham called. He's scared, I could hear it in his voice. I think we need to rethink our association, especially since he put us in jeopardy."

"I was thinking the same thing. Where is he?"

"Jersey turnpike. I talked to our friend downstairs. His home is on Mountainside Drive in Ridgewood. He showed me a picture. It's quite nice and big. He called it an English Tudor home, stone faced, a lot of shade trees in front."

"Follow him home."

"He invited us both to come see the house. I told him I might be interested in buying in the area because I wanted to retire. I asked if he would mind if I came alone. His face reddened. I told him you and I weren't a couple traveling together. I called it a ruse we used to ward off suitors. He suggested supper tonight and I thought it was a wonderful idea."

"Call the hotel in Teaneck now. Tell them to stay put; Joseph will come for them when we get into the house. We got to move fast, Reba. Graham shortened the timetable with his attempt to thwart Ethan Edwards. I should have seen it coming. It was stupid of me."

"Don't blame yourself. What do I do about Graham? He won't get here in time."

"Leave a note for him with the night manager. Tell him not to worry. I'll settle with him. Got to go."

"Write down his address. His home is number 401 on Mountainside Drive."

"I have it. Got to go." He hung up just as Harry stepped into the office. "Well, Harry, tell me I own a van."

ON THE RUN

"Adam, it's Frank Graham on the phone."

"What do you want, Graham? People are dead. I thought you would have put a bullet in your head. Your boyfriend is dead. Palmer killed him." He said this to reinforce the narrative that Palmer was the enemy.

"I'm retiring Mister Cahill. I won't kill myself. I'll simply disappear." Palmer killed Christopher I knew it. He is going to kill me next. Out loud he said, "First you need to know where Palmer is. He is presently in Fort Lee, New Jersey. He has a spectacular view of the Hudson River and, of course, the George Washington Bridge. The woman is with him. I don't think I need to tell you who she is. Five in all, but you already know that don't you?"

"What's the address, Graham?"

"I think I have given you enough clues. You just need to fill in the blanks. Goodbye Adam. You won't hear from Frank Graham again. "

Adam put the phone back on its cradle, leaned back in his chair, sighed, and folded his hands on his lap. Was there a clue in Graham's monologue aimed at Palmer or was he orchestrating a clever distraction? Cahill tapped his thumbs together. He had already made one mistake in judgment, which caused five people their lives.

"It is the view, not so much of the river . . . It's the bridge . . . or maybe the bus terminal?"

"You're mumbling, dear heart. What did Graham say?"

"I need to call Timmons."

"Is it about Ethan?"

"No. Could I have a brandy, Beatrice? I need to call Timmons. I also need to talk to Mona." He dialed Timmons private line. When Timmons answered he began. " I just received a call from Frank Graham--- He's going dark. I told him Palmer murdered his friend. He said he assumed the same thing--- Graham gave me a hint as to where Palmer may be."

"Mona is here as you requested Adam."

"Good, put her on the extension."

"Mona, pick up the extension phone."

"I'm on Good afternoon, Mister Cahill."

"Hello, Mona. You used to live in New Jersey. I believe you said in Bayonne?"

"That's right, Mister Cahill, I grew up there."

"There used to be an amusement park in Fort Lee--- Please call me Adam."

"Yes, above the Palisades--- Adam."

"Describe the view across the river, Mona. Tell me what you see"

"Well, we went at night, mostly. I guess the lights of the city, the bridge all lit up."

"Was there a lot of activity on the river at night?"

"Truthfully, I didn't pay much attention. I was in high school, boys were a priority then, not the river. Anyway, the park is gone, replaced by high rise apartments, very expensive homes. I think Jackie Gleason lives there."

"Where are we going with this, Adam?" Timmons cut in.

"I'm getting to my point. I just needed background, Ronald. Mona, stay on the line. Graham called me. I am sure there has been a break between Palmer and our boy Graham. I believe Graham has given me a clue about Palmer's plans. I can't be sure, but I think—"

"The bridge is the target," Timmons blurted out.

"I think so—either the bridge or the terminal itself."

"Ethan needs a detailed layout of Fort Lee: main streets, connecting highways, hotels, and condos with a view of the river and bridge. He needs it as quickly as you can get it, Ronald."

"May I say a word? It's the terminal, you two. More carnage.---More death."

"I think you may be right, Mona."

"What about Frank Graham?"

"He's in the wind, Ronald. He'll find a hole and crawl into it and wait for events to play themselves out. If I know him, he has already changed his appearance."

"What if Palmer speeds up his plan?"

"Palmer isn't ready. He will need a vehicle, maybe two vehicles. I would guess cargo vans, and he needs seclusion to build the bomb inside the trucks. He can't just throw a grenade at the bridge. He will need high explosives to wreck the bridge or the terminal. I agree with you on one very important point, though. We haven't much time."

"What about the liberty statue?" Mona interrupted. "He can reach it by boat. I remember a serial killer was talking to the police and mentioned a statuesque female known all over the world. We already knew he was a serial killer from that Dupree fellow."

"Ronald, my boy. I think you should be working for Mona."

"I am fine right where I am, Mister Cahill. It was a thought only. I am sure your idea is the right one. It certainly makes more sense."

SWEDESBORO, NEW JERSEY

A fresh haircut much shorter than he was used to, a visit to the local army-navy store where he purchased a wide brimmed cotton bucket head cover, a replica from the Vietnam era and a pair of pilot sunglasses. He exchanged small talk about the Marine Corps while paying special attention to the general appearance of other customers. He needed to do a little shopping before he returned to the hotel.

He drove into the parking lot of the Swedesboro Town Place Suites, drove to the rear of the building, and parked. He removed the rental stickers from the rear bumper of the car, went into the building and directly to his suite. He showered, changed into clothing more fitting his surroundings, and turned on the television, watching it for only a few moments. He decided to eat. The desk clerk recommended the Swedes Inn for its dining and history and one could walk there.

He ordered half a roasted chicken, French fries, and string beans, telling the waiter he had high blood pressure and he needed to watch his salt. He ordered iced tea.

He thought of Christopher. The waiter brought fresh hot rolls.

"Enjoy your meal."

"It smells wonderful, thank you for suggesting it." He picked off the wing, pulling the meat off between his teeth. The wing was the measure of the bird. If the meat was good and plentiful close to the bone, the bird was good. He needed a plan. He needed options. He picked up a leg and bit into it.

First replace the car with sedan. He chose a four door Ford. He had cash in the apartment a small savings and checking account in a local bank in Hoboken; these accounts were useless. The police would surely monitor them. If he wrote a check, it could easily be traced. He'd planned it this way for just the outcome he now faced. A nice comfortable amount of his ready cash, nearly one half million dollars, was in the Sun Trust Bank of Charleston, South Carolina, under a false business name and address in Tampa, Florida.

He owned a home on Pawleys Island, less than an hour drive from the city. Charleston was perfect for him. He was anonymous. The port of Charleston gave him ready access to transportation south. The rest of his holdings were in the Grand Cayman island, totaling nearly four million dollars held by RBC Wealth Management. He remembered mentioning the home to Palmer, but doubted Palmer would try to get to him now even if he remembered. His attention would be elsewhere until he got his revenge. By then he would be dead, so the matter of the house on Pawleys Island was moot.

He finished the leg, wiping his hands and mouth with a linen cloth, and began cutting the white breast into thin slices. He thought of Christopher. How much he loved sitting on the beach on Pawleys Island. Christopher, the sweet, gentle man. It was time for a strategy. When he was settled, he would mourn. He cut a roll in half and filled it with the thin slices of chicken.

"Is everything satisfactory, Mister Chester?"

"It is a wonderful meal, Le Mar, thank you again for suggesting it. I will have coff no cream. I think I'll skip dessert."

RIDGEWOOD, NEW JERSEY

Rita Alaura stood by the bay window in her living room with her long-haired Dachshund mix propped on her sofa, its paws on the flowered cushions, its snout resting on the back of the sofa. She crossed her arms over her cotton robe just as a silver four-door Mercedes turned into the driveway across the street.

"Isn't that nice, Chloe?" she said out loud, patting the dog. "Mister Underwood has guests. What do you think about that, Chloe?"

The dog looked at Rita, let out a low growl, and once again rested her snout on the back of the sofa.

"I hope he is having some fun; God knows he has been so lonely. Let's go out back so you can pee, and then to bed. Maybe tomorrow I'll take you for a walk if my hips hold up." She padded to the rear of the house and opened the screen door. She waited, tapping her fingers on the frame. Chloe did not like being rushed. Finally giving up, she called the dog inside. "I know you, Chloe. No pee now, but in two hours you'll wake me up. Let's go to bed. I'll read and wait. I'd like a bit of peanut butter on a slice of white bread. Maybe you'll change your mind." Chloe let out a low yawn. "I'm tired, too, little girl."

CHAPTER TWENTY-SEVEN

401 MOUNTAINSIDE DRIVE: JULY 11

Palmer came around the car. They approached the house. Reba knocked on the oak door after unscrewing the entrance light. She waited with her ear against the wood, listening.

"I hear him."

Underwood opened the door. "Hello Reba, I'm glad you made it." He smelled as if he'd just come out of the shower. There was the scent of Canoe lotion on his freshly shaven face. He was dressed in a starched white shirt and black slacks. Even his shoes were polished. Come in, come in. Mister Preston is not coming after all?"

"I'm here, Underwood." Palmer pushed his way into the foyer, drawing his weapon and pointing at Underwood's face. "Step back Underwood, and don't make a sound. Are you alone? Answer me and don't lie or I'll blow your fucking brains out."

"There is no one here," his voice cracked.

"Reba, call our friends and give them directions to the house. Tell Joseph to come in."

SATURDAY : JULY 12

Rita slipped the harness through her dog's legs. "Try to stay still, little girl, and let mommy finish. I know you want to get going. It's beautiful morning-- warm." Chloe, standing on her hind legs with her paws on the back of the

374

sofa, let out a low growl to alert Rita to strangers. Rita looked out the window.

A tall man with light-colored hair was cutting across Underwood's lawn. A younger man was working in the flower beds, removing weeds, and a woman was sweeping the entrance way.

"Mister Underwood has either hired a grounds crew or has guests. Either way is good, isn't it Chloe? Are you ready for your walk?" The dog jumped from the couch, tail wagging furiously, and ran to the front door.

The man with the sandy hair waved and said good morning. He had a nice smile. She waved and said good morning as she walked along the slate path to the sidewalk. "Maybe I'll stop and see how Mister Underwood is doing on the way back. What do you think, little girl, shall we stop?"

Palmer turned to Reba.

"Go inside, Reba. Talk to Underwood, and find out what you can about the old lady across the street. Warn him about making trouble. Get a list of neighbors and their hours. Find out where we can find two large drums, gas cans, electrical wire, etc. I'll make a complete list for Moshe. He can pick all the stuff up. Joseph, you watch her house. Jot down when she gets up in the morning, when lights go on at night. See if you can detect an alarm system."

"We could have done this before moving here, Palmer."

"Yes, we could have Joseph, but seeing as we were in a hurry---Reba call the apartment and see if Graham was there. If he is, tell him we're in Teaneck and to wait until I come to him." He looked at Joseph. "Start watching the movements of the neighbors, okay?"

Rita didn't come right back. After she crossed the street, she took her dog down a side street. Both men shrugged their shoulders and went back to what they were doing. A car passed, containing a woman with two small children in the back seat. She paid no attention to the men in Underwood's yard.

"I am going to take you out for a drive later, Underwood. I will allow you to walk on your property for the neighbors, especially for the old woman who lives across the street. I need you to tell me all about her. I need to know the routines of all your neighbors. Are you hungry?"

"Can't you at least untie me?"

"No, I cannot. I will remove the rope from one arm if you wish to eat something. I can cook very well."

"Why don't you kill me right now? I've seen your faces and can identify you."

"We have no intention of killing you. We need only the use of your home for a week or so."

FRANK GRAHAM

He felt better as soon as he turned onto Sand Fiddler Road. A third house was completed a door down from the corner. One lot with a sold marker separated him from his home and the home of his neighbors, Nick and Mary Martino. To his left, five completed homes with tall trees and thick foliage hide the golf course and club house, which were under construction.

Nick was in front of his garage, washing down dust and debris from the empty lot next door. He cursed the wind that seemed determined to make a mess of his driveway. Graham honked his horn and parked at the curb.

"Hey, look who's here.," Nick turned off the hose valve and padded across his lawn. "You home for good, Roy?" Nick asked, shaking the hand of the man he knew as Roy Chester.

"I retired from government work. I'm done, Nick. I'm looking for a life of leisure and kicking your ass on the new golf course a couple of days a week. What do you think about that?"

"I know all about retiring; I don't know about your golf game. I have been practicing, Roy."

"I thought all the lots would be full by now," Graham said, looking over Nick's shoulder.

"I was hoping . . . You look beat up, man."

"I am. I drove all night to get here. I'll tell you what, give me about six hours of sleep. Make reservations at your favorite eatery in Charleston. Help me get this loaner turned in and I'm buying supper for you and Mary; what do you say?"

DOUBLETREE INN - FORT LEE

Two men and a woman entered the lobby. The woman walked over to the restaurant, made a quick inspection of the occupants, turned, and shook her head.

"Good morning, gentlemen, are you checking in?"

"Not today," Shevchenko answered, taking the photos out of his coat pocket. "I would like you to look at these photographs. Let us know if you recognize any or all of them. They may be guests here." Shevchenko produced his ID.

"FBI . . . what's going on?"

"Please look at the pictures," Edwards answered. "Can you identify anyone?"

"Two stayed here. Am I . . . is the hotel in danger?"

"Relax." Shevchenko looked at the nametag on the young man's jacket. "You are in no danger, Jesse Smith, unless you've done something wrong that we need to know about. You haven't, right? His drawl was smooth, with a hint of playfulness.

"No, sir."

"In that case, young man, just answer my question. Did they check out together?"

"I never saw him. He must have come in after my shift. I only have one name on the form. She checked them both out." The nervous tick in his throat made him cough. "She said they had found other accommodations. She didn't say where; she paid cash. She seemed very nice. Soft spoken. She is beautiful; the picture doesn't do her justice."

"I guess it is safe to say the room has already been cleaned?"

"Not only cleaned but occupied. Are they very dangerous?"

"Yes, they are." Edwards gathered up the pictures and handed them to Shevchenko. "Could we see the registration card she filled out?"

"Of course, give me a moment." He returned and handed over the card.

"Thanks. Calm down, young man. You or the hotel are in no danger. I'll bring the card back. Relax, Jesse. If there was a problem you would know, okay?"

"They may have multiple IDs, Ethan, one for the rental and one here. Our friend Jesse would not check rental papers against the registration card. The license plates may also be stolen."

"Well hell, Peter, I feel better already."

"We are all hungry. I suggest we eat here while you make calls for tracers on the rental." Shevchenko took the card and padded back to the lobby. "Excuse me. One more thing . . . could you tell me where you would suggest we can go to hire a cargo van or perhaps buy one?" He apologized to the young couple he interrupted.

"I would try Paramus Chevrolet on North Route 17. They have the biggest lot in Bergen County. In fact, they are the only place you can buy a Corvette in the county. If they don't have what you want, no one does."

"Thank you for your help and your patience; I will not bother you again." Once again, he apologized to the couple at the desk. Shevchenko walked back to the center of the lobby.

"Jesse tells me if you want a cargo van, which I would suppose one would need, it can be found in Paramus on North Route 17. What shall I order for you, Ethan Edwards? Palmer, wherever he is, will be there when we find him and kill him, along with his little brood."

"I like that, his little brood."

"Make your calls, Ethan."

"I'd like pancakes with a side of sausage. extra syrup, juice, and coffee. I also hope to meet your wife one day."

"Maybe we could go to a Red Sox game in Boston? We will eat hot dogs, peanuts, and drink beer, yes. Timmons told me you were a fan."

"THE BROOD"

"I do not believe Underwood, nor the old woman across the street, will be a problem, from what he has told me. Her house is laid out like this one. She has no alarm system and no close family except for a daughter who lives in Atlantic City. She is alone with her dog. I still think we need to take Underwood for a ride. I also have the name of a large hardware outlet. Underwood says we can find whatever we need. Have you completed the list for Moesha? He is anxious to go John."

"Yes Reba, it is smaller than I originally thought. His garage is well stocked."

"He is very frugal John. He has an eye for quality. He built the pool table downstairs. I do not see any reason for killing him, John. I want to leave him behind. By the time he is found, we will be dead anyway. I called the apartment complex. Graham never showed up."

"He's gone, if I know him. We will be long dead before they find him, if ever. My only fear is he may try to make a deal before he becomes a ghost."

"Why would he do that?"

"My guess is he thinks we turned on him; when he did not return to the apartment, I was convinced."

"You are frowning, John; what are you thinking?"

"How could I be so stupid? How could I have missed the obvious?" He began to rock back and forward, his clenched fists pounding his knees, his face reddening. He opened his mouth trying to scream, but no sound emerged. He saw his dead parents for only a second, but it was enough to make him gag.

"Stop it John. Calm down." She jumped from her chair and knelt by his side. "Relax, John, I am here for you. Take a deep breath." She put her hand, palm down, on his member and slowly massaged him. "Relax, John, this will pass. We are safe." He was beginning to become erect. "That's good. Relax, let me help you. Let's find a quiet corner. After, you can tell me what caused you to be so angry with yourself. Do not cave on me now, Palmer. Pick yourself up and make love to me."

"Feel better now? I know I do. I think I climaxed four times."

"I was rough on you. I'm sorry, Reba. I'm so sorry." A tear slipped down his cheek.

"Do not be, John. A woman like me enjoys it rough on occasion. It brings the animal out in me and it makes me anxious for more." You have him, sex is your cookie. Hold onto the power.

"I won't brush my teeth."

"Save that thought for later," she said. Turning to the mirror, she spied the bruising on her shoulders. "Now tell me what sent you into such a rage?" He is better, compliant, more relaxed. Control. He is butter in your hands and doesn't realize it.

"I know where Graham is!---We need to get to him and quickly. I don't think he gave us up completely but, if he is convinced by the CIA, we turned on him? He might to save himself."

Maury Taylor, the weekend manager, led the two men into his office. He excused himself, offering seats to his visitors while taking a phone call from a tenant. He apologized, putting the phone back on its cradle.

"I want to answer your questions, but we have to address our resident's right to privacy."

"We have been up and down the boulevard, Mister Taylor, and we need to see even more apartments. You are the first to question us. I applaud your attention to your clients. The people we have pictures of are not permanent residents and may not even be staying here." Edwards pulled the pictures out of his coat pocket. "If we need to get a warrant, we can. Getting one takes time. I'm afraid time is the one thing we do not have."

"I am only the weekend manager. Our full-time manager, Mister Underwood, isn't here not on weekends. In fact, he is off until Tuesday."

"We understand, Mister Taylor, we only want you to say yes if you recognize the faces." Shevchenko held himself in check, reminding himself he wasn't in Moscow. "Please, Mister Taylor, just look at the photos? You won't be in trouble. No one will ever know we were here. Look at the pictures."

Maury was a man who followed rules. This managerial job was probably the best job he ever had. He was a man who allowed others to direct his actions.

"Tell me, were you in the military?"

"Yes, how did you know? I was a career army in the maintenance division --- twenty-five years. I made staff sergeant---E6. It was a good life."

"I was in the army as well. Help us out, please?" Edwards put the pictures of the men and woman on the desk. "Take a moment, Mister Taylor."

"I never saw these men." He put the pictures face down and picked up the other picture. His expression changed. "I met her. She was here, but she left. The only reason I saw her was I was picking up my paycheck. Mister Underwood had already gone home, so she asked me if I would accompany her up to the 12th floor. She wanted to leave a note on the door of an apartment. She said it was for a friend, but she couldn't wait."

"Did you take her upstairs?"

"Yes. I gave her a piece of tape and she put the note on the door. She never came back. She called this morning and asked about the envelope. I told her nobody came for the note. I make rounds every morning; that is how I knew."

"How did you know the envelope had not been opened?"

"The tape had not been disturbed, Mister Edwards."

"Do you know where she called from?" Shevchenko asked.

"No, I don't, but I think it was a private residence. I didn't hear any traffic noise or people in the background."

"Would you do me a favor, Maury? We will wait in the lobby while you go upstairs and retrieve the note and bring it to us. Would you do that?" Edwards saw immediately the hesitation on his face. "She isn't a resident and it is obvious the person who was to receive the note isn't coming."

"You will wait in the lobby?"

"Yes, as soon as we have the note we will leave. You will never see us again. You don't have to get permission, Maury. It is okay to help your government."

"It is a matter of national security," Shevchenko added. "Which means you must never discuss this meeting with anyone. You were a good soldier; be a good citizen, okay?"

"Okay." He led them out of the office, locked the door behind him—twisting the knob to be sure—and walked off toward the elevator bank.

"I like that last line about being a good soldier, Peter."

"I am sure he was. He did as he was told; he needed direction. I was impressed by his attention to small details. The lack of outside sounds when the woman called and the small thing about the tape most people would not notice. I think the army missed an opportunity, and I am sure he never offered it. Afraid to overstep. The perfect soldier."

Maury stepped off the elevator waving the note.

"She knew how to dress, nothing cheap about her."

"What was she wearing that caught your eye, Maury?"

"A fur coat—I think it was sable—with jeans, a pullover sweater, and high heels. Wasn't a damn thing wrong with that body either. I noticed because the weather is so warm. She seemed overdressed for the season. I think she might be Arabic. Does that help?"

"Immensely, Maury," Edwards answered. "Remember, not a word about us being here."

"My lips are sealed. What if she comes back? Who do I call?"

"I doubt you will hear from her again. She may call and ask you to throw away the note. Just say you will, and then call the number on the back of this card. Ask for Ronald Timmons. Goodbye, Maury."

"How many did the CIA help resettle, Peter?" Edwards asked, when they returned to their car.

"Not including us? Five stayed behind: Comrade Vlad Kozlov and his wife and Boris Molotov's his wife and children. They will be safe, Mikhail will see to it. And you, Ethan, where will you live?"

"We want to live in New York when this is over. We've already made plans and Anna Lee has a job waiting." Edwards peered into the rearview mirror. "Tell me, Dmitry, what are you thinking?"

"Elsa and I want to live in Arizona for the climate: no more Russian winters. I want to build a home with my own hands and have a pool. Have cows, horses to ride and sheep. I want to sit on our porch smoking a pipe in the cool of the evening. Elsa will like that too." His face flushed. "We have many years between us. My only regret is we will have to stay away from our good friend Peter."

"Kasparov is correct, Ethan, "Shevchenko interrupted, "we will be a thorn in the side of our government as long as we are alive. We will have to be cautious."

"Not if we can convince Moscow you were killed by Palmer--- What if you used my comic strip? We simply devise a code that will allow messages to be sent back and forth. Like sending messages through the newspaper personal columns. Who considers a comic strip as a vehicle to keep in touch?"

"You would do that?"

"First, we need to concentrate on getting through this alive, Dmitry."

"Yes--- alive," Shevchenko lamented.

"Palmer and the woman stayed at the Double Tree and the apartment in Fort Lee. The other four stayed at a different hotel, we have no idea where. I won't waste time looking."

"You are betting they are staying in Jersey, right?"

"They must be. A private residence. Check and see if the Israeli Embassy has a safe house."

"That's new," Timmons answered. "I'll take care of it. We are also monitoring police calls throughout the county. I think we have covered everything. Tell me, what are your plans for today?"

"We're checking dealerships throughout the county, starting in Paramus today. We believe he has or will purchase a van."

"Mona suggested the bus terminal might be his target. I think she might be right. We've notified the authorities through the FBI office in New York to be watchful. Of course, we couldn't give them a time frame with what we know. They took it seriously."

"They had better. You said you had news for me, Ronald?"

"Graham is dead; he was murdered in South Carolina. He had a home on Pawleys Island under the name of Roy Chester. We sent pictures of the Israelis to the FBI office in Charleston. A neighbor, his name is Martino, told the police Graham was in front of his house, they were kibitzing about a game of golf and both were drinking coffee. They spied a young man with one of those roller tape things measuring an open plot across the street, a corner plot. Martino figured the young man had either bought the plot or was a broker. He says he went inside to get dressed when he heard the shot--- I almost forgot---"How are you doing with cash flow, Ethan?"

"We're good. I'll call and check in with you this evening, Ron. Are you working on a hotel for us?"

"Let's see . . .wait, there is a large shopping center where Route 17 and 4 converge. It's called the Garden State Plaza Shopping Center. It seems to be in the middle of everything."

"See if you can put us close to it."

"I'm on it, call me later. Oh wait, I have a message for Kasparov, 'Your friend left Moscow yesterday morning, arrived in Paris safely and is now on a flight to America. Expected to land at Dulles airport at eight o'clock our time.' You got all that, Ethan?"

"I got it; where will she stay?"

"I will make all arrangements. We'll pick her up at Dulles. I'll call you with your hotel and hers."

"That's great, Ron." Edwards hung up and walked back into the main restaurant. "I'm glad we waited to eat. We learned a lot."

"Your food is getting cold, Ethan. Does Timmons have any news?" Shevchenko asked.

"Graham is dead, he was in South Carolina. He had a house there. Timmons says the hit was very professional."

"Hurry and eat; we need to go. I suggest we go to that big dealership in Paramus first."

"Sergei and I need extra clothing. The women are complaining as well."

"There is a very large mall on our way, Boris." Ethan looked at Sergei. "And no one has told me your last name. I'm curious."

"Only use one name. " Sergei answered.

"I guess that makes sense. The Garden State Mall, Boris, is on the way," Edwards said, putting another wedge of steak in his mouth before pushing the plate away. "It is on Route 17 where it passes over Route 4. We'll drop you off on our way to the dealership. What are you thinking, Peter?"

"I remember Palmer once said that Chevrolet was the best car in America."

"My basic training platoon Sergeant Clark, had a 1963 Corvette. I really liked him. He prepared me for parachute training. He always referred to us as his 'young warriors.' I own a vintage Corvette. It's a '64."

"Maybe I will buy one. Dmitry, go with us to the dealership?"

"You do not have to ask."

"Always my shadow, Comrade?"

"I also have news for you, Dmitry. The woman you have been waiting to hear from arrives in Washington today. Timmons will call with information when he finds us hotel accommodation. He will also find something for—"

"Elsa . . . my Elsa. She will want to join me."

MOUNTAINSIDE DRIVE: JULY 13

"I brought coffee; it is time to get up."

"What time is it?" Palmer asked, rubbing the sleep out of his eyes. "The sun's up?"

"It is after nine. A glorious day: warm, no clouds, no humidity. You were tired from all the work last night. I thought you should sleep." She put her hand under the covers. "Daniel knows about us. This morning I saw him in the garage. He was sniffing the air around the interior of the van like a dog sniffs meat."

"I need to get out to the garage, but hold that thought."

Reba frowned and pulled her hand out from under the covers. "Talking about smells, Underwood needs a bath, he stinks."

"Have one of the boys watch him."

"Abram has arrived in New York from South Carolina."

She sensed the agitation in his voice. He was worried. All his cleverly laid plans were partially being dismantled. She had to refocus him and settle him down. "We are all alone and you want to rush out to the garage. I guess you are already tired of me." She climbed off the bed and slipped out of the robe. "If you don't want to, then you can watch me leave."

"I'm sorry, Reba. I'm sorry."

He is like a puppy needing a treat. Let him wait. "Underwood still needs a bath."

"Then give him one. Watch him shower while you stand there naked. Watch the thrill in his eyes as he looks at you, knowing he can't have you."

"You are a cruel man, Palmer. I am cruel as well, but I have limits."

Ethan climbed out of the car. Behind him, on Northbound Route 17, a white van passed unnoticed with two men inside. "I'm not here to buy. We need information on a man who may have bought a van recently. You do sell vans, right?"

"We have a nice selection in the back."

"Is the general manager inside?" Shevchenko asked, reverting to his southern accent."

"You a cop, buddy?"

"Sort of, buddy. You want to answer my friend's question?"

"His name's Paul Goldsmith. His office is in the back of the showroom, on your right, behind the pickup truck." He cleared his throat to cover the nervous tick in his voice.

"A bit harsh with that salesman, Peter?"

"I do not like smart people whose attitude does not extend to their balls. My father taught me as a young boy to keep peace with strangers you meet. Never to show weakness, which they will use against you, but be careful not to show strength unless you are sure about the other person."

"Your father must have met my father except for one point. My father told me never to show strength or they will learn to defend against you."

"You never told me if your parents suffered, Ethan." They spied the general manager in his spacious office. A couple sat across from him. He looked up, seeing the three men in the hall. He excused himself and stepped around his desk to greet them.

"We need a few moments of your time, sir, a question first."

"Paul, call me Paul."

"Did you sell a van in the last few days, maybe a cargo van?"

"As a matter of fact, we did."

"We are FBI agents. We need to know who purchased the van."

"Oh, in that case . . ." He looked past them at the woman stepping into the hall from the showroom. "Madge, can you take these FBI agents to see Harry? He's probably in his office making dry calls."

"Of course, Paul. Follow me, gentlemen."

"Thanks for your help, Paul."

"Whatever you are here for . . . it's nothing serious, I hope."

"We just need to know who bought it."

"To answer your question, Peter, they didn't suffer." Edwards responded in a low voice as they followed Madge through the showroom. "They were killed instantly."

"He was punished for his crime, I hope?"

"He was a repeat offender, a man who abused drugs and alcohol. He had no license and had multiple DUI convictions. He was a menace. It was only a matter of time before he caused harm to others. I took care of the situation, Peter. I believe we had this conversation once before."

"I wanted Kasparov to hear it."

"I have decided to wait outside, Peter, if you do not mind?"

"Go ahead, Dmitry, we will not be very long."

"Harry, these two gentlemen need a moment of your time," Madge said, tapping lightly on the doorframe of Harry's office.

"Sure, c'mon in. How can I help you?" Harry extended his hand to shake theirs. He was small, with reddish receding hair and a porn star mustache curving down around his mouth, disappearing under his chin. "Have a seat."

"You sold a cargo van to a man a few days ago. We need to see the paperwork."

"I'll get it."

"You Americans are so full of yourselves, you can't see danger all around you, Ethan Edwards. Here we are getting information about a man whose business is none of ours just because we identified ourselves as government agents. No one asked to see our identification. The most powerful country in the world . . . no matter what European governments think. One day, you might pay a terrible price for your foolish acceptance of people you do not know. It is sad."

"I get your point, Peter."

"Here we are, gentlemen." Harry placed the invoice on his desk with the brochure. "He lives in New York on Eighty-First Street. He's planning a move to New Jersey to expand his plumbing business to the tri-state area."

"Did you verify any of this information, Harry?"

"He paid cash, so it wouldn't have been a problem. We filled out registration forms, which are required. He signed them and drove off. Oh, wait, he asked about a hamburger place for lunch. I told him about the Fireplace, up Route 17. You can't miss it. Is this guy a crook or something?"

"Or something, Harry."

Perry Underwood brought a fresh bath towel, a pair of clean underwear, a shirt, and jeans into the bathroom. He purposely left shoes, socks, and even slippers behind. He had one chance of survival: squeeze out of the bathroom window, stay close to the hedges lining the perimeter of the yard, and run to a neighbor's house. The hedges were thick with new foliage. He would be able to easily jump them and find help on the next block.

He stripped and turned on the spray of water, adjusting the handle to hot so it would steam up the room He began to sing "Love me Tender" not too loud, but loud enough to hide the sound of the window opening. He slipped the lock and slowly raised it. He took the folded clothes, tossing them through the opening. He lifted himself up using the lip of the tub and pushed out the screen. He then turned onto his right side and started to climb out, pulling his stomach in to clear the enclosure. His body stuck out to his waist. He put his left hand on the outside ledge and with his right arm, he forced himself forward and downward to help break his fall. At that instant, a carving knife was driven into the back of his skull.

Palmer removed the apron and plastic wrap that protected his clothing from blood spray, balled them up together, placed them in a bucket, and went into the house. "Reba, where are you?" he called, padding to the foot of the staircase.

"I'm downstairs in the game room, cleaning up."

"Come up here. I want to show you something."

GARDEN STATE MALL

"Did you get everything you needed gentlemen?

"I have changed my mind. I think I would like to stay here," Sergei said. His companions laughed. "I have made a joke, yes?"

"Wait until you see what they call grocery stores."

"I have seen them in New York. The shelves are full of canned and boxed food, rows of fresh meats and vegetables. I love this country."

"Let me introduce you to what Americans call a food court."

"What is that?" Boris asked.

"C'mon, I'll show you. We'll discuss what we found out at the car dealership."

"I will wrap the torso and get it ready.

"Take the Mercedes rental, Daniel. Find dumpsters that have just been emptied behind local stores. Use several to get rid of the corpse. Do not bring the Mercedes back to the house. Park it a couple of blocks from here. Reba has a map of the development; she will show you where to park it."

"Where will we take his car?"

"Some place where it will go unnoticed: a large lot, perhaps a commuter lot or possibly that shopping center at the junction of Route 17 and 4."

"I know the one. I saw it when we drove here. I will leave it at the mall."

"I'll get started on the wiring for the fuses." Palmer patted Daniel's shoulder. "We are very close to finishing what we came to do." He turned on his heel and stepped over to the work table. He picked up a utility knife and cut two, six-foot plastic sheets. He grabbed a role of strong shipping tape and went inside.

"I left the shower on to make sure the blood and residue went down and did not clog the drain. You want my help wrapping him?" Reba asked standing in the doorway of the bathroom, "I was wrong. I didn't think he would be so stupid."

"It doesn't matter, Reba, does it?" Palmer answered, without looking up. "Take a shower and get dressed. I want you to take his car away. Daniel will follow you once he has dumped Underwood and bring you both back." He looked up at her, his eyes shaded. "Get your shower and get dressed." He played a game and lost Reba. We will not." He began to wrap Underwood's legs in the sheets of plastic. "Don't waste time. Drop the car off at the mall and make sure you remove all the contents."

JULY 16

"Mona, it's me. Is he in his office and is he alone?"

"Yes Ethan, I'll put him on. You're all right?"

"So far so good, I guess."

"How are your friends holding up?"

"They very much like American women, and today I introduced them to the food court. They are like kids on a roller coaster."

"I'll put you through," she said with a muffled laugh. "Do you want me to contact Anna Lee and let her know where you are and that you are safe?"

"I will call her. Thanks, Mona, for asking."

"You need to check out of your hotel and move to the Hilton Inn in Hasbrouck Heights, it's very near the routes 17 and 4 exchange an overpass to be exact. You will be pretty much in the center of the county roadways.

They are expecting you."

"What's the address, Mona?"

"Ronnie has it. Oh shit, Ethan."

"It's okay Mona. I didn't hear a thing. Put me through."

"Ethan, I'm glad you called, you must have something for me?"

"He bought a Chevrolet cargo van in Paramus the other day; it's white."

"He is planning a massive explosion."

" I will give this new info to New York," Timmons answered.

"Tell your friend Oates to make up a crisis of some sort, not too drastic. We don't want them spooked. They might just set it off on the ramp or near the toll booths. One more thing, Ron. He told the sales rep he was a plumbing contractor. He may have put decals on the sides of the van."

"Got it, what else?"

"Tomorrow we are going back to talk to the regular manager. Mona tells me you have us in a hotel near the highway?"

"I do--- It's the Hilton Inn of Hasbrouck Heights. Use the west ramp just past the Garden State shopping center. Turn left at the top of the ramp it will be on your right. It also has a ramp on the East side of the roadway What else have you for me, Ethan?"

"I'm worried, Ron. It could happen in the next seventy-two hours. Now that he has a truck, he only needs to rig it and boom . . ."

"I'm on it. Tell Kasparov his friend is in our hands. Have him call my office. I will arrange for them to speak to each other."

Reba turned the Lincoln into the parking lot. She came very close to being sideswiped while maneuvering across lanes. She cursed the driver entering the lot and parked to give herself time to catch her breath. A security officer went by in a golf cart. She checked her watch, making a mental note of the time. She paid close attention to his uniform; he wore no gun. He was short, portly. Next to him on the seat a large cola drink.

She turned off the engine, slid out of the driver's seat, and walked back to where Daniel had parked three spaces away, facing the on-ramp. She explained the delay and told him to try and get closer to the main entrance while she drove around before making her decision on where to leave the car.

"I will come out through the main entrance to be picked up."

She went back to the Lincoln, got behind the wheel, and checked her watch. Four minutes had passed since the guard went by. She waited. Twelve minutes passed and then she spied the golf cart with the portly guard. No later than fifteen minutes to make a round.

She backed out of the spot and started up the lane to the right of the main entrance, driving slowly past the two-lane exit road to Route 17. At the top of the lot, she turned left, Daniel followed until they reached the entrance to the Mall. He pulled into a spot marked Shoppers Pickup Only and waited. Reba spied the restaurant bar, its entrance facing the lot.

"Perfect," she said out loud. She turned right and right again into the second lane and found a space.

She went to the entrance next to the restaurant and entered the shopping center, walking toward the main entrance at a shopper's pace. She passed the escalator leading to the food court. Reba went out the main entrance where Daniel was waiting. She got in the car.

"Let's get back to the house, Daniel." They drove off, just as the five hunters exited the main entrance.

Rita awakened, looked at her dog, and smiled.

"Okay, what is it now, Chloe? You need to go out?" She got up, scolding herself for not getting dressed properly for this time of day. "Okay let's go out back. Do what you got to do and I'll give you a treat, but nothing more until I get cleaned up and dressed, okay?" She gave a quick glance out of her window and saw the woman approach the house in the car driven by a young man. He parked in the driveway. Chloe led out a loud indignant bark.

"Okay, okay . . . when you got to go. I know the feeling."

"I'm almost done with the incendiary devices for the barrels." Palmer sighed. Reba, Tomorrow I'll add the gasoline and detergent. Let them ferment together overnight and then I'll connect all the final wiring. You and I will pick up the car and drive down the turnpike. We will leave for the island twenty minutes after the team leaves for the port authority. We get off at Exit 14, drive to the ferry landing, and cross over to Liberty Island. By then, the terminal will be in flames."

"What if they close the island?"

"Then we will go down into different subway stations and explode our vests." He opened the door to the garage and froze. "I told Daniel not to bring the car back here after he picked up Abram."

"Listen to me. If by chance we need to move fast, we need the car here and not two blocks away. We are so close. I've learned over the years it is the smallest missed detail that can lead to tragic outcomes."

"Yes, of course. You are right, Reba." He turned on his heel and faced the young man. "How did it go on Pawleys Island? Are you sure he is dead?"

"He is dead, Palmer."

"Get some rest. Sorry about the drive."

"You were right, Palmer, it was worth it. How is the bomb making going? Are we close?"

"This Wednesday. It will all be over on Wednesday or Thursday at the latest."

"You will have your revenge, Palmer. Perhaps one day someone will write a book about this Wednesday coming. Of course, we will never have existed, the pages of our lives will be blotted out. No one will ever know what sacrifice we made for our homeland."

"Maybe it is better that way. What do you think, Reba?"

"Let us think of it this way. We are pawns; the important thing is we saved our country and our people from destruction by our enemies."

CHAPTER TWENTY-EIGHT

Edwards stepped out of the shower. Memories flashed like snapshots. The hospital, Quentin Morgan. The twenty-six-year-old Green Beret medic from Knoxville, Tennessee. His second month and second tour in the country, shot in the head by a woman. He thought was a civilian after he helped deliver her daughter's child. The missions, the battles, the loss of friends, a closeness that could never be repeated in civilian life. The old Thai woman. Holding Captain Lovett in his arms, watching his life slip away. Christmas Eve. Ethan sang "Silent Night" until His Captain took his last breath.

He folded the towel in half and placed it on the floor and then slipped on a pair of underwear and jeans. He combed his hair. He ran hot water while shaking the can of shaving cream. He put the razor under the flow to warm the blade. Absentminded rituals. He lathered his face. A memory returned as clear as if he were there again, sitting by Quentin's bunk reading passages from the second book of Moses.

Edwards folded the face towel in half and placed it on the floor on top of the bath towel. He opened the door. Shevchenko was standing at the coffee bar pouring two fresh cups of coffee.

"Good morning."

"Good morning, Ethan Edwards. I have coffee with a delightful pastry called a maple bar."

"Is everyone up?"

"Ah, my friends are quite content this morning. Sergei, Olivia, and Boris went to that bar on Highway 17. Boris and Olivia enjoyed a little too much vodka and once back here, they found an even better way to relieve the tensions of the day. Sergei discovered the love of his life and they are together in his room. Olivia chased Boris out early this morning. I heard him enter his room. Food Courts, clothes shopping, and now true love. Sergei has decided he loves America and wishes to stay. Kasparov spoke to Elsa last night and Lila to her friend in Vienna. Both are now sad and missing their mates."

"Thanks for the coffee…I need to call Anna Lee."

"I will leave and make a call of my own. By the way, our Mister Underwood called in sick today."

"Did he call?"

"I did not ask. My mistake. I will call back before I call Ladas. Make your call, Ethan."

"How much more has to be done before the van is ready?"

"I'm adding nails, ball bearings, and detergent. There is a bit more wiring to be done. It will be controlled by the radio. When you park in the terminal, leave the key on and turn the radio on. The station is pre-set. You will have sixty seconds to clear the area before the device goes off, Joseph."

"That should be enough time. I counted the steps from the landing to the escalator and stairs. It took twelve seconds to be on the stairwell and five more to reach the level below. We should all be on the lower level or close enough to it to make our escape."

"Did you calculate travelers being on the stairs and escalators, Joseph?"

"No, Abram I did not. Does it matter?"

"No. Thursday we strike. The night before the attacks, we will fill the barrels with gasoline. We will have to leave the garage open because of the fumes."

"That could be dangerous, John."

"Why, Reba?"

"An open garage is an invitation to thieves."

"She makes a point, Palmer."

"I'm open to suggestions."

"We take out the panels on top of the door and place a fan facing the opening."

"Okay."

"I suggest a dry run instead of going into the terminal. We cross the bridge and leave by the ramp."

"No dry runs. We go on Thursday."

"What if they have increased surveillance?"

"Why would they? They do not know the target."

"I have been looking for restaurants, John." Reba said changing the subject. Abram will you excuse us? I found one in Fairlawn that sounded most interesting. It is called Chan's Waikiki; they serve Chinese and Polynesian food. It is not far from the mall. Our last supper, so to speak."

"Chinese and Polynesian. Make a reservation. What about the men?"

"They will make do. I called for two at six o'clock Wednesday evening. We will eat, come back to the house, and . . . make love for the last time."

"A woman called saying Underwood was sick. She left a message. Maury told me he was sure he recognized the voice. It was the same woman who left the note. He is sure of it. Underwood's home is located in Ridgewood. I wrote down the address."

"We have to verify if it is Palmer. We can't just drive over there, guns blazing. We have to think of the neighborhood Peter. It is probably well established. I'll call Timmons. Order us food. Tell the others to order breakfast sent to their rooms. Give them no more than an hour, Peter." Edwards picked up the phone and dialed the operator. Seconds passed before Mona answered. "It's me, Mona; is he in?"

"Of course, Ethan; hold on."

"Thanks, Mona."

"Have you news, Ethan?"

"We think the son of a bitch may be in Ridgewood. I have an address, Ron. The owner of the home is a guy named Underwood."

"Isn't that the manager of the apartment where Palmer stayed in Fort Lee?"

"The same. Today someone called in sick for him: a woman's voice, according to our source, definitely accented. We need to get into that neighborhood and we need to do it quietly. We need to get close to that house. Can you do it?"

"You think this fellow Underwood is part of the plot?"

"No Ron--- I don't . I would wager he is probably dead."

"How will I reach you?"

"We will be right here, Ron."

"Give me time. I am contacting Ronan Ambrose, FBI Newark. I will contact locals as a courtesy. We must get them in the loop. We do not have a choice. I will keep involvement to a minimum. I'll call as soon as we have a plan in place."

"What about you? Any news from your end?"

"Christopher is adjusting. I feel sorry for the young man."

"Funny how heartache--- never mind. Ron, I don't trust them. We don't need a couple of suits going against professionals. They'll be slaughtered and we will lose Palmer."

Stay put, wait for my call." Timmons hung up. "Mona, get me FBI Newark, Ronan Ambrose. Only talk to him, then come in. I want your input."

"What about Angela and Sidney?"

"Yes, of course; thanks, Mona. They think they found Palmer, possibly in Ridgewood, New Jersey. He made a mistake. I'll bet it has something to do with Graham."

"I have to agree with Ethan, concerning the locals."

Ernesto Gomez climbed into his security cart. He turned the small fan on to full. He shrugged, wiping his forehead. The fan only circulated the hot July air. He began to patrol the lot. Near the entrance to the restaurant-bar, he noticed the car with a thin layer of soot covering the hood and front window. He spied the flat tire. Ernesto took a sip from his drink, pulled his notepad out, and wrote down the license plate number. He would notify his supervisor when he stopped for a piss break.

"Ethan."

"Talk to me, Ron."

"Stay put. Feds need time to set up. It's a complicated situation, a lot of moving parts, Ethan. They want to get it right the first time."

"Who's running the show, Ron?"

"Ronan Ambrose. He is good at what he does, Ethan. He says he needs the time, he needs it. The clock starts at 10:00 a.m. today. If it is Palmer and the Brood, we can hit them tonight and end it."

"Every minute we wait is a minute wasted, Ron."

"I get the point, Ethan. We got to do what we got to do, so does Ronan."

"Hello, I need to speak to Mrs. Rita Alaura. Is she home?"

"Who's this?"

"Are you Rita? It is important I speak with her."

"Yeah, I'm Rita. What is it you're selling? I don't need nothing."

"My name is Ronan, Ambrose Rita. I am the special agent in charge with the FBI in the Newark office."

"For God's sake, my husband is dead. He ran a couple numbers for some people. He was not a wise guy, a made guy. You FBI guys still go to break his balls. You can't let him lay in his grave?"

"Rita. May I call you Rita? I'm not interested in your husband's criminal history. Listen to me and listen carefully, we need your help. Do you understand?"

"Call me Rita. Help with what? I'm an old lady."

"Rita, calm down and stop shouting. Listen to me, please. Take a deep breath and relax. I need to talk to you about your new neighbors across the street."

"Quiet, Chloe. Yeah, a woman, young. four or five men. She says she's his niece."

"I want to send an agent to your home. He will be dressed like a PSE&G employee. His reason for coming is you complained about the smell of gas in your kitchen. He will explain everything to you when he arrives. Can we please come to your home?"

"Yeah, okay, you come. When is he coming? I'm not dressed."

"He is at the Suburban diner on Route 17. How much time do you need?"

"I will need a half hour or so. What has mister Underwood done?"

"Nothing. My man will arrive in forty minutes, okay?"

"Yeah, it's okay."

"He will explain everything…Don't talk to your neighbors. Wait for him."

"Okay, okay. I'll get ready."

HILTON HOTEL

"Ronald, what have you for me?"

"I've talked to Ambrose. He worked out a surveillance plan---"

"No Ron. No FBI all we want is for them to identify the occupants. We'll take it from there---I mean it Ron."

"Okay Ethan, it's you're call."

"What's the plan? I'm putting you on speaker, Ron. Everyone is here."

Timmons spoke for fifteen minutes, laying out every contingency that could arise. When he was finished, he asked, "What do you think . . . any suggestions?"

"We need a utility truck. Bring it to the hotel and leave it. Bring a change of clothes for a woman of five foot eight. Write down sizes. I will need a change of clothes for a man as well." Ethan relayed Boris's sizes. "Relay that information to Ambrose after his agent verifies if it is indeed Palmer."

"Why them, Ethan?"

"They will react to any situation with deadly force without waiting for permission."

"I've understand. What else?"

"Reba is Israeli Mossad: dangerous and methodical. You had better have someone at the PSE&G substation in case she becomes suspicious and checks on the gas leak story."

"Good thinking, Ethan. Anything else?"

"How much time do we have?"

"I'll get back to you." Timmons hung up.

"Sergei of Latvia, I understand you met a young lady last night?"

"Sergei Folic of Latvia. I love America. Now I have two names, yes?"

"What do we do in the meantime?"

"We wait for Dmitry to come down and for Timmons to call, verifying it is the Brood."

"I would like hot tea from a glass."

"Order tea, Leonaa."

Reba stood next to Daniel and watched the PSE&G panel truck pull to the curb. A man with a clipboard, a shoulder bag, and a hand-held telephone got out, locked the door of the truck, and walked up to the house, studying his clipboard.

"Get Palmer in here."

He rang the doorbell. The door opened and there was Rita, her dog by her side, growling. She opened the storm door and he disappeared inside.

"What's going on, Reba?"

"A man in a uniform of the utility company just went into her home. That is his truck."

"Just in case, get her number from directory assistance and call her. You know, like a concerned neighbor would do."

"I will, Palmer. Daniel, keep watching the house. I think Joseph should watch the side yard."

"I will tell him. I'll be in the garage." The hint of sarcasm in his voice did not go unnoticed, nor was it appreciated. Reba dialed directory assistance. Later, when he looks for comfort, I will remind him. Take away the cookie and the child will pout, she told herself.

"I have the number. I marked it under her name in the telephone book."

Reba called the number. Rita answered.

"Hello, it's me Reba, Perry's niece. I noticed the utility company truck. Is everything okay, Rita?"

"I have a gas leak. This young man seems to think it is something to do with the valve on the stove. He says it's no trouble. He is going to have a maintenance truck come out. He's calling his boss now. I got to open the window in the kitchen. You want to talk to him?"

"Oh no, that isn't necessary. I was just concerned."

"He isn't too worried about it. He's a nice young man. Okay, thanks for the call, we're fine."

"Did I do okay, Mister Mahoney?"

"You did great. Please call me Derek."

"Ah, you call me Rita. You want a drink of something?"

"Nothing, thanks. You picked out three people from the pictures I showed you."

"I'm sure of those three. I see a couple more, but only far away. I don't think I can recognize them. I'm sorry."

"Do not be. Tell me, Rita, when was the last time you saw Mister Underwood?"

"I saw him go out with that Reba woman twice a couple days ago. I haven't seen him since. You think they hurt him?"

"We don't know. What kind of car does Mister Underwood own?"

"A Lincoln. I think a couple of days ago, I saw a woman leave with his car. I did not see her bring it back. I could have missed it. I don't stare out the window all day, Derek."

"I understand, Rita. Any other cars over there you might have seen?"

"A foreign car. I don't know the make. A big white van. I thought it was Mister Underwood. He does a lot of his own work over there, but then I didn't see him again. Chloe, stop sniffing Derek's trousers. He's okay, Chloe . . . go lay down."

"I don't mind, really. We have a dog at home. She's a mutt, but a great dog. I'm going to call for the truck now."

"Yeah, it's okay . . . You married, young man? I don't see no ring"

"Yes, I am, Rita. It will be eight years this September. We have a daughter. She is four. Her name is Alexandra Nicole after her two grandmothers."

"You take care of what's yours, young man. Family, it is the most important thing. You should wear a ring so people don't think you are ashamed of your marriage. My husband always wore a pinky ring. . . fifty years, he never took it off. He was a good man, my husband . . . a good provider. He made mistakes, but he was a good man. You wear a ring and don't look like you are ashamed."

"He's leaving. I guess it wasn't that serious."

"Is he looking over here?"

"No, he's writing something on his clipboard." Daniel watched the man get into his truck and drive off. "He's gone."

Reba stood in the door frame separating the den from the kitchen, her hands on her hips. She frowned, unable to shake the feeling of insecurity. Small worry lines formed at the edges of her eyes. She had to be sure it was really a gas leak and nothing more.

Felicia Newton answered on the second ring.

"Good morning, thank you for calling PSE&G. How may I direct your call?"

"Hello. I'm calling about my neighbor. She has a gas leak. I guess I want to know if the problem is serious."

"What is your name and address, madam?"

"Underwood. I live at 401 Mountainside Drive in Ridgewood. My neighbor lives directly across the street." Reba gave Rita's name and the address to the operator.

"Let me switch you to our service department. Please be patient and hold; it might take a minute. Calls are picked up in the order of the call."

"I understand. Thank you, operator."

"Thank you." Newton switched on the recorded music, got up, and walked into the hall. "The call you thought might come, Mister Winters. She is asking about a neighbor's gas leak."

"Thank you. Direct the call to Mister Thompson's office. Count to thirty, then put it through." Agent Cole Winters dashed down the hall and disappeared into the vacated office. He plugged in the recorder to the phone and waited. When it rang, he switched on the recorder. "Cole Winters, how may I help you?"

"Mister Winters, my name is Reba Underwood. I am calling about a gas leak at our neighbor's home. One of your people was here, but he has left."

"What is your name and your address?"

"Reba Underwood, I live at 401 Mountainside Drive in Ridgewood. My neighbor is Rita Alaura and she lives across the street. She is an older woman. I am worried about her."

"Hold on, ma'am, let me look up the work order. You say our man already left, so he should have called in. Hold on." Winters began typing out a message to his supervisor.

Call received, caller a woman. Middle east accent who calls herself Reba Underwood checking validity of gas leak.

"Ah, here it is. I found it. It is a gas leak that seems to be behind the stove. It needs the valve replaced. I'm sure our people shut off the gas. We are dispatching a maintenance crew as we speak to your neighbor's home. I'm sure it is no danger to neighbors. We'll make sure the problem is handled when the crew arrives."

"Thank you, Mister Winters, it is certainly a relief."

"Happy to be of service. I wish all our customers looked out for a neighbor like you do. The truck should be arriving soon. The crew has already been notified. Did you notice windows opened, by the way?"

"Yes. They are."

"Good, it's just a precaution. Thank you again for calling PSE&G."

"Feel better now?"

"Yes, I do, Palmar . . . much better." She hung up.

"So, we are back to Palmer, are we?"

"You should take your own advice about loose ends, Palmer."

Palmer stepped toward her, his fist clenched.

"Are you going to hit me, Palmer? I've been beaten by the best; ask Abram, the quiet one who stays in his room and prays. He beat me until I thought he would finish me. The instinct to cause great harm has a name, Palmer. It is called Abram." Get a hold of yourself; let it pass. He will cave. Hold the cookie from him.

"Reba, a utility truck."

Palmer stepped toward the window. Daniel stepped aside so they could look across the street. Abram stood in the hall watching Palmer.

"It is all right, Abram, go back to your prayers. Daniel, how many in the crew?"

"I see a man and a woman carrying tool sacks. I wish I had a pair of binoculars so I could see their faces and name tags."

"No need, Daniel. I called the utility company." Reba side-stepped, avoiding Palmer's hand on her shoulder.

"Reba don't be . . ."

HILTON HOTEL - HASBROUCK HEIGHTS

"Boris and Leona are in. The FBI is not very happy. I think I made my point. I told Ambrose to be patient, it was nothing personal."

"Good Ron, what else?"

"Rita positively picked Palmer, Reba Klein, and Daniel Berg. Couldn't ID the other two, but she said there were two. We're sure they are all there. Rita also said the white van is there and she saw lights in the garage late at night. She hasn't seen Underwood in days."

"We've given Palmer and his people a code name: the Brood."

"I like it. Ambrose called the local PD. He spoke to the chief and gave him a description of the car in case they dumped it. He told the chief it might be involved in a drug situation."

"You don't see a problem inviting the Paramus PD in?"

"You made me skeptical at first, Ethan. They could help us locate the car. We were specific, that is why we didn't notify Ridgewood. Ambrose was very implicit in telling Paramus to immediately notify him if the car is found. Ambrose wanted his people to inspect the car. He mentioned possible booby traps."

"Did it work?"

"I'd say so," Ambrose said. "The chief was cooperative. Also expect a call from your people as soon as they get set up in the house."

"Thanks, Ron, we'll take it from here."

"Elsa Lebedev is coming up to Paramus; we couldn't stop her."

"I'll let Kasparov know. Maybe she could be a help." Edwards put the receiver close to his chest. "Peter, tell Dmitry he is getting company."

"Dimitry will be happy. Now he won't worry."

"I'm back, Ron."

"Got any ideas how you will approach?"

"I'll be in touch." He hung up. "Elsa coming here could be a distraction, Peter."

"Do not worry about Dmitry, my friend. He is a man who will not be distracted. Shall we begin?"

"Yeah, we need to."

Leona sidestepped the window in the upstairs bedroom. She pulled the bolt back on the Dragunov 79 sniper rifle and pushed it forward, sliding a 7.62 high velocity round into the chamber. She checked the safety and set the weapon next to the window. She backed out of the room, closing the hall door behind her. Chloe stood on the landing to the staircase, her tail wagging. "Come here, little dog. You do not want to? It is okay, I will come to you." She picked the dog up, holding her close to her chest. "I like dogs, you know that?"

Boris was just completing the assembly of his weapon. She noticed the fearful look on the face of the old woman.

"Boris, must you do that here?"

"I am almost finished."

"Finish it in the kitchen and hurry; we must leave soon." Olivia sat down. Chloe made quick work of folding herself on Leona's lap. "I think I have made a friend. I am sorry, Rita. I know you are frightened. Trust us. You are in no danger. We will leave soon and return in a little while. Please leave your back door open so we can return unnoticed."

"Must you go?"

"Yes, or we will make those people across the street suspicious. It will be only a short time." Leona took the old woman's hand in hers. "I must use the phone. Do not be afraid. I will not let any harm come to you."

"Mister Underwood is dead. They killed him, didn't they?"

"We do not know that, Rita. I will not be long. One question: Your neighbors behind you are home this time of day?"

"They all work. The only one I know is home is the lady that lives up the street. Maybe I could go to stay with her?"

"We will see. For now, stay calm." Leona got up and walked into the kitchen, Chloe cradled in the crook of her arm. "Are you finished, Comrade?"

"Yes. I have two more clips for your Makarov and three magazines for the rifle."

"Good, thank you. Please call the hotel and ask for Edward's room. Give me the phone when you are connected. Sit with Rita; she is terrified." A moment of silence passed before the connection was made. He handed her the phone and walked back to the dining room.

"Ethan Edwards, it is Leona. We are ready now. We need to remove the truck."

"I know. I will ring once when Lila and Ivanov are in position to take the vehicle. When you leave, drive south, straight to the second cross street. Turn right at the corner, drive up the street, make another right turn at the first cross street. They will be waiting in front of the home behind the one you are leaving. Go back to the house. Can you do it without being seen?"

"Yes. I am sure of it. When do you think you will move against the house?"

"We are addressing that problem as we speak."

Reba watched the two workmen get into the utility van and drive off. She counted to ten and went out into the front yard, standing behind a tall bush. She watched the truck go straight down Mountainside Drive and through the intersection. It was then that she stepped further out, her hands in a fist against her hips. The truck made a right turn.

A minute later, she pulled the Mercedes out of the garage and followed the path of the truck. She turned right at the second intersection, sped up, and stopped at the next corner. She moved into the intersection, looking to her right than left. There was no truck and no sign of the utility people. She drove to the next block and stopped, peering up the street. She went to the third street, then the fourth street slowly. Satisfied the utility truck was gone, she drove back to the house.

The two Russians waited, hidden by the tall shrubs. Boris checked his watch: two minutes since the Silver Mercedes passed the cross street. He smiled. "She will go back to the house now. We are safe to move, Leona."

"How did you know she would follow the truck?"

"I would have done the same thing. Let's get into the old woman's house."

"If you were not married, Boris, I could like you."

"If I was not married, I would let you, Comrade." They made their way over two yards and went inside. "We are back, Rita," Boris called out. Chloe barked.

PARAMUS

"Are you buying the FBI story, Leonard, my boy, about drug people living in your town?"

"I guess so. That Mahoney fella was pretty direct, from what you told me. He did mention a joint effort when they take down the bad guys. We know all about getting warrants from some unnamed judge, so it does make sense."

"I guess you are right. Unless we find the car they're looking for. That might change things. You got to admit busting a drug ring in your town has consequences, if you know what I mean Lenny."

"I think I do, Zack. Both our towns have mayoral races in November. Something to think about. Keep in touch. No, wait . . . I have an idea. Why don't you pick me up and we take a little ride?. Just a look-see. You know what I mean?"

"I like it. It can't hurt, Lenny, you know them damned Feds? We might hit the jackpot. I'm on my way, buddy."

"I am going out for a while. Palmer."

"I'm almost finished here. Another half hour on the vests and . . . I'll go with you."

"It isn't safe for you to be out. I am even thinking of canceling our reservation at Chan's. It is just too dangerous, and we are so close now." Control. He mustn't make the decision. Only think he is.

"Is this shit about what happened this morning, Reba?"

"No, Palmer, it is not about you--- never mind. I do not want to have that conversation again. I am going to the Riverside Mall in Hackensack. I will not stay long. I will bring food back from Chan's. I will reheat it and we will eat. I will get extra if they are hungry. They will not be. They are performing the ritual of shiva. It will not be completed, but it will help them face what is to come. I am going. Do you want the food or not?"

"Why aren't you in shiva?"

"I've brought enough shame to my name. My mother is still held in high esteem. I will not insult my God by praying."

"I'm sorry about this morning, Reba. I'm very sorry. I acted like a child. It won't happen again. You were right to be cautious."

"It isn't important now. I will be back before dark." Hold the cookie away from the child. She backed out of the garage and drove off.

"Hello, Wayne."

He started to close the rear doors of the cargo van and froze, hearing the high-pitched squeal of his mother's voice. Her skin seemed to be peeling away from her frame. He could see her bloodless black veins under the leafy skin. He almost gagged.

"I thought you were gone to the west coast, you and Dad. What are you doing here, mom? I don't want to see you or hear that rattle in your voice."

"I was worried about you, Wayne. That Jew woman, I don't like her."

"Get out of here now. Where's your husband?"

"I told you, he's found a new friend in Seattle, Wayne. I don't like it there; it rains all the time. I get very cold."

"You're cold because you're dead, Mommy. You were dead even when you were alive."

THE HILTON - HASBROUCK HEIGHTS

Dmitry and Elsa entered Edward's room, their faces flushed, clinging to each other. The phone rang.

"Hello."

"Yes, Leona. Silver Mercedes a rental . . . She is alone. I understand . . . We can't move against them unless they are all there together. Have you seen any of the men? Palmer only, okay . . . Call when she returns . . . I'm holding . . . You've seen what? Are you sure? Stay on the line." Ethan's face darkened.

"The woman is out of the house; she's driving a silver Mercedes rental. She is alone. Leona has seen Palmer standing in the driveway. We may have a bigger problem. Leona says an unmarked police car passed the house slowly. Two men in civilian clothes inside . . .detectives probably."

"They may live in the area, Ethan."

"I don't believe in coincidence, Peter. Didn't an FBI agent visit the Paramus PD today?"

"Yes, they did send an agent. You need to call Timmons. What about the woman?"

"She could be anywhere. She might only be going out for gas, for all we know. Call us the moment she returns. Watch for that police car; let us know if it returns."

"It just went in the opposite direction. Ethan . . . She is out for another reason. A woman who looks like that does not pump her own gas."

Ethan hung up. "I better call Timmons."

"She is a woman like any other woman in the world. They go out alone for a reason Ethan. It maybe to forget about the hard day they have had? It may be because of an argument with a loved one perhaps? You men have never understood these urges."

"I agree with Lila," Elsa added. "I have done the same thing in the past. Shopping is where they go. I have heard so much about America. Shopping and food markets with shelves stacked up to the ceilings. I want to go shopping myself."

"What if Lila and Elsa use the car?"

"I do not think that would be wise, Dmitry. Any wrong move . . . a look, perhaps an awkward glance. I'm sure she can recognize familiar faces always seeming to be where she is. She will recognize trouble if she is being watched. We want her to feel safe. It is better for us to trap them on Mountainside Drive then having to fight her or all of them in a crowded mall."

"What if they have decided to change the plan and attack a mall?"

"It is up to us to stop them, Dmitry Kasparov." Shevchenko looked at Ethan, who simply nodded agreement. The phone rang.

"It's Leona. she has returned. I guess she changed her mind."

" The car radio crackled to life. Supervisor 13. K "

"Is Sergeant Gibson with you, boss?"

"He's still with me; what have you got?"

"We have a positive ID off the engine block of that Lincoln. Paramus just notified us. It is registered to a Perry Underwood, 401 Mountainside Drive, Ridgewood. We called the house, but got no answer."

"I'm not surprised; We just rolled by the house and we haven't seen any movement. Thanks for the update, Sergeant. We're going to take another drive by. Supervisor 13 . . . out."

"We have to make sure who's there, how many, when we hit it, Len . . . Smell that air."

"What air, Zack?"

"You get it: the smell of awards and promotions, Len, like that old movie with Tony Curtis and Burt Lancaster . . . Sweet Smell of Success. I'm definitely feeling that smell, Len. Let's get patrol to make a stop at the house."

Corporal Clay Harbaugh opened the passenger door in front of 401 Mountainside Drive. He took a few seconds to look at the property and the house. Lights were on in the front rooms and one room on the second floor. The lawn and front door lights were not on.

"Sure as hell doesn't look like there's anything out of place, Glen. I'm going up to the front door. Radio the boss; tell him we are at the house."

"You sure you don't want me on your back, Clay? Remember what the sergeant said about the occupants?"

"You stay with the car, Glen. If there is trouble, get out of here quick as shit through a goose."

"The local police are across the street, one officer going up to the front door. The door is opening. . . what do I do? You want me to do nothing? . . . Yes, I understand. No, I will not give away our position. Boris is downstairs. We have a high and low clear path of fire if necessary. Wait--- the officer is going into the house. The door is closed. There is another shadow on the window. It is a man's shadow; I am sure of it. Wait--- the upstairs light has gone out. You are leaving now? Good. Wait --- the officer is leaving. The door is closing; it is Palmer with the woman."

"Stay on the line. Tell me what they are doing."

"The garage light just went on . . . The cops have left. Palmer and the woman are in a Mercedes. They just pulled onto the street in the direction of Paramus."

"Can you see what they took with them?"

"No. The white van is leaving, going in the opposite direction. I can see two men in the front seats. The other one must be behind the driver. You want us to go over to the house?"

"They're running dammit. Those locals spooked them." Ethan picked up the phone and called Langley. "Locals; the bastards went to the house. The Brood is on the run, all of them. Get the locals off of us, Ron. We're going in. Get them to stand down."

"I'm on it, Ethan."

"We had them, Ronald. I told you no locals---We had them.."

WEDNESDAY, JULY 19

Leina stood in the front yard of Rita's home, wearing a long coat.

"It is a new day, Boris." She started across the street with Boris in tow.

"You both go in through the garage. Ethan and I will clear the upstairs; Dmitry will go with you. Boris, go back across the street to Rita's house. If anybody comes out besides us, shoot them to death. How is Rita doing?"

"She is a strong woman. She is better now than she was when the Brood was here. One of us better stay outside in case neighbors look to see what is going on. Sergei you stay."

"I stay here, no trouble . . . I love this country, and look at these homes." His voice drifted off.

"Good. Leona, starting with the garage, do a search of the first floor, every inch of it. We'll do the same upstairs. Maybe they left something behind that will help us find them." Edwards drew two 9 mm pistols from his shoulder holsters.

"Be careful. Palmer may have set traps," Edwards added. "We called the FBI; agent Mahoney is on his way, don't shoot him, Boris." Nervous laughter, then a few seconds of silence.

"You think they may have left someone behind, Ethan?"

"No, I don't." Edwards turned to Shevchenko. "Shall we?"

"Lead the way, Ethan; you have the two guns."

HILTON HOTEL - SECAUCUS: JULY 20

Abram steered off the ramp on Route 3, turned left onto the access road, and then right onto the driveway. He spied the Mercedes parked in a spot reserved for check-in patrons. He pulled to a stop and opened the driver side window.

"Where shall I park, Palmer?"

"Pull it into the garage. Find a space on the first level and wait. I'm going to check you three in."

"Are you going to stay here?"

"No, Abram. I'll explain after I find rooms. Go ahead and park." Palmer went up the stairs and into the lobby. He recognized the desk man and smiled inwardly. The shortened night here with Maxine crossed his mind: the sex and the murder delighting him at first. He put the thoughts aside. Now was not the time to dwell on pleasant memories.

"Welcome to the Hilton, sir. Are you checking in?"

"Four young men will be staying here overnight. I hope to have company for them this evening. I expect the women to be available through the night. They will need a suite and privacy ---You understand my request; can you help me?"

"In that case, I'm glad you chose a suite." The desk manager produced a picture. "We're inundated with conference people staying here, something to do with the hospital next door."

"How convenient. If someone should get sick. "" He took a quick look. "The suite is perfect for our needs. One of the young men is getting married this Saturday." Palmer placed three one-hundred-dollar bills on the counter.

"I understand completely." The desk man took the bills and folded them into his jacket pocket. "I will gladly be of help," the desk man glanced at the admissions card, "Mister Preston."

"You understand the girls must be clean; no surprises. They must be attractive; color is not a problem; young, good bodies and of course, they must be clear of disease. I do not want my nephew to be dripping anything on his bride other than what is expected. You will promise me this?

"Of course Mister Preston."

"We will settle with you financially in the morning, Is that satisfactory?"

Twenty minutes later, four young men entered the lobby, each carrying two small bags. They nodded to the desk man as they passed him.

401 MOUNTAINSIDE DRIVE

"So, what do we know, Peter --- anyone?"

"They left in a hurry: clothes, suitcases, cosmetics, all left behind, even essentials like aspirin and menstrual pads. A woman wouldn't leave them unless she was really panicked or forced to," Leona said.

"They made sure they took all the explosives. I found one bar of C-4 at the bottom of a steel container. A lot of wiring is cut into twelve and sixteen-inch pieces, only a few longer, maybe ten feet. Eight empty gas cans, all used. I smelled gas in all of them. And other things: boxes of ball bearings, boxes of ten-inch concrete nails and two Togo switches. The windows were missing in the garage door. I am sure to release the smell of gas and pressure."

"What do you think, Dmitry?"

"I believe he has two fifty-gallon drums in that van, filled with gasoline, along with explosives and other materials. I think it is all wired to a trigger . . . more than likely the radio."

"You mean like a mercury switch?"

"Yes, Ethan. That is what I think."

"Are you getting all this, Agent Mahoney?"

"Yeah, I am. We all agree the van is the weapon?"

"Yes."

"I need to make a call."

"Before you do that, Agent Mahoney, listen to Dmitry. Tell the agent what else you found in the garage."

"I found cloth material cut in eight-inch perfect squares. When I placed them together. the pieces formed a pocket."

"He made at least one vest?"

"That is what Dmitry and I believe. What none of us found were documents or any cash."

"Make your call, Agent Mahoney. We'll put our heads together and try to figure out where they might go."

"I can't believe I let you make love to me in the front seat of this car. In a parking garage, no less. What were you thinking?"

"I was agitated; I needed a release. I needed you like we were before this morning. You can't tell me you didn't enjoy it."

"That is the problem. I enjoyed it too much. Where are we going, John, and why are we not staying with the others?"

"We are going to the La Quinta Inn in Clifton. I don't want to take a chance on all of us being together. We'll hide there until tomorrow morning. I sincerely doubt they will find us in time to stop us, but why chance it. You want me to get off the highway. A lot of side streets in East Rutherford and dark enough for privacy Reba?"

"No. I want you to find a drugstore. I have no cosmetics and only one more pair of underwear. I need clothes and so do you: at least one fresh change."

"The hotel may have both."

"I am not wearing a sweatshirt that says, I got laid at La Quinta Inn in Clifford, New Jersey.

"It's Clifton not Clifford."

"Whatever you call it. I am going to the mall in the morning."

"It is too dangerous, Reba."

"The mall is big; I know my way around. I know the exits. It will be safe in a crowded place, and as you say, they will never imagine me going to a mall. I am going. I refuse to wear the same clothes and underwear. You should have let me pack for both of us."

"We couldn't be sure if time permitted that luxury."

"I am not going to spend my last day on earth without at least clean under-wear. I need you relaxed. Are you relaxed, John?"

"Yes, completely relaxed."

"What did Mister Timmons have to say, Ethan?"

"A red alert has been issued on the car and the van, Peter: state and county north to West Chester and South to as far as Philadelphia. All three governors have been notified."

"We were so close."

"There's more, Peter. It seems three individuals traveling from Russia with false IDs and travel papers are being held in Paris by immigration. A fellow named Gusev alerted the Frogs."

"He heads our state police agency."

"Timmons is sure they were coming here for you. There is something else. Our people have Mister and Mrs. Kozlov in residence in our embassy."

"That is good news."

"May I make a suggestion, Ethan Edwards?"

"Of course, Boris, please do."

"If we are to put our heads together, we should go back to the hotel and involve everyone. We are finished here. We know what we know."

"An excellent point, Boris."

"Boris and I will stop at a diner. I have never seen such places. We will bring tea, coffee and pastries. No one will sleep, but we must eat."

" A wonderful idea Leona." Boris patted her head. "If I were not married, I could like you." Everyone laughed except Shevchenko, who only smiled.

"I think we are going now. The sun will be up on this new day in a few hours." Two cars left the house on Mountainside Drive.

"I am going to close my eyes, Ethan Edwards. I will not sleep, but I must rest and think about our next move. What time is it?"

"Two thirty-five, to be exact."

"If he is panicked, he could strike today."

"I am not so sure. Today he hides and plans. He has to. Every law enforce-ment agency is on high alert. Liberty Island will be shut down. Tomorrow,

Peter, or Friday at the latest. We need to locate the van. Take that tool out of his hands. Isolate him and the woman. It's our only chance."

"Either way, I am afraid many will die. He Has too many alternatives to prevent it."

CHAPTER TWENTY-NINE

HILTON INN - HASBROUCK HEIGHTS

"Sergei, we need your input. Come sit down with us."

"I can hear very well, Ethan Edwards."

"All right. This is what we know. They are on the run or they have a contingency plan like Fort Lee. I want to think they are desperate, but something tells me Palmer is too smart not to be ready for any emergency. So, where am I going wrong?"

"You are not wrong, Ethan Edwards, but only partially right," Leona answered. "The mistake was not knowing where to go. We must look at the speed with which they left the house. They are without personal items, most likely only the clothes on their backs."

"What is your point, Leona"

"My point is, Peter Shevchenko, as I said before, clothing and body essentials might not mean anything to a man, but to a woman it is different. Where they go will be near a locations she can go to find clothing and personal items. They are somewhere in New Jersey where they feels safe, and she is within driving distance of stores."

"If he had another plan of action, he might go to Teaneck or Fort Lee. He would assume we would not look there," Boris added.

"A normal person might think that. Palmer is not ordinary. He will think like we do and eliminate that as an option. I believe he has something else in mind." Peter rubbed his chin. He will go to a location he knows. Maybe visited in the past. A location he convinced himself we would not suspect."

"A place obscure to the hunter, but close enough for his next action." Sergei spoke from his post at the door. "We must think like him to get into his psychotic mind: feed off his arrogance and then we will know where to look."

"That is excellent, Comrade--- A place Palmer thinks we will never look, but where?"

"It has to be a place in his recent past, Peter. He may change the date, but not the plan."

"Wherever it is, he will need easy access to main roadways. I do not believe he is still in this area. He must know it will be searched thoroughly. The van will be his downfall if found. He needs to find refuge where he can keep the van out of sight of prying eyes."

"Good point, Dmitry."

"Points do not make results, Ethan Edwards."

"Not always, but it is the conversation following the point made that matters, is it not?"

"What do we know? Palmer has a vehicle capable of doing great damage, which he must hide from view. He cannot chance a home invasion or a hotel with open parking. He needs a garage, Ethan. A hotel with a garage: airy and close enough for him to finish what he has started, but far enough away so he can—"

"Secaucus," Edwards blurted out.

"What is a Secaucus?"

"Secaucus isn't a thing, Lila. It is a town on Route 3. It is an access highway that goes directly to the Lincoln tunnel with connections to the Turnpike, Route 4, 17 and Route 46, all of which will put him on or near the George Washington Bridge."

"There must be many hotels close to the bridge; he could easily hide. How can you be sure, Ethan?"

"I was watching the news one night. A North Viet officer was shot to death on Broadway in New York City. I remembered the officer. He led the attack on one of our— Never mind that now, the point is Palmer was the man who killed him to protect himself and—"

"The woman murdered in Secaucus," Shevchenko interrupted.

"Timmons told me that Barnett was having an affair with Palmer."

"We need a phone book."

"Why waste time looking up numbers and making calls? I will call the desk clerk downstairs. He or she will know which hotels in Secaucus have covered garages."

"Good, Lila, very good."

"You were a very good teacher, Peter Shevchenko, as was your assistant Marina."

"Let us not forget the woman. She has needs, personal needs, and she will get them. Her vanity may play a role in finding the two of them and their little psychotic brood, yes?" Leona added. "She will shop for personal items and clothes. Do not ignore my thoughts. He will not go with her and chance being seen. If we are lucky, we can get to her . . . kill her. At least separate them."

The group fell silent while Lila dialed the operator.

"Hello, operator, I have a question. A friend of mine is staying at a hotel in Secaucus. I do not remember the name, but I do remember it was a popular hotel. She said it had a covered garage and that is why she stayed there . . . Yes, I will hold a moment." Lila crossed her fingers. "Yes, operator. Yes, I am, as a matter of fact. I live in Moscow . . . I remember now. Thank you so much for your help." Lila hung up; the smile broadened on her face. "The Hilton Hotel off of Route 3."

"Lila, go to your room and call the hotel. Talk to the desk clerk at the Hilton. We need to know if they are staying there. Get all the information you can without creating undue curiosity. Desk clerks are like fish in an open market: no matter the smell, they will be bought. If they went there, they should already be checked in. Call now and ask for the night manager. In the meantime, we need to plan how we will approach the situation."

"I think they will rest and relax. They will feel secure. I am sure of it, Ethan Edwards. They must be as tired as we are."

"I agree. Let's take care of our personal needs and meet back here."

"What about her personal needs?"

"Later this morning. Malls do not open until ten o'clock, Leona She will shop. She will rest with Palmer and finalize their plan."

"I agree with Lila."

"I had a good teacher as well, Peter Shevchenko."

"I see by the look on your face you have good news," Shevchenko said when the group met again in Ethan's suite.

"Good news, yes, Comrade Shevchenko. The desk manager was more helpful than I expected. Four are staying there in a suite on the sixth floor. An arrangement was made for women to join the Brood this evening. I told him me and a friend are also guests of the gentlemen. Palmer and the woman are not staying there. He did not know where they were. He offered that piece of information. I did not ask. He also told me that two young women were already chosen. I told him we would be arriving soon and would meet two of the young men in the bar. Could he arrange that for me? He was most gracious. I also told him guards would be with us to ensure there would not be any problems. He was most agreeable to that."

"We only have half of the puzzle without Palmer and the woman."

"I have more information which might be favorable. The desk man also told me the four are there for a bachelor party. The man who made the reservations told him to expect noise. I repeated we were invited guests for the entire night and were invited by the man who signed for the suite. He gave me the name James Preston without me asking. The desk man is too helpful. I would not trust him to remain quiet after we visit the hotel. I did good, yes?"

"You did fine, Lila," Edwards answered. "We need to get there. Find the van and disable it. Agent Mahoney, you want to make that call now?"

The AAA truck backed into the space beside the Mercury. The car doors opened, and three men jumped out. Kasparov, driving the blue sedan with Leona and Lila, followed the truck in and parked the Ford next to Agent Mahoney's Mercury. Boris and Sergei joined the rest of the group, carrying weapons for each of them.

"My names Rich Collins. What am I looking for? I was told explosives?"

"We believe this van is carrying explosives in large drums in the rear compartment," Agent Mahoney said. "Be very careful. One of them was just out here looking over the van. He paid particular attention to the latch on the hood and the seam between the rear doors and body. He might have booby trapped it."

"Thanks for the tip. You are?"

"My name is Mahoney. We met once before, Agent Collins. Time is important. It is a joint action with the KGB. You must never write this up on a 302 or any piece of paper for that matter. Tonight, as far as you are concerned, never happened.

"What the hell—"

"It means Kentucky Grain and Bran it's used in cereals," Shevchenko answered in his best North Carolina drawl. Do you understand the need for selective ignorance, Mister Collins? "Please, can you get started?"

"I get it, I get it now---Okay, get back all of you. Keep an eye out for civilians. Get behind the cars and get down. I'm going to start with the hood latch." Collins padded to the rear of his truck and returned with a medium-sized cloth bag. With fingers barely pressing against the grill, he reached under the face of the hood and followed the same motion until his fingers found the string. Slowly, he moved a single finger over the latch. He leaned forward so he could see the piece of string in his hand.

"It's not wired to explode if tampered with. The explosives are probably on a timer. I'm going to make a hole in the driver's side window and we are going to take this van out of here after I checked the back doors. I smell gas." The agent stood up. "I found a sliver of rubber in the seam under the door with no wires. It wasn't a trap. Seems whoever placed the objects just wanted to make sure no one tampered with the vehicle. It's on a timer; take my word for it." Collins took a small tool with suction cups out of his bag. He walked around to the driver's side.

He put the small object against the glass and pressed the suction cups. He reached down and pulled a pair of pliers from his bag. In seconds, the glass exploded into small fragments. He put the flashlight into his mouth, brushed away fragments of glass still in the window well, and leaned into the van.

"Oh yeah, we got a masterpiece here," he exclaimed. He reached in, feeling the inner door for a trip wire. Feeling nothing, he opened the driver's side door. He jumped in behind the wheel, took off the emergency brake, and put the gear lever in neutral. "Let's move this rig, gentlemen. Right now."

"I understand your concern for civilians and this lovely garage, Mister Collins," Shevchenko said. "You have to disarm this device in here. We do not know in which direction their room faces, but if they are vigilant and they see this van being pushed across the lot, we are going to have a possible hostage situation, possibly a bloodbath."

"I guess I'd better get started. The wiring is very good, but I think I know how it will all work. I'm betting it is all controlled by the radio dial or on-off switch. I also think it is a timed response mechanism. It is going to take time. I got to be sure. I won't get done before they close the bar. Somebody better keep the patrons inside."

Shevchenko and Edwards exchanged glances. Both looked at Kasparov and nodded.

"Mister Collins, the FBI chose a wise man for this important work. I applaud your analytical mind. I, for one, would not have thought the problem out so carefully and reached a most rational decision." Shevchenko turned to Edwards. "Shall we take a walk and discuss our next alternative? Ladies, would you be so kind as to change into more revealing clothes? Two of our targets are waiting for you and you are late as it is. Lila, would you bring the satchel please, the brown one?"

Edwards turned to Mahoney. "How fast can an assault team be here?"

"Hard to say; I'm on it. I'll call Newark from the truck."

"If I may," Shevchenko added, "we might want to notify the Israeli Embassy right away. I am sure they will be most interested."

The night manager walked out of his office apologizing to the two gentlemen.

"We are in no hurry," Shevchenko said. "We are not guests." Shevchenko turned toward the entrance to the bar. Leona was in the entrance, lighting a cigarette. She looked up, put two fingers to her cheek, and went back inside.

"How can I help you gentlemen?"

"You are the night manager, I presume?"

"Yes, I am. I came on duty at seven."

"I assume you know why we are here with the young ladies?"

"Yes."

"Do you know a gentleman by the name of James Preston?"

"Why, yes. In fact, he made the arrangements for, shall we say, special attention. North Carolina: Have I guessed right?"

"That is very good."

"So, how may I help you?"

"We are here with two ladies. I believe Mister Palmer required two ladies? We were told you have two. Plans change. Our ladies are in the bar now getting acquainted."

"I am all alone except for the operator. Plans change, as you say, so do costs, if you get my meaning," the clerk said in a conspiratorial tone barely above a whisper. "I apologize. Was it one of your ladies who called earlier?"

"Yes, it was. I hope we are not going to have a problem?"

"Not at all, I assure you. There is a gentleman standing in the hotel entrance. I believe he is trying to get your attention."

"Ah, the AAA man, I'll see to him while you two complete the arrangement." Mahoney, dressed in mechanics clothes and holding a work order, stood in the entrance.

"Is our car ready, young man?"

"There is a problem with your car. A flat tire."

"I believe you told our caller they were on the sixth floor, Suite 616?" Shevchenko asked. Diverting the desk man's attention

"Sorry for the hold up. I mean, who checks their spares, right? Edwards wrote 616 on the paperwork."

"No problem. I'll come back when we're finished." Mahoney spun around and walked outside.

The desk clerk turned and said in a low voice, "The suite faces the lot and the garage, but I don't think the view is the issue." He smiled, exposing cigarette-stained teeth and snickered. "Damned cars are like women. Can't live with them nor without them, am I right?"

"I couldn't have said it better myself." Shevchenko hid his concern about the view from Suite 616. "So, I can assume the problem with the ladies is solved."

"How much is your advance--you know?"

"Well, gentlemen, since you have been so obliging, we could manage a lesser charge for you. One thousand dollars for the girls---cash of course." Shevchenko looked at Edwards. "Sound about right. We will see that James has the correct amount when we see him."

"That sounds good to me. You've seen the ladies when they came in. I am assuming the other ladies are young and easy on the eyes? We do not mind paying the price for prime."

"Your friends and you will not be disappointed."

"Let's go check on the girls. I better not catch them doing side financing.

We're done here, right?"

"Yes, of course. Please tell the girls not to get too rambunctious."

"If there's any howling going on, it'll be those boys, and of course we will take special care of you above Mister Preston's bill when the ladies are through," Shevchenko answered. He spied Agent Mahoney out of the corner of his eye. "Triple A is back."

"We're ready outside when you are."

"Give us a minute, will you?" Edwards walked over, put a hand on Mahoney's shoulder, and whispered, "Wait until we go upstairs. Shut this floor down. No one leaves the bar. No one comes in. No calls."

"No problem, sir. You just need to sign off on the slip and new tire."

"Sure, let me do that now. The suite faces the garage and lot. Have you notified the CIA and the Israeli Embassy?"

"Both. I spoke to Timmons at CIA and the head of security at the Israeli Embassy.

"I'll call you on the field radio when we have breached the room." Edwards stepped away, waved to Shevchenko, and started to walk toward the bar.

"Now you won't bother our friend Mister Preston, sir. He is with his special friend and has directed us to see to the gentlemen upstairs. Can we trust you to keep this between us?"

"My lips are sealed."

Shevchenko pressed two one-hundred-dollar bills into the clerk's hand. He shook it and followed Edwards into the bar. The women were talking to two of the Israelis. Elsa was getting up with Kasparov, who paid the bill in cash. Arm in arm they walked out. Chekov sat at the bar, her arm draped over the shoulder of the young Israeli who was known as Moody. Leona stood very close to Joseph. Her foot rested on the lower railing of the stool, so that her knee touched his crotch. His hand was on her hip, which she maneuvered so that he would not feel the 9 mm weapon tucked into the small of her back.

"I see you have become quite an item," Shevchenko stated, his smile widening as he approached Lila and Moody.

"Moody and I have an understanding. Moody, this is a friend of mine. He arranged for us to be part of your stay here."

"So, you know--- I like it rough.

"Well, that is good to know. What about you, Lila, is this arrangement suitable to you?"

"I like strong men. Shall we go now?"

"There are supposed to be four of you; what about your friends?"

"The other ladies are on the sixth floor waiting for us," Moody said.

"I can't wait to get you naked Moody." Lila teased.

"Are you ready, Elsa?"

"Yes, Dmitry." She stood up, picked up her glass of wine, and sighed. When he stood up, she put her arm around his back. "When we reach the door, I am to keep walking until I reach the far end of the corridor and wait for you to come for me."

The door to the elevator opened and the two couples stepped out. Moody spied the couple from the bar coming in their direction; they were laughing and hugging each other. He dismissed them and led the women with their overseers down the corridor to Suite 616.

Lila kissed Moody on the cheek and started to unbutton her blouse as Moody knocked.

"Who is there?"

"Moody and Joseph with two beautiful women." Moody opened the door with his key and was pushed forward. Leona, her weapon drawn, rushed in behind him, pointing her weapon at the back of his neck. Lila drew her weapon and hit Daniel just behind his left ear, knocking him down to one knee.

"We want you all on the floor--- move, " Edwards said, stepping in behind Lila.

A woman screamed; she was young, maybe nineteen or twenty. Joseph grabbed her before Lila could react. He pressed the 9 mm Glock handgun against the side of her head. The other young prostitute naked on the sofa, pinned herself to Abram her legs straggling him.

"Let me see your hands, Abram," Leona commanded.

"Let her go, Joseph, you aren't going anywhere," Edwards said, in a flat voice as he gauged whether he could take a headshot without hitting the young prostitute.

Lila and Dmitry tied and gagged Daniel. When Moody began to move,

Leona quickly pointed her weapon at him, her Makarov steady in her hand.

"Do not be foolish. Stay very still. You have no way out. Where is the other one . . . Moesha. Where is he?"

The door to the bedroom opened.

"I surrender. Do not shoot." Moesha put his hands in the air and dropped to the floor.

"That leaves only you. Let me see your hands, Abram," Edwards said.

"I demand you notify our embassy. We are Israeli citizens." As he spoke, he reached into the space between the cushions and pulled out a weapon.

Leona, without hesitation, fired twice the bullets entered the young prostitute's body, went through, and struck Abram. When the young woman slumped over, Leona fired a single round into Abram's head, exploding bits of brain matter and blood on the window and drapes. She then turned her and turned her attention to Joseph. "Your life means nothing to me. I will kill you."

Joseph dropped the weapon and fell to his knees, putting his hands on top of his head.

The young woman screamed.

"No more shooting. Dmitry, find Elsa."

"I'm calling down to Mahoney to be sure he has the first floor locked down. We need an ambulance to cart the dead girl off. Shut her up. Will someone get her clothes on and put her in the bedroom?" Edwards shouted. "Leona go with her and keep her calm."

Shevchenko took Leona's gun.

"Sit down with the young woman. Calm her down before she awakens the entire floor. You did what you had to do. The death of the young woman was unavoidable."

Dmitry and Elsa came into the room. Elsa covered her mouth and gagged.

"A resident next door is quite upset. I explained I was head of hotel security. One of the ladies screamed that the occasion was a party for a guest who is getting married and things got out of hand; he will not be a problem," Kasparov said from the doorway.

"You are sure of this fact, Dmitry?"

"It seems the woman he is with is not his wife. I am sure he will not be a problem. I told them to stay in their room and make no attempt to leave. I have his driver's card."

"Here is where we are," Edwards said, hanging up the phone.

"Mahoney contacted the Israeli Embassy before we came upstairs. Until we hear from them, we do nothing. Mahoney is in charge downstairs. His people took over the security operation and phones to manage incoming calls to the hotel. No one leaves; Mahoney is on his way up."

"I do not trust the desk manager to be quiet concerning this matter. I do not believe him when he says he doesn't know where Palmer is," Shevchenko added.

"Allow Leona to speak with him," Lila said. "We will find out exactly what he knows or does not know. Ethan Edwards?"

"You're right, Lila." A knock on the door. "That is probably Mahoney, let him in."

"Holy shit," was Mahoney's reaction when spied the two bodies on the sofa and the three Israelis bound, gagged, and with their eyes covered with tape lying on the floor. " What the hell happened here, Edwards? At least cover them up."

"Relax, Mahoney. He went for his gun. It was unavoidable. He had the woman by the hair. We had to shoot. There is another young woman in the bedroom. I need to call Langley. Timmons needs to tell us what to do about her. Elsa, will you sit with her, let her know she is safe, offer her whatever to keep her quiet?"

"I need to call my boss."

"No calls. Take care of matters downstairs. I'm calling Timmons. He will contact Mister Ambrose."

"You know what time it is, Edwards?"

"Yeah, I do Mahoney. We don't have Palmer."

"Let me talk to the woman first. Gauge where her head is at."

"She is frightened. Her friend is dead, and she is still a girl. Not even twenty. She uses her body for money. Where the hell do you think her head is at? Go talk to the agents downstairs. No one leaves. Tell them we have a power failure and a possible suspect in custody. Go. You can talk to the girl later."

"If it is okay, Elsa doesn't need to be here."

"Yes, we can finish this, Dmitry Kasparov. Take your woman back to the hotel. I am sorry, Elsa, that you had to witness this tragedy. Try to rest as best you can. You as well, Dmitry Kasparov. There will be little time for rest after this night."

She is very afraid. She thinks she will be murdered. This FBI man . . . he has work to do. What time is it?"

"Why, Lila?"

"I think we have twenty-four hours, not much longer, or there will be a disaster. We need to interrogate the night manager. We will go now. Is it all right gentlemen?"

"I think it is," Shevchenko answered. "Do what is necessary."

"May I have my weapon?"

"I do not believe you will need it Leona. Lila is armed and there is no threat."

The lobby doors stood open in front of Mahoney. Outside those doors was a different life. He started for the doors, but halfway across the lobby he stopped, surrounded by sofas, end tables, and chairs in paisley colors. Upstairs, a very frightened young woman whose life may have been shattered forever waited to hear her fate. She is what matters now, not the personal needs of a single FBI agent. He turned and walked toward the group of agents keeping vigil on the bar while other agents stopped guests from entering the hotel.

"We need to have a conversation, just the two of us, Ethan Edwards, after we are finished here," Shevchenko began. "It concerns that French fellow Dupree and the KGB assassins that were stopped in Paris." The phone rang.

"That has to be Timmons," Edwards said, picking up the room phone. " Should we hold them, Ron?"

"No, we shouldn't, Ethan. They are the Israelis' problem, not ours, and to hold them could create a national security problem that could literally blow up the Farm. What about the young woman?"

"Mahoney wanted to call his boss at the FBI."

"Bullshit! Do not, I repeat, do not turn the young woman over to them. Keep her safe and with you until we can get her moved here. Where are we on Palmer?"

"We are nowhere. He is in the wind, Ron. I don't think these three know where he and the broad are. As soon as we can get out of here, we'll start the search again. He could be close. He will find a place. He won't sleep in his car."

"What are we looking at?"

"Very little, Ron. If what happened here gets out and he knows he's lost a big part of his brood, no time. He'll move right away." Edwards sighed. "What if Ambrose doesn't want to go along and demands we turn the girl over?"

"He won't. He likes his damned job and he isn't about to put his ass in the hot seat. He knows if he takes her, it will stay a goddamn secret for about five minutes."

"Mahoney, what do I tell him?"

"The broad stays with us. Like I said."

"No call's Derek Mahoney. Timmons is calling your boss as we speak. How is it going downstairs?"

"It's covered."

"Take a deep breath, Derek. You did nothing wrong. You are a very good agent on a very bad day. It will pass. Go home, Derek Mahoney, to your wife and kid. Forget us and pretty much forget the whole goddamn mess. We live in a world you have only heard of. Goodnight. It's been good knowing you and working with you. Turn it over to whomever is in charge downstairs."

"What will you do after this?"

"First, we are going to turn these men over to agents coming from the Israeli embassy, then the search begins again. We will need the borrowed cars a little longer. Will your boss allow it?"

"You have my permission, Ethan. Let's leave it at that, okay?"

"Fair enough, Derek." Edwards shook the agent's hand.

"Goodnight, Derek Mahoney, and goodbye. Go home, kiss your child goodnight," Shevchenko said, kneeling next to the young Israeli named Joseph. "Your embassy is sending people to take you and your brood away, Joseph. I have only one question: "Where is Palmer?"

Edwards walked into the bedroom and sat next to the young woman.

"I'm not going to hurt you; you are safe now. What is your name--- your real name, not your street name, and your correct age?"

"I'm afraid to breathe."

"I know . . . tell me your name and age."

"Shana Moss. I'm eighteen. I have no family; Rhea was my only family. I'm fuckin' lost man, I got nothing. "

"You have us now. Where would you like to live?"

"Florida, man . . . Miami, lot of paper in Miami. Dudes will pay big for young ass like me. I just got to get there. Can you do that?"

"There is no future in what you do, only pain and loneliness. If we can help you—

"Help with what, a job at Mc D's? No, man."

"Education, for one thing; you can become anything you are willing to work for. You've got to change your verbiage. If I can do this, will you do it? Will you take the chance to get out of this life?"

"What if I can't make it--- what then?"

"Think of your friend. Do it for her memory, Shana Moss. Do it for Rhea."

"The Embassy people are here," Shevchenko said from the door. "Daniel Joseph and the one they call Moody do not know where Palmer and the woman are. I believe them. I think they fear the Embassy people more than they fear us."

"I don't blame them, Peter. Close the door until they take them away."

"Why should I believe you, man?"

"Because I am your way to freedom and a life, Shana Moss. I'll give you a minute to think it through. As far as Rhea is concerned, she will get a better resting place on the farm where you can visit her. Okay, Shana?"

The passenger side door opened. Jonah Shapiro got out, walked around the rear of the van, and climbed in, closing the doors behind him. He took a seat on the opposite wall and knocked on the thick screen separating the cargo space from the passenger seat.

"So, we finally meet." He took a gun from a small cloth bag next to him on the bench. The van moved slowly to the exit road.

"We are being taken back to Israel for trial?"

"No, that is not an option for you three. Nor is it an option for Reba Davidoff- Klein."

"What is to become of us?"

CHAPTER THIRTY

"Its eight o'clock, Peter?"

"You have my bottle of vodka. How is Shana?"

"Asleep I hope. Elsa is with her. Dmitry wasn't pleased. The bottle is on the bar. The agency has someone coming for her. She will be here at ten. One of the ladies can stay with her until she's picked up."

"Would you like to join me?"

"Why not: get a buzz on the first thing in the morning."

"Sergei called a few minutes ago. He and Boris checked hotels up Route 3 all the way to the Lincoln tunnel. No one registered under Preston or her name, Klein, and no one fit their description. Here is your drink. The media is broadcasting a shooting. The night manager was killed. They suspect robbery."

"Was it truly necessary, Peter? I mean killing the manager."

"Do you believe that man would not turn on us?"

"I think Langley could have convinced him." Edwards drained half of his drink. "I had an occasion once," he began. The memory sent a shock through his body.

"The old woman in the apartment the day you hunted the two traitors. I know Ethan Edwards. "I have Minsk. It still haunts me no matter the reason." Shevchenko raised his glass in salute." To those who committed no sin and those who did." He lowered his glass and sighed. "I have another matter I need to discuss with you before the others are awake."

"What is it, Peter?"

"More vodka?"

"I can't finish this glass, Peter." He put the glass down on a side table. "What troubles you, Peter, besides Fedorov and the three assassins in Paris?"

"Fedorov wants to rule Russia after Brezhnev steps down or dies. No one is truly safe from his grip. Not even Leonid Brezhnev." Shevchenko took a sip of his vodka and put his glass down on the bar. "The three people in Paris are not a diversion. I believe they are a backup. The head of the Moscow State Police knows this. The real assassin is here among us."

"You trust this man, Peter."

"I do. Colonel Gusev is a good man. If he is found to have aided us, he will lose more than his job. I would take his words seriously. I must remember to see he receives a case of Camel cigarettes through your embassy in Moscow. Can you see to it, Ethan? That way, he will know I received his message."

"I will call Timmons. Who will betray you?"

"I need a shower, shave, and a change of clothes. I need to call Ladas. You might want to call your woman." Shevchenko drained the last of the vodka. "In one hour, we will continue our discussion, yes?"

"I'll come up when I'm dressed."

One hour later, Edwards entered Shevchenko's suit. "Are you almost ready, Peter?"

"I was just about to call and wake up the others."

"I have news: The cigarettes will be delivered within three days. The bartender and her family are being held in seclusion. The other patrons were sent home."

"That is good news. The sooner we can let her return to a normal life, the better."

"Yeah, we'll keep our fingers crossed on that one. By the way, the Kozlov's landed in Sweden late last night. How do you like your eggs?

"Cooked."

LYNDHURST DINER : JULY 20

"Would you like more coffee, Comrade?"

"Remember where you are, Sergei."

"Of course, you are correct. I am sorry Boris. I cannot believe we have been at this all night and have not found those two. Where can they be?"

"They are close by. I feel it in my aching bones. They have other identities at their disposal. We can be sure. I am going to call the hotel. I want to stay out. If nothing else, they may go out to eat. Do you have American money?"

"Yes," Sergei answered.

"Good. Pay for the food and leave a large tip for the waitress. It is the custom here when the service is good, and the waitress is friendly. Wait in the car."

"I love this country."

"What does this wonder of womanhood do for work?"

"She is a labor nurse at the local hospital in Secaucus."

"You have balance in your thoughts, Sergei Folic. It is refreshing."

"What you are saying is a good thing, Boris?"

"Yes, Sergei, a good thing."

"Good, then Sergei is happy too . . . We must go."

Elsa could not get over the lavish servings. After devouring a large breakfast and two bear claws, she belched with satisfaction and took a long drink of orange juice. "Americans are spoiled. It is no wonder you are all so fat. It isn't fair, it should be like my country: to everyone the same."

"And what do the powerful leaders and oligarchs share, Elsa?"

"That is enough for both of you," Shevchenko interrupted. "Leave the politics to those who can change it. Elsa, see to the young woman. Edwards and I need to talk."

"I have a mind, Peter Shevchenko. I can think." Elsa huffed, picked up another bear claw and a glass of orange juice, and walked to the bedroom, closing the door behind her with a distinct click.

"You must forgive her—"

"There is nothing to forgive, Peter. I expect you want to know if I have made a decision on my choice of traitor in our little group."

"I would be most interested in your opinion."

"The woman who calls herself Leona."

"Interesting, Ethan."

"You disagree?"

"I did not say that."

"What do you think of the women's idea concerning a woman's needs? I assume she is talking about Russian women of stature."

"It's the same here, Peter. Shopping will depend on the most important factor and that is, she isn't spooked."

LA QUINTA INN - CLIFTON

Palmer rolled over onto his back. The room was dark, the drapes pulled tightly closed, the only light was the bathroom light, the only sound, Reba singing softly. Palmer glanced at the bedside clock; "9 o'clock," he mused, congratulating himself for the previous night's lovemaking. There was mindless intensity in it, a fierce, rugged all-out fest. He smiled.
"What are you doing in there?"

"Getting dressed."

"Come back to bed; I'm not finished with you."

"I have coffee and bagels ordered. They will be here in a few minutes. I am going shopping. I need sizes for you. I have no intention of leaving this earth in underwear I have worn for two days. Get up now. Pull the drapes, let the sun in."

"I'm going to call the hotel and check on the boys."

"They are not children at summer camp, John. I am sure they are fine. Get dressed. At least put on the hotel robe, I am hungry. Maybe later, when I return, I might be hungry for other things. We will see." The lovemaking was intense, but he didn't hurt her.

"Make love." He smiled inwardly and mouthed the words. Make love.

"I need sizes." She opened the door just enough so he could see her face and the toothbrush jutting out from the corner of her mouth. A knock on the door.

"My breakfast is here; I'm starving." She closed the door.

"Room service."

"I'm coming, hold your horses." He got out of bed, pulled the drapes open and slipped on the hotel robe, barely noticing the scratches on his shoulders.

"She is as depraved as you are, Wayne; maybe I will like her after all."

"Shut up you miserable bitch." He opened the door with a boyish smile on his face. "I'll take it from here; my wife isn't dressed. Take this." He handed the young waiter ten dollars. Is it very warm outside?"

"Ninety-five degrees already and humid."

"Food's here. Get it while it's hot."

"Did you call the hotel?"

"No, you're right, of course, let them sleep. I need to go there and take care of the manager Where are you going, by the way?"

"The Garden State Plaza. Did you write down your sizes, John?"

"I will. I'm still not thrilled with you going out."

"Discussion over. Write down your sizes, including shoes or sneakers. I'll need some ready cash." She bit off another chunk of bagel, wiping the excess cheese from her upper lip with the tip of her tongue. She knew it excited him, so she slid her tongue slowly from one side of her mouth to the other, then back.

"You sure you want to wear that fur coat with jeans and a sweatshirt in this heat, Reba?"

"I will be seen as just another rich bitch, flaunting her wealth. It will conceal my weapon. What will you do while I am gone?"

"Finalize bus schedules and boat times from both the Jersey side and Battery Park. I'll call the boys later for one last meeting before the attack. I'll watch some TV. I'd rather come with you. Here are the sizes."

"That would not be wise and you know it. Two hours at most and I will come back. I'll hurry. I want to get there before the stores are too crowded. One more thing, John, shave the beard before I return. It scratches me." Without waiting for an answer, she stepped out into the hall, closing the door behind her. She shook her head—letting the loose curls surround her face— slipped on a pair of oversized sunglasses, and walked to the elevator landing.

Sergei slumped in his seat. "There is a hotel La Quinta. Pull into the lot." Suddenly he sat up. "It is her, Boris, look. She is getting into the silver car."

"Are you sure it is her?"

"I am sure, Boris; a woman as beautiful as her stands out. Maybe she is going to the Hilton. She is alone. Palmer must have stayed at the hotel. Follow her."

Boris waited for her to enter the roadway and pulled out into traffic behind the Mercedes. At the next overpass she passed over the highway and turned taking the ramp down in the opposite direction toward the Hilton Hotel.

"She is driving under the overpass. She is not going to the Hilton. She is going on Route 17. I have to phone the hotel. You are sure she is alone?"

"I can't be sure if Palmer is with her, but I am sure It is her."

"Stay calm, my friend, I am going back to the diner and calling."

"That was Timmons, everyone. They have found the dealer where Palmer rented the Mercedes. It is to be returned by 6:00 p.m. today. The agency is three miles north on Route 17."

The phone rang. Edwards answered on the first ring.

"Hello. Yes, Boris. Are you both sure it was her? Hold on. She is on the move. They do not know if she is alone or if they are together. They want to know what we want them to do. C'mon, everybody, think about the options Keep holding, Boris."

"Where did he see her on Route 3?"

"She came out of the La Quinta hotel parking lot and is now on 17 North. He's angry with himself; had they gone West instead of toward New York, they would have found them a lot earlier."

"Don't blame yourself, any one of us would have done what you did. Call the hotel to see if they are registered under Preston. Call me back."

"They could be turning in the car, knowing we have its description and picking one that's not so conspicuous? One thing is obvious, they do not know about the trouble at the Hilton."

"You are right, Lila, they cannot possibly know."

"If she is alone, she is going to the Garden State Plaza to shop," Lorena added with conviction.

"You may be right." The phone rang.

"Yes Boris? Thank you. Stay at or near the hotel. If Palmer emerges, kill him." Ethan hung up. "No one by that name registered."

"Leona, you and Lila take Elsa with you. Elsa will be the perfect companion since she has no knowledge of American malls You will see she is kept from harm if the woman comes to the mall?"

"No harm will come to Elsa, Peter Shevchenko."

"You understand why she needs to be there Dmitry as a distraction only."

"I understand. I do not worry when Leona tells me no harm will come to Elsa."

"Then it is settled. We will give her time to get to the mall. Dmitry, go to Elsa. Explain the situation to her. Ethan, can I offer you another coffee?"

As soon as the two men were alone, Shevchenko turned to Ethan and in a quiet voice said, "One thing I will add to your theory, Ethan Edwards. No attempt against me will come until Palmer is dead." Shevchenko poured a half shot of vodka into each cup. "If I should be assassinated. I want you to murder my assassin. Promise me you will take care of my wife. Keep her safe and see to her needs. Will you do that for me, Ethan Edwards?"

"You have my word."

"We will drink." They raised their cups in a toast just as Kasparov and Elsa came out of the bedroom. "Join us in a drink to our success, Dmitry. The ladies are in the lobby waiting for you, Elsa."

"I told Shana Moss to shower and wait in the bedroom. A woman will come for her with fresh clothing." Elsa blushed. "That girl wanted to make love to me and Dmitry as her way of thanking us. You Americans have strange customs." Her face burned bright red. The men laughed.

"She also said she is very hungry."

"I will order her a big breakfast, Elsa."

"There is a Mercedes in the lot. It has a rental sticker on the front bumper. I am assuming it is her car. It is the only one with a sticker. A woman drove it here. The driver's side window is open partially. I smell a woman's perfume. Here is the number of the public phone and the number on the license plate. Call me back with the identification--- No, we have not seen her--- Call me back." Leona hung up the phone.

"Elsa, you stay with me. Lila, if it is her, we will separate after disabling the car. You take the left side of the main concourse. Americans call it window shopping. You can look into the stores with limited vision, but more importantly watch the women in the concourse."

"I cannot believe the extravagance of this place."

"Wait until you see inside these stores, Elsa. Be careful not to express awe at what you see. Remember, the woman we search for is a trained Israeli agent. We must fit in—" The phone rang. "Yes, I understand, Peter. You three will be coming now. Good. I do not know if she is alone. I imagine she is."

"Where is the car?"

"Behind the Macy's department store. She is smart, she parked facing the exit lane with the back of the car against the wall."

"Did you disable the car,?"

"I cut the air valve on the tires . . . We are in the mall. Wait, Peter, Lila is coming . Peter, she has the target in sight. It is Reba. Hold on, I will put Lila on."

"She is in the food court ordering a coffee. She is carrying a single package of beauty supplies in her left hand and a shoulder bag on her left shoulder. She is wearing jeans, a man's tee shirt and flat shoes. She is wearing a fur coat. Cold-blooded like her heart."

"Can you make contact?"

"No---too dangerous. Three policemen are here. They are not store security. They are local, otherwise I could simply step behind her and shoot her in the head. Palmer is not with her. She only orders for one."

"We need to take her alive. Wait for us in the food court and do not follow her."

"I see a Saks Fifth Avenue store. She is going up the escalator. Looking at the windows to the store."

"We are leaving now and will arrive soon. Goodbye."

"Elsa, here is some American money. Stay here in the food court. Find a table close to the police officers."

"Yes, Lila I understand. Elsa moved her hand, making the eastern sign of the cross. "Be careful."

"I thought the men wanted me to be with you as a distraction?"

"It is better if you are not. Leona told Dimitry we would protect you. This is the best way."

"As you wish, Lila."

"Lila, if she goes into Saks, I will go to the parking lot entrance and wait in case she leaves that way. Tell Shevchenko."

Palmer stepped out of the bathroom. The hot shower had been refreshing. He shaved his beard, a small admission or subjugation to her will. Whichever it was, he was pleased with himself. One hundred fifty pushups and sit-ups.

Make time for her when she returns.

"Is this love?" he said out loud. "Is this how love makes you feel?"

He glanced at the clock on the side table next to the bed: 10:43 a.m. He picked up the phone and called the hotel.

"Good morning," he said in a cheery voice. "Could you put me through to Suite 616 please?" A moment's hesitation by the operator went unnoticed. He was still in the Reba moment.

"One moment, please," the operator answered. The line seemed to go dead. Seconds passed and then the phone rang and was picked up. A woman's voice.

"I am sorry. My name is Benedict. The boys are sleeping. May I ask who is calling?"

"I am a friend of the young men who were using the suite." Without waiting for a reply, Palmer put the phone back on the cradle. His mouth tightened. His next thought: turn on the TV. Who the hell is this broad Benedict? Maybe he should have asked if she was one of the guests. The picture brightened and then sound. A reporter stood outside the Hilton. Police were everywhere and reporters were fighting for space. The local reporter was explaining the situation.

"Son of a bitch!" he screamed, and fell silent. His mind racing. He shut the TV off. "They are all dead. We've got to hide. Keep moving until morning." He slipped the 9 mm pistol into the belt of the jeans and quickly scanned the room. "If they are dead, the hunters have the van ."

He was dressed in the same clothes he wore the day before, the underwear he discarded in the shower stall. The only important thing was to find Reba. The phone rang.

"The cab you ordered is out front, sir. Will you need assistance with anything?"

"No, thank you. I haven't much and I'm here until tomorrow morning. Please inform the driver I am on my way down. Wait a moment, please have the driver come around back. I will meet him there." What if I killed the taxi driver and used the cab? No one would pay attention to a taxi driver. Something to think about.

The cab driver turned into the entrance ramp and stopped. A heavyset guard with a container of Pepsi cola in his left hand approached the cab.

"What's happening man, I need to get my passenger up to the main entrance."

"No can do, buddy. No more cars in the mall. It's shut down until further notice."

"What's the problem officer," the passenger asked. Noting the time on his watch. "It is past eleven the mall is open isn't it?"

"They say some woman got shot outside the Saks Fifth Avenue store. All I know is the lots are closed and this cab is blocking the pathway for emergency vehicles."

"Thank you, officer. Driver, tell me, how much will it take to get me to the Port Authority in New York?"

"Ronald, she's dead. Palmer is alone. You had better contact the Israeli Embassy. I am sure they will want the remains." Edwards switched the phone to his left ear. She's in Paramus. It couldn't be helped. She wasn't going to give us Palmer and she wasn't going to give herself up. She killed a saleswoman to prove her point."

"Any clue as to where he might be, Ethan?"

"No. They stayed at the La Quinta hotel on Route 3, but we didn't find them in time."

"Have they removed the body? Where did they take it?"

"It is still a crime scene, Ron. She hasn't been moved. We didn't stay to discuss it with the police. Leona grabbed her shoulder bag after she shot her. She's going through it. I'll call you when we get back to the hotel. Wait. We got a room key."

PALMER

He got out of the cab at the rear entrance to the port of authority terminal, walked the length of the main concourse, and out onto Eighth Avenue. He jumped into another cab and told the driver to take him to Barneys, the men's store. He checked his watch: 11:48 a.m.

He purchased a pair of corduroy slacks, a pullover, a short-sleeved shirt, white socks, Adidas high top sneakers, and underwear. He went upstairs and was fitted for a double-breasted blue pinstripe Armani suit. He gave the tailor two crisp one-hundred-dollar bills to ensure the alterations would be quick. While he waited, he called the Plaza Hotel. He bought a medium blue snap tab collar shirt, two pairs of blue socks, a pair of cordovan shoes, and a brightly colored paisley tie. He needed one more item to complete the outfit: a fine leather briefcase; the one he had would never fit the image he needed to create.

The cab slid to the curb in front of the Plaza Hotel at 2:12 p.m. Palmer paid the driver. The door swung open. He was immediately greeted by the doorman with a welcome hello and a glad-to-see-you smile. Palmer was treated no differently when he checked in and was taken up to his room on the eighth floor. The room was large and airy with a view of the park. He put the bag containing the explosives next to the bed. Palmer tipped the handler and did two things: First he called for room service, a steak, medium-well, a baked potato with extra butter and bacon bits, string beans, and a pot of coffee.

"It will be about forty minutes, sir, to prepare your order."

He added the bottle of his favorite Russian vodka almost as an after-thought and was not surprised when he was told it was in stock. He showered, slipping on a clean pair of underwear and the hotel robe. He flipped on the television and switched channels until he found the news. He called down to the front desk and requested a haircut and manicure for 3:30 the following morning.

The camera was focused on the yellow tarp covering the body. She was dead.

"You're right, Wayne, it's her. It happened earlier. I was just getting to like her. Now that she is dead, I'm sure I do." His mother lit a cigarette and leaned on the window sill. She blew a plume of smoke out of the rotting hole where her throat once was. "She wants to see you, Wayne."

A tap at his door, metal on metal. "Room Service,"

"Go ahead, Wayne. He will not know I'm here. I promise to be quiet until he leaves. Then we'll talk while you eat."

"Put the setting by the window."

"Of course, sir. Would you like me to open the bottle of vodka and pour a glass?"

"That will not be necessary. By the way, could you tell me where the closest hardware store is located?"

"Walk up to Ninth Avenue and south three blocks to Columbus hardware. They carry everything."

"Thank you. The food smells wonderful." Palmer took money from his wallet and gave it to the server.

"Forgive me, sir, but the suite is smoke-free."

"I thought I smelled smoke. I intend to call the desk after I eat." Palmer opened the door to let the server out. "You said Columbus hardware on ninth." He glanced at the server's name plate over the pocket of his white jacket. "Thanks again, Carl." He closed the door. "Are you still here?"

"I told you, Wayne." She dragged on the cigarette. "Carl is nice looking. I could go for him."

"I am ready to have my drink. I'm sure Carl would be thrilled to see you. Get out, Mom."

"Reba is waiting for you at the Port Authority bus terminal uptown. She wants to see you once more before you do what you two had planned."

"Tell me we will never have to do this again, Ethan. Promise me?"

"I promise you, Anna Lee. We will marry and be normal and we will raise our son the best way we can. I promise."

Edwards put the phone down. For a long minute, he stood next to the bedside table deep in thought, his thumb and index finger absentmindedly stroking his chin. He nodded. The decision made, he picked up the phone and dialed.

"Hello Adam Cahill, it's Ethan."

"I was wondering when I would hear from you. Timmons has been keeping me updated. I've followed your movements. The news media is completely in the dark so is the administration. The shootings at the hotel in Secaucus and Paramus are being handled as separate incidents. Ridgewood didn't even make the news. You have done well, Ethan."

"He is still out there. We have another problem, Adam. Shevchenko is sure one of his team will attempt to kill him after Palmer."

"You think he is right, Ethan?"

"I know he is right, Adam."

"There is nothing like a chilled bottle of Russian vodka with a single ice cube to complete a trying day." Shevchenko placed the glass on the table next to Edwards and took his seat. "I am amazed by your country's ability to place such a plausible blanket over events like yesterday and today. In Russia, we simply control the situation and what narrative is put forward. Here it is so sophisticated in its nuance." Shevchenko took a sip of his drink.

"Do not make the same mistake we did, putting our faith in Stalin. Be careful of these people you think you are fooling. Never allow a government or its news outlets to control thought. I have been awed by your free press for years. There is danger as well . . . Enough of that song. I think we have the right plan for tomorrow. He will strike the bus terminal. We will be waiting."

"What convinced you, Peter?"

"That little item Mister Timmons passed along about the man and woman coming too close to the Statue of Liberty last week and had to be shoed away like an annoying puppy. With her dead and the rest of the Brood dead, he has no choice but attack what was once more likely a distraction."

"I agree Peter. That boat couldn't have been a coincidence. No possible way."

"I have one more item to discuss. There is someone you will meet very soon. Her name is Tatyana. She is the assassin who will—"

"Kill you when Palmer is eliminated?"

"She will attempt to kill me, Ethan. You will help me stop her. How ironic when you consider the situation. For years you hunted me and I hunted you. Now you may very well be my savior."

"You know who it is, Peter. You asked my thoughts, knowing how I would answer."

"I am afraid so, Ethan. Your logic was impeccable. You couldn't have known what I knew."

"So, tell me Peter, it's Leona Sokolov isn't it?"

"I met her once briefly at the residence of Fedorov's Dacha. She brought me tea and a pastry while I waited for Fedorov to see me. She looked different then. She wore thick glasses, her hair was blonde, cut very short; she wore a hair net. Now it is brown and longer. Even with the heavy clothing, one could see she had large breasts. I am a man; I notice such things, Ethan Edwards. She hides her true feelings quite well, don't you think?"

"What amazes me is how you were able to remember all this from a quick glance?"

"Yes. There was one more thing. Her shoes were polished black leather with thick crepe soles, long thick laces. Laces to strangle an enemy. Soles made for stealth: a killer's shoes. Her real name is Tatyana Poriszkova."

"Why wait, Peter?"

"We need her expertise and her ability with firearms she would have never put in the position she now holds. She cannot live."

"You have my word, Peter Shevchenko."

"Good. Now let us enjoy our drink and speak of more pleasant subjects. The sun is still with us, so drink up. Tell me how you spent your time when you were not hunting. How did Ethan Edwards relax and manage his life?"

"I wrote a book about my experiences. I burned it after my first date with Anna Lee. I wanted her in my life. I can't explain the attraction, but it was real. I didn't want her to read it and run off on me."

"I knew it the first time I saw Ladas. Your woman doesn't seem like the type to run at the first sign of trouble, Ethan. She is like my Ladas, very strong in a quiet way."

"Yes, she is, but I'm still glad I burned it. Your turn, Peter."

"One more question, please?"

"Go ahead and ask."

"Once, on a lark, Maxine and I drove across this country in a Volkswagen bus to New York. It was August, if I remember, in 1969. We went to this farm where a concert was being held."

"Woodstock?"

"You heard of it, of course."

"I was there, Peter, six rows from the stage. I wanted to see Janis Joplin in concert. Why are you smiling like a fool? Can't believe an ex Green Beret would like stuff like that?" "Finish your little story first."

"I met this girl there; she wore only black outfits, a big Johnny Cash fan. We shared those three days like it was the last three on earth. Her name was Loretta. I brought two quarts of Ballantine Scotch with me and a lot of Wise potato chips. She helped me drink it and eat my potato chips."

"I think I remember who this singer was: long hair and had a real gravel voice?"

"That's Janis all right. She finished her song and I stuck my hand in the air, holding that scotch bottle to salute her. And what did she do? She pulled a pint of Southern Comfort out of her back pocket and waved to me. The crowd went crazy. We left after three days. I never saw that girl again." Edwards drained his glass, a hint of melancholy in his voice.

"If you are ready, so am I, Ethan Edwards." Shevchenko brought back two full glasses, raised one, and announced, "For the women we knew even for only three days and the fond memories they left with us."

"I hope wherever you are, Loretta, you are happy and content." Ethan raised his glass into the air. A salute to a memory.

Shevchenko raised his glass: "Schastlivy i dovolni."

"Tell me, what were you smiling at?"

"Behind you, Ethan Edwards, three rows and slightly to your left a couple who'd driven from California watched, laughed, and cheered for you and Janis Joplin. At that moment, I felt a shiver go down my spine looking at you from behind. I couldn't understand why until just now." Shevchenko drained his glass in a swallow and stood up. "Drink up Ethan Edwards; who knows what tomorrow will bring."

CHAPTER THIRTY-ONE

FRIDAY, JULY 21

At 3:30 AM precisely, John Palmer walked into the salon in the Plaza Hotel for his shave and haircut. He was greeted by Brandon Taylor, the young man who would tend to his hair while a young woman by the name of Mara, looked after his nails. He expressed his wishes for his hair and nails in a casual falsetto voice. He ordered an orange juice while explaining he was preparing for an important job interview and that his look needed to be impeccable.

Brandon assured Palmer there would be no error in his grooming. First impressions could make or break an interview. Palmer put his hand over the stylist's hand and squeezed it.

"I knew you would understand Brandon, I knew the moment I laid eyes on you."

"Where is Sergei?" Shevchenko asked. "And why is he not here, Dmitry?"

"He is awake, Peter. I knocked and told him to hurry."

"Remember, we cannot be in the terminal later than six o'clock. I need to make a call. You all have been issued the clothes you will wear and your assignments. Be in the lobby in thirty minutes. Ethan, give me a moment."

When they were alone, Shevchenko said, "There is a change in plans." Shevchenko reached into his pants pocket and produced two similar tubes of poison. "We will use these ampules Ethan. This poison attacks the nervous system. It will shut down all bodily functions and render Palmer motionless; but alert."

"Both ampules; For what purpose, Peter?"

444

"Nothing must be left of Palmer or the woman. The bodies must vaporize. I want them to be able to count the minutes left to them. Do not argue this point with me."

Ethan picked up the phone and dialed the hotel operator.

"I need to call long distance . . . Good morning, Ronald. Sorry to get you up so early."

"We've been up all night. Both Angela and Sydney are with me. I have the information you requested. I'm looking at her picture as we speak. Tell Shevchenko he is correct. Sokolov is on the security team. Her real name is…"

"We already know her real name. Peter acquired it from Gusev of the Moscow state police."

"She is very dangerous and very good at her job. At least eleven kills to her credit."

"What about the terminal cameras, Ronald?"

"The security office is on the second level. I spoke to the police commissioner and he is giving us all the support we need . . . no questions or changes. The mayor knows nothing."

"That is a plus."

"He is taking a big chance, Ethan. We better not make any mistakes. What are your intentions with the woman?"

"That situation will be handled once we have Palmer. You understand, Ronald?"

"Completely."

"I've got to go. We need to get to the terminal. Once we're in the security office and able to monitor the entire terminal, I'll call and set up an open line."

"We'll be here, Ethan . . .whatever it takes, Ethan."

"Yes . . . I know."

"Just as a side note, Ethan . . . the woman and the other four Israeli agents' bodies have been cremated along with all personal effects. We have been in contact with Shin Bet and Mossad. They were killed when their helicopter crashed during a training mission. They are putting the story out as fact. You'd better go."

"I'll be in touch, Ron. How is the young woman doing?"

"She is going to be all right. Christopher and Shana have bonded. The bartender and family will be just fine. Be safe, all of you."

Palmer rolled up the note with Brandon's number on it and tossed it into the wastebasket.

"Another time, young man. You have no idea how close you came to death." He smiled, thinking of the scenario he cooked up in his mind for Brandon's last moment on earth. He pushed the thought aside. "Today is for you, Reba Klein." He kissed the mirror. "I will see you at 6:30. I will look for you in the window of the dress store. I bought a suit, a very expensive suit, just for this occasion. I hope you like it."

"You look very nice, Wayne. I wish your father could see you."

"Shut up, mommy."

Don't be rude. I am nice enough to bring you messages. You should be grateful.

"Oh, I am, mom--- I certainly am."

At 6:05 a.m., the team entered the terminal. Edwards, Shevchenko, Lila, and Sergei went directly to the second level. They clipped the special identification tags onto their jacket pockets and approached the police officer's desk.

"My name is Ethan Edwards." He produced a driver's license and the special FBI badge, placing them both on the desktop. "We have permission to use the security office."

"My name is Stevens. We got the memo and we were told to supply you with diagrams of each floor, if you need them. I'll take you in. What the hell is going on? Can't you give us a heads up?"

"We have the diagrams, but thanks. As to your other question, I'm sorry I can't. What I will tell you is be very alert," Shevchenko answered, his drawl thick. "This is a photo of the man we are looking for. He may have changed his appearance. I'm sure he has. Under no circumstances are your people to approach him."

"If this is so important, why don't you people let us increase our—?"

"We don't want to alarm him. I am sure he has been here and knows the movements of the security guards and police. Everything must look like a normal morning. We will need six handheld radios, a gurney, and a wheel-chair. Do you have an evacuation plan should we need one?"

"Now just a damned minute; What the hell is going on, bud?"

"What are your orders, Sergeant Stevens?" Edwards answered.

"To comply with your requests, whatever they may be. Nobody said shit about an evacuation."

"It is a precaution only, Sergeant. Now, please take us where we need to go. Time is short."

"This really is piss poor shit man."

"You've said a mouthful, Stevens. Show us the control room. Stay alert and out of our way . . . please."

"I'm responsible for those commuters out there."

"The control room, Stevens; now."

"Yeah, okay . . . step around the desk."

"Is there a phone to call out on in there?"

"On the wall next to the door."

"Thank you . . .One more thing, if all goes as planned, it is very important we have a clear path to the exits."

"But don't ask questions?"

"No questions."

Palmer carried the briefcase close to his body, with the explosives neatly tucked inside. The timer was ready to be set. He patted the 9 mm pistol under his left shoulder.

He entered the Forty-Second Street entrance to the Port Authority bus terminal at 6:05 a.m. The second explosive pack under his shirt was strapped to the sides of his rib cage and tied with a belt across his chest. A small hole cut just under the left armpit with the wiring for the plunger nestled in his shirt pocket. If it was not for Reba waiting up town for him, he would have set off the explosives now.

His lips moved, a barely audible sound escaping. The train entered the station with a rush of air. He took a step back on the platform and waited, his lips trembled ever so slightly, his eyelids fluttered.

"I'm coming, Reba . . . Wait for me."

"Next stop, Fifty-Ninth Street," the conductor announced.

"I'm coming, Reba. I am going to leave visas for four Middle East students on the train next to the conductors' door when I get off."

Shevchenko clipped the Port Authority maintenance badge onto the breast pocket of his green workman's shirt and entered the men's room. He heard a toilet flush in a stall and waited until the door opened. A man who looked about fifty with salt and pepper hair and matching goatee emerged. He was dressed like Shevchenko. He had a wide expressionless pock-marked face. His eyes were deep set and blank, his shoulders slumped. He looked like a man whose life had a story with very few bright moments.

"I am an agent with the FBI." Shevchenko produced his identification, holding it out in front of him. "I need your help; What is your name?"

"Is it important knowing my name?"

"Not really, but since you obviously don't want to give it, I'll just call you 'Hey You.' Now, Hey You, let me explain why I am here dressed like you. Are you with me so far?"

"Yeah, I'm with you."

"Well, bless your heart." Shevchenko took a step forward. He could read the name on the faded ID card now. "I need you to go into one of the stalls, Edgar. Sit down and don't move until I know the bomb threat has been neutralized." He was interrupted by his handheld phone.

"We are in place, all monitors activated, no sign of subject; time 6:08 a.m. Acknowledge with a single beep."

Shevchenko pressed the key on his phone. "Now, please do as I say, Edgar."

"Fuck that, man. I'm not sitting on no toilet waiting for some asshole to blow me up."

"If you don't do as I say, I am going to drag you into each stall and make you drink all the water from each toilet until you explode. Now, if you understand I am not playing games with you, take one step back. Do it now, Edgar. I will not repeat myself."

"I don't want to die. I'm not much. I don't get much—"

"I know, I see it in your eyes. I will not let anything happen to you, okay?" He blinked. "Think of me as a friend, an angel on your shoulder, and do as I say." Shevchenko put out his hand and waited for Edgar to shake it. "Do you have 'Out of Order' cards for the bathroom?"

"Yeah, I do."

"Please, place one on the door while I make a call. I want to alert the authorities about the closure."

"I won't run."

"I believe you. My name is Peter Grant. You may call me Peter or Pete."

"Next stop, 110th Street."

"Here I come, Reba. I thought about blowing up this train and the station at Forty-Second Street, but I would have missed seeing you. Just three more stops."

"You look wonderful in your suit, Wayne."

"Shut up."

Handheld radios crackled to life on both levels of the terminal. Lila's familiar voice said, "I do not understand how these people can stand this cooped-up space; it stinks in here."

"Get to the point, Lila," Edwards said from the base of the escalator.

"Time is 6:12 a.m., clear both levels. Wait one second . . . never mind, acknowledge with a single beep."

"Sorry about the smell." Edwards beeped once and slipped the phone back into the waistband of the transit police uniform: black slacks and blue shirt. The loose-fitting leather waist-length coat hid the two 9 mm Glock handguns. The uniform was comfortable, but the shoes squeaked when he walked. "Lila, tell the desk sergeant to bring the gurney and medical supplies to the first floor east wing men's room and leave it outside the door."

"Next stop 125th Street."

At the top of the moving stairs, Ethan spied Boris and Leona. Boris was in the wheelchair. Leona sat next to him on the long bench.

Boris tapped his cane on the tile. His thick dark glasses hid his eyes. He tapped his cane and softly hummed a tune to the beat of the cane on the tile. He stopped tapping when his message was received in the control room.

"Will you need some assistance, sir?"

"No, thank you. My daughter has our tickets."

"All right, sir, you have a nice day." Edwards pressed his hand on the Russian's shoulder and stepped away, pulling his cap close over his eyes. He checked his watch: 6:14 a.m. Where are you Palmer?

"Next stop 175th Street, Washington Heights. Port Authority Bus."

"Kasparov, where are you?"

"In this disgusting overcrowded control room; it reminds me of a freighter I was on many years ago. I am here to monitor the crowd, freeing Lila to work with you. She is a very useful tool and completely without fear. Is Boris acting accordingly, Ethan?"

"Yes, playing the role quite well, I assure you. I thought Leona was to act as his sister?"

"Peter wants to exchange her for Lila. I think you know why, Ethan Edwards?"

"Yes, Peter told me. I understand his concern."

"Peter knows what he is doing. I am sending Lila out now. Meet her at the top of the escalator and give the ampules to her."

Edwards spied Lila on the escalator landing. He turned to Olivia, who was holding two bus tickets and staring at him. He signaled her to approach by tipping his hat.

"Here are the ampoules, Lila." Edwards, blocking Leona's view, slipped the ampoules into her hand. "You know what to do; bring Boris in the wheelchair. Shevchenko will distract Palmer and—"

"I know what I must do, Ethan Edwards."

"Officer, I have a question." Leona said, stepping between Lila and Ethan.

"Why of course, ma'am, how can I help?" Edwards turned away from Lila, who sidestepped him and Leona, and walked to the bench, sitting down next to Boris.

"What is this, a change in plans?"

"Peter is in the downstairs men's room, the one marked, 'Out of Order.' He wants you close by to assist him in managing Palmer. Go now."

"What about Lila?"

"She will bring Boris down on the elevator. Peter is sure he can distract Palmer without endangering her or Boris."

"The ampule?"

"Lila has it. Go now and get in position." Edwards watched from his perch on the aisle side of the escalator until Leona was down on the first level before he followed.

"He's standing in front of the woman's clothier. Ping once."

"Reba, you are beautiful. I've come. It is almost time."

"You see what your eyes tell you to see, John. I like your suit. Perfect for the occasion, and your glasses are a nice touch." She lifted her finger and put it in the jagged hole where once there was an eye and a cheek bone. The skin partly burned away. "Do what you came to do. Be watchful of your enemies. They are here, darling, in the terminal. I've seen them."

"She is lovely isn't she, Wayne?"

"Take your hand off her." His eyes fluttered; his lips quibbled. He made no sound. "Don't bring that miserable thing with you, Reba."

"Do what we came to do, and don't worry about her. I will be waiting ---waiting for you to pick me up on the river. Will you come for me, darling?"

"Yes , I will come for you. Is that the message?"

"Yes. They are here waiting for you. Do not fail, John. Do not disappoint me."

"Never, Reba. Wait by the shoreline. I'll say it again; don't bring the hag."

"I won't. It will be just you and me, darling. We will sail on the River Styx of Greek mythology forever more."

Lila emptied the ampoules into the two syringes, tested them, and capped both before slipping them into her coat pocket. She stepped out of the cubicle and walked to the sinks in the front section of the restroom, washed her hands thoroughly, and walked out into the main concourse. She gripped the handles on the chair and began pushing Boris toward the center of the concourse.

"Shevchenko stepped out of the restroom and calls out to Palmer."

Lila removed one syringe from her pocket and flicked the cap off. "We are ready. Palmer is taking a step toward Shevchenko. He must have a detonator on his person or he would have exploded the device. All his attention is on Shevchenko. Be mindful of the case. It is big enough to hide a dangerous explosive."

"Shoot him!"

"No, I am directly behind him, he is not aware of me. He is reaching inside his coat. Get ready, Boris," she whispered. "I am going to push you into him."

Palmer's mind was a swirl of disconnected thoughts. He should have put a plunger on the case. Too late to think about that now. The plunger in my shirt pocket. Move slowly; don't panic, he has drawn a weapon. The crowd is large enough the explosion will be strong enough to kill hundreds. Put the briefcase on the floor and distract him while you reach for the plunger.

He felt a sharp pain in the small of his back from the point of Boris's cane. Out of reflex, he straightened up. His hand came out of the jacket. The wheelchair struck him again, forcing him to lose his balance and topple backward. The last thing he heard was Reba screaming at him from inside the large window, just before Lila plunged the syringe into his neck, releasing one half of the contents into his carotid artery.

Boris, minus the dark glasses and cane, hoisted the limp body of Palmer onto the gurney, covering him with a sheet. "Where is the car, Dmitry?"

Shevchenko waited for Edwards to disperse the curious, then walked over to the gurney. He leaned over the limp body of Palmer and said without mimicking the drawl, "We meet again, Palmer. Do not worry, you will not die from the injection. It will only stop your body functions You will hear and see everything going on around you. You will be helpless to change the outcome." He opened the suit jacket, found the plunger in the shirt pocket, and pulled it up just enough to remove the trigger.

"Time to go Palmer. Leona, helps Lila. I am giving you the honor of disposing of him. Dmitry, bring the car."

"A gracious thought, Peter Shevchenko. I would have thought you would keep that honor for yourself."

"You will be witness to his death. You will be with us when we return to the motherland. Take the credit and accolades. You deserve what awaits you. Lila, you also ride with Kasparov and sit in the back with Palmer. Do you have everything you need for the ride?"

"Yes, Comrade, I have everything I need."

"We will meet you as planned and finish this. Go now." Shevchenko turned on his heel. "I need a moment."

The curious were already moving away. "Thank you for your assistance, Sergeant. Please wait a moment."

He turned and walked quickly back to the restroom, removing the sign on the door

"You may come out now, Edgar, the danger is past. Do not waste the days you have left."

"I called for an ambulance to assist you."

"Thank you, but we can handle this. No ambulance," Edwards answered. "The crowd is already dispersing. Just keep the busy bodies at bay until our people have removed the problem." He turned, looking through the glass at the mannequin sitting on the sofa, a quizzical look on his face.

"Can't you tell me what all the fuss was about? I got to write a report."

"No reports, Sergeant Stevens, and no more questions. We are leaving. Thank you for helping us. Paperwork will go into your file from the FBI stating that your assistance went beyond the call. I might add, possibly resulting in a commendation. Good bye, Sergeant Stevens."

"This must have been some sick son of a bitch."

"You have no idea, Sergeant Stevens. Do you have a wife at home? Kiss her when you get home and hug her tightly."

"That's funny," Edwards said, staring at the mannequin seated inside the window.

"What is it, Ethan Edwards?"

"I thought her legs were crossed the other way and her right arm hung beside the chair. Kasparov also noticed something different about Palmer. It was more than the clothes. He thought he could see Palmer talking to the glass."

"I think you imagine things, Ethan Edwards."

"It was her legs. They were crossed and now they are not. The mannequin was smiling and now she is not." Ethan felt Peter's hand on his shoulder. "Maybe, I'm going freaking nuts."

"You have been under great stress, as have all of us. You are coming down . . . reality is taking its natural course. We must go."

"Tell me Peter," he said. "You think that Frog . . . I forgot his name . . . was right about Palmer?"

"Francois Dupree was his name and the answer to that is unknown and may never be known. Unless some evidence magically appears one day."

Palmer's head rested on the headrest. There was spittle on his chin, his eyes were blinking, wet and glassy, his right hand trembled.

Lila wiped his mouth with a tissue.

"You can hear me. I know you can. You are going to die soon. You will be awake, counting the seconds, powerless to stop it." Lila turned away from Palmer and leaned forward. "I am honored to have served with you, Leona Sokolov. I have learned so much by listening and watching you." Lila slipped her free hand onto Sokolov's shoulder, close to her throat. "I wish to kiss your cheek . . . May I?"

"You are very kind, Lila Chekov, and a good agent. You will do well. I will see that your actions this day are rewarded. I think—"

Lila plunged the needle into her artery. Lila's strong grip held Sokolov in place, leaving her unable to move or defend herself.

"You will join Palmer soon, Tatyana Polizkova, for your treachery. Rest now and think of your own death." Lila slapped the woman hard across her face, sat back, and wiped the spittle from Palmer's chin.

"Are we there yet, Dmitry Kasparov?"

"Soon, Lila."

"I am reminded of my childhood in Leningrad. Boris understands, don't you, my friend? The things we did for the motherland . . Alas, the motivations of men are still filled with hatred and mistrust. Power and greed. Twenty million dead and for what?"

"I remember. They are like a scar on my mind."

"We're coming to the turn off for Route 3, Peter."

"The explosives in the briefcase and the vest he wore, when detonated, will obliterate them both."

"What will Moscow be told?"

"The embassy will be notified that Polizkova, Kasparov, and I died bravely while attempting to stop Palmer. We died in the explosion. Ivanov will notify the embassy in New York that nothing was left. Our remains were lost. You and I will disappear into our separate worlds, along with Kasparov. Boris will return to Minsk and his wife. Sergei will return to Latvia. Chekov will return to her lover. They both will seek asylum within a year." Shevchenko sighed.

Edwards pulled off the highway, circled around to the base of the ramp, and stopped.

"They are waiting for us."

"Boris mark the time from the moment we enter the dirt road until we reach a safe distance."

"I am sure the explosives are of high value. We need to get far enough away from the hospital and those apartments so that the explosions and shock waves do not blow out windows, harming civilians," Ethan added, a pained expression clearly visible on his face. "The car will draw attention with all of us in it once it is done."

"I thought of that possibility, Ethan Edwards. Have Kasparov pull off the road and wait for the detonation. We will have them pick us up where the road begins and then we will drive to the bus station and separate. We will be running. We must allow enough time to reach the hard surface road."

"You are taking a chance sending them back, are you not?"

"We know the risk, Ethan Edwards," Boris Molotov answered. "It is the only way. If we do not return, agents will flood your country looking for all of us. The KGB will use their informants in your government and in the media." Boris turned and looked at Sergei, who nodded agreement.

"Our leaders will never be satisfied if some of us do not return. Peter, I want to open the briefcase."

"If I am wrong about the contents of the briefcase being on a timer, you will lose, Comrade, and that will create different problems. I will open the briefcase."

"Then Fededov will have what he wants, Peter, yes?"

"Then he will have what he wants. Ethan will see to Ladas if it becomes necessary"

Edwards stopped next to the tan sedan. He repeated the plan and drove off. They passed the hospital and apartments beyond. The maintained city road shifted to a small bumpy macadam drive as it passed the parking lot of the apartments.

Edwards spied Boris in the rearview mirror, studying his watch.

"I think a mile in should be quite enough."

"I agree. I think we will go unnoticed."

"Measuring time and distance from the hotel, I calculate we will have seventeen minutes to fully clear the blast area, which is, of course, without knowing exactly the strength of the explosive charges."

"Seventeen minutes. Not a lot of time."

"We will have to run very fast."

"I agree."

"Before we do anything, may I make a suggestion?"

"Of course, Sergei."

"I love this country, but I am first a citizen of Latvia and a soldier. I should be the one to open the briefcase. I am alone with no one who will miss me."

"Let us not forget the young lady in the hotel, Comrade."

"I think she will manage without me. You know I am right, Comrade Shevchenko."

"I have no argument against your observation, Comrade."

The three men climbed out of the car. Shevchenko walked up the right side of the sedan and peered in at the two prisoners.

Palmer was bare-chested. Chekov had removed the explosives from his vest and put it on the seat next to him. His eyes flashed anger, resentment, and the hatred that lived inside of him like a cancer.

Shevchenko looked into the eyes of the woman. Her eyes were fluttering and glazed over, her lips quivered, perspiration flowed down her cheeks, staining her blouse.

"Tell Comrade Fedorov when you both meet again how you died. You did not think I would recognize you, Comrade? Look at the two of them, Ethan."

"So, you are Palmer the traitor. If I had not missed you years ago, we would not be here today. I regret it to this day for reasons you could never understand." He stood up straight as Sergei approached.

"I am ready to open the briefcase. I suggest you find refuge near the edge of the water."

"We will never get far enough away to save ourselves. Open it." No one breathed, blinked, or moved. Edwards stared at his watch.

"Go ahead, Sergei."

"Sergei opened the trunk, took a deep breath and opened the briefcase slowly. In a moment, he sighed with relief. "I love this country," he whispered, raising his head above the trunk lid. "You were right, Comrade Shevchenko, it is on a timer." The three men breathed a sigh of relief in unison.

"I believe your FBI will not be happy to lose a car, Ethan Edwards." Shevchenko said.

"They'll get over it believe me. This is one case they won't advertise."

"Comrade Sergei Folic is the explosive expert, if that is your question."

"Seventeen minutes is all we will have after the timer is set. Seventeen minutes to run a mile to the car and be off."

"We will give a few more, Ethan, if you wish."

"No, we have been here long enough. Set the time, Sergei."

Shevchenko leaned forward, reached into the open window, and patted the woman's face.

"Ahh," he sighed, "what a waste of a lovely pair of breasts. Goodbye Tatyana Polizkova."

They ran, threading their way along the rutted road until they were clear of the reeds. Kasparov waved them on. "Hurry."

"Three minutes."

"Plenty of time. I'll pull up to the entrance lane next to the hotel and turn around."

A police car leading an ambulance, sirens shattering the silence, turned into the emergency entrance of the hospital. The ambulance stopped under the concrete awning as the sedan passed. "Two minutes."

"What about the police car?"

"He will go to the area of the explosion. We will be long gone before more police are alerted."

Kasparov crossed his fingers and whispered a silent prayer. It was the first time he prayed since he was fourteen, when he watched Boris, with Shevchenko gripping his shoulders, as he climbed the ladder in that trench with ice and snow making movement dangerous on the roadway above. In the far distance ahead of them were the spires of Leningrad. Behind them, the grey-green slugs searched for them in the trench.

"Did everything go well? I assume it did."

"We will know in," he looked at his watch. "forty-five seconds, Lila."

"Ivanna Kamenev should have been here. It is too bad she had that terrible car accident. She was a very good phone operator."

Kasparov nodded.

"Yes, she was too good . . . ten, nine, eight, . . . three, two, one. Nothing. I did something wrong. A connection perhaps. I will—"

Explosion.

"You are slipping with age, Sergei, three seconds off."

The ground shook, the car swayed, red-orange flames appeared and a thick black cloud rose into the cloudless sky. The black cloud widened, obscuring visibility beyond its growing perimeter until it reached hundreds of feet in the air.

"It is time to go."

"Let me drive, Dmitry."

"If you wish to drive, Comrade Edwards. Please take the wheel."

Shevchenko and everyone sighed with a sudden rush of relief as Edwards drove onto the service road toward Route 3 East.

"You three know what you must do. Good luck to us all." Shevchenko looked at his three comrades and smiled, then fell silent with a look of finality on his face.

When they reached the Park & Drive, Edwards pulled behind a cab in the arrival zone and got out with Shevchenko. The five of them hugged and kissed. They shook hands with Edwards, who got back in the car to allow them their last moments together.

"Our people will monitor events and see that you all get out of Russia. Be patient."

"How will we know? How will we find you?"

"When it is time Lila, you will know. We will not meet again, but Ethan and I have worked out a code. That will be explained. For now, ask nothing more."

Shevchenko and Kasparov got back in the car with Edwards behind the wheel.

"We all have women waiting for us. Women who love us. Let us get to them as quickly as possible." Shevchenko tapped Edwards on his shoulder. "When we get back to the hotel, I would like a moment with you, Ethan Edwards."

"Certainly."

"You are also invited, Dmitry." Brief laughter, then silence in the car for the rest of the ride to Hasbrouck Heights.

"You have something important to discuss, Peter?" Edwards asked, when all three had gathered in Shevchenko's room. Vodka was poured into glasses.

"Listen to me, Ethan. Fedorov will become the next president that is preordained. After his tenure will be a man I most respect, a tough man who will do what is necessary to make Russia more productive. He will improve the wellbeing of its people. He will have enemies in the KGB and ruling class.

He must be protected and allowed to reach the position of general secretary. He sees the need for change or my country will die. I am talking about my friend Mikhail Balandin."

CPSIA information can be obtained
at www.ICGtesting.com
Printed in the USA
FSHW011950231121
86442FS

9 781525 574245